DEDICATION

For Emma & Matthew; Ellen & Claire.
The pair who helped build Thea and the pair that first lived inside it.

FATEWEAVER

There is no frigate like a book
To take us lands away,
Nor any coursers like a page
Of prancing poetry.
This traverse may the poorest take
Without oppress of toll;
How frugal is the chariot
That bears a human soul!

Emily Dickinson

PROLOGUE

The old man sat hunched in a chair, his crooked frame completely still. A few splintered rays of morning sunlight broke through gaps in the boarded windows, illuminating dancing specks of dust that filled the cabin. It had been nearly two days since he had heard the news, two dreadfully long days in which he had worried and fretted over what he should do. The brown letter lay unfurled on the desk, its edges curled from repeated readings, for the old man had kept coming back to its words in the futile hope he had misread or misunderstood the current situation.

With great effort, the man pulled himself to his feet and shuffled slowly to a towering timber bookshelf. Running one gnarled finger along the dust-covered volumes of almanacs, history books and faded fictions, he stopped at one particularly thick book. Pulling it delicately from its place, he carried his heavy, leather-bound quarry to his chair. He awkwardly seated himself, setting the book flat on his lap, and studied its cover carefully. It looked as old as he did. The hard maroon-coloured leather was extremely worn, and thin black cracks had spread their way across its surface like tiny veins. In the middle, embedded almost like wax, was the dull imprint of an infant hand. The old man placed his much larger hand over the imprint and a reluctant smile broke his wrinkled face.

Opening the book he flicked through the pages slowly, stopping here and there to read for himself. He continued to read until the last vestiges of sunlight had all but disappeared from the hut and he was left in near darkness. The old man sighed heavily and withdrew a silver knife from a side clasp of his belt. He held the knife in a quivering hand, his mouth offensively dry as he felt his entire body shake with fear. One lingering beam of sunlight danced off the perfect blade as he raised the knife above his head. Slowly, the old man opened his mouth and whispered two words to the empty room: "Forgive me."

Then with a great cry, he slammed the knife into the book.

In another place, another time, another altogether everything, a young girl woke with a start.

1 - AN ALMOST ORDINARY GIRL

Charity Walters scrambled about in the darkness for the bedside lamp, finding it only after knocking over several things, including her wind-up alarm clock and a half-empty bottle of water. She clicked the lamp and flooded her room with reassuring light. What a strange dream that had been, she thought, something about an old woman with a knife, or was it a man stuck in bed? She rubbed her temples trying to remember but her head was cloudy with sleep and what little vestiges of the dream she could recall were soon lost in one long yawn. It didn't matter anyway, she thought distractedly, if it was really important it would come to her sooner or later. She gave the room one last furtive glance and then lay back down on her soft mattress, letting sleep envelop her; A second later or so it seemed to Charity, she was jolted awake once more, this time by the tiny alarm clock, which was now screeching noisily on the floor at the foot of her bed. Its shrill call echoed around her bedroom in the semi-darkness. Charity slipped her feet out from the warmth of her blankets and almost immediately trod on something sharp and painful; an upturned plug. Cursing inwardly she kicked it aside and reached for the clock, now intent on ripping out its batteries. However, as she grasped her hand around its cold, tin casing, the clock ceased its noisy protests and fell silent once more. Charity sighed heavily, glaring down at its tiny face. It read one minute past midnight. "Broken," she muttered to herself, before tossing it away, flopping back onto her bed and drifting into slumber for what she hoped would be the final time that night.

"Charity...breakfast!" yelled a voice from outside her bedroom some hours later. Charity was already awake. She had been for some time now, just waiting for a reasonable excuse to get up. She groped across her bedside table, feeling her way along the scrunched up pieces of paper, pens, tattered bookmarks and overdue library book notices. She reached all the way down to the carpeted floor, patting the fibres expectantly for her quarry; she could feel all manner of things that littered her bedroom but still not the item she yearned for. Charity knew she could've simply opened her eyes and checked but she liked to play this little game every now and then, relying on her fingers, refusing to use her sense of sight. She greatly enjoyed these personal challenges and would rarely abstain from one until she succeeded. Sure enough, after several long and frustrating minutes she placed her hand on something large and flat. Her heart beating excitedly, Charity squeezed her new discovery and felt the comforting sensation of worn leather. She pulled the item up to her with some difficulty. It was quite heavy and she found that she had to reach over and use both hands. Still her eyes remained resolutely shut until the prize was safely positioned in front of her. Finally she opened her eyes and as they accustomed themselves to the light pouring in from the window, they brought into focus a copy of her favourite book: 'Alice in Wonderland'. By Lewis Carroll.

"Charity, breakfast! I'm *not* going to call you again!" The voice echoed from downstairs once more and Charity, recognising her mother's shrill tones bellowed back. "Alright, I'm coming, I'm coming!" she pushed the book away regretfully; right now was not the time it seemed. She swung her long legs out from the covers and strode to the full length mirror in the far corner of her bedroom, appraising herself.

Charity studied her image carefully. She had a long thin face, a round button nose and two very brown eyes, in fact she looked almost ordinary. There was one particular thing that set Charity apart however, something that grabbed people's attention as soon as they caught sight of her, something that had spawned countless conversations among adults and sparked hundreds of taunts from her peers. She was the owner of some rather unusual hair, for her hair was not one of the more mundane shades of brown, black or blonde, or even red. No, Charity's hair was enchantingly, brilliantly, almost impossibly white.

When she had been much younger, Charity had wondered how she had gotten such unusual hair from such plain parents, after all her mother, Wendy Walters, was a teacher in a local primary school whilst her father, Richard Walters worked as an estate agent, selling houses far superior to their own, and both *their* heads remained dull shades of brown. In her quiet moments alone Charity used to imagine that perhaps she had been adopted by these parents from some white-haired stranger, someone who would arrive at her house one day and whisk her off on a series of marvellous adventures in exotic, far off lands.

Whenever she had questioned her parents on this intriguing topic, her mother would always say it was, "just one of those things" and quickly change the topic. They had both seemed fairly content to ignore her obvious distinction. Unfortunately for Charity, however, her peers had not been so willing to turn a blind eye to the issue and Charity had come across her fair share of unwanted attention as a result of having such vibrant locks, and nowhere was this more pronounced than at school. From her very first day, all those years ago, she had stood out like a bright, white beacon among the other heads of brown, black, red and blonde, and being a shy, uneasy girl she had not found this upsurge of attention welcome. As the years rolled by Charity had tried earnestly to keep her white head down and blend in as best she could, but she was always unpopular and thanks to her striking locks, had at times found herself on the receiving end of a school bully or two.

Charity shook her head, trying to rid herself of such depressing thoughts. It was the first week of the summer holidays after all, time to be optimistic, besides, she sniffed the air inquisitively as she headed out of her room and downstairs, she could smell something that almost always cheered her up. Her favourite food in the world, bacon, was obviously sizzling away in the kitchen, just waiting for her to come and claim it. She bounded the last three stairs and pelted into the kitchen, muttering rushed apologies to her mother who was busying away at the stove, her back to Charity. Wendy Walters was a tall, elegant woman, with mousy brown hair and a very long thin face. She had always struck Charity as being a worried sort, the type of person who frets when loved ones leave the house on short errands. Charity used to notice how distracted and agitated she got when her father was not around, something she had taken heed of when sharing the same house for the duration of the summer holidays. She had quickly learned it was best to avoid her during these stressful moments.

"I called you five times," her mother said tetchily, as she poked and prodded at a solitary egg that was sizzling noisily in the pan.

"Well I only heard you twice," said Charity truthfully.

"And why didn't you come the *first* time?" snapped her mother.

Oh dear, thought Charity, she was trapped. "I…I was getting changed," she said guiltily, hoping her mother wasn't in one of her moods.

"Hmmm." Her mother pursed her lips and gave Charity a withering look that told her that she did not believe a word of this excuse. "Well no point in worrying now, sit, sit! Your food's almost cold!"

Charity squeezed herself into an empty chair and eyed up her plate which was brimming with pancakes, bacon and sausages. She smiled contentedly and wasted no more time, scoffing it into her as fast as she could manage. She was so focused on eating that she didn't notice a third figure enter the room, kiss her mother cheerily on the cheek and take a seat opposite her. She looked up from her now sparse plate to see her father staring down at her, a wide grin stretching across his surprisingly youthful face. He was tall, like her and her mother. He had wavy brown hair and thick black glasses which he wore all the time, except when reading the newspaper, which always made Charity laugh.

"Morning, little 'un!" he said, happily.

"Morning, Dad," she smiled back at him, some of the bacon falling from her mouth as she did.

"Charity, honestly!" sighed her mother, turning away in mild disgust.

"Wha'?!" Charity gesticulated in mock innocence, letting yet more bacon drop back onto her plate.

"Mouth closed, you little savage!" snapped her father playfully, brandishing a fork in her general direction.

Charity resolutely closed her mouth and chewed her food quickly. She was eager to question her father about the day's activities he had planned for them and besides a silly thing like speaking with your mouth full was hardly anything to get worked up about. She was sure her father wouldn't have even mentioned it unless her mother had done. Charity swallowed a great mouthful of breakfast with difficulty and made to speak but her father did so first, fixing her with a look of unmistakable concern.

"Charity, you look tired. Your mother and I heard you bumping around last night - is… everything alright?'

"What? Oh…yeah, I suppose."

"You're sure? You didn't have another nightmare did you?" he fixed her with a suspicious look, as if he already knew the truth.

"No, not really… I was just… my alarm clock went off, dunno why." Charity hated lying to her father but knew that the alternative would simply worry him. For you see, ever since she was little, as far back as she could remember, Charity had been plagued with unsettling nightmares. These almost always involved her being stranded on top of a tall, isolated tower, thunder, wind and rain all hailing down upon her. The tower would swing from side to side and Charity was soon thrown this way and that as she desperately tried to cling onto something that would save her from hurtling down into the impenetrable darkness below. No matter how hard she clung on, however, she would invariably lose her grip and slip back into the reality of her darkened bedroom, sweating and terrified. Understandably, her parents were greatly concerned and she was paraded in front of person after person, all intent on tracing the cause of these disturbing visions. To their surprise, however, Charity was not the victim of any form of childhood trauma or emotional distress, and she wasn't even afraid of heights, something her mother had thought of when Charity told her of the tall teetering tower. Charity herself had quashed this theory by scaling the huge tree in her back garden without so much as breaking a sweat. In truth she was simply a shy little girl who greatly enjoyed her own company, and all involved were forced to admit that there was no discernible reason for her nightly distress. The common assumption was that with time they would subside, but her parents continued to worry and the nightmares continued to torment her until eventually, after what had seemed like an eternity, the nightmares began to come less frequently. Soon they would only bother her once or twice a month, and then after a while not at all.

"You're sure?" her father repeated. "You'd tell us if they'd started up again, wouldn't you?"

"Yes," Charity chimed. "I'm too old for nightmares, Dad."

"Oh my, yes of course, how silly of me!" her father bellowed, his face breaking into a smile once more. "My daughter is the bravest, wisest and least nightmare-prone daughter in all the land!"

Charity grinned and threw a piece of sausage at him. It hit him on the side of the head and he fell back into his chair, his head slumped against the wood, his tongue lolling out of his mouth in a creditable impression of a dead body. Charity giggled as her mother coldly poked her father in the back of the head.

"Well now that your father's finally snuffed it, I can run off with that lovely postman!" she said loftily. Instantly her father burst back into life, standing up and whirling to face her mother.

"It's a miracle!" he pronounced to the entire kitchen. "The love of a good woman, eh, of two good women, has cured me!" He nodded regally at Charity, who bowed her head in imitation.

Charity laughed loudly as he dragged her increasingly embarrassed mother around the kitchen in a perfect impersonation of a ballroom waltz, all the while humming a classical tune for the whole kitchen to enjoy.

"Daaad!" groaned Charity loudly over the humming. "What are we doing today?"

He released her mother, who turned to the dishes, mumbling something about "living in a mad house".

"Well I was thinking…library!"

Charity's face lit up. "Brilliant! When?"

"Now! Get your duds on, I'll warm the car up!"

Charity bolted from the kitchen and thundered up the stairs, ignoring her mother who shouted sarcastically behind her, "You're welcome for the breakfast, MUM!"

She threw on the first outfit she had to hand and hurtled back downstairs and out the door. Within minutes her father had joined her in the car and she was en route to her favourite place in the world.

....

Charity and her father ascended the stone stairs of Sarsfield library, Charity pulling her father along impatiently as she strained towards the glass door that led inside. They made their way past the revolving bookstands and through the automated sensors that searched for any non-checked out books on your person. Charity bounded forwards towards the many rows of neatly organised books, leaving her father standing by the checkout desk.

"I'm going next door. Got to get something for dinner, little 'un," her Father said in a loud whisper. Charity gave him a thumbs up to show she had heard and then turned back towards her books. She walked up and down the shelves, running an index finger along the many spines, their colours and titles blurring into one as she sped past them, searching for something that would catch her eye, her latest literary discovery. Charity loved to be surprised by a book, to let it catch her completely off guard, and she had found that this was most easily achieved by choosing books at random, books that sparked her interest from the spine or cover alone. And so she resolved to keep up with this well-rehearsed process, moving up and down the aisles until she had reached the very back of the library, where she knew the old educational textbooks where kept. These were of no interest to Charity and so she skulked back to the fiction section, preparing herself to start over.

She had just made her way once more to the end of the first row, when she spotted something that she was sure hadn't been there before; a very old, very worn, dark green book was poking out from its shelved brothers and sisters. Charity couldn't imagine how she had missed such a thing, something this out-of-place would almost certainly have grabbed the attention of her wandering eyes. So, sliding the book from its place, she savoured the excitement which usually came with the discovery of a new book. It was deceptively heavy and Charity almost dropped it once free of the confines of the shelf. It was covered in dark green leather which was worn and scratched, so much so that whatever title the book had previously worn had long since faded away. This was obviously a book considerably older than the ones she usually read, and one that most likely didn't belong in this section of the library. All the other books were new or at the very least clean. Nonetheless it was something of mystery and so Charity carried her discovery over to a nearby armchair, curiosity slowly creeping up inside her as she wondered what sort of adventure these aged pages held for her.

Flopping down into the chair, she flipped the book over several times on her lap but saw no title, no blurb. There wasn't even an author's name printed onto the leather binding on the spine. Perhaps, she thought, this was one of those really old books her father and teachers spoke about, printed when there wasn't enough ink for such trivial things as covers. Rather than wonder anymore, she opened the front cover tentatively and peered inside, expecting to see an old-fashioned font emblazoned across the crisp pages. She was instantly deflated. The book was empty. There wasn't a single word printed on the first, second, third or fourth page. She rifled past each crisp, white page but saw no writing whatsoever. Flicking along the cover so the pages blurred past each other into a mirage of white, she keenly scanned for a blot of black or colour but found none. Her heart sinking, she reached the final page and flicked it lazily aside - nothing. Charity made to snap the book shut, annoyed at what an unnecessary distraction this had been from her usual enjoyable reading time, but just as she did so, something caught her eye; a glimpse of writing, writing that had been scrawled on the inside of the back cover of the book, just visible in the bottom right hand corner. She was sure that she wouldn't have noticed it had she not been so intently studying the book's contents. Charity quickly repositioned the book, eager to see what had been written. She squinted, concentrating hard. Two words had been scrawled in untidy handwriting in the corner of this final piece of canvas. Both words were printed in the same dark black ink, and upon recognising what they said, Charity felt the book slip from her hands and lay flat on her lap, her heart rate increasing significantly. At first she had thought her eyes had been deceiving her, but she cast them over the words again and again. There was no mistake, it was there in black and white, written on the inside of this odd little book: **'For Charity.'** The words seemed to reverberate around her head, she ran a finger along them, hoping that the ink would disappear as she smudged her forefinger along the hard surface, but there they remained. She read them aloud in a hushed whisper: **'For Charity'**.

Charity was breathing very fast. The air around her seemed suddenly lighter and her head throbbed uncomfortably. She racked her brains, thinking hard. A book *just* for her? This was obviously a coincidence, she thought to herself. The rest of the pages were blank, so it must be a diary or a journal or something. She felt herself starting to calm, rational thought taking hold of her once more. Someone's handed it into a charity shop and it somehow made its way to the library that was bound to be it. Charity felt slightly reassured by this idea but decided in order to sate her paranoid curiosity that the lady at the desk might be able to shed some light on where this strange book had come from. In any case it certainly didn't belong *here*. So she carried the book, a little more tentatively now, towards the long wooden desk near the entrance to the library, where she knew the woman who checked the books would be working. Sure enough, when she reached the desk a startlingly old woman greeted her with a familiar toothless smile.

"Ah hello, dearie, lovely to see you back again," she said warmly. The old woman saw Charity at least once a week, but Charity had never been bold enough to properly introduce herself, and so she had remained 'dear'. Charity for her part had managed to avoid the embarrassment of asking for her attention without the knowledge of a name by resorting to only approaching her when she wasn't busy when a simple throat cough was enough to gain her an audience.

"Um, hello," Charity replied and she was shocked to hear her voice quivering slightly. "This book, this book."

"Yes?" the woman reached out a bony hand to take it in but Charity did not relinquish it.

"It's… I think it's been put here by mistake." She waved a solitary arm around at the surrounding library.

"Oh and why's that?" the woman asked, raising her faint eyebrows in surprise at such an odd announcement.

"Well it's blank you see, there's no writing, or title or anything…I think it might've been meant for a *charity* shop." She placed great emphasis on the word, hoping upon hope that the woman would put her out of her misery and confirm her suspicions. The old woman continued to look perplexed, however, so Charity placed the book on the counter.

"Dear, dear, dear," she tutted in a frail, gentle voice, "that won't do now will it?"

Charity said nothing, not sure how to respond. At least she was now vindicated in bringing the book to the woman's attention.

"Not sure how that got there, dear. Not to worry, these things happen, I suppose. Well thank you, I'll just -" the woman grabbed a hold of the green book and made to pull it towards her, but Charity quickly placed a hand on the back cover, resisting her.

"It's meant for a charity shop I think, I mean it says so…" Charity squeaked in a panicked voice. She did not know what had made her do it, nor why she was still holding onto the unusual book.

At first the woman did not say anything. She looked extremely affronted and even alarmed at having been stopped in her usual duties. She pursed her lips and eyed Charity with rising suspicion. "A charity shop you say?"

Charity nodded silently, her hand still on the book.

"Well that is *odd*" she said, in a tone that was soaked with genuine bewilderment, "because we don't nor have we ever accepted donations or used books. All our books are bought wholesale from vendors or publishers."

Charity, now increasingly worried the old woman thought her mad, hurriedly opened the back cover and pushed the book towards her face.

"See, it's been donated to a charity or hospice or something like that."

The woman looked down at the contents but showed no sign of understanding. On the contrary she looked more confused than ever.

"Dear, I don't see anything."

"What?" said Charity confused. "It's here, here!" She pulled the book round to face her but to her astonishment the back cover was now completely empty.

"My dear, are you sure you're quite alright?" the old lady asked, her already wrinkled face crinkled in concern.

"But I don't understand, it was…I mean…it was…" Charity trailed off, rubbing her head in utter incomprehension. She was sure of it, she had seen writing, it was just there mere moments ago, but now, now it was gone. 'What was happening to her?' she thought, her panic rising once again.

"Look, I'll just take this and make sure we get it back to wherever it -" Once more the librarian made to pull the book towards her but again Charity stopped her, grabbing hold of the book with both hands and yanking it to her chest.

"NO!" she yelled before she could stop herself. "I mean, sorry, could I, can I check it out instead?"

"Check it out? But why? There's nothing in it!" the old woman was definitely looking at her now as if she had gone quite mad.

"I know that, I just...I like it," said Charity feebly. She didn't really know why she wanted it. The old lady was quite right -what use was an empty book you couldn't write in?

"There's not even any checkout card, I doubt there's any record of it for the library."

"I don't care. Can I just take it?" asked Charity desperately.

The woman looked conflicted for a moment and then her face softened slightly and she held her hands out towards Charity,

"Oh, I suppose so. Well let me give you a card for it then."

Charity spluttered her thanks as the woman took the book from her and fixed a stiff piece of card to the inside front cover. She stamped the card roughly, made some handwritten notes about the appearance in a very old ledger and finally passed it back to Charity, who took it gratefully and rushed towards the exit, the book now clutched tightly to her chest.

2 – A GLIMMER OF GOLD

This was certainly not the first time Charity had shown a peculiar attachment to a book; in fact it was a scenario everyone in her household was quite accustomed to. Her parents had always told her that ever since she had been able to make her tiny hands into clenched fists, she had yearned to hold a book. Charity had not been a little girl of extraordinary intelligence and although she would've loved to claim it, she was also never an amazingly gifted reader. And yet, books had still always given her a great pleasure for some reason. Whether it was the enjoyment of a good story or the mystery of not knowing what was coming next in a tale, Charity found that as she grew up, books had always proven to be a much more enjoyable option than anything her peers took part in.

Charity was still clutching the green book to her chest as she descended the steps of Sarsfield Library and began searching for her father, who was nowhere to be seen. The events inside had shaken her and she had absolutely no idea if he was late for their meeting, or she early. Charity walked up and down the busy high street, craning her neck for a sign of him but she couldn't even find his car and after fifteen minutes she was just beginning to panic. She had just started to consider that it may be best to return to the library and wait for him when a familiar voice called out from nearby. Charity whirled around to see her father emerging from the door of a nearby corner shop, struggling with several heavy-looking shopping bags and fumbling for something in the inside pocket of his long overcoat.

"Dad!" called Charity, sprinting towards him, mild relief coursing through her.

"Charity, love, come help me with this shoppin', will you?"

"Sure."

Charity bounded forwards and grabbed two bags from her father, who looked much more comfortable now his burden had been significantly lightened.

"You done?" he asked inquisitively, eyeing the green book, now tucked under her arm.

"Yup."

"That was fast, usually you…you know…take your time, savour the precious moments of solitude."

"No, it's bit too busy," lied Charity, not meeting her father's eyes. "Besides I found what I wanted."

"Did you now?" her father's voice answered. Charity thought it sounded less jovial than usual, almost as if he was accusing her of something, and Charity couldn't shake the distinct feeling that somehow he knew there was something she wasn't telling him.

As they made their way back to the car, Charity made no more mention of the book or the library and her father took no more notice of her new discovery. Instead they spent the journey home discussing what shopping her mother had wanted picking up. Charity had no interest whatsoever in this topic but had brought it up, knowing that it would allow her to idly chat without much thought, leaving her mind free to focus on what had happened in the library. *This,* she thought to herself as her father happily talked away, was obviously a *much* more pressing issue.

The more she thought about it, the more she was convinced that she had imagined the writing. She had clearly been thinking about a book just for her as she perused the choices and her brain had played a very convincing trick on her. It had happened before, lots of times she'd thought someone was watching her, or could've sworn she'd heard someone listening in on her conversations or phone calls and yet when she'd turned to confront these feelings, no one was ever to be found, and it always turned out to be just the product of an over active imagination.

By the time their car pulled into the driveway she had managed to calm down enough that she now found the whole thing quite laughable. How could she have believed something so absurd? A talking book! She even briefly thought about sharing the story with her father but in the end decided not to; he might think she was losing her marbles and she really didn't want to worry him. She helped her father in with the shopping and then mumbled that she was, 'going to her room for a bit', but her father called back to her as she climbed the stairs.

"Dinner'll be soon, don't get too comfy up there little 'un!"

"'K!" she yelled back, hurrying into her room and slamming the door shut behind her.

Charity couldn't help herself. She knew she had been imagining things, she realised her brain was obviously playing tricks on her but she had to be absolutely sure. She slammed the book onto her bed and immediately flicked through its pages, searching for something, anything that might've looked like writing, a blot of ink or spot of grime or dust, but the book was blank. She checked the whole way through, including the front and back cover just to be sure, but found nothing but spotlessly clean, white pages. She closed the book and abandoned it on the bed, getting up and pacing the room distractedly. She was frustrated at herself. Why had she even brought the thing home? She should feel relieved as clearly she wasn't going mad after all and yet for some reason she felt disappointed. The notion that a book could communicate and was doing so with *her* was an idea so exciting it could've been ripped straight from one of her own adventure novels.

All of a sudden a small flash from somewhere in her dimly lit bedroom made her jump. Something had given off a tiny burst of light, like the flashing of a powerful torch being clicked on and off very quickly. Charity had almost fallen over in shock; she spun around, searching for the source, praying she wasn't again imagining things. Maybe she *was* going mad after all, she thought frantically. Then another pulse of light flashed around her tiny bedroom and Charity jumped back again in alarm, her breath catching in her throat, and her heart racing so wildly she was sure it was trying to climb out of her chest. She had seen where the light was coming from. She stared wildly at the spot where the last blast of light had issued from - her bed. She knew what lay there, she knew that the only thing that lay upon her pressed linen duvet was the book.

She edged towards her bed, her whole body bristling with tension as she tiptoed towards where she knew it lay. She raised a trembling hand towards a portion of blanket that partly obscured the book from view. Charity gently peeled back the fabric of her duvet and revealed a corner of the book. It looked quite the same, there was no flashing light or wondrous change in its appearance, she pulled back more of the cover, and then, gritting her teeth, whipped off the rest, exposing the whole thing. She dropped the duvets suddenly, and clasped both her hands over her mouth to stop herself from screaming. The book's cover was no longer blank - the previously untarnished leather had been emblazoned with a swirling golden font, as if someone had scratched the writing onto its surface without being noticed. Charity couldn't move, she was frozen with fear and confusion. All she could do was read what had been scrawled onto its leather surface: '**3, 8, 1, 18, 9, 20, 25**'. The numbers made no sense to her as she racked her brains. What did she do now? What *could* she do? What if she took this to her parents and the numbers disappeared? She'd be thought insane - maybe she was insane! She stood silently in the semi-darkness of her room, her mind racing, only her heavy breathing and the faint glint of the numbers clouding her thoughts.

Charity felt truly lost as hundreds of scenarios ran through her head. What could happen? What might happen? What was the best course of action? When suddenly, an ear-splitting scream brought her back to reality with a bump. Her mother's high pitched shriek was coming from downstairs and Charity immediately flew out of her room and came crashing downstairs to see what had happened, the book momentarily forgotten. When she tore into their small kitchen, fearing the worst, she found a very odd sight; her mother was bouncing up and down on the spot, a euphoric look on her thin face and her father was bent over, staring open-mouthed at a small television, in the corner of the room.

"Well, folks, that was the midweek draw! I'm Simon Banton, and I hope it's been a lucky one! Now back to Michelle and Alan in the studio, how'd those numbers work out for you guys?" A handsome blonde man in a smart blue suit was grinning emphatically out at Charity from the television screen, behind him a large glass sphere still whirring away, tumbling myriad colourful numbered balls.

"Um…what's going on?" Charity asked the kitchen at large. Her mind felt like one of the balls as she desperately tried to keep herself calm. Her mother and father both turned on the spot, surprised by her sudden appearance but positively beaming at her.

"We…we…won," croaked her father in a very restrained voice.

"WE WON!" her mother burst out, apparently unable to contain herself.

Charity understood at once but was apparently unable to translate this with her face. She tried to speak, to utter more questions but none came out. Her mother, taking this as a sign of confusion, grabbed her jovially with both hands. "THE LOTTERY!" she bellowed happily, "WE'VE WON! WE'VE WON!!"

Charity did not have time to react before her father leapt at her and began to whirl her around the kitchen like a marionette, whilst her mother shrieked happily down the phone at their assorted relatives. Charity managed to disentangle herself from her father and stepped back to view the scene before her. This was too incredible to be real, she thought, it was all too coincidental, the book, those golden numbers. "The numbers," she said audibly, her eyes widening suddenly. "Dad, Dad do you have a ticket?" she asked urgently, yanking at his lapels.

He was still dancing what seemed to be a blend of a tango and ballroom waltz with her mother, who was deep in conversation with one of her sisters, the phone pressed to her ear with one hand, the other clasped by her father.

"Ticket, what for - oh, yes," he fumbled in his jacket pocket with his free hand and produced a small white piece of paper with the lottery symbol and seven numbers printed in faded red ink on the front. Charity took the ticket wordlessly, almost too afraid to look. "What if, what if it's…" she thought, as she turned it the right way up and read.

3, 8, 1, 18, 9, 20, 25.

She handed back the ticket and managed to mumble that she needed some air, before racing up the stairs to her room, leaving her parents to their celebrations. For some reason she did not feel quite the same as they did. Her insides were churning like a washing machine and her brain was racing with so many questions that she was surprised it didn't burst out of her head. It was just too much to take in, she thought. Winning the lottery? The book? "What is happening?" she thought desperately. The book, she would show her father the book, who cares if he thought she was mad, she thought defiantly.

Charity barged into her room. Her parents *had* to see what was going on. Upon entering her neatly ordered room she found herself face to face with an empty bed. Her book had been here, she'd left it right here on the mattress. Charity immediately dropped to the floor, grabbing handfuls of items and pulling them from underneath her bed in case the book had slipped off somehow, even though she knew it had been laying perfectly safely in the centre of the mattress when she had left. Still she searched, and the more time it remained hidden, the more frantically she searched. Something was happening to her, she knew that now, either she *was* indeed going mad or someone was playing the most elaborate practical joke on her that had ever been conceived.

By the time her father was hollering up the stairs to her, "Little 'un, we're leaving! We're heading to see your Gran!" she had managed to tear apart most, if not all of her belongings and still the little book remained out of her sight. She heard the door downstairs unlock and her mother's high heels clink on the tiled kitchen floor as she rushed outside. "Charity! Come on!" her father shouted from the hall. Charity stared frantically around her room. It was no use - she had to put it out of her mind for now. Something was happening, she was sure of that but not something that she seemed to be able to do anything about. Besides, she thought, as she listened to the sounds of her parents singing as they made their way from the house, they *had* just won the lottery.

....

Later that evening Charity found herself sitting in one of the most expensive restaurants in Sarsfield town, her beaming parents either side of her and a nagging pain in the back of her head, something she was sure was to do with the mysterious disappearance of the green book.

The waiter came and went, congratulating Charity's parents as he went on their prize, her Mother had wasted almost no time at all telling anyone that so much as met her gaze about the lottery win. Before long Charity was presented with a sumptuous plate of curried chicken, rice and two types of naan bread, she stared down at the food savouring the smell. There really did appear to be nothing she could do about the book now and so she tried desperately to push the thoughts from her mind and instead focused on questioning her parents about their unexpected win.

"So how -" started Charity,

"Much?" finished her father.

"Well, yeah." said Charity, grinning at her father, who returned it warmly.

"It's not as much as you might think. I mean it's A LOT, it's more than we've ever had, so it's plenty to be gettin' on with, but it's just not, like, a billion squillion pounds."

Charity laughed, "Does that amount even exist?"

"Don't know little 'un, and doubt *we* ever will. No this is our one chance, we'll not get this lucky again, so we best enjoy it!"

"I think we should tell her now Richard, get it over with." her mother whispered in an anxious voice, and Charity noticed that her father's brow furrowed with sudden concern. He turned his gaze to her, his eyes staring deep into her own, he seemed to be appraising whether or not she was ready for this new piece of information.

"I want to know!" she exclaimed, "Whatever it is, I don't care jus-" Charity fell silent as her father held up a long thin finger, he chewed his food thoroughly, then opened his mouth as if to speak and then quickly dropped in another piece of curried chicken and began chewing slowly. Charity smiled indignantly at her father's stalling and he too smiled at her frustration, his mouth still full of steaming chicken. Her father had opened his mouth once more, in imitation of his first trick and when he moved to shovel in a third helping of chicken Charity had hit the table, indignantly,

"Dad!"

"Sorry, sorry, couldn't resist, oh what FUN you are!" he said happily. "Ok, now you may not like this," he looked incredibly serious once more. "But your Mother and I feel it's the right thing for you, for us, for everyone really."

Charity's elation at the unexpected lottery win was quickly being replaced by an unpleasant sense of foreboding.

"Marion, d'you want to explain more?" asked her father as her mother turned to look kindly at Charity.

"Charity, dear, you're thirteen years old now and that means you're old enough for some responsibility in your life. Now your Father and I, well we aren't rich."

Charity's father made a move to interrupt but his mouth was again full of chicken so he waggled his fork in the air, making her mother tap him agitatedly on the arm. "Yes, yes, yes, alright we *weren't* rich but blah blah blah! This lottery money has…erm…changed things a bit, dear. You see, we've always wanted to be able to set you up properly for life, give you a better future, something your Father and I didn't have when we were *your* age and now well, we can. Your Father's made a couple of calls this evening and well, he got a place at St. August's!"

Charity opened her mouth to speak, then closed it when she could think of nothing to say.

"Saint August's, Charity isn't it wonderful!" said her Mother positively beaming.

"Saint what?" said Charity, wrinkling her nose as she pulled a perplexed face.

"Saint Awwwwguuuust's," her father replied slowly. "It's a private boarding school just outside of Kent, not too far from Sarsfield actually. We've always wanted to send you to a posh place like this but we just didn't have the means and now, with most of this lottery money…we do."

One word reverberated around Charity's head, fogging all her other senses and making her heart drop right into her shoes: 'boarding'. Did this mean they were fed up with her? Did they simply want her out of the way? What if they had had enough of her lounging around the house constantly reading a multitude of books? Why now, why her? It simply wasn't fair! Hundreds of questions and objections flew around her mind but in the end all Charity found she could utter was, "Oh…ok."

The rest of the dinner passed by without any more drama or surprises. Charity attempted to keep her face light and impassive throughout the meal but her insides felt like they were trying to jump out of her mouth. Her parents said nothing more on the issue, instead choosing to discuss what extravagances they could now afford but she knew that her father could sense her misgivings. Sure enough, when they arrived home later that night and Charity had excused herself and trotted quickly off to her bedroom, it didn't take long for her father to find her.

"Knock, knock," he said, opening the door slightly. "Can I come in little 'un?" he asked kindly.

"Yup," said Charity airily, her eyes focused with difficulty on her weathered copy of Alice in Wonderland as her father seated himself on the edge of her bed.

"Little one, you're almost a proper lady now so I'm not going to spoon-feed you some excuse or make you go to anything you don't want to but just understand that St. Augusts' could be the best thing for you." When she did not react, her father squeezed her foot and seemed to reconsider his words. "I know it sounds like not *your* type of thing, but that's all part of life, doing things you're not familiar with. That's how we learn," he finished sagely.

Her father seemed to be waiting for a reaction but Charity simply continued reading and only gave a mute nod to show she had heard his words.

"Well…anyways, read this, it's from St. August's, I think you'll like *it*," he said pointedly, dropping a folded paper brochure at the foot of her bed.

Charity made no move to grab the paper, "Thanks," she uttered quietly, barely opening her lips.

Her father nodded in an understanding way and made to leave. At the door he stopped and as he opened it, he turned to look at her, his blue eyes twinkling mischievously. "Be a shame to miss out on the library though, apparently it's quite outstanding," he whispered softly and then quietly closed the door with a wry smile.

Charity stopped reading and stared at the closed door. She waited until she could hear the muffled footsteps of her father descending the stairs, then she dived for the brochure.

Many more conversations occurred before Charity consented to attend St. August's School for Young Ladies. Her father hadn't been exaggerating about the prize fund; it wasn't enough to support the family without working but it was more than enough to send one child through private boarding school. Charity had gone to the local comprehensive, Woodvale High School, for a year now and whilst she had no real attachments to the place she did still see some appeal in being that much closer to home.

So before any decision had been reached about her future school, Charity had sought categorical assurances that she would be allowed home on holidays and that this library was indeed as magnificent as described in the school's brochure. Charity had read and re-read the little pamphlet hundreds of times since her father had presented it to her. It was clearly quite out of date, for it showed no pictures of the school or the library but instead described its surroundings as 'magisterial' and 'a perfect platform for young ladies moving into adulthood.' When it came to the library a brief description had been written about it being, 'an ideal place for studying and furthering the enjoyment of reading.' and below this, was a glowing review from a prominent literary critic, "In terms of sheer scale it's a must see. Some of the rarest volumes one is ever likely to encounter in the mainstream market. If, like me, you seek more from your books then this is the place for you." – C. Calville (1902)' It was this ringing endorsement that had piqued Charity's interest and after a week or so of deliberation she had agreed upon the idea, on the provision that she would be allowed home on holidays and if she really didn't like it, could leave after a year or so.

Charity was astonished at how quickly her parents seemed to have her year-long expedition to this foreign place planned and organised. Indeed it took barely a couple of days before Charity was presented with a set of brand new school supplies, including a very fetching faux-leather pencil case, a hefty brown satchel that Charity thought looked like something a brainy academic or professor would wear and had therefore taken to wearing it around the house, and a beautifully pressed school uniform. This was something she had been used to of course. Her old school uniforms had also been mandatory but never this formal or posh looking, she had thought. Her mother, tears leaking from her rather red looking eyes, had lovingly handed over a blue skirt which went down to her knees, a crisp white shirt, a blue white and red striped tie with a small golden crest imprinted at the bottom and a beautiful striped blazer. The blazer was easily the most spectacular item of clothing, with three tiny buttons that gleamed and shone in the light of the lamps and the St. August's crest, a golden shield of battle encompassed by a wreath of leaves and a tiny flame atop the shield stitched into the right breast pocket. Charity couldn't deny her father's proclamation that it was, "Worth every penny."

As the summer breezed by Charity found herself becoming more and more conflicted at the idea of beginning her new school. St. August's seemed like a wonderful place, seeming almost as if it had been designed with a girl like her in mind, and yet she couldn't shake the nagging feeling of worry that seemed to cloud her excitement. It would be the first time she had been away from her parents for a meaningful period of time. However there nothing she could do about it even if she wanted to, her parents seemed set on her trying out the school and she had given her word that she would at least attempt the idea.

Something else was concerning Charity, something that had concerned her greatly ever since the evening of their unexpected lottery win. Charity had not forgotten what had happened in the library that day nor had she forgotten that a strange book had managed to tell her the numbers of a national lottery draw moments before it had been revealed to her unsuspecting parents and the rest of the general public. The book had gone of course, this was what concerned her most of all. Books do not just get up and walk away, and she had torn her bedroom inside out and upside down in her quest for the little green book to no avail. It was as if it had never existed to begin with. There were times when she had seriously considered telling her father what had happened, that she was worried she might be losing her marbles after all, but what could she say? "Hey Dad, a magic book told me we were going to win the Lottery and then disappeared." No it was no use, she had decided to keep quiet about the whole thing, even managing to convince herself that it might have been a figment of her imagination although deep down she knew this was not the case. A fresh start would do her good, she had thought, as long as she could keep the book from her thoughts for the final week of her holidays everything would be fine.

Her plan had been going well right up until two days before she was to attend St. August's. Charity and her father had gone on one last trip to Sarsfield library in order to return some overdue books her mother had borrowed some weeks earlier. This was the first time Charity had visited since the incident and she was overcome with nerves. Entering the library she scanned the floor for a sign of the old lady who had stamped the green book, but she was nowhere to seen. Relieved, she moved to the aisles she was most familiar with and scanned the shelves but found nothing that piqued her interest. Several minutes later she approached her father who was deep in conversation with a plump blonde woman behind one of the many wooden desks. She was chatting animatedly as she waved a digital scanner around like a conductor waving a baton in front of an imaginary orchestra.

"It's awful, I know, very unexpected but that's not even the worst of it as we're under-staffed now," she was saying in a thick accent. "Can't get a lick of help now, I mean they're all over us when we fail to fine peoples for late returns." Her face shifted from a look of annoyance to a simpering smile, "That'll be £3.20 by the by, dear," and then back to pursed lips, "But now that we actually need a bit of help, nooooo, they stay *far* away, they daren't darken the doorway."

Charity's father was nodding in a sincere way. He looked to Charity like one of those dogs that sits on the back shelf of a moving car, his head bobbing up and down as he forked out some change and handed it to the woman who was still droning on and on. She spotted Charity slink behind her father and broke off from her ramble to focus on her. "Oh, hello Charity, haven't seen you round these parts in a bit!" She said cheerfully, "Why you been away, what you been up to?" Charity instantly turned scarlet and stammered something about, 'being busy'.

The librarian tutted and smiled knowingly at her father who was now ushering Charity out of the library and explaining he had to get on and make the dinner. Charity rounded on him as soon as she was safely in the car and well out of ear shot.

"What was she talking about for so long?"

"Oh nothing really little one, just well...you know Mrs Tanner?"

Charity blinked at him, nonplussed. "No…"

"You do, dear!" he said agitatedly, pulling out of the car park and onto the main road. "The elderly woman who scanned all your books. Cripes, you've been here enough, you're bound to have come across her dozens of times!"

"Oh…I…never learnt her name, she always seemed a bit sharp," Charity said timidly.

"Yes, I know what you mean, no time for dillydallying. Well I'm afraid," her father looked hard at the road in front of him, "she's passed on."

"She's dead?!" Charity spluttered, aghast.

"Well that's *one* way to put it honey, yes," Her father answered reasonably.

Charity felt her heart thumping madly in her chest. "Do they know what happened?"

"As a matter of fact no. Mrs Pew told me it's all everyone is talking about, just seemed to drop dead…it's quite the mystery. Imagine that happening in a small town like yours. It's like something out of one of your books eh?"

3 – A SECRET AT ST. AUGUST'S

Charity had attempted to make as many enquiries as she could into the death of Mrs Tanner and its apparent connection to her mysterious missing book in the brief two days of summer she had had left. To her great disappointment, however, she had made no progress whatsoever. All she had managed was to make everyone very suspicious of the amount of interest she seemed to have in the death of an elderly woman, which was really none of her business.

She spent a great deal of time talking to the other librarians, eager to learn more about her demise and where the green book may have come from but they knew little about Mrs Tanner's death and even less about the book. She soon realised that she was not going to solve either mystery in the brief portion of summer remaining to her.

The final two days of Summer passed in a blur of unanswered questions and before she knew it the first day of school day had presented itself. Arriving at St. August's with her parents was not nearly as daunting as she had imagined. The lottery money had certainly given her access to a beautiful campus and they had wasted no time in touring the entirety of it. When it finally came time to say goodbye to her parents Charity was pleasantly impressed with herself, she was not nearly as upset or panicked as she had thought she would be. Her Mother on the other hand was almost inconsolable and leaning on her Father had wailed her goodbyes as he hoisted her into the car and trundled down the long drive and out of sight.

The first few days of life at St. August's passed by just as quickly as the final days of Summer, a haze of new faces and new places and soon the first day of classes came and went, then the first week and before long she had almost reached the midterm break.

All in all, month into her first year of St. August's, Charity was delighted to find that it wasn't nearly as intimidating as she'd thought. The other girls were relatively friendly and even though she couldn't honestly say she had made any actual friends, she had found enough reasons to enjoy her brief time there. The teachers were pleasant, the work casual and the grounds beautiful - all in all it was quite satisfactory. Besides, she had reasoned that she was extremely fortunate to have had such an opportunity and it was best to make the most of it whilst she could.

One sunny morning in early November, Charity awoke to the sounds of bustling feet and shrieking students, only to discover that she was, once again, late for class. This was becoming an alarming habit of hers. Not having the luxury of her mother to wake her in time for classes she had been forced to rely on her own, inconsistent alarm clock. She bundled her school uniform on, grabbed her brown backpack she always carried to classes and hurtled from her dorm room, leaving the place in a considerable mess, and sprinted off towards the main building.

Charity checked her wristwatch reluctantly. She knew it would simply confirm her tardiness but she had to at least know how late she was in case an excuse was required. To her surprise it was only a quarter past nine and class started at nine, which meant if she got across the campus in ten minutes or so she would only miss part of her chemistry lesson. She quickened her fast walk into a jog, hiked her backpack up slightly and broke into a run, hurtling down the flight of stairs and out into the sunlight grounds of St. August's.

Charity ran as fast as her legs would carry her for five full minutes when she was forced to stop or she thought her lungs might explode with the effort she was exerting. Leaning on the wall of the rectory clutching at her sides, which ached dully, she considered her situation carefully before continuing. The chemistry lab was just around the corner but what was she going to say to Mr. Speers? She racked her brains searching for a believable excuse, the usual 'slept in' line was beginning to wear thin with most of her teachers and privately Charity could understand their frustrations. She thought hard but her brain seemed to still be tucked up in bed, and she fought the urge to just run back to her dorm and pretend she was sick. Gritting her teeth. She decided to simply tell the truth, and if she was lucky Mr. Speers would be lenient. So after a moment or two she gave herself a motivating little shake and made the last three hundred yards to the chemistry lab. When she reached the familiar plywood door she knocked loudly, as she turned the handle and entered the room.

For a while she couldn't see anything at all, nothing but a strange cloud of white smoke that was billowing from somewhere deep within the classroom. Charity looked around for the other pupils but it was impossible to see anything through the fog,

"Hello?" she called out hopefully.

"WALTERS!" a shrill voice called back, from the depths of the mist. "LATE AGAIN…COME CLOSER GIRL, WE'RE CONDUCTING!" Charity recognised the nasal voice of Mr. Speers and holding her breath she ducked under the initial wafts of cloud and groped her way to where a babbling crowd of excited girls were gathered in the centre of the classroom.

Mr. Speers, who was a small man with a greying beard and drastically receding hairline, acknowledged her with a nod and then continued addressing the class. "This ladies, is hydrochloric acid," he announced, holding up a beaker half full of a colourless liquid. "Now I'm going to be doing a couple of experiments with this and some other *fascinating* little ingredients today. This will be mostly practical and I'm afraid due to the volatile nature of the results you girls will not be participating, so just watch and eh, try to enjoy them as much as I will!" Mr. Speers laughed wheezily, and some of the girls joined in with him sycophantically. Charity meanwhile, had lost all interest as soon as this pronouncement had been made. She knew that this was one of those classes that didn't require her to answer questions and that meant she could let her mind wander…and wander it did. In just over six hours she would be engrossed in a world entirely unlike her own, a world where anything was possible, a world of fantastical stories, daring adventures and mind-bending fantasy.

So the rest of Charity's day dragged in without incident, as days often do when you have something pleasurable waiting for you at the end of them. Finally, however, after what seemed like an eternity of waiting, the last bell of the day rang loudly throughout the campus and Charity bounded to her feet and made for the door. She tore from Miss Kipsin's arithmetic class before the final bell had even finished shrilly trilling. She hurtled along the bustling corridor and burst out of the main building and through the aviary. This, she knew, was the quickest route to the library. Charity squeezed her way through the crowds that were making their way to and from classes, clutching her backpack as she went. As she neared the library she happened to peer inside it, but to her horror, it was empty. Her books were gone! She must've left them in one of the classrooms during the day. Making a mental note to leave the library an hour earlier to find them she pushed on, her white head bent low amongst the throngs of students now heaving their way past her in the opposite direction.

Whispers followed Charity as she walked. They often did, as her striking hair generally got her noticed wherever she went. She had attended St. August's for a whole month and still people continued to stare at her. "Can't they think of something more interesting to gawk at?" Charity asked herself under her breath as she blushed furiously as yet another older girl openly pointed at her, whispering something, apparently very amusing to her friend, who laughed giddily. She was so annoyed at the unwanted attention that she almost bumped into Mrs. Graham who was standing outside her Spanish classroom chatting animatedly to a suited man that Charity didn't recognise. She saw that he wore a handsome pinstriped, grey suit and had a grey fedora hat perched jauntily on his head, "Oh, s-s-sorry," she spluttered apologetically, barely glancing up from her boots.

"Do watch where you're going Walters!" Mrs. Graham said, sounding agitated as Charity bundled past, still uttering rushed apologies.

Charity was relieved to reach the sanctity of the library and immediately rushed inside, shutting the double doors tight behind her, drowning out the fevered noise in the neighbouring corridor and savouring at last, the sound of silence. Charity truly loved this place but even she had to admit that it was not nearly as grand as the brochure had made it out to be. In fact on her first visit to the library she recalled how she had thought she was in the wrong place. A disappointingly modest room with wood panelled walls and mouldy, olive green carpet was hardly the 'grandeur' she had been imagining. There were plenty of sections and choices though and it did have several quiet spots to sit and read, so Charity had supposed that the place, as a whole, could have been a lot worse. In any case, it was easily the best thing about St. August's'.

Charity read long into the late afternoon. Soon the sun had set and the elderly librarian had packed away the last of her rubber stampers into the old wooden cabinet she used behind the checkout desk. Charity had been nestled snugly on a cushion in the back of the library, deep in the middle of her latest literary find when she heard the library door slam shut. She looked up suddenly and then jumped as she heard a key turn in a lock somewhere. Getting up, she made her way quickly to the front desk but found it deserted. She tried the handle of the wooden doors but they were locked tight. She called out loudly for someone, for anyone, but no answer came and she knew that since the library was at the far end of the campus there would be no one around until very early the next day. She moved to the huge bay windows but they were the type of antiquated windows that didn't open and close and she daren't break something so old. Slowly the realisation of her situation dawned on her - she was locked in the library.

In her youth Charity had fantasised about this very situation, being locked inside a library for days on end, having nothing but the stillness of the night and thousands upon thousands of stories all to herself. It had seemed an idealistic scenario but Charity soon realised that missing the comfort of her familiar bed was enough to distract her from any substantial enjoyment in such a place. She wandered the shelves, picking out random books here and there and flicking through their pages and after about an hour Charity had resettled herself among the pillows at the back of the library, intent on trying to get some sleep for a while. She had just started to doze off when she was again interrupted by another unexpected noise. A snapping sound, like the breaking of a stick, sounded above her head and Charity craned her neck quickly to see the source of the noise. Seeing nothing, she stood up and checked the nearby rows of books but again found no sign of a disturbance. Attributing this mystery noise to her over-active imagination, she returned to her pillows but when she stooped down to pick up a particularly lumpy pillow, something cold and wet tapped her on the back of the head. A droplet of something had splashed down from the ceiling above and landed squarely on her white mane of hair. Charity felt where the drop had struck her and then inspected her fingers, which were now stained an unmistakable shade of jet black.

"What –" she exclaimed, sniffing the substance in utter bewilderment, "Is this…ink?!"

Charity strained her eyes. Through the darkness she could just make out a broken panel in the wooden slated roof above, but had she not been alerted to that very spot she doubted very much if she would've ever noticed it. In fact, the lack of any proper light made it virtually invisible. Charity fingered the splintered panel, running a finger along where the black substance seemed to be escaping from above. There's so much of it, she thought, wondering how nobody had noticed such a thing before now. Very puzzled but determined to get to the bottom of this oddity, Charity gently pulled back one of the broken boards, hoping to reveal the source of the black substance. The panel was surprisingly loose, in fact Charity noticed that it was barely held in place and had come away with hardly any effort whatsoever. She certainly hadn't meant to damage school property but there was obviously a serious flaw in the library and whilst she was stuck here she thought she could at least do something constructive and find out why. So after some hesitation, she dug her fingers into the widening gap she had created and pulled away another section of panel, again it came away with surprising ease and Charity threw the ink-sodden wood onto the ground with the other piece.

I've gone this far, I may as well go a little further, thought Charity, as she hopped onto a nearby table to get a better grip on the panels above. Charity pulled off three more pieces of panel until she had made a hole just big enough for her to fit through. When no obvious culprit to the leak had emerged she had come to the conclusion that she was going to have to climb into the attic of the library herself and investigate what the problem could be. So, stacking a chair on top of the table she began to climb towards the gap that one hour ago had not been present in the library at all. She teetered nervously as she righted herself on top of the chair and with difficulty, reached up and placed her hands through the hole and onto the floor of the room above.

The floor was damp with what Charity guessed was more of the ink-like substance but she gripped tightly nonetheless and yanked herself up through the hole. She had pulled herself onto the floor and managed to stand up straight, slipping slightly in more of the dark liquid that lay all around the floor at her feet. Glancing around, she suddenly realised that it was much darker up there than in the main library. Charity supposed she would need some source of light; she sighed heavily and began her descent back down the rickety ladder she had assembled. Ten minutes later she had found what she had been looking for, one candle and a set of matches, both 'borrowed' from the librarian's store cupboard. She won't notice anyway and there's plenty in there, thought Charity, as she climbed into the darkness for a second time that evening.

When she was once again standing on the ink-splattered floor, she lit her candle and flooded the room with a warm glow. Waving the candle around, Charity gasped in astonishment. She was surrounded by books, thousands upon thousands of books piled high in the shelves around her, and what shelves they were. Majestically decorated mahogany shelves that towered right up to a ceiling that must have been ten, fifteen, or even twenty feet high, Charity couldn't tell. She began to walk, her feet squelching in the liquid below. Bending low she found that it had certainly pooled where the hole was but there was a definite trail. Part of Charity told her she should climb back down and attempt to fix the panels that she shouldn't have broken in the first place but something else her urged her onwards, away from the library and along the mysterious trail that lead deeper into this hidden section.

Charity moved slowly, keeping her candle low so she could accurately follow the trail. She walked for what felt like the full length of the library below but the path did not stop. It kept going, further and further it went. Charity wondered where this extra area of floor had sprung from. The library was one of the smallest buildings in St. August's and there was no way such a large room could've gone undiscovered right above it. After what felt like an age of walking with her back bent low as she tracked the little trail, Charity finally bumped into something small and hard, a dead end. In front of her was an ornate, stone pedestal that looked quite out of place in the wood covered library. Charity wondered what its purpose was until she noticed, lifting her candle higher, a dusty book laying on its flat surface. Its cover was largely unreadable due to a thick layer of dust and grime but Charity could see that it was leather-bound and ancient-looking, and the pages were gilt-edged and smattered with the same black ink as the floor.

The ink, Charity now noticed, was trickling all the way down the shaft of the pedestal and even from the pages of the book themselves. Charity reached out and touched the thick leather front cover and as she did, she could suddenly feel something wonderful. An inexplicable sensation spread itself right through her entire body from the soles of her feet to the tips of her white hair, and for a whole wonderful minute she stood savouring the astounding feeling coursing through her veins. Then, as suddenly as it had started, it stopped. Charity could not explain what she had felt or why it had happened but she was starting to get the feeling that the library at St. August's was perhaps not as ordinary as it had first seemed. She reached out instinctively towards the book sitting on the little pedestal, reaching out as she had done hundreds of times before and flipping over the front cover, eager to gaze inside at its contents.

Without warning, a blast of black liquid engulfed her face, head, arms, her entire body. There was a sudden torrent of noise all around her, and mingled screams and shouts of joy whirled about the room penetrating her senses. Charity screamed as loud as her lungs would let her. Confused and disorientated, she groped for the pedestal, for a nearby bookcase, for anything to steady herself as she felt like she had been lifted off her feet. She felt the candle slip from her grasp as she tumbled over and over, panic turning quickly to outright terror. She had been screaming for so long she thought her lungs might burst and then just as suddenly as it started it stopped. The noise, the liquid, and the movement all ceased as Charity, still screaming, fell to the ground with a crash so terrible that she knew, in that instant, that she had died.

4 – THE OLD MAN AND THE BOOK

Charity could hear something, something new. The terrible noise that had split her ears moments ago had stopped, but she kept her eyes shut tight, afraid to open them, afraid of what she might see. What had happened when she opened that book? "This is a nightmare," she thought desperately. "If I stay here and don't move, don't open my eyes everything will be alright. I'll just wait here on the floor and soon I'll wake up in my bed", Charity promised herself. But deep down she knew that *this* was nothing like any nightmare she had had before. Everything was too real, too vivid, the way the floor felt beneath her, the relentless pounding of her heart, was all too horrible to be a product of her over-active imagination. The noise was growing louder now and Charity strained her ears despite herself. "Panting, heavy breathing, sounds like some sort of animal," she surmised logically to herself. She kept up a relentless stream of conversation inside her head, willing herself to keep calm. "Ok, Charity open your eyes, just open them on the count of three. Ok *one*…" Charity steeled herself, "*two*…" she spoke the word in her own head once more and then, "…three!" This time Charity spoke the word out loud and for the first time since she touched that old book, she opened her eyes.

It took a few seconds for Charity's senses to adjust to her surroundings; she noticed with rising apprehension that she was definitely not in the library anymore. She was lying on the filthy, dust covered wooden floor of a small room. The old oak panelled walls were bare and infested with mould and the windows patchily boarded up, allowing only a small amount of light to shine through in thin shafts. Charity wiggled her toes checking if her legs still worked, which thankfully they did. She righted herself and looking around, began to panic. This was definitely not the room she had been in thirty seconds ago. "Or has it been thirty seconds?" she asked herself desperately. Time was not something she could be completely confident about at the moment. The rasping, panting sounds were becoming louder still, and, looking around the room, she saw that it seemed to be coming from a small armchair in the far corner of the room. Warily, Charity made her way towards it, her heart rate increasing alarmingly as whatever was making those noises snorted and spluttered from the chair. She slowly moved closer to the back of the chair, her hands outstretched. Dread flooded her body as she reached for the worn fabric. She held her breath once more and pulled the chair roughly around to face her. Instantly she fell backwards in horror. A blood-soaked old man was slumped astride it, his breathing ragged and his face blotched with sweat and patches of dried blood. "I – I what what's wrong?!" Charity gasped, horrified, righting herself once more and moving closer to the stricken man. "Oh my! You're hurt, I know, I can help, I think I can help, wait!" Charity pulled off her school blazer and pressed it softly on the man's chest. There was so much blood. The old man grimaced in pain as she patted his wound and with difficulty he seemed to control his erratic breathing.

"You…" he croaked, "I knew, knew it…would…" To Charity's utter bewilderment the man's face had broken out into a watery-eyed smile.

"I'm sorry, I don't understand! What do you want me to do? Should I get help?" Charity asked urgently and made to move away from the chair and closer to the door of the room, but the old man grabbed her roughly by the hand, stopping her.

"NO…WAIT!" he hissed through clenched teeth.

"Ow! Please, let go…of…me!" grimaced Charity, wrenching her arm from the old man's surprisingly strong grip.

The man lurched back against his armchair and for a few horrible seconds Charity thought he was dead, but then very slowly his eyes flickered open, he opened his mouth and spoke, his eyes locked upon her own.

"Please, listen to me…I…I need you to listen." His breathing had grown sharper and every few words were punctuated with a terrible rasping sound he made as he clutched at his throat and chest with shrivelled, long-nailed hands.

"I – alright, I'm listening, but you really need help."

The man airily waved a hand in the air. "No point, the wound…it is irreparable." Charity couldn't help admire his bravery, this man was surely going to die and if she didn't do anything… "You will…have a lot of questions, girl, but I'm afraid," he grimaced in pain and shifted in his chair, "I do not have long."

Charity opened her mouth to speak but closed it instead, waiting for him to continue, "You were brought here for a reason…*you*…can read!"

Charity raised her eyebrows in derision, but kept her voice calm and reassuring. "Well, I mean, of course I can read, I'm thirteen, it would be *strange* if I didn't know how to read."

"I don't mean reading a book, girl!" the man snapped in frustration. "No, you can read Journals." This last word was whispered in an unmistakable tone of reverence, escaping his mouth in a mere whisper. Charity could tell that this was something quite special, something that the man wanted to keep between just the two of them.

"I don't understand, I'm sorry," Charity said hesitantly, still eyeing the dark unyielding patch of blood issuing from beneath her blazer, "Please, let me go and find help!"

"Aren't you listening to me girl?" he retorted angrily. "You are a reader, a translator, a Regalis!" the old man's eyes bulged out of his head. She could see he was trying to underline its importance of this statement but Charity could only stare down at the near lifeless figure, misunderstanding and confusion welling up inside her.

"PLEASE!" he yelled, losing all sense of secrecy. He groped for Charity but she took a step back from his chair, terrified, wanting to run, to get away from this wretched figure. The man clutched roughly at his wound, screaming out in what looked like intense agony. Charity moved back further still, towards the door, her hands clasped to her mouth, tears welling up in her eyes. "I'm sorry," she wept, "I don't know what you want!"

The man was flailing his hands about wildly now, he made one huge effort and leaned out of his chair, his blood-stained hands flapping through the air in front of him. With immense difficulty he managed to grasp onto a small side table in front of his chair, on which was placed a large leather-bound book, not dissimilar to the book she had opened in the strange room all that time ago. The man placed one trembling hand on the book and flung it off the table and across the dust covered floor. It skidded to a halt a couple of inches from Charity's feet but she did not pick it up. He leant back but kept his manic eyes fixed on Charity's tear-stained face.

"I don't…" she started.

"Forgive…" he stammered breathlessly, and then with an awful finality he laid his head back against the cushioned armchair, closed his eyes and was, at last, still.

Charity did not move. She had never seen a person die, never mind a stranger in such odd circumstances, and she was unaccustomed to the feeling of mingled dread and guilt that was now coursing through her. Somehow his stillness terrified her far more than his ranting had done. She continued to eye the body warily, not daring to move for if she did she knew she would have to face the reality of her terrible situation and that was something she did not want to do.

Charity knew it was no use panicking; the first thing she must do was compose herself. She was finding it hard to breathe and if she continued like this she would surely collapse. Her hands shook as she clumsily felt for the pulse on her neck, and finding her heart beat she slowly counted out the beats inside her head, willing them to slow down, to bring her heart rate back to normal but the more she worried that her heart or lungs might explode from the stress, the more it sped up. She shut her eyes, concentrating hard, trying to silence the little voice in her head which was screaming in terror at the unexpected and inexplicable events she had been through in the past hour, if indeed it was that long. After a while she had managed to calm down enough to lower her pulse to a relatively healthy level. She opened her eyes and the horrible sight of the old man greeted her once more.

Moving towards the worn armchair she immediately tripped over something large and heavy, and, bending low she saw that it was the book the man had thrown at her some moments ago. She hadn't even registered its presence due to what, she thought, was the more pressing issue of a dead body in the corner. Charity picked up the book, which was surprisingly light, she carried it away from the chair and began inspecting it carefully. "What's so special about it anyway?" she muttered to herself; the man had seemed almost mad with insistence that she read it. It wasn't even in good condition, she thought, running her fingers over the cracked cover and noticing a huge gash in the centre of it, where something had clearly penetrated the books initial pages. It certainly wasn't an ordinary book though, that much was obvious. For a start instead of a title, a man's name was written across the cover in familiar gold handwriting, 'Vincent Dunluce' and just below that, the words: 'Year of Birth: 4033'. As Charity inspected the cover more thoroughly, wondering who Vincent Dunluce could be and why the old man thought this so crucial, a curious thing happened. The book gave a little shudder and then almost at once the gold writing on the cover began to vibrate minutely, each of the tiny golden letters pulsated in their places and the space below the writing was unexpectedly filled with more of the shining words, as if a ghostly hand was expertly scrawling them onto the cover in the same exquisite handwriting. Charity had dropped the book in alarm but as it fell to the floor she could clearly read the finished line of text: 'Year of Death: 4105'.

She whirled around to stare open-mouthed at the body slumped lifelessly in the chair, "Could this be something to do with him?" she asked herself disbelievingly. This had happened before, she thought terrified, that old book in her room all those months ago, the same golden writing. The situation was ludicrous, she knew that and part of her screamed that she should burst out of the room and find someone, a policeman, an adult, anyone who could help, but something nudged her onwards, something that had come into being when she first touched the dusty old book back at school. On any other day Charity would have turned on her heels and torn out of there but instead she bent down and opened the mysterious book, lying quite innocently on the floor in front of her. She would not bury her troubles this time, this time she would find out what was going on. She flicked through the pages, her heart full of trepidation and if she was honest – a little excitement. However, to her disappointment, the ivory white pages of the book seemed completely blank. As she rifled quickly through them she spotted nothing of interest, not one passage, message or sentence - in fact the book was devoid of any writing whatsoever.

She stopped turning pages near the end of the book and left it spread open. Charity ran her fingers along the edge of one of the pages thinking hard. Perhaps the man had hidden something in the cover of the book. She picked up the book, feeling a small indentation on the back cover as she did, when something happened that made her drop it to the floor once more. All of a sudden she noticed that a very faint letter had formed in the top left hand corner of one of the pages, a letter that had not been there before. She squinted hard at the book now lying open on the dusty floor and could just make out the outline of a miniscule letter 'T'. Charity focused harder still, staring at the pages with intense concentration and as she did the 'T' was joined by an 'o' and then more letters, dozens, perhaps hundreds of characters swirled onto the page in unison, spelling out a clear passage of writing.

'Today I might go for a short walk near the Four Falls, I get so lonely at times and the terrible guilt isn't pleasant. *Must remember to get supplies for later on*, I'll have to stop at the market. Walking to the lake is one of my favourite pastimes I think, it does a lot to ease my worries, *What if he comes back? I knew there was something wrong with him, he wasn't meant to... I don't know if I should've done it.* Think about something else, think about the lake, the calming lake.'

Charity had read quite a few books, even by the tender age of thirteen and yet she had never read anything quite so odd in all her life. The language in this book was strange and erratic, broken up by random thoughts and feelings; it was a bit like a diary she thought to herself but a diary where *all* the writer's thoughts spilled onto the page in one long passage. She flipped several pages further and noticed to her great surprise that *all* the previously blank pages were now filled with words, the entire book from the very first page to the last was riddled with the same curly black handwriting. Charity sat dumbfounded, and for a long time she simply stared at the old book, her brain frantically trying to rationalise the situation she found herself in. Instinctively she ran her forefinger and thumbs along the book and flicked through the pages to somewhere near the end. She read:

'I knew it would happen, I knew it would happen! *I should have done more to get rid of him...* It wasn't a normal situation and poor Maria oh my sweet Maria why did you leave me? *It was HIS fault, he took her from me! I'm scared;* I don't think I've ever been so scared. He will come for me, Oh Thea! *...I must be mistaken.* I must read the letter once more...no, no **NO NO!** *It's all true, all of it!* I could hide, I could run but where to? Oh Thea he'll find me, I know he will.

No, I can see what must be done, I must repent for my sins, only then can I find peace. This is the only way, besides *I'll be with her again.*'

Charity was shaking, she was struggling to comprehend what this could all mean, a cavalcade of questions bounced around her head and she wanted nothing more than someone, anyone to answer them. The letter, she thought suddenly, if she could find the letter the writer had mentioned then it was bound to tell her something that could help her. She shut the large book with a snap and again saw the golden writing etched onto the front cover. It glistened at her, mocking her confusion as she got to her feet and moved silently around the room searching for the letter. The old man lay quite still and Charity attempted to ignore his presence as she scoured the room quickly, in search of the one thing she hoped that could give her answers. After half an hour or so of frantic rummaging, pulling out books from a nearby bookshelf, checking under piles of old abandoned laundry and, despite Charity's intense disgust, checking the pockets of the old man's waistcoat, she moved back disappointed to where she had left the book. It was still there, the golden writing still flickering in the light now shining through the cracks in the boarded up window. Just then Charity spotted something protruding from below a nearby desk leg. It was a tiny fraction of brown, very creased paper. She slipped the paper out and unfurled it flat on the dust-covered floorboards, she felt her begin to race as very carefully she began to read:

Vincent,

I truly hope this letter finds you. I know you have lived a difficult existence since the passing of Melody. It is unfortunate that I should have to contact you under these circumstances but I must inform you; I know about the boy. None can be blamed if one's kin does not graft, and Thea can be cruel as well as kind, Vincent and - I'm sure you thought you were doing the right thing. A child without a Journal in Thea is but a mere shadow and alas that is where darkness often treads. My sources in the Castlands have reported disturbing events that all point to the boy. I cannot be sure but he talks of returning to the Mainland, returning to find you.

I will not be so bold as to assume that you will take heed of the words of a stranger without question but I can only ask that you trust me, Vincent. I have seen and read many things, these things to come will all spawn from him. It is not over yet, you can still do the right thing, your sins can still be forgiven but a heavy price must be paid.

There is but one capable of stopping what is to come but she is not of our world. I will see to it that she is drawn to us but the gate must be opened. You know what act must be committed to open the link.

But understand that if you fail to act, Vincent then it will be all of Thea that pays the price for what you have borne.

With your help a worthy Regalis will rise once more.

A Friend

Charity read the letter through three times, checking each line for hidden meanings or hints. She stood up, her head swimming with information. Charity had no idea what was happening, the myriad questions she had had swirling round her mind before had now multiplied tenfold, was *she* the girl being written about? What did the writer mean by 'this world'?

Charity was now more convinced than ever that she had lost her mind, and she felt sick. She was finding it increasingly difficult to breathe in the dusty old hut and quickly stuffed the letter into the pocket of her skirt before stumbling to the door. She needed to get out of this room, and she wanted away from the old man, away from the dust and away from the strange book. Flinging the door wide open, she stepped out into crisp, fresh air but stopped in her tracks almost immediately. Charity gasped in amazement at the sight that unfolded before her eyes. She was standing, not in the grounds of St. August's, but in a small village of tiny, single room huts scattered sporadically around, and just behind these huts was a monolithic waterfall, bigger and more incredible than any she had ever seen in all her life. The water cascaded down from miles above at four separate points, crashing into a veritable ocean below. Charity clutched at her head - this was all too much. Her vision was fading and she could just make out blurred figures rushing towards her as she stumbled, some stopping in front of her whilst others moved past her into the hut.

"Help the poor girl!" someone cried from somewhere. "What *is* she wearing?" Voices bombarded her senses, blurring into one.

"That's the Dunluce house, why was she - oh my!"

"His Journal!"

"Call the Order!"

"HELP!"

"She's not right, she's -",

"Catch her, she's fainting!"

5 – THE IVORY ORDER

Charity hit the mud hard. The only thing she was sure of was that she had fallen with a considerable splash on to the cold, sodden ground. Muffled voices and noises sounded from just above her and she was finding it increasingly difficult to think clearly. Charity could feel several pairs of hands roughly grab at her, pulling and prodding at her limbs, and then a voice echoed the loudest among this bustle:

"Stand yerselves down there folks, stand back! Give us a bit of room now! Lemme through!"

Charity opened her eyes and a blurred white form moved towards where she lay and bent down. "S'ok, girl, I got yeh," said a kind voice, and Charity smiled weakly as she was effortlessly hoisted up into the arms of a huge figure.

When she next awoke she was lying in a soft, comfortable bed, her whole body enveloped by fluffy blankets and her head propped up by a squishy feather pillow. Charity smiled to herself, opening her eyes to get a better look at her surroundings. She was almost too drained to register much except a huge arched window that looked out over a vast expanse of water that she did not recognise. Making the conscious decision to find out just where she was, she reluctantly slithered out from beneath the blankets. As her feet touched the cold tiled floors she realised her boots and socks had been removed, however she still had on her dark school skirt, St. August's tie and her navy school shirt. After some searching around her new surroundings she found her socks and boots in a cream coloured laundry basket beside the window but her school blazer was nowhere to be found and try as she might she could not locate it. Frustrated she moved towards the large arch window at the far end of the room and goggled at the sight that met her. Charity stared open-mouthed at a crystal clear blue ocean that seemed to go on forever, as far as her eyes could see. Such an incredible spectacle would almost certainly have taken her breath away were it not for the sight of a bright *red* sun which was hanging motionless just on the horizon, bathing all before it in a pleasant cherry-coloured glow.

A curious realisation dawned on Charity as she stood watching this new sun make its way across the sky, something that some part of her had known since she had first awoke in the strange cabin. She was *not* on Earth anymore. This was like no place she'd ever heard or read about and the latter was something that ultimately concerned her the most. Charity knew enough from the times she had read books on geography that there was absolutely nothing on Earth that compared with the sight that greeted her now.

Charity found the rest of her clothes on a chair by the bed and had just begun to pull on her boots when the door was thrown open and a large bottom squeezed through the frame. This large behind was followed by the equally large body of a smiling red-headed woman, dressed head to toe in a cream-white uniform. She was beaming and chatting away merrily to the room at large, and Charity noticed she was carrying an intricately-detailed silver serving tray which she set on a bedside table, still with her back to where Charity stood.

"Nathaniel has been in a foul mood all morning, but then, you don't know him, I suppose you don't! Well not to worry, you'll meet him soon enough, he's fine once you get to know him, A PUSSY CAT HE IS! We'll get you fed and then it's off to work…that's right, it's not all free breakfasts and comfy beds, gotta do your bit, s'all part of the…" Charity noticed that the huge woman spoke incredibly quickly and didn't seem to need to breathe between sentences, it all just came spewing out in one long burst. Charity smiled awkwardly as the woman turned and seeing her standing there, jumped back in surprise. She had clearly been expecting to see a slumbering girl lying peacefully in the bed but instead she found Charity, quite awake, fully clothed and standing at the window.

"OH!" she yelled dramatically, her substantial frame wobbled furiously, "My girl you gave me a fright, why on Thea would you not tell me you weren't in the bed? I coulda been holding the tray and then what? BOOM that's what, all that lovely breakfast would be on the floor, what a waste that'd be!" The woman glared at Charity with beady blue eyes.

"Oh I'm sorry, I just didn't really know when to speak. You sort of surprised me." Charity smiled hopefully at the glaring woman but as she did the glare slipped off her face and she reverted quickly back to her upbeat disposition, "Oh well not to worry," she said bracingly, "Well why *are* you out of bed? You had a nasty fall, a nasty 'un, bed's the best place after a fall like that, make no mistake girl."

"I'm fine, honestly I am," said Charity in a tone which she hoped would convince the woman, and then spotting the silver tray laden with food she added quickly, "Although, I am a *bit* hungry I suppose." The red-headed woman beamed at her.

"Then it's time yeh got something in yeah, got plenty of stuff here to keep yeh going." she bellowed to the room and after several moments of rustling and bustling about the room she had seated Charity on the edge of the bed, the silver tray perched, quite perilously, on her knees.

"Well eat up, eat up." The woman encouraged Charity giving her a slap on her shoulder, which now felt like it might drop off. Charity winced in pain and eager to avoid upsetting the large woman again, grabbed a fork from the tray and shovelled in a portion of unfamiliar looking pulses.

"I'm Giselle, by the way, can't believe you didn't even ask my name, rude, rude!" said Gisele pouting dramatically and then seeing Charity's concerned face burst out, "Ahh now calm yerself, I'm only pulling yer pages, you've had a fall, s'only natural you'd be a little forgetful of your manners." A reassuring grin split her wide face, whilst Charity, whose own face was too stuffed with food to respond now, nodded in agreement.

"Oh my, I've forgotten your drink, back in a moment girl, don't move, and keep eating – you could do with a good feed by the looks of yeh."

Gisele could move awfully quickly for someone so big and Charity noticed as she whipped out of sight that she wore a brown leather belt around her ample waist and holstered to the belt was something small and olive coloured, something that made Charity's heartbeat increase rapidly - a book. Not as big or grand as the one in the old man's hut but she could see again a flash of familiar golden writing on the front. A couple of minutes later she was back, this time carrying a beautifully decorated clay jug in one hand and a silver goblet in the other. Laying the goblet on the tray she tilted the jug until a splash of sapphire blue liquid trickled into her goblet.

"Opal berry juice, it's a specialty in Agua, just glorious!" Gisele said answering Charity's unasked question with a broad grin. "You'll love it trust me ye will, take a sip, go on." Gisele continued to coax Charity as she raised the goblet to her lips and drank deeply. She had to admit that it was truly delicious, the blue liquid fizzed and popped yet she could see no bubbles in the goblet. Some of Charity's feelings were clearly present on her face because Gisele had begun to laugh affectionately, "Yeh like that eh? Aye you'll fit right in ere girl. But oh," her face fell comically as she looked intently at Charity, "I haven't even asked yer name, can't be calling ye 'girl' the whole time now can I? Oh and there's me complaining about you not asking me name and I haven't, ah dearie me!"

"Charity, my name is Charity Walters." Charity said concisely,

"Noooo, don't know any Waters, nor any Chartys round these parts, ner anywhere else really." said Gisele looking thoughtfully out of the window, "Well, Charty Waters I suppose you'd like to know where in Thea you are, would that be right?"

Charity was conflicted between correcting Gisele's mispronunciation of her name and finding out more about where she was. She decided that the correction could wait until she discovered more about her current whereabouts.

"Yes, oh yes, I would." said Charity happily, thinking excitedly that perhaps she was on the verge of a simple answer for once.

"Well," said Gisele seating herself on a corner of Charity's bed, Charity feeling her end of the mattress rise at least a foot into the air as she did so, "To be exact Charty, you are in Agua's Ivory Order Chapter." Gisele tapped a small badge that was embroidered onto the front of her glisteningly white uniform. Charity stared at the symbol, which appeared to show an open book atop a red circle. Charity definitely didn't recognise this symbol and privately began to wonder if she had been taken in by some sort of cult. Absolutely none of the words Gisele had said meant any sense to her. What was the Ivory Order Chapter? What was an Agua? A million different questions sprung to the forefront of her mind but she couldn't decide which one to ask first so she just looked helplessly at Gisele, who considered her, creasing her brow in concern. Her blank stare was obviously not the reaction she had been expecting. Charity supposed that this announcement should have been followed by a look of clear understanding or sudden realisation.

"Not heard of us eh? My, that is odd I'll say, well then we'll take things nice n' slow…you're in Agua, you'll know about…that…at…least…" Gisele tailed off at the blank look Charity continued to fix her with. "My, my, oh my, you did bang yer head didn't you, umm well…Best to start off with the basics, you're on Thea, Thea the planet, this big spinning thing we all live on." Charity was not enjoying being made to feel so stupid. She had certainly never heard of this Thea but thought that if she was to fit in, even a little, that it was best to at least play along with this part of this explanation.

"Oh of course, Thea, well I *know that*," she exclaimed in an understanding tone of voice, "I just forgot whereabouts I was *ON* Thea." Gisele's worried look fell away as she breathed out, clearly relieved.

"Oh thank goodness, thought you'd lost all sense there Charty. Well like I said, you're in Agua – eh Ag-wa is one of the three Mainlands on Thea, there's Agua, Dura and Imputtia."

"Oh, ooooohhhhh" feigned Charity, "I remember. Of course, Agua." She was sure her face was flushed with embarrassment but attempted to look as though she understood. "So would you know anything about where I can find Earth then, Gisele?" she asked, in what she hoped was a casual manner. She knew her question was a lost cause before Gisele opened her mouth to answer, her face cracked with concern once more and Charity felt her spirits plummet.

"Uhh well earth's in the ground love, isn't it? I mean that's what earth is, y'know? Dirt." Gisele again seemed worried about Charity's mental condition, fixing her beadily with another concerned stare as Charity felt her heart sink down into her boots. "Oh yeah, sorry, I knew that, thanks." she said, still trying to keep her voice light, despite the nagging voice in her head which was screaming, *This isn't right, she doesn't know where Earth is! Ask something else!*

"Well we should be getting to work, it's almost time." Gisele briskly stood up, causing Charity's mattress to sink downwards once more.

Charity watched as Gisele made to bustle from the room, her arms full of the silver tray. She could think of nothing else, her brain seemed to be screeching at her to tell the truth, to tell Gisele where she was from and that she needed to get back home. "Gisele!" she barked in a high pitched voice that almost a scream, and Gisele whipped around in fright, staring at her.

"Blimey Charty! Wha's the matter with you, scared me half to death th – Charty, what is it? You ok love?"

Charity wasn't listening. She was thinking hard, her brain aching to make sense of the insane situation she was in. She stared out the window at the ruby red sun and then back at Gisele, she steeled herself and let the thought that had been plaguing her mind ever since she had woken up in the strange little shack tumble from her mouth.

"Gisele, I don't know how to put this but…well, I'm lost! I mean - I'm not from A-Agua and…" she faltered - how could this stranger understand? If she didn't know where Earth was then how was Charity to get home? Wherever this organisation was they had no idea what 'the Earth' was and they'd surely think Charity mad for suggesting she lived there.

But Gisele did not look perplexed, on the contrary, a knowing look was clear on her round face, the sort of look Charity thought a mother might give her child, "Oh Charty, I'm so sorry! Where are yeh from exactly?" asked Gisele setting down the tray and coming closer to the bed once more.

"Oh, umm, it's a really faraway place, like *really* far!" Charity knew she couldn't tell her the truth, but how could she find out where she was or how to get back home? She hesitated for a moment and then had a sudden idea.

"OW! That bang on my head, ohhhh it stings, I can't quite remember…where…I'm from." Charity clutched her head in mock agony, straining her eyes dramatically.

Gisele clapped two enormous hands over her mouth in shock. "No! Don't strain yerself, Charty, I'll help yeh, umm… I know, no wait, far away, far away," she said slowly, "That would be, YES! Imputtia, it must be, is it Imputtia? Is that where you're from?" Gisele was speaking very slowly and very loudly to Charity, as if she were talking with a dazed toddler. "IM-PUSH-EE-A?? YES?"

"Imputtia… of course!" exclaimed Charity in mock excitement. "Now that would be *very, very* far away from here wouldn't it?"

"Oh my yes, miles and miles Charty, miles and miles and miles!"

"Well can you maybe help me get there perhaps?" Charity had no desire to go to *anywhere* in this strange place, but she figured that if she could engineer herself a means of transport it might mean she was closer to a way home.

"Charty dear, that would cost an awful lot, an awful lot, more Odes than I has, that's fer sure, but you could just stay here fer a bit, you'll be working in the kitchens anyway I mean, be able to pay yer own way eventually."

"What's that now?" Charity asked pointedly, her eyebrows raised. "I'm working here? Why am I working here?"

"Well…I mean, like I said, this is the Ivory Order, it's the place with the most intelligent people in all of Thea, s'our job to pick up urchins like you and bring em here to work…fer a wage o' course. Trust me it's a lot better than being on the street."

"But I don't want to work here!" said Charity heatedly, thrusting off the now depleted silver tray onto the bed and standing up defiantly.

"I wouldn't say you've a choice Charty," said Gisele calmly lifting up the silver tray in one large hand. "Most urchins that come here leave eventually once they've earnt enough to pay their way, all the Order want to do is make sure you have the fortitude to make it on yer own. If we let all little ones out early they'd be out there in the mud and the rain with no food or shelter. Nah, this way is better in the long run."

Charity raged and ranted whilst Gisele went about the tiny bedroom patiently rebuffing her arguments and questions with a calm smile spread across her face. She threatened to storm out of the room, to run off but she had no idea where she was or how to go about getting back home. Gisele meanwhile was adamant that Charity was to work her way to a self-sufficient amount of money and before she did that she'd not be going anywhere.

Eventually, after over an hour of annoyance and frustration, Charity had sufficiently calmed down to see that this arrangement may, in fact, work in her favour. Gisele had told her that there were intellectuals here: explorers, teachers, leaders. Someone was bound to know how she could get home. In any case, thought Charity, if she was to survive here she would need money – that much was obvious.

So with her mind made up - not that she had had much choice in the matter - Charity followed Gisele out of the room, grabbing her bag and swinging it onto her shoulders as she went. She patted her side pocket and felt the reassuring crinkle of the old man's brown letter snuggled inside. Whilst she had made up her mind to work, she had not forgotten about the intriguing mysteries of the letter and the strange book. That was something she intended to find out much more about if she was to spend some time here in the Order Chapter.

On their way to the kitchens, Charity passed marble figures of men and women, pictures of strange sweeping landscapes and suits of white armour glistening brightly in the sunlight streaming in through the small circular windows set against the wall of the building. Gisele, who had been extremely friendly to her so far, had begun chatting animatedly to Charity just as soon as they had left the small bedroom, "The Ivory Order is a place for the top end of society to meet, share ideas, socialise with each other. Their main job though is to hand out Journals, yeh know these things," she wiggled her huge hips letting the book flop up and down against her waist. "Where is yer Journal by the way?"

"Um…It's in my bag." Charity lied quickly. There were a lot of things unclear about this strange place, but one thing that was abundantly obvious was that these people held these funny little books in the highest of regards.

"Oh right. That's fine, each to their own I guess. I'd be scared of losing it - too forgetful." She shuddered. "Imagine if you never found it again."

"Yeah," said Charity, in what she hoped was a convincing tone, "That'd be awful!"

The rest of the of the journey passed in semi-silence, every now and then Gisele would burst into talk, explaining the history of various statues they passed or to point out the types of wood used in the grand stairs they were descending. She spoke with such love and reverie on these occasions that Charity would've forgiven herself for thinking that she owned the incredible house. After traversing what felt like the length of two football fields they found themselves outside a small white door with the words, 'Kitchens - Staff Only' printed on it in black, block lettering.

"This is the Kitchens, Charty," Gisele said jabbing a finger at the sign. "Now it gets a bit er… rowdy in there, so keep yer head down and just follow me." Gisele pushed the little door open and squeezed through with what looked like a great effort. Charity followed her and saw that she was now in a long room with about two dozen cookers and stoves all piping out wafts of unusual coloured smoke. Charity could barely see a thing in this place, she bent down low and followed the sound of Gisele's voice, which was now booming over the din of the others in the kitchens, "CHEFS AND COOKS! COURSE THE ODD KITCHEN MAID TOO, MOST FOOD TENDS TO CAUSE A BIT OF A MESS SO WE HAVE TO LEARN OUR OWN WAY THROUGH THE HUBBUB!"

"OK!" shouted Charity as loud as she could. She wasn't even sure Gisele had heard her; being several feet taller than Charity and having her face currently obscured by an acrid blue smoke cloud currently engulfing this section of the kitchen. Gisele hurried off into the thick clouds ahead of her and Charity hurried forwards but before she stumbled, landing hard on a cold, tiled surface. She righted herself and tried desperately to listen for Giscle's voice but it was almost impossible in the din of the kitchen. Charity continued to grope her way through the maze of legs and falling utensils towards where she assumed Gisele was heading. She looked around for something, anything that would lead her to Gisele but she could barely see her hand in front of her face. Charity had really begun to panic and just as she was starting to think about turning back when a large hand appeared out of the smoke beside her, it grasped her arm tightly and yanked her forwards as if she were a rag doll. Charity was pulled through a cloud of green smoke and emerged on the other side, a beaming Gisele staring down at her.

Gisele released her and indicated a white wooden door in front of her, it was almost identical to the one they had come through moments before except for a small sign that was nailed to the top which read, 'East Wing'. They hurried though and slammed it hard behind them, and instantly the noise and commotion was silenced.

"Takes a while to get used to it, sorry." said Gisele

"No it's fine. It's a bit, er, busy isn't it?" said Charity, extremely relieved to have escaped the noise and commotion.

Gisele laughed heartily, "Oh! Yer a kind one, I can tell, go on…" she leaned in close to Charity's face, "tell us what ye really think, no niceties now."

Charity looked conflicted for a minute and then said hurriedly, "That was terrifying, I thought I was gonna get cleaved in two by someone. They're so noisy too and the smoke, how can anyone cook in a place like *that?!* I could hardly breathe!" Her words tumbled from her mouth so quickly she sounded a great deal like Gisele usually did.

Gisele gave another huge laugh and slapped Charity on the back, nearly knocking her flying. "Tha's brilliant, girl! You are a funny little thing aren't yeh! Come on, we'll cut through the gardens, nearly there, jus' heading for the Helper House."

Gisele set off once more, Charity again following diligently in her wake as she moved down another flight of ornate stairs and out a side door. All of a sudden they were outside in the bright sunlight and in front of a lush, green garden; Charity felt wonderful finally being outside. A cool wind whipped her face and the rays gently warmed her face and arms. The two walked along a stone-covered path that lead around the edge of the greenery. Charity was savouring the glorious weather and frequently stopped to marvel at the different varieties of flora and fauna that inhabited these odd gardens. They had just turned a corner, past a particularly interesting purple rose bush with spikes that vibrated and pulsed when their short-lived peace was shattered by a loud scream coming from nearby. Both of them stopped dead and listened intently, Gisele agitatedly whirling around on the spot, searching for the source of the commotion.

"Please somebody! She's had a baby, she needs help, SOMEBODY!" A man's voice was yelling from just beyond a small row of hedges. Gisele gave one look at Charity and then tore off. Charity, eager not to get lost, followed in haste, sprinting as she attempted to keep up with Gisele. They arrived at the source of the noise and found a crowd of people jostling each other for a view.

"Clear the way folks, clear the way, Ivory official!" Gisele called out in her booming voice, parting the crowd as she went, Charity slipping easily in behind her as she moved. What they found in the centre of the crowd was a very sweaty woman and an increasingly anxious man, the woman lying on her back holding a tiny new born baby in her arms. The infant was mewling but the parents, at least Charity supposed they *must* be the parents, did not look very happy. On the contrary they looked mad with worry. Upon seeing Gisele, however, the man, who had been kneeling beside the woman, jumped to his feet and ran to her.

"Oh thanks be to Thea, thank you. My wife and I were out, she went into labour all of a sudden, and I didn't have time to get the book. Please I need a book, if she doesn't get one, I didn't know what else to do, please help us!" he finished imploringly.

Gisele patted the man reassuringly on the shoulder. She was at least his height and twice his width. "Sir, everything will be fine now, we'll get her grafted and then we'll get you two home where you belong," Gisele said, putting one of her hands inside the cream jacket and pulling out a maroon coloured book with difficulty. Charity noted with interest that there was no writing on this one; in fact to anyone else it would seem to be entirely normal. The man seemed to feel differently, however, as he fell to his knees in gratitude.

"Oh thank you, thank you, thank you! Thank you so much, Miss!"

"It's my job, sir. Now 'scuse me whilst I begin," Gisele said, moving towards the tiny crying child, the new book clutched tightly in her hand.

"No, no problem," said the man, moving to the side. He continued to hover anxiously behind Gisele, peeping over at his newborn with a look of intense apprehension etched onto his face.

Charity watched on, fascinated, as Gisele silently picked up the infant from the woman who gave it up gratefully, a tired and relieved smile now present on her sodden face. Holding the child delicately in one hand, Gisele placed the book face down on the ground in front of her, then taking great care, she leant the newborn forwards and lightly set its hand on the back cover. The small pink hand fidgeted on the maroon cover as Gisele reached out and pressed it into the leather. Charity could hear murmuring from the people around her and could see that Gisele had her eyes closed now and whispered something in a hushed voice:

"Know Thy Self.".

Charity had no idea what was going on and she looked around at the crowd for some sign that they too shared her confusion, but most were nodding in recognition and some were even repeating the phrase under their breath. "Know thy self, know thy self, know thy self." Charity could see their lips miming the words, some eyes closed and others full of reverie.

Charity turned back to the newborn. The infant's hand had stopped wriggling atop the book, and she clapped a hand over her mouth to stop herself from shouting out in surprise. The tiny hand was sinking into the leather of the book, as if it were made of custard. Slowly it began to sink down a couple of inches or so, until it was pressed in so firmly that she was sure the baby would be stuck onto it forever. Charity could see the previously solid cover ebb and flow about the child's tiny hand. Then out of nowhere, the entire book gave a small shudder and suddenly creaked open of its own accord, splaying its fresh white pages to the assembled crowd. The woman on the ground shrieked with joy, clapping her hands together, whilst the man, who had been bobbing up and down behind Gisele, finally struggled past and grabbed at the book. Charity was sure the child would be stuck to it and be dragged from Gisele's arms in the process but to her continued astonishment the hand loosed free almost at once, leaving only the tiny imprint as evidence of the event.

The man held the newly impressed book aloft in front of the crowd, shrieking with joy and waving it triumphantly above his head, "It worked, oh thank Thea it worked, I have a daughter! AH HA!"

Charity could see once more the front cover of one of these strange books, previously untarnished become decorated by familiar, swirling, golden writing, this time spelling out the phrase, 'Belle Pearson, Year of Birth: 4105'. The man glanced at the book, then at his child, and picking her from Gisele's outstretched hands he held her close and whispered, "Belle, what a beautiful name!"

Gisele turned back to Charity who was staring open-mouthed at the scene in front of her. She quietly uttered her congratulations and then silently ushered Charity through the crowd and back into the gardens. They walked without talking, but Charity, who was suddenly bursting with questions, was finding it increasingly difficult to quell her inquisitiveness. She kept quiet nonetheless, somewhat content to simply wallow in the incredible nature of what she had just witnessed. Something was at work in this world, she thought, something impossible, and yet it had occurred right in front of her eyes. Gisele stopped suddenly. They had apparently reached their destination, a round, domed building that looked to Charity like a large, stone igloo. Before it, a sparklingly-clean gate glistened over their heads with a sign that read: 'Helper House'.

"Welcome to your new home!" beamed Gisele, "No time to get comfy though, it's time for work!"

6 - BELLS AND JOURNALS

Gisele wasted no time in ushering Charity through the two large double doors and into a spotlessly clean circular hall. Dozens of metal framed beds were arranged along the walls, their white sheets clashing with the ivory floor tiles. Charity craned her neck to get a better look at the whole room as Gisele continued to shepherd her forwards. She could see that there were no windows set along the cream coloured walls, in fact the only light sources Charity could see were emanating from several large torches that had been placed haphazardly around the room. These wooden torches burned merrily away as Charity moved further into the centre of the room, some set up beside the little beds, others attached to walls and one or two Charity spotted hanging from the ceiling.

In the centre of the room, clear of any beds or torches, was a platform. Charity could see that it was raised ever so slightly above the tiled floor and for some reason it drew her immediate attention. Squinting hard at this dimly lit platform, Charity could see something sparkling but could not immediately make out what it was. She tried to tear herself away from Gisele and get a closer look but just as she did Gisele cleared her throat loudly and thrust her towards a crowd of people Charity hadn't yet noticed. A large group of chattering girls and boys, all around her age, were talking animatedly to one another as Charity was hurled into their midst, and she glanced about them red faced and awkward, not knowing what to say or what to do. However despite her sudden arrival into their midst the group did not cease their conversations and despite some sneaking surreptitious glances at her they all but acted as though she wasn't there.

Gisele moved right up to the tiny platform, blocking out its contents behind her massive frame. She turned to face the group, straightened herself and then called to them in her own characteristic manner

"Alright listen up helpers! It's almost time to get to work, new day, new start, time to go an' all that. Now this right here -" she paused momentarily and took a giant step forwards, yanking Charity, who had crept out to the edge of the group, up to her side, "-this ere is Charty, Charty Waters, she's a lovely young lady and I know she's gonna fit right in cus you lot will make her feel very welcome now, won't you? Uh huh, of course yeh will!"

Charity noticed that Gisele did not wait for an answer but ploughed on with her speech - this was clearly not a question that required a response. However from the looks of the assembled crowd of helpers Charity did not feel confident that they were as welcoming as Gisele seemed to think. Most of them didn't really seem at all interested, on the contrary they looked bored by Gisele's whole speech, as if they had heard it many times before. Charity caught some of their eyes and tried to give what she hoped was a friendly smile but no one in the crowd returned her grin.

"And that's the schedule for today, helpers," finished Gisele, brightly clapping her massive hands together. Charity looked up alarmed. She had been so concerned with what the other helpers had been thinking about that she hadn't listened to another word Gisele had said. She immediately began to panic: what if she had said something incredibly important? She looked desperately from the helpers who were now nodding obediently, to Gisele who was smiling proudly down at all of them.

In a matter of seconds, the group of helpers had disbanded, flowing out the double doors Charity had entered earlier. Charity made to move after them, unsure what, if anything, she was supposed to be doing, when Gisele grabbed her by the lapels and hauled her back.

"Actually Charty, you're with me today! Yea we'll be -" Gisele let go of Charity and suddenly jumped back in shock, "Oh Thea! Forgot your bell, you'll need one before we pop off, big place the Chapter, lots of places to get lost." She rummaged again inside one of the pockets of her huge cream uniform and pulled out a minuscule silver bell. It was about the size of two of Charity's fingers and was intricately decorated with lots of black swirls and curls. Gisele placed it into Charity's already outstretched palm as gently as she had picked up the newborn baby.

"This is a handheld Order location orchestrator. Only tha's a bit of a mouthful so we jus' call 'em HOLOs for short. Take it." She pressed the cold metallic HOLO into Charity's palm. "Now, you take good care o' this,

Charty," she said, looking deadly serious. "We don't give em to just nobody, there's protocol, only official Order helpers in the capitals get a bell and you best give 'em back when yer leavin', that's the rule, always been the rule."

"Is it expensive then?" asked Charity, wondering what was so special about the tiny bell.

"Course, but that's not why it's special is it? It's been enchanted, hasn't it? Those elemental types did something to em, made em all special like, that Igniculus stuff is mighty powerful I tell yeh. Anyway, that there's none of our business all that fancy stuff, we just take what we get down here and if it makes our lives easier so be it." Gisele reasoned smiling broadly at Charity.

Charity wondered what Gisele had meant by 'Igniculus stuff' but thought that it could wait until later, as the HOLO had completely captured her attention. She stared at it for a long time - she had never seen anything so small and so beautiful. After a time she reached out and picked up the little bell with two fingers. It felt oddly warm to the touch and yet Charity was sure that nothing had been heating it. She hesitated for a moment and then began waving it around expectantly however to her great surprise there was no soft tinkling, in fact the bell seemed unable to make any sound at all. Charity turned the bell over, confused.

"I think it's broken," she said looking up at Gisele who was still smiling at her, an amused twinkle in her doleful blue eyes.

"Well that's because yer doing it wrong ain't yeh? Here, give it ere." Gisele picked up the bell by a small leather tassel which was fastened to the top of it, held it up and then very gently, almost without moving her hand at all, she moved the bell from one side to the other. Charity stared, captivated by Gisele's strange behaviour. It looked to her that Gisele was barely moving the bell at all. To Charity's increasing amazement the bell instantly began shuddering and vibrating so hard she thought it would surely snap away from Gisele's grip but it did not, and continued to tinkle violently in place. Then very gradually, the entire bell began to shift of its own accord, moving not from side to side but in one noticeable direction. The bell writhed and twisted on the end of the leather tassel like a snake being charmed from a basket and after a couple of seconds stood suspended horizontally in mid-air. Charity looked from Gisele's beaming face to the little bell which was now pointing quite obviously at the tiny table in the centre of the room. Charity pulled her eyes from the little instrument and moved towards the centre platform on which stood a spindly wooden table with one item suspended above its surface, a large golden bell.

"It's…it's pointing at that bell!" Charity said excitedly. "That's, I mean, how? How does it do that?!"

"No idea, like I said, just take what yer given and if it's better fer one, it's better fer all." Gisele said sagely. "Oh hey watch, it works both ways too, you see Charty if yer lost and you need to find yer way back ere, just ring the bell very softly and it'll point the way home, dead simple. Sometimes though I need to call all of yer together, y'know for helper meetings an stuff and when I do I jus hit this -" Gisele hit the large golden bell with an outstretched hand and immediately Charity's bell, which had fallen back to its limp starting position sprang into life, once more vibrating madly and straining to reach out to the golden bell hanging over the tiny table. Gisele grabbed the golden bell quickly with a massive hand, stifling its ringing, "Don't want all those helpers flooding back in from their work, keep em busy, busy is best," she said happily, smiling down at Charity who was still staring open-mouthed at her little bell.

Charity bombarded Gisele with questions about both *her* bell and the great golden bell in the middle of Helper House but Gisele rebounded all of her subsequent interrogations with an airy wave and excuses mostly revolving around her, "not needing to know that sorta thing". When Gisele did finally manage to get a word in, she informed Charity that she would be working with her today whilst they cleaned the main dining hall. Charity's heart leapt, as not only did this mean that she would have a first-hand look at what helpers were supposed to do in the Order Chapter, but it meant that Charity would have a perfect chance to find out more about this strange land.

Gisele lead Charity from Helper House, through the gardens and back into the main Order Chapter Manor. They walked what felt like the full length of the great house whilst Charity ran over the things she knew about Thea in her head. She knew that these books were prized very highly by the people here, she had seen that the books were capable of extraordinary things. Charity thought hard, remembering what she had read in the old man's letter, she knew that someone had wanted *her* to come to this place and it definitely had something to do with *those books*. Before Charity knew it, Gisele was leading her into a huge room adorned with crystal chandeliers, a long wooden dining table and lots of peculiar heads of animals Charity didn't recognise.

Gisele had told Charity they would be cleaning the entire room for an upcoming banquet that evening and she was subsequently handed a wooden dustpan and fine bristled brush and told to start in the far corner of the room, which, not wanting to put Gisele in a bad mood, she dutifully did. Unfortunately for Charity, Gisele had decided to start cleaning in the opposite corner of the room making the task of questioning her a lot more difficult than Charity had imagined. So they cleaned and cleaned, Charity bending low and sweeping what dust she could find into the wooden pan and checking every now and again how far away Gisele still was. When eventually after an hour of cleaning they had finally worked their way towards each other, Charity straightened up, cracking her back.

"Gisele, sorry, can I just ask a small question?"

Gisele grunted, still sweeping up. Charity supposed this meant yes, so she continued.

"What was that thing you did earlier, with the baby? I've never…"

She trailed off as Gisele dropped her brush to the ground and stared at her with a shocked and confused expression on her face. Charity had expected this, something that caused that much of a stir was quite clearly something that everyone should know about and her increasing ignorance on the topic of these 'books' was undoubtedly a strange thing indeed. Charity racked her brains thinking of something that would excuse such ignorance.

"My head is getting a bit better, Gisele but I can't quite remember about the whole baby…book…thing," she finished lamely.

Charity felt her face go red, it was a pretty pathetic bluff she thought but she could think of nothing else. Charity was sure that Gisele would not be won over by such puny lies, however looking up she saw that Gisele now fixed her with a look of intense sympathy, her brow furrowed and when she spoke to Charity it was in a soft, reassuring whisper.

"Well, I suppose, if yeh really av forgotten… I mean…cripes it's hard to explain, Charty!"

She took a deep breath looking around the room wildly for inspiration.

"Well…" she said finally, "It's how you got *your* book, how *I* got *mine*, how *we* all got em. What I did out there, that was a grafting, 'sa special technique the Order members do, free a charge o' course, we've always done it for hundreds of years now. When a little baby is born we don't want em growing up without a Journal, so we create a sort of bond between em."

Gisele paused, struggling with how best to explain the situation.

"These Journals," she proudly patted the book strapped to her side, "are no ordinary books as you know. They are made from Ordium," she said in a hushed voice.

"Oh, what's Ordium?" interrupted Charity, eager to hear more.

"Keep yer cover on girl, I'm getting to that!" said Gisele as Charity fell silent, deflated. "Now Ordium comes from an Ordium tree, well s'pose I should say *the* Ordium tree as there's only ever been one, for 's long as I can remember. Don't know where it is mind, no ordinary folk do, only the higher ups in the Order know that. It's them yeh see that make the Journals and sends them out from the Chapters, there's an Ivory Order Chapter in every Mainland on Thea."

"What make these books, er, Journals I mean, what makes *them* so special?" asked Charity, who by now had completely forgot about cleaning, her brush hanging limply at her side.

"What makes em so special?" asked Gisele incredulously, "Blimey, Charty you must know that!"

"I…" Charity faltered. She scanned her mind for yet another excuse but it seemed to be filled to bursting with new information and all she could do was stare up at Gisele. She returned Charity's look with one of mingled shock and pity, and placing a large hand on her shoulder, stared deep into

Charity's eyes and spoke so softly that Charity had to strain her ears to hear. "Charty, your Journal is *you*. It's your past, present and your future, it's everything you have done, all your thoughts, feelings and worries. It's, I mean, it's your loves, your losses, it's everything you have ever experienced *written* by *you*. That little baby you saw, as soon as her Journal accepted her it'll have started to write down all the things she's doing, the things she's thinking, though I expect that wouldn't be too fascinatin' seeing as she's only little."

"But she couldn't write, how's she supposed to write dow -"

"You don't write it down yerself girl, the book does it for yeh. That's why they're so special, that little ceremony, that 'grafting' allows your book to channel everything about you onto the pages…if they accept yeh that is."

"Journals have to accept you?" Charity asked, intrigued.

"Well now," said Gisele who in an uncharacteristic move seemed to consider her words slowly. "Most folk'll graft no problem, your hand will be imprinted in the back of yer book and yer name goes on the front when yer born. Something to do with the Ordium I think, reacts with yerself - don't ask!" she said quickly as Charity opened her mouth intent on probing further. "I don't know how it works, like I said the learned types sort all that out. Anyways, the name on the front is just a way of recording who you are and making sure yer book is yers."

"Oh I understand. So it keeps it from being lost. What happens if it gets damaged or destroyed though?"

Gisele shuddered, "Yer Journal is tied to you, so yer Journal gets damaged then so do you, it gets destroyed then, well you get the picture."

"But how?!" asked Charity astounded.

"I dunno Charty love, it's just always been like that hasn't it? Yer Journal is like you soul. If your soul is destroyed…" Gisele finished looking ominously down at Charity who now understood why she had been shuddering.

"Does everyone have a Journal like…us…like us then?" asked Charity, trying to move the topic away from the destruction of peoples souls.

"Oh, umm…no," Gisele said flatly.

"No?" asked Charity,

"No" Gisele repeated, then glancing at Charity she bit her lip and stared around the banquet hall, and when she was sure they were quite alone she dropped her voice to a low whisper and bent in low to Charity.

"Well I mean it's like I said, not all folk get a Journal, some aren't…aren't…worthy. The Journal, it rejects em, it just lies there, their hand does nothing, the book does nothing."

"The grafting doesn't always work?"

"Well, yes, I mean, no! It's complicated, girl! It's not like it don't work, not the fault of Journals neither, sometimes people just aren't *meant* to get a Journal," said Gisele frustrated.

"What happens if you don't get a Journal?" asked Charity, suddenly wary.

"A Thean without a Journal is nothing, yeh see, the Ordium has seen no good in em and no good can come of em being in normal society so they're taken to…the Castlands."

"What's the Castlands?"

"It's where all the folk without books the…Laccuna, tha's what we call em, are left to their own devices. They're better off out there I say."

"And you get grafted at birth?"

"Tha's right."

"But what about if like a baby *was* rejected, what happens?"

"Like I said, if that happens… well…" Gisele looked suddenly intensely awkward glancing around the room surreptitiously. "The baby is taken to the border and cast out, all the countries have their own little rituals or ceremonies to see off their kin, it's not pleasant but it's for the good of the many."

"That's horrible!" Charity said, disgusted. "People actually give away their babies just because a book doesn't *like* them?!"

"Hey now girl, calm yourself, I'm just telling yeh like it is, those Laccuna are bad news, have *you* ever been out there in the Castlands?"

Charity shook her head. "Well I have," said Gisele, now leaning over Charity imposingly. "Laccuna would happily tear out your bones and eat em for supper, they're savage, with no Journals to keep em in check they do anything they please." Gisele finished sharply and gave Charity such a stern look that she dropped her arguments instantly and fell silent. With their conversation seemingly at an end, Charity started cleaning again, but she could not shake the feeling of outrage that this place seemed to think it reasonable to treat people in such a cruel and passionless way.

Later that night, after a full day of cleaning, Charity had taken herself to one of the free beds inside Helper House. She went early, eager not to discuss anything or socialise with any of the other helpers; since Gisele's explanation she did not really feel like making new friends. She lay on her bed and closed her eyes. This world, wherever it was, had seemed strange, almost magical to her and despite her feelings of worry she had to admit she had enjoyed her time on Thea. However, now the world seemed darker, colder, harsher. The revelation about the Journals, whilst amazing, had shown Thea to be a place of danger and at this moment Charity wanted more than anything to simply be back home. Pulling the sheets around her head she forced such thoughts from her mind and after a while slowly drifted off to sleep.

A loud scraping sound jolted her awake moments later, or at least it felt like mere moments she couldn't be sure. Charity stared bleary-eyed at the surrounding darkness, she could just make out dark lumpy shapes tucked up inside the many beds surrounding her and it took her a several long and confusing minutes to realise that she was not in her own bed back home. She bit back a sudden urge to bury her head into her pillow and cry. Then from somewhere in the darkness the scraping sound issued once more, this time from just outside the chamber.

Charity hesitated, the temptation to dive under her covers was becoming stronger by the second but she forced herself out of bed and listening hard she crept across the cold floor and towards the door that lead outside. As she neared it thin shafts of light peppered her feet, she could see that the door had been left ajar. Someone had just made their way outside it seemed. She pushed it open further still and the heavy door crunched against the tiled floor as it swung forwards. Charity's hands flew from the door as if she'd received an electric shock, the noise was bound to wake someone and the last thing she wanted was to get into trouble. She stood frozen for a long time, listening hard for signs of disturbance but heard only the heavy breathing of her fellow helpers. Tentatively she squeezed herself through the crack and out into the gardens.

Charity scanned the Chapter gardens before here. It was just as silent as Helper House had been, it appeared as though the visitor had simply disappeared. She glared around at the many trees and bushes that enclosed the garden, then up to the imposing Chapter building she'd explored earlier that day. If someone had been sneaking around in their dorm she was not likely to find them now, the grounds were sprawling and hiding places were plentiful. Sighing to herself Charity turned to go back inside, glancing up to the night sky as she did and wishing desperately that she was home.

Her hand hesitated before the door, her eyes locked to the sky as though in a trance. Something large and red was hovering high in the night sky, something that she had not expected to see and something that had her blood run cold. A dark red moon was clearly visible in the starry scene above her head. It stared down at her, imposing and awe-inspiring, it's crimson surface a stark reminder that she was very far away from home.

The thoughts of the silent visitor now gone from her mind Charity stumbled inside Helper House as quietly as she could. Her brain felt like it was sagging with new information, new sights and new realities. It did not seem possible that all of this could be happening to her and yet here she was and here she continued to be. She lay down on her bed and let herself sink into the soft mattress. If she closed her eyes and slept she might, just might awake in her own bed she thought desperately. Slowly the comforting thought that this might all be some strange dream lulled her off to sleep.

When she awoke the next morning she felt groggy. The rest of her sleep had been punctuated by dreams full of wailing children, skulking black figures and terrifying white knights. She awoke with a palpable pang of disappointment stabbing her somewhere near her heart. She was still here. Rubbing her eyes, she saw that the torches on the walls were still alight and judging by the large collection of empty beds most of her fellow helpers had already left. Charity pulled on her school uniform and placed her bell in the pocket with the brown letter. Thankfully the bell did not make a sound as she moved. This was a welcome coincidence for Charity, because today she had decided would be a day that may require a bit of sneaking and exploring. Gisele met Charity outside Helper House and took her to another large stone room not far from the gardens where Gisele said the Ivory Order staff ate.

Charity ate alone as Gisele left to sit with some other members of staff at a large square table near the back of the hall. She smiled at her apologetically but Charity didn't mind, she was still finding things difficult to process at the moment and some peace was probably for the best. She had seated herself at the far end of the one of the long tables and had just begun eating something that closely resembled a type of sugary bread when a small boy appeared at her side. He couldn't have been any older than eight or nine but was bouncing excitedly on the spot.

He leaned over to Charity and whispered, "Hey new girl, you hear about the Regalis?"

"The what?" asked Charity, puzzled, though somewhere deep in the recesses of her mind a spark of recognition flickered - she had heard that word somewhere before.

The boy fixed Charity with an odd look. "What you mean what? The Regalis of course, a reader, one of the Journal readers."

Charity widened her eyes in shock and remembrance. She hadn't just heard that word, she had *read* it, on the brown letter currently residing in her side pocket.

"What about them?" she asked hurriedly.

"Them? You mean *her*. Well she's dead see, went a week ago but the Order been keeping it all hush since then but you didn't hear it from me," he whispered. He made to go but Charity grabbed his arm roughly, pulling him back.

"OW, gerroff! What are you, ow!" The boy struggled but still kept his voice low.

"Listen to me," Charity said, "I'm going to ask you a very stupid question and you are going to play along and answer me. Don't ask why, just do it ok?" she said menacingly and just for good measure she gave his arm a little twist, not enough to really hurt him, but enough to keep his attention.

"Ow! Ok ok, fine! What is it?" the boy asked, scowling at Charity,

"Why is this Regalis so special? It has something to do with the Journals, doesn't it?" she said fixing him with an intense stare.

"Yes, yes, course it does."

"Well?" she blurted impatiently, "What's the link?"

The boy looked at her as if she'd lost all sense but he answered none the less, "They are the only ones that can read Journals that aren't theirs aren't they? They can read any Journal anywhere!"

Charity released him, her eyes widening in shock and he left quickly, rubbing his arm and cursing under his breath.

She sat back in her chair, her breakfast completely forgotten about. A 'Regalis' was someone who could read other people's Journals, but that meant they could read other people's feelings, other people's thoughts. Hadn't the old man called *her* a reader? Could she be the person the letter was referring to when it said, 'The Regalis will rise' or was this all one big misunderstanding? Things were starting to fall into place and Charity resolved that there was really only one way of finding out the truth -she would have to get her hands on someone's Journal.

....

The exquisite dining room bristled with noise and anticipation as the guests took their appointed seats at the long mahogany tables. Men and women all dressed in their finest wares had made their way to this event, seeking the most extravagant food, powerful company but above all information. The most disconcerting rumours had been flying around for days now, whispers of corruption, foul play, thievery and even murder. The men and women pouring into the Great Hall were ravenous for a thorough account of recent events and all were sure that tonight's hosts would surely clear things up once and for all.

Amongst the hustle and conversation, three figures sat at a long black marble table in three very large, high-backed chairs. The figures were startlingly different to one another. There was a small blonde woman with very dark skin, a tall bespectacled man with a mop of black hair, and an older bald man with a thin white beard that reached right down to his knees. The three had settled themselves quietly in their seats and only once the guests had fallen into a familiar buzz of hushed chatter did one of them break their silence.

"Thank you all for coming," said the old man, drawing his chair back and standing up to his fullest height. His deep voice commanded respect and no sooner had his first word boomed around the hall than the chattering guests ceased their conversations and fell silent, watching the top table with great expectation. "I, that is to say, we," he gave a small nod to the two people on his left, "felt it best to organise this little get-together to clear some things up."

No sound followed this and yet the man paused, seemingly waiting for someone to interrupt. When no one did he continued.

"I am very sad to inform all of you that seven days ago our beloved Katherine, the *last* known Regalis on Thea, passed away peacefully at her quarters in Imputtia." This time some noise did break out, whisperings and mutterings filtering around the hall, worried voices heard from every mouth and troubled looks seen on every face.

"Now, now there is no need to be concerned, none at all. In truth the role of the Regalis has been greatly diminished in recent times, in fact Katherine's role was mostly advisory in her final years and therefore her passing shall not affect our, that is to say, *your* lives. We have managed for some time now due to her debilitating health without the assistance of a reader so I promise you that very little will change in your day to day lives."

Some nodded, others frowned, and a wave of whispers swept around the hall once more. The speaker ignored this interruption, clearing his throat for silence and when it fell once more, he continued.

"Nonetheless, I know how much the position of Regalis is cherished and revered in my country and all over Thea. Therefore I have gathered you all here to reassure you further that, as Chancellor of Imputtia, I will be making it my chief priority to assist my country's Ivory Order Chapter in their search for the next Regalis. The people of Thea want a new Regalis and whether it takes one year or a hundred we are determined to find them one."

There were significant nods and impressed looks being shared by the audience now and the old man continued, spurred on by their encouraging faces.

"As prominent members of your own country's political and social hierarchies you're all obviously aware that the Order are constantly on the lookout for anyone who possesses any form of Journal reading skills no matter how minor. Now I have been in very close contact with senior members of the Order and they have assured me that regardless of the Regalis' passing, men, women and children will continue to be supplied with Journals when necessary."

Suddenly an angry voice broke out from the listening crowd, "Why doesn't the Order send word with the Cardinal, show they *really* want to help?!"

This outburst was followed by a smattering of angry mutterings from some in the crowd, whilst others tutted and frowned at the uninvited interruption. The old man showed almost no reaction to this, giving only the smallest of grimaces before addressing not the speaker but the room at large.

"Now friends, you know that the Ivory Order is rather fond of its rituals and secrecies and one of those being that the Cardinal remains a hidden figure, only those in the higher echelons of the Order ever having the privilege of knowing his identity. I say again, they have sent me a cast-iron guarantee that absolutely *nothing* will change in day-to-day life for the Theans of your countries and that is what you can take back to them, that proclamation. Babies will be born and Journals will be readily available to *all!*" He finished emphatically, with the heir of a man not intent on discussing this issue any further.

The angry man had simmered down now and merely looked grumpy at having his point batted away with such ease. The rest of the guests, however, showed a happier and more content disposition as the old man smiled warmly at them, wrapping up the first part of his speech.

"I *believe* I have the full support of my colleagues here and they have consented to assist their own Order Chapters in Dura and Agua." He acknowledged his compatriots with a small hand gesture, first to the woman who looked haughty but willing and then to the bespectacled man, who merely gave a nervous smile. "They will be assisting the Order in any way they can and I urge you *all* to do the same." The three figures nodded reassuringly at the crowd.

"Now, the other issue I would like to outline is the concerning reports coming from the Castlands. It is no secret that touring Order Knights have been noticing increasing signs of in-fighting and violence among the Laccuna, nothing hugely out of the ordinary for such savages. However, there have been whisperings of Laccuna being spotted on the Mainlands and whilst these remain unconfirmed, even the hint of such an incident is quite unacceptable. Laccuna are not to be permitted anywhere on the Mainlands. Can I urge you all that if you notice anything unusual to contact an Ivory Order official or your local heads of state immediately. It is of the utmost importance that we stay united, only then can we stamp out such things…for the good of all of Thea! Ladies, Gentlemen, I thank you for listening so patiently to an old man's ramblings."

The crowd laughed and the man smiled to himself. "Please enjoy your meal."

A polite round of applause broke out as the old man sat down.

"Very nice, Euphestus," the blonde woman said leaning across the table to pat him on the hand, "Yes nice and clear," the bespectacled man added, shifting in his seat uncomfortably. Euphestus nodded in appreciation.

"Thank you friends, I just hope they listen. In the meantime, have you given any more thought to dear Katherine's words?" he asked seriously.

The woman scoffed. "C'mon, Euphestus you didn't actually believe her did you? She was seconds from death - Thea knows what she thought was happening."

The old man considered his words and then spoke quite calmly. "My dear Mosia, I am not saying she was right nor am I saying she was wrong," he fixed a spotlessly white handkerchief to the front of his robes, "However I was forced to leave one particular incident out of that little report and I wonder if you too have heard tell of it?"

"What, what incident?" snapped Mosia impatiently.

"Well, some days ago, my men were called to a huge disturbance on the northern border of the Castlands. When they arrived they found four Laccuna trying to invade a small household. I mean they've never dared come so close to the plains! The report was most disconcerting these Laccuna were completely deranged!"

Mosia raised her eyebrows in derision and looked as though she was about to interrupt but Euphestus placed a long bony finger meaningfully on the table in front of her and kept speaking.

"I mean more so than usual, Mosia. They kept going on and on about 'the boy', never explained themselves, 'the boy, the boy' they shouted, 'the boy will save us!' I was told of how they laughed and cheered, even under interrogation…they were still laughing when my men disposed of them."

"Nothing unusual about that, Euphestus, savages will fall behind any cause, no matter how frivolous," said the bespectacled man.

"They claimed," continued Euphestus, ignoring the interruption, "that one of their own had entered their dreams and told them to take the Mainlands, that soon the Laccuna would take the Order Chapter in Imputtia."

"Nonsense. Jossent's right, Euphestus, they were clearly just riled up," reasoned the woman, now skewering a piece of dark meat on the end of her fork. "Such savages cannot be reasoned with, they were mad, that's it!"

"They claimed he was a Regalis, Mosia, a Regalis among the Laccuna, such a thing is not possible," said Euphestus.

"Precisely, it's impossible, don't give it another moments thought, I've told you before they're all mad in the Castlands."

"Perhaps you are right," said Euphestus, stroking his long white beard and staring out the window at the ruby red moon hanging high in the night sky.

7 – THE BOY

A rabbit with deep amber fur darted across the damp forest floor. Pausing now and again, its keen yet weary eyes sourced for any signs of danger. Its black nose twitched wildly and its ears pricked up at the sight of the bright, dusty-red lands that stretched out up ahead. With one final check, the rabbit bounced out from behind a stump and shot towards the gap in the trees. A little red blur, he hurtled under branches, over tree roots and through thickets of nettles. He had almost reached the clearing when he heard a snapping noise, saw a blur of steel, and the rabbit crumpled to the ground with a soft thud.

The thin young man kept his pose, bow held firmly and straight ahead in his left hand, his right hand open at the side of his head, one eye closed and a smile on his pale, chiselled face. *"Too easy."*

He slung his bow over his shoulder and set out to claim his prize. He had not eaten in days and the rabbit would provide welcome sustenance for the final leg of his journey. He had grown weary as time wore on, his arms were still corded with tough, rope-like muscle, but his face was pallid and his eyes gaunt in his head. As he reached his kill he pulled the arrow from the body, wiped the blood from the tip and replaced it in his quiver.

"One arrow could be the difference between life and death."

The young man picked the dead rabbit up by the scruff of the neck and turned it round so as to stare into its vacant eyes. He noted they looked remarkably like his own, empty and dark, quite the contrast to his ash white hair.

His hair had always been a burden growing up, its distinct colour making him an obvious target for bullies and slavers. He recalled countless days being taunted and beaten by the children in his village, their jests and jabs cutting him deeply at first. However, he was no longer the defenceless and weak child he had been when he was abandoned in this wasteland. It shamed him to think on how they had tormented him, but he had taken his revenge, on each and every person who had wronged him. *Oh, how they begged for mercy.* He smiled as his thoughts turned to each of them; Bowden, the fat carpenter's son; Morag, the girl who had pretended to like him, only to lure him into an ambush; Endawin, Martin, Godfreyed, Talla, the list went on. How many had there been? He had lost count.

As he recalled these precious memories he went about preparing the rabbit to eat, his trusty dagger having proved more than a match for many of his meals. He had never gotten used to the taste of raw meat, despite almost everyone growing up around him pressuring him to do so. He had always known that he was different in ways far more important than that. There was a power inside him unlike any other, of that much he was certain. How quickly his instinct and prowess with both blade and bow had advanced were testament to this. Who else, at the age of seventeen, could say that they had trekked the near length of these savage lands alone? Word of his actions was spreading like fire through the villages and huts in the surrounding land, yet there was but one man he hoped would hear tell of them. *I hope these stories reach you, old man. I hope they creep under your door and through your windows like shadows. I hope they torment you day and night. I hope you know, I am coming for you.*

Still, for the past few days he had felt even more 'different' than he usually did. Several mornings ago, he had been sleeping in the hollow of a gigantic elm tree, curled up in the dark when he was plagued by the strangest of dreams. He was standing on the top of a pile of rickety old chairs, wobbling and shaking perilously beneath his feet. Only the feet he saw were not his own, they were far too small to be his. Like a flash he was standing in near total darkness, a candle illuminated what looked like an old library. *How he hated books.* All of a sudden he was standing in front of an altar, a large tattered book in front of him, dripping with an unknown liquid. *Could it be blood?* The hand that reached out to touch it was not his own, delicate and much smaller. When he touched it an ear-splitting scream had torn through his head, splitting the skies and a flash of brightest white had burned his retinas. He saw the faintest glimpse of an old derelict cabin, heard a noise that sounded like a wounded animal and all of sudden woke with a start. He sat up in the hollow. The sun had almost risen above the tree tops, making the greenery around him glow auburn in the morning light. He did not feel normal. His heart was beating slower than it had ever done and he had the strangest sensation running through his body. It was as though his veins were filled with warm gold, his body tingled and his fingertips felt like they had a million tiny lightning bolts surging through them. He stood up and left the hollow, walking several metres towards a fresh pond that lay near the elm tree. Bending over the pool's rocky edge, he gazed into the water's reflective, glassy surface. The rippling reflection staring back was quite the same gaunt face he had always known.

He worked feverishly and before long he had a small fire burning. He must keep it as small as possible; he knew he was only a day away at most from a city. A city he knew must be Dura, the sprawling red desert that lay before him could only be the arid lands that he had heard tell of. *Is this where you are?*

Once he had finished, he doused the fire with damp wet grass to stifle the smoke and began to gather his things. He carried with him a satchel that looked as old as the forests around him. Tattered and mangy, its jet-black fabric was split in places and bore the unmistakable signs of something that had been very well travelled. Indeed his entire outfit shared this theme, from his dirty vest jacket, to his lightly-woven plaid shoes. He had chosen not to wear boots on his journey, wanting to remain light as a feather, black as the night. Remaining unseen was a problem, however, when your hair shone like burning phosphor. So he had taken to wearing a shawl that covered his mouth and wrapped its way around his head to cover his eye-catching hair. When fully clothed, all that was visible were those dark and empty eyes. On his back was a bow carved from the wood of an Atra tree, a tree famous for its bark as black as coal and as tough as most metals available in the Castlands. He holstered his jagged dagger into the side of his belt carefully, its job done.

His bag repacked and his weaponry adjusted, he set off towards the red and barren landscape ahead of him. It was almost a full day before he saw any sign of life. Climbing the brow of a moss-covered hill he spied his destination, a colossal red palace rising up ahead of him, its peaks dusty and partly concealed by the swirling sand that engulfed the whole area. From his perch atop the hill, he could see that all around the palace were ruby red huts, their walls worn and bearing signs of old age and around this area, a huge wall enclosed everything, shutting it off from the sand and surrounding desert. The stranger stole his way quickly to the wall and nimbly ascended it, his crooked fingers grasping the minute crevices with surprising ease. He moved so quickly that none of the city guards had any sign an intruder was present.

The young man was ravenous. The rabbit had provided him little sustenance for his tiring journey and he needed food before he could proceed any further. His nose followed the smell of baking bread to a busy market place, children, men and women happily chatting as wares were bought and sold and gossip exchanged. *I ought to be able to sneak past a stall and snipe a few stray loaves,* he thought, as he slunk down over a small gate, keeping his body as low as he could, his fabric-covered feet barely making a sound on the dusty ground. He stopped under the shadow of a balcony and pressed his back up against a wall, and he could hear the voices of a small crowd marching towards him.

"Vartas' been jabbering on about a lot more disturbances in the Castlands of late. I reckon those savages are up to summit."

"Vartas?! Wouldn't listen to a word that blind old fool says. Came to my house just last week looking an Ode or two for his 'Ordium Substitute, almost as good as the real thing he said! Well I told him, I said, I weren't throwing my money away on junk like that! He started yammering on about how 'The Order's running out of the stuff', trying to scare me into buying, he's nothin' but a con artist, that one."

Many voices murmured in agreement as at least seven men walked past, all dressed in the same white uniform with heavy metallic belts bearing a symbol of an open book encircled by a red moon attached around their waists. The young man noted the presence of swords that sparkled in the oppressive sunlight. *I could pick them off one by one, but first I must eat.*

He moved silently in behind the troop and headed off towards the stalls. Using a crowd of elderly shoppers as a disguise, the young man slipped a pale hand through the wall of people and grabbed a small loaf of brown bread. He retracted it quickly and buried it deep in his satchel. He performed this move several times on other stalls, and before long he had two loaves, a piece of fruit cake, and several sticky buns. As he was about to set off back into the shadows he saw a stall with a display of finely-crafted, steel-tipped arrows. Making his decision in an instant, he sped off towards the stall, this time planning on passing the stall at a brisk walk and merely swiping as many arrows as he could under the black guise of his shawl. As he strode past he swept a cloaked hand out over the arrow-strewn table, but just as he was about to grab a hold of one, a strong, brawny hand grabbed hold of his wrist. Looking up sharply he saw the face of an enormous looking blacksmith, muscles bulging out from under his smock and with several prominent teeth missing.

"This hand is mine now, you filfy rotten fief, you'll be lucky if I don't 'ave you're head neitha." The man spoke in a thick accent the young man could barely understand.

"Guards!" The smith bellowed.

The young man put his free hand inside his pocket and grabbed a handful of red dust that had been swept into his cloak on his journey across the red desert. Quick as a cat he flung the dust into the smith's face, who recoiled in pain, freeing the wrist he had been holding tightly. The young man spun on the spot and hurtled through the crowds. He had no idea where to go, but he could hear people taking up chase. He bundled over those too slow to get out of his way and darted round stalls and carts. He hurdled a small wall and sped down an adjoining alley. *Find the shadows, you are safe in the dark.* He ran, twisting and turning down narrow side streets, surrounding him on all sides where the walls of many red clay bricked houses. He could hear footsteps getting closer and closer from behind but he dare not look back. Instead he ploughed headlong through a labyrinth of twisting alleyways, until he rounded a corner and was met with a sickening sight. A huge wall of flat white marble was blocking his path, so tall it blocked all sunlight. He stood panting in the near darkness, his brow wet with sweat, his heart pounding in his ears. He could hear voices growing louder, "THIS WAY!"

He did not move as six of the same white-clad men he had seen earlier rounded the corner and advanced upon him slowly.

"Thieving is it?" A tall and well-built man asked as he panted, trying to regain his breath. "Not in my city, lad. Throw me your Journal."

The young man stood perfectly still, he smiled under his cowl.

"Are you deaf, lad? I said throw me your Journal!" repeated the guard.

When the young man did not move, the guard grew angrier.

"Tollas, grab his Journal and give him a boot for disrespecting the Order," demanded the guard, who the young man was sure had not noticed the dagger that was now grasped tightly under the thief's black cape.

As the guard named Tollas strode forward, the young man noticed the small book clipped to the side of his metal belt. A pretty looking thing, with ornate gold lettering that sparkled in the thin shafts of sunlight that penetrated the alleyway. *So this was a Journal.*

The guard made towards the thief. He stretched out a hand so as to grab the thief by the scruff of the throat. It happened in a flash of silver and red, the guard crumpled to the floor in agony, writhing and screaming in pain, holding the stump of his arm where his hand had once been attached. The thief held his position, his dagger tip pointed to the ground, crouched over on one knee, his head bowed, his muscles taut.

The rest of the guards roared in anger and sprinted towards the youth, bellowing all manners of expletives, none believing what they had just witnessed. Two ran straight for him whilst three more cautiously stayed several meters back, choosing to draw bows instead. *Clever men.* The youth realised he was in trouble. The two guards approaching him he could deal with, but not even he could evade three archers at such close range.

The two guards in front of him had drawn their swords but the thief did not plan on giving them time to advance upon him. He whirled on the spot, his black cloak engulfing him as he spun his dagger round in an arch towards the oncoming guards. The first guard parried the blow only just, but the force of it knocked him off balance. The youth grabbed him from behind and held his dagger to the bare throat of the guard. *They dare not fire lest they hit their friend. What a burden love must be.*

To the thief's disgust he saw that this guard too had a book strapped to the side of his belt, similar in size but far more regal looking. This man was clearly of some power in Dura. "They'll have your Journal for this boy, you're finished," grunted the guard, wheezing as the youth pressed his blade closer to his throat, a thin red line appearing at the point where the silver met flesh.

"Finished?" questioned the youth in that velveteen voice, calm and cool like an ocean breeze. "My dear man, I am only just getting started." He made to walk the man forward so as to make his escape using him as a shield, but before he could take a step he was knocked to the floor, his head ringing with pain. The now one-handed guard, had crawled his way round the back of the thief and had struck him on the head with the hilt of his sword.

The youth's vision blurred, he struggled to keep conscious as dark figures loomed over him. He saw swords pointed at his throat, one, then two, then finally five in total all drawn about him.

"We'll have your head for this, believe me", whispered the head guard, staring down at the youth before ripping his cowl from his face. To his utter shock, the youth was still smiling, a cold, thin smile that made his eyes look like thin lines of black ink. "Trust me, you won't find it funny when we bring you in front of the Clergy. They'll…" the man stopped mid-sentence as the youth raised his hand from his side. *I won't give you the pleasure.*

In his hand he held the book that had been attached to the second guard's belt. "My Journal!" yelled the guard, who had been holding his throat to stem the small beads of blood that had been leaking from his thin wound.

"YOU DARE! YOU DARE TAKE ANOTHER'S JOURNAL!" screamed the head guard, his face blisteringly red, his eyes showing utter disbelief. He could barely speak for choking on his rage.

The youth felt disgusted holding the wretched thing. It almost vibrated in his hand. *Is this what it feels like?* He was shaking now, shaking with anger. *This is the reason he did it?* He no longer cared for his life, he was going to have his small revenge, in this moment. He would die in this alley, he knew it, but he would go out of this world with one final act, he would cut this man's very soul from within him and maybe then they would know how it felt.

He made for his blade that lay at his side, the guards above him frozen with horror. He could see it on their faces, but did not expect such shock and fear. They backed away apparently too horrified to move. The strange vibrations had grown stronger and as he reached out and touched the cover of the book something unexpected occurred. A wonderful, blissful sensation coursed through this body, more brilliant and euphoric than anything he'd ever experienced in his entire life. A million tiny lightning bolts were exploding inside his fingertips, synapsing a thousand times a second. His heart had slowed, when a moment ago it had been shaking his ribs like prison bars. His blood felt like molten gold and time itself seemed to slow down.

The book on his lap opened of its own accord, its pages unfurling and opening somewhere near the middle. Lines of swirly black writing were appearing on the ivory coloured pages. Letters, then words and finally full sentences formed. At once he knew what he was reading, he knew only too well what these wretched things did, these *Journals!*

He stared down at the words in the pages, the inner most secrets of a life exposed for him to see. This man's thoughts and feelings, the events and moments of his life, no matter what he did to lock them away from Thea, were now his to peruse. He had no idea why or how this was happening and yet something deep down inside him told him that he deserved this power, that he alone was powerful enough to wield it. He had never even set eyes upon a Journal until today and yet now he found that he possessed a skill that most Theans would kill to obtain.

"*Blimey this kid is quick!* Where in blazes did he go? Ah, there, down the alley, wretched little worm'll pay for this.'

The boy read the words aloud so all the alley could hear, a horrible grin splitting his gaunt face.

"What is happening? Where did this lad learn to fight like that, *oh if I lose another man, Mosia will have my head and then who will provide for Dwenaline and Haemus?*"

"Is this *all* you think about old man?" asked the youth in a spiteful voice, "How mundane an existence you must live, Dwenaline and Haemus are your *children?*" He spat the last word out as though it were a curse. "You should keep your mind on your sword not your kin, it will serve you better."

"How did you…? I, my Journal -" stammered the guard as the youth smiled at the appalled look on his face.

The guards were all staring open-mouthed at the youth on the ground in front of them.

The head guard sheathed his sword, his hands were trembling and his previously authoritative voice shaking with fear. 'Bring him in, no blood shed… just…bring him to the Chapter."

8 – ADVENTURES IN FRIENDSHIP

Charity was frustrated beyond words. She had spent what felt like several weeks working for the Ivory Order, receiving good compensation for her hard labour but was no closer to unravelling the problem of how to get home. The situation she now found herself in seemed utterly hopeless and after many sleepless nights of pining for her familiar bed and the comforting arms of her mother and father she *still* didn't have the first idea about how to find her way back. She had initially thought of travelling back to the old man's shack, wherever that had been, but a glance out of the window of the Order Chapter had doused these ideas immediately. The sprawling oceanic lands surrounding her seemed endless and she had no way of crossing. She imagined that most people used boats, but even if she were to get her hands on one how would she find the old shack when she had absolutely no idea where it was?

Then there was the mystery of the Journals and why, unlike anyone else she'd met on Thea, she was able to read them. Her own innate curiosity coupled with the impossibility of her current whereabouts meant that she had spent as much time focusing on solving this curious problem as she had on getting home; however the result had been the same. It was not all bad news however as after five gruelling days of hard work Charity had been presented with something that lifted her mood considerably. Gisele had called her into her office and handed her five fat, little, round coins stating proudly, "Your wages Charty, it's been a fine week's work Charty, knew you'd fit in here, now don't go spendin' them all at once though." Like everything else on Thea the coins had proved to be most unusual and highly mysterious, for one thing Charity had no idea quite how much five gold coins was worth. She yearned to ask more but Gisele had bustled from the room as soon as she had handed over the payment and Charity had not had an opportunity to question her since. She had since decided that the solution to the mysteries of the coins and the Journals may be solved by doing something she was not at all used to doing, making friends. She had seen her fellow helpers with the coins and noticed their Journals strapped to their sides as they went about the Chapter. The solution was obvious, she knew that to get close enough to actually read a Journal or ask them about the coins she'd need to befriend one of them unfortunately for her though this was something that Charity had never found to be easy.

To Charity's surprise she was presented with an opportunity to achieve one of her goals the very next day. It was a particularly sunny day and Charity was on her way back from completing her daily job of cleaning the rectory rooms, when she spotted a group of her fellow helpers just outside one of the larger common rooms. She knew it was one of the common rooms having had the valuable opportunity to explore as much of the Ivory Order Chapter as possible in the early days of her time in Helper House. She had felt that it was sensible to familiarise herself with her new abode as it may come in handy. This, however had been no easy feat. For a start, the Chapter was enormous, consisting of one colossal mansion-like building and the sprawling grounds around it which themselves contained at least five different smaller buildings including Helper House. Charity had initially thought from a distance that the bricks of the Chapter's buildings looked as though they had been smattered with brown and red but up close she saw that this was merely layers upon layers of dirt and grime, possible built up over hundreds of years. During her cleaning she managed to get close enough to see beneath this layer of grime and was shocked to discover that at one point the bricks had been the purest shade of lily white. Charity imagined what the main house would have looked like when new, a glistening blotch of white rising up from the great green gardens around it.

During her investigations, Charity had moved all around the Chapter but didn't dare go into any of the rooms she wasn't supposed to, instead sticking to the corridors and stairwells as Gisele had commanded. Even these were tricky enough to work their way around and Charity found herself lost at least a dozen times in her very first week. Luckily for her, however, the tiny silver HOLO bell Gisele had given her became a vital ally in her explorations. Grasping the leather tassel and deftly twitching the bell would cause it to vibrate excitedly in the direction of Helper House. By now Charity had gotten used to checking the bell was in her pocket every time she left Helper House, as Gisele would, from time to time, call all the cleaning staff together either for their meals or simply to update them on jobs that needed doing.

Charity always explored the Chapter alone as the other helpers did not seem in a hurry to make her acquaintance, in fact not one of them had as much as spoken to her since the incident with the small boy in the dining hall which clearly had done nothing to persuade them that *she* was *their* type of person. Charity had seen the little boy pointing at her animatedly nearly every time they were in the same vicinity; this was usually followed by giggles or hushed whispers that always made Charity blush and hurry off in the opposite direction.

It was with great trepidation, therefore, that Charity took several deep breaths, strode around the corner and made her way towards the assembled group. There were four young boys, and six girls cloistered together in a huddle. Charity thought they looked about fifteen years old; she also noticed with relief that the little boy was not present. She stood awkwardly for a moment, just outside their circle, rocking up and down on her heels as the group continued to whisper in hushed tones.

She cleared her throat, noisily - too noisily in fact. She *had* meant to catch their attention subtly, but instead two of the girls jumped in surprise and the whole group stopped chatting at once and glared at her.

"Yeah?" asked one of the boys, easily the tallest, with dark black hair and a sneering, swarthy face.

"Oh, eh, hello, I'm Charity."

"We know your name. Giselle told us, *remember*?" the boy retorted, his lips curling as the girls in the group giggled.

"Oh yeah," she laughed nervously. This was a huge mistake, she thought desperately, she really was dreadful at this sort of thing., "Well… anyway, I've been here for about a week now and thought it was about time I -"

"Where you from anyways?" the boy interrupted. "Those clothes of yours are weird, they Imputtian clothes?"

"Imputtia! Yes!" said Charity, remembering the lie she had told Gisele on their first meeting, "I used to live there but I needed money so I came to Agua to find work, must've got knocked out or something because the last thing I remember I was begging for food on the streets and then I just woke up here.

"Oh," said the boy, his sneer slipping from his face slightly.

"Yeah, well I'm from Dura actually, got shipped here ages ago for stealing, lost count of how long I've been stuck here for. It's not easy but s'pose it's not all bad." The boy said, smiling ruefully at Charity for the first time.

"I'm from lower Forfal, just got to get enough Odes to get back down the water rail, it's pretty expensive now," said a small boy with red hair.

"I think the Order's a nice place," said one of the girls, who was so small and round that Charity had hardly noticed her at first. "I come here now and again to earn some Odes too, they're real nice to me."

"Odes?" said Charity in a confused voice. She'd been unable to control herself and had blurted out the word without thinking and immediately regretted it; the group gave her the now all too familiar look of perplexed concern she was getting so used to.

"You not got any Odes for working yet?" asked the red-haired boy. "They must've paid you!"

Charity thought quickly. The coins Gisele seemed to spring into her mind as realisation dawned on her.

"Well yes, of course I've been paid, I meant I just pronounce it differently to you…O-deees, that's how we say it in Imputtia." Charity said, hoping she sounded confident and inwardly hoping that no one in the group was actually *from* Imputtia.

There was a strained silence as they continued to stare at her, and then one spoke.

"Yeeaah," the tall boy said slowly, "I think my cousin pronounces it that way, she's from Imputtia. I visited her once when I was tiny."

"So is that all the money we get?" asked Charity, eager to change the topic slightly.

"Well it's enough, innit? Ten Odes'll buy you a crane-cart to Dura, three'll get you a night at an inn in lower Forfal. Besides most people trade anyways, y'know, you take my sword I'll give you an ox or two. My old man used to tell me that people can do business with just about anything."

Charity felt that she was starting to get the hang of this now and she reasoned that she would work it out more as she went along. In any case she seemed to have a respectable amount of Odes stashed away and once she was done with the Order she could see where it took her. Charity stood listening to the group chat about a variety of different topics, still feeling very awkward but delighted they had at least been pleasant enough to consent her to stay.

"Well we better be off then!" said the tall boy, after about twenty minutes of conversation she had taken no part in but had listened to enraptured. Charity looked quickly to his Journal, a thin purple volume that was sticking out of his side pocket. She tried to think of something to say, to keep them around and give her more time but it was too late. The group had already dispersed and were moving off down the various corridors, all shouting their goodbyes to one another.

Frustrated, Charity turned quickly and bustled off round the corner but as her white hair whipped out of sight she heard several of the group shout something from behind her.

"Ok, bye Charity!"

Charity beamed at the paintings as she hurtled past them, an unfamiliar feeling washing over her. Her heart swelled with excitement. *I think I've just made friends*, she told herself and she skipped the rest of the way back to Helper House, thoughts of Journals and her parents momentarily forgotten.

When she got there however she found that she wasn't alone. Gisele was speaking very softly to someone inside the circular dorm room.

"Now dearie, no need to be upset, a couple of days here an' you won't know yerself, c'mon buck up!"

Gisele was patting a very small girl on the top of the head in what Charity assumed was a reassuring manner although the difference in size made it look like Gisele had merely attained a very lifelike puppet. The girl had a thin pale face, huge green eyes and the longest black hair Charity had ever seen; it swept down her back and nearly touched the back of her knees. She was wearing a pair of dark navy trousers which were covered in black stains and blotches, a red formal jacket and brown knee high boots, all in all Charity thought she looked extremely odd indeed but then, she reminded herself, many people probably thought the same about her when they eyed her extraordinary hair.

"Ah Charty!" said Gisele in a relieved voice, turning to see Charity standing in the doorway. "Wonderful! Great timing girl, oh yes indeed. Now, now then this ere is Soapy, er didn't catch her second name. Soapy this is Charty, Charty Waters, great girl she is, great girl!" Gisele happily slapped Charity on the back with a massive hand, knocking all the breath out of her. "She came ere jus' like you, Soapy, ah you'll be best of pals ya will."

Gisele dropped her voice to a very loud whisper and leaned over to Charity, "Do me a favour Charty, give her a quick tour would yeh? Needs a friend I reckon." Gisele winked at Charity who nodded quite sure that the small girl had heard every word of Gisele's secretive request. However Gisele seemed quite unaware of this and scampered quickly out of the dorm muttering about, 'mopping the dining hall before tonight's feast', as the double doors swung shut behind her.

Charity considered the girl for a moment, unsure of herself or what to do next, before remembering her earlier success at befriending her fellow helpers. Enthused with a newfound confidence, she opened her mouth.

"So…" she said bracingly, and then after no more words seem to come she fell silent almost immediately, her mind completely blank.

The small girl turned her huge green eyes upon her. Charity supposed she must've been about ten or eleven years old. She looked quite terrified.

"So…umm, what was your name again? Didn't catch it." She spoke as kindly as she could.

The girl sniffed, wiping her nose on the red sleeve of her jacket. "Sophie." She spoke in a high-pitched, caring voice, "You're Charty…Charty Wat -"

"It's not Charty Waters," responded Charity quickly, rolling her eyes but smiling to herself. "It's *Charity Walters*. Gisele's called me that since we first met and well I was gonna correct her but it's been far too long now. I just don't have the heart to tell her anymore," she said exasperated. "You're sure you're not called Soapy then?" she grinned hopefully at the girl.

"No!" laughed the girl, smiling for the first time. Charity noticed how brilliantly white her teeth were.

"How'd you end up here then?" Charity probed eager to keep the conversation flowing.

"Well, I used to work at the Records Department in Forfal but I was ummm...I left." Sophie replied in a small voice.

"Oh. Right, but... you're a little young to be working aren't you?"

"I'm fifteen!" said Sophie in a disgruntled voice. "People *always* think that!"

"Sorry it's just -"

"Yes I'm small, I know." Sophie interrupted, then looking guilty she said exasperatedly, "Oh sorry! I've only just met you and I'm biting your head off."

"No, its ok I understand." Charity smiled reassuringly at Sophie, which felt like the right thing to do at this current moment. "What is the Records Department, by the way?"

Sophie looked positively agog at Charity's lack of information. "The Record Department...The RD? It's where all the records of Thea are written down for publication and storage... you don't know about -"

"Oh yeah!" interrupted Charity in what she hoped would be a convincing tone. "Sorry I'm a bit dozy today, just forgot. What was your job there, did you record...a...lot?" she asked awkwardly. What an incredibly dull question to ask, she thought.

Sophie, however, did not look like she thought it a dull question; on the contrary, she looked delighted.

"Wow, no one ever really asks about what *I* did!" she said, beaming at

Charity.

"I was a copier, you know, I'd copy down important events and significant discoveries about all of Thea into some of the many History Books. It's a really important job and they take it very seriously. I was there for nearly four years. I learnt loads, it was a brilliant way to find out more about Thea and earn a living while you're doing it!"

"Wow! Cool! How come, how come you're not there now?" asked Charity, impressed.

"Oh, ah, well…one day," Sophie's thin face darkened considerably, "I accidentally copied down the wrong passage into the wrong book, ruined a whole year's work. They just don't allow you to make mistakes - every record has to be flawless…so they kicked me out. I had nowhere to go so I had to come here, thought maybe I could earn some Odes to go somewhere *different.* "

"Don't you have family?" asked Charity,

"Well…no…I don't, my mother and father disappeared when I was very young. I've sort of fended for myself most of the time, spent more than a few years in different foster homes before going to the RD, managed pretty well up until now." Sophie's face was now pointing solemnly at her brown boots. Charity looked at her, guilt welling up inside the pit of her stomach, here was another lost girl, just like her except *she* didn't have anyone to go home to.

"Sophie," said Charity slowly, realising something, "you grew up here yeah?"

"Um yes,"

"Well how'd you like to show me the sights? I reckon Gisele wouldn't miss us if we're back for mealtime."

"Oh, ok sure, I guess…Are you sure they won't notice we're gone?"

"Nah, there's loads of workers at Helper House they'll never know, plus we could have some fun!" Charity grinned and Sophie grinned back excitedly.

Charity moved quickly to her bed, grabbed the bag of Odes from under her mattress and stuffed them into her empty pocket, then motioning to Sophie exited the dorm and ran past the gates of Helper House and out into the gardens. Sophie then took the lead, moving quickly through the gardens and out onto a cobbled path that led out of the Chapter grounds and into a bustling high street. Charity looked up and down the street which was crawling with people moving in and out of shops, stopping to converse in the street or pursuing wares at stalls and stands. Charity and Sophie moved slowly as Charity kept stopping to peer into shop windows or read posters hastily stuck to walls and stands. She stopped firstly at a bright red one and read:

'Finnegan's Book Safe – When you and your family leave the safety of the home, your Journals' safety is tantamount, so rest easy knowing they're locked where danger doesn't dare to tread, a Finnegan's book safe! Comes complete with room for up to seven full size Journals, an anti-break combination lock and is portable enough for transport between destinations. Whilst stocks last.'

Moving along the same window she read another, this poster was larger than the last and had been stuck to the inside of the shop window.

'Clunky Journal stopping you living your life? Want to keep it close but out of sight? Then you need Brandon's Journal Holsters, simply attach the customisable clasps around your Journal and snap it to any belt, buckle or fabric! Perfect for the Thean who's on the go all the time! Warning: Brandon's are not responsible for Journals burnt, lost, broken or damaged during high risk ventures.'

Charity moved further along the streets reading as many signs as she could, and had just finished reading about a new branch of a shop called '*Silvus' Supplies: open now in Galcia, Forfal and Duradon*' when suddenly without warning a woman with a voice as loud and booming as Gisele's let out a howl of laughter from right behind her. Charity jumped back in such alarm that she almost crashed into one of the many wooden stalls located on the main thoroughfare of the high street. She managed to stop herself with difficulty and turned to stare in annoyance at the source of the surprise. It turned out to be a very round woman with two strawberry blonde buns of hair who was so deep in conversation with another woman - this one was so grey and shrivelled that Charity thought she greatly resembled a tiny talking raisin - that she didn't seem to notice the small child currently zooming in and around them like a giant, extremely loud bee.

Charity leaned in curiously, listening hard to their conversation.

"Oh well you'll never guess who died last week!" said the large woman, matter-of-factly.

"Not Benny?!" replied the other, answering the question but still sounding engrossed all the same.

"Benny," said the first, nodding vigorously, "Was out after hours, down in Lower Forfal, went on a bit of binge I heard, took a few wrong turns, didn't come home, the Order said."

"How'd they know he died? He could be lost though! That'd be just like old Benny it would."

"Found his Journal, didn't they?" said the large woman, looking positively delighted at being able to deliver such grim news. "Cut to ribbons it was. Well I said to my Arthur that's bound to be the Laccuna's doing, must be."

"Oh Thea help him!" said the other smaller woman sounding equally delighted at this unpleasant news. "Well that'll happen if you hang around the Castlands, wont it?"

"It will indeed my love, it will -" the large woman cut herself off and bellowed at the small child who throughout the entire conversation was still streaming around them. "Joan! Will you calm down love, just, here Phyllis wants to ask you something, c'mon love stop running for Mummy now, come on - oh I give up!" She shook her head in desperation but smiled all the same.

The grey haired woman called Phyllis smiled back. "How's her lessons going?" she asked.

"Not well, not well, I try my best, so does Arthur when he's the time but she just can't keep still. She moves about so much I'm surprised her Journal can keep up."

"Ah well you know kids - she'll grow out of it."

Charity pulled herself away from the fascinating conversation with difficulty, she could hear Sophie's shrill voice calling her from somewhere in the bustling street and she moved towards it, dodging and ducking through the oncoming bodies.

She found Sophie on the other side of the street staring at a violet coloured poster stuck to one of the shop windows. "Look, Charity, I heard about this but... but it was just rumours and hearsay, nothing confirmed until now." Sophie touched the poster warily as though it might suddenly snap her hand off. Charity looked at the poster and read:

'WARNING: All citizens of Agua, please be aware that Laccuna have been spotted on the Mainlands. If you see, hear or notice anything suspicious contact your local Ivory Order Chapter immediately!'

Below the writing was a blurry hand-drawn picture of a man with scruffy hair and sharp pointed teeth, he was bearing them menacingly and although Charity knew this was only a sketch she couldn't help recoil a little at this first impression.

"I knew a kid once," said Sophie suddenly, making Charity jump. She had almost forgotten she was there. "I knew a kid that went into the Castlands *on purpose*. Said it was all make believe and that he'd never even seen a Laccuna so they weren't real."

"What happened to him?" asked Charity, afraid of what the answer might be.

"Don't know, we never saw him again. His poor mother used to drink too much after that and go on and on about Laccuna taking him."

Charity shuddered, "That's awful!"

"Yeah, I know, but Laccuna hardly ever come to the Mainlands. Plus we have the Order here to protect us," said Sophie bracingly.

Charity continued to stare at the horrifying image of the lacuna, her mind wandering to what Gisele had told her about those without a Journal. Was this what became of the babies abandoned in the by their parents? She was just about to question Sophie about this when Sophie spoke from somewhere behind her.

"Shall we head in here for something to eat? I've been once or twice, it's not bad," she said warmly and Charity, tearing her eyes away from the violet poster, followed her inside a red doorway, her imagination whirring with images and stories of the savage men and women of the Castlands.

The two girls made their way through the cafe, at least what Charity thought it was a cafe, customers sitting at circular tables eating whilst others ambled around chatting with fellow diners as they sipped from steaming mugs. Charity noticed that Sophie seemed to be leading her into the very depths of the room. They walked until they came to small wooden table near the back of the cafe. Charity looked around and realised that they were now completely out of sight from the rest of the diners; in fact even the women serving at the long wooden counter didn't seem to know they were there as after ten minutes nobody had appeared to take an order from them. Sophie had pulled them up two chairs and then sat down adjusting herself so she could lean her elbows more comfortably on the table.

"I always used to come here to relax," she said wistfully. "No one ever checks this corner for customers. I once came here to eat and nobody came to serve me, I just sat here for ages. I liked it so much I came to the same place the very next day. It's nice to have a little solitude you know?"

"Yeah, although, I get plenty of that back home," said Charity absentmindedly.

"Where *are* you from exactly?" asked Sophie.

Charity gave a great sigh and looked deep into Sophie's emerald green eyes. Something about them reminded them of her father's eyes and in that moment she decided that she could trust Sophie.

"Sophie I need to tell you something, I need to tell *someone*. If I don't I don't how I'll ever get back!"

"Get back? Back where exactly?" asked Sophie, who was watching Charity, a wary expression on her pale face.

"I'm not… I'm not…" Charity sighed again. This was difficult. How on earth did she begin to explain her situation to someone she barely knew? Charity understood this was foolhardy, borderline crazy and almost definitely the wrong thing to do, but there was something about Sophie, she wasn't quite sure what, that made Charity trust her. She was the first person to really spend any time with her on Thea besides Gisele who was almost always rushing somewhere or working at something. Sophie might run off, she might tell everyone that Charity was mad but what if she believed her? Sophie knew things she didn't, hadn't she worked at this 'Records Department' for years? Mightn't she be just the person to help her find a way home?

Sophie continued to stare at Charity, her bright green eyes shining like beacons in the dim light of the cafe. Charity clenched her hands defiantly and met her gaze. She was going to tell her the truth and she was going to tell her everything about her journey so far, from getting stuck in the library at St. August's, to finding the old man, to making her way to the Order Chapter.

"Sophie, I'm not from round here." She began nervously as Sophie crinkled her brow in confusion.

"Huh? You from Imputtia? Dura?"

"No not quite," replied Charity a calmly as she could, "I mean I'm not from *anywhere* on Thea."

"I…don't understand." Said Sophie a noticeable sense of panic creeping into her voice now.

"Well, and this is going to sound a bit mad but just let me finish ok?" pleaded Charity

"Ok. I guess," said Sophie, moving her chair ever so slightly back from the table.

"I'm from a place called England and I know you won't have heard of it." Sophie had opened her mouth, possibly to stop Charity but she ploughed forwards, desperate to tell her everything she could, "There's a really good reason you won't have heard of England and well it's because it's not on

Thea. I mean to say, it's not in this world…or this time…or reality, frankly I don't really know where I'm from or where this is. Up until a week ago I'd never heard of Thea, no one had where I'm from, it didn't exist. At least not back there."

Charity did not give Sophie a second chance to question her, launching straight into her story from her first visit to the library in Sarsfield right up until she'd met Sophie. It took a long time for her to tell her tale and to her credit Sophie sat willingly and listened to everything. Charity had tried, whilst recounting her story, to gauge Sophie's reaction, but her thin face had remained impassive and unreadable. When she finally finished she waited for Sophie to speak, her heart thumping in her chest and doubts seeping into every corner of her mind.

"Charity… I, I don't know what to say," said Sophie slowly.

"Say you believe me!" said Charity quickly.

Sophie was grinning but it was not a pleasant smile that spread her pale face. It looked more like a grimace of pain than one of mirth.

"Believe you?" she whispered through clenched teeth. "Tell me, which one of the other helpers put you up to this?"

"What?" gasped Charity, her stomach lurching horribly as Sophie glared at her.

"Oh don't act all innocent!" Sophie snapped, "How'd you expect me to react? If you were going to mess with me for being the new girl you might at least have chosen something vaguely believable. I was supposed to swallow your story and you'd all have a good laugh about it later tonight, is that it?"

"Sophie no! I'm not messing with you honestly, it's the truth!" cried Charity desperately but Sophie had already thrust back her chair and was getting to her feet.

"Just save it, all right, you've had your fun." She made to stride off but stopped just behind Charity, she turned to face her, a revolted look on her face, "And do you know what the worst thing is Charity? I thought you actually liked me, I thought we could maybe be friends." She gave hollow sort of laugh and turned to go but Charity launched herself at her, catching her around the arm and dragging her back to the table.

"WAIT! JUST WAIT!" she shouted as some of the other customers in the café looked up in surprise.

"Charity…get…OFF!" growled Sophie as she squirmed under Charity's grip.

"Ask me anything! Anything at all and I'll answer it. I'll prove it to you, go on ask me anything."

Sophie stopped struggling and stared right at Charity, cold fury behind her huge eyes, "I admire your commitment to the joke Charity I really do, it's all *very* clever. I ask you something about this other world and you make up a bunch of cobblers about it until I believe you. Nah, I'm not *that* stupid!"

Charity felt sick, she looked desperately around the café for something that would help her convince Sophie but saw nothing that could possibly help. Sophie was still glaring at her, tapping her foot impatiently, "Well, anything more or can I go?" she demanded sulkily.

"No, no you can go." said Charity listlessly as she released Sophie's arm and felt her pull away. There was nothing she could say to convince her, it was just too much to ask of someone she'd just met. Somewhere in the back of her mind she wondered vaguely whether anyone would *ever* believe her.

"Next time you want to mess with me just write it all down in a letter. It'll save us both a lot of time and effort!" said Sophie haughtily.

"What did you say?" asked Charity suddenly, an idea bursting into life at Sophie's words.

"I said-" began Sophie but Charity wasn't listening, she was digging in her pockets for something. How could she have been so stupid? she thought as she pulled out the crinkled brown letter she'd taken from the old man and slammed it onto the table in front of Sophie.

"THERE!" she exclaimed triumphantly, "You want proof? There's your proof."

Sophie stared down at the ragged letter unfurled on the table, she bent low and began to read, her eyes skimming from left to right over the page, her taught face slackening as she sped through its contents. Charity skimmed the letter to the man named Vincent, she wondered would Sophie know more about the man than she'd done. After two minutes had passed Sophie glanced up from the letter and stared intently at Charity as though she was seeing her for the first time.

"Not of our world? The gate must be opened. You're saying this is how you…you got here?" whispered Sophie hoarsely.

"I think so."

"How do I know…I mean how can I be sure you didn't write this yourself?" said Sophie but her voice was different this time. It was no longer accusatory or angry, she sounded desperate, like she was begging for the letter to be a trick now.

"You don't." she said quietly, "You can't know that, just like I can't be sure you won't run off and tell everyone about this. I don't want anyone to know about this Sophie. This isn't some practical joke, it's the truth, it's what happened to me and I have honestly know idea why or how but it all happened."

Charity looked at Sophie who shook her head and mouthed the word 'mad' to herself. Charity felt her spirits plummet, she covered her face with her hands and slumped onto the table. It was no use she thought, there was nothing more she could do.

She heard a door slam as if from far away and glanced up from the table only to find Sophie sitting in front of her once more, her eyes wide and her mouth half open.

"Sophie? What-"

"Oh Thea, I'm mad. I must be mad, I *know* I'm mad." Sophie whispered to herself.

"You're not mad." replied Charity, hoarsely.

"I must be…I… well… I don't know why, this is completely ridiculous you know? I mean c'mon a different world, if someone heard, they'd lock you up for sure." Sophie paused, reaching out and touching Charity on the arm. "I just feel like…you're telling the truth."

Charity felt like someone had blown her up with a pump, she couldn't believe what she was hearing. Without thinking she burst from her chair and leapt at Sophie grasping her tightly around the shoulders.

 "Ah! What are you - ?" gasped Sophie in alarm.

"Oh Sophie! I don't know how to thank you," Charity said, still crushing Sophie, who was attempting to wriggle free. "I know it all sounds impossible but I just needed someone to believe me, I've no idea what to do here and I need to get home. Thank you, thank you, thank you!"

"Oh, don't mention it I guess." Sophie's muffled voice replied from somewhere underneath Charity's armpit.

Charity leapt back, apologising profusely as Sophie righted herself, looking ruffled.

"Look Charity, I do believe you, Thea knows why but I do, I mean I guess you'd be hard pressed to make up something like this on your own. The thing is though, I'm not sure everyone else will be so trusting and if that letter is really genuine." Sophie gave a little shudder glancing down at the curling letter once more, "This all sounds like some pretty big, scary stuff, who knows who's involved. You have to keep this quiet, no telling anyone else, not… one…Thean can hear about any of this. Got it?"

Charity nodded looking serious but feeling elated, someone actually believed her, perhaps her plan had not been such a foolish idea after all. Talk soon turned to what Charity's old life had been like, Sophie asked dozens of questions including what people wore, what the houses were like, how people travelled about and even what kind of food they ate. Charity told her everything she knew for even she didn't quite know exactly how cars worked and Sophie had seemed most interested on the topic.

They left the restaurant soon after to find the sun beginning to set and started back up the high street towards Helper House. On the way Charity managed to ask some of the questions that had been bothering her since her arrival on Thea, although this proved difficult as Sophie continued her own onslaught of questions to Charity the whole way to the gates of Helper House. She did inform Charity that they did not have cars but used horses, that most large or complicated things were powered by something called Sparks, Charity had tried to ask what this meant but Sophie had quickly moved onto another question of her own.

A short time later Sophie and Charity moved silently through the open gates of Helper House and slipped through the door into the dorms. It had been one of the most unexpectedly wonderful days of Charity's life, she had found someone who she could confide in, someone who didn't think she was odd or strange. Sophie seemed to love books just as much as she did and Charity had found herself wishing that she had known Sophie back home - maybe then she wouldn't have felt so alone. Charity was just considering inviting Sophie along with her on her journey when something unexpected happened that drove the thoughts of friendship from her mind.

"Where have you two been!?" bellowed an unfamiliar voice from the shadows.

The two girls nearly died of shock, and stumbled backwards, falling over each other. A tall man dressed all in white, a great metallic belt fastened around his waist and a huge sword attached to his side strode purposefully from the shadows. His face was partly obscured but Charity could see his fury clear as day.

"I have been waiting an age, where in Thea have you been?" he bellowed, standing before them, large and terrible.

"We - we were just in the city and -" babbled Charity.

"The city!? What do you think we're paying you for girl, to go sightseeing?!"

"I didn't know, I'm sorry!" Charity said feebly.

"I couldn't give an Ode for your petty apologies. There *are* no second chances at the Order. It's out on your ears, the pair of you!"

He grabbed Sophie and Charity by the hair and pulled them roughly from the dorm. They shrieked in pain as he yanked them through the doorway and out into the gardens. Charity was scrambling her feet along the ground with great difficulty as the huge man continued to tug them onwards. They had just reached the gate when Charity, who had managed to turn herself around, spotted something nestling behind the man's silver blade on his belt. It was a Journal, about the same size as Gisele's had been. Charity reached forwards but it was just out of reach, and her hand swiped through the air aimlessly as the guard gave one last almighty tug on her white hair and dropped both girls suddenly to the ground.

"What are you doing, girl?" he spat, and Charity, looking around, saw they were right in front of the Order Chapter, the gardens around them completely deserted. Sophie was snivelling silently on the ground beside her, her now tangled black hair resting on her lap.

Charity felt a bubble of rage build up inside her.

"Stop your crying, get up!" The guard made a grab for Sophie who attempted to scramble out of reach but he caught her by the leg. His attention was taken up by Sophie's squeals of pain so he didn't see Charity leap to her feet and throw herself at his hulking form. Charity barely came up to the man's shoulder and was not nearly strong enough to throw him to the ground but she caught him hard around the waist and hung on as tight as she could.

The man instantly let go of Sophie and stumbled backwards. He struggled to free himself of Charity, swinging her around like a merry-go-round.

"Girl, you better get off… I'll have you locked up for this, you little -"

His threat was cut short, as a small clicking sounded from the side of his belt, a click that echoed around the deserted gardens and made Sophie's head snap to attention, her focus suddenly all on the guard's large metal belt. Charity released herself from his waist and fell to the stony ground with a crash, the guard's Journal clutched triumphantly in her outstretched hand.

The man bellowed with rage and made a swipe for the Journal but Charity pulled it from his reach just in time. Sophie had her hands clasped to her mouth; her green eyes wide and terrified.

Charity slammed the book onto the ground and rifled through to random page. It was now or never, she thought determinedly, either this worked, or they were done for.

Unlike the last time she had opened a Journal, the words did not spring into view in front of her eyes, this book she saw was already full of them, the same glistening, curly black writing she had seen before. The guard had unsheathed his mighty blade by now and was whirling it around his head, his eyes popping with fury

"Close it girl, close it or I'll cut you in two. I MEAN IT!"

Charity looked at the guard, determination burning in her eyes and then back down at the Journal. She prodded a finger down onto the page and read loudly:

"This is ridiculous! How long have I waited now? *How come I always get these boring jobs?* **I should be running this Chapter's security, not following up on bleedin' helpers.** *Who does Gisele think she is bossing me around?* **When I find the little blighters, it's the door for the pair of them, I haven't waited all night to dish out warnings, I don't care what Gisele said."**

The guard had dropped his sword limply to his side. He mouthed a couple of silent words which looked to Charity like, "How did you? How can?" He continued to stare at her as she shut the Journal with a snap. She did not look at Sophie but could feel her eyes boring into the back of her head.

For a long time nothing made a sound and then the guard raised his eyes and looked at Charity.

"Come with me..." he said in a low voice and then seeing Charity's furious glare, adding, "please?"

Charity and Sophie got up silently and followed the guard inside through the huge double doors of the main Chapter.

9 – THE JOURNAL OF CHARLES CALVILLE

"Why didn't you tell me you were a Regalis?" whispered Sophie.

"I wasn't sure I was one, I didn't even know what a Regalis was until about three days ago, remember, I'm not from round these parts!" Charity retorted in a pointed whisper.

"But the letter…you don't think it was talking about *you*? Do you?" asked Sophie sounding awed.

"I dunno do I?" snapped Charity irritably, "I told you I'm not - "

"OI!" barked the guard looking furious, "Not a sound! You hear me?"

They did not need to be asked twice. Charity fell silent at once and followed the guard diligently with Sophie trailing behind her looking terrified. They proceeded to walk what felt like the full length of the Chapter in complete silence save for the sounds of their footsteps on the carpet below. They ascended and descended staircases, stormed through deserted rooms and moved down seemingly never-ending corridors until finally they were brought to a halt. The guard had stopped them outside a beautiful wooden door with a brass handle, the front was engraved with gold trimming and had fine markings all around the edges. For some reason the door gave her a feeling of unease. Whoever resided behind this door was likely to be very important indeed and Charity knew that could only mean one thing: they were in a *lot* of trouble.

The guard did not immediately approach the regal looking door, instead disappearing down a neighbouring corridor and returning two minutes later dragging two spindly wooden two chairs behind him. He set them down wearily, pushing them up against the wall, indicting with a twitch of the head that Charity and Sophie should sit. They complied without hesitation. Turning his attention to the door he knocked very quietly with his left hand. His right, Charity noticed, was still gripping his Journal tightly - he had not reattached it to his great metallic belt, and the white of his knuckles conveyed his panic at briefly losing it. The three figures waited for a response in silence, the only sound that could be heard was a distant shouting that seemed to be emanating from a nearby window on the opposite wall. Charity stared at the tiny, circular window which was slightly ajar, and despite its size could just make out the crimson moon still hanging high in the sky. Its light was so much more vivid than the one she remembered from home. Charity squinted, she was sure she could see something that looked like thin wafts of smoke drifting upwards. She craned her neck to see more but one glance at the stiffened guard beside her convinced her *not* to leave her chair. It was no good, she couldn't see *anything* from here. She resettled herself on the hard wooden chair, listening intently. The three waited for what seemed like an age and then finally a small voice answered from beyond the door.

"Enter," it commanded, and the guard turned the brass handle and strode into the room, closing the door tightly behind him.

"Have you always been able to read?" Sophie asked softly after a furtive glance at the door.

"Well I suppose so, I mean ever since I came here I have." So Charity told Sophie about her experiences with the old man's Journal and how she had pieced together the information about Regalis from Gisele and the small boy. "But I didn't know if it would work again. Sorry I kind of skipped that part of the story, everyone seems to take it a bit too seriously. Is it really *that* big a deal?"

"Yes it is," Sophie said seriously. "A Regalis is someone who can have access to anyone's thoughts, feelings or fears, it's an incredible power!"

"But I don't want to know anyone's thoughts or feelings or any of that!"

"That doesn't matter, the fact is you *can*," Sophie said heatedly. "Theans sometimes have to wait hundreds of years for a new Regalis and with the last one dead," Sophie drew breath excitedly, "you could be the Order's new Regalis!"

"I don't -" began Charity.

"You could, you could, I think even the last one could only read after intense concentration, took her days to pour over Journals to decipher them but you, you can do it just like that." She snapped her fingers together, looking admiringly at Charity.

"Sophie I just… I just want to go home, I don't care about any of this," Charity said, sighing heavily.

"Oh." Sophie stopped looking disappointed and falling back against her chair, which gave a great groan.

Charity suddenly felt dreadful. All the euphoria of finding her first friend had evaporated as she sat awaiting whatever judgement was being decided in the room behind her. She'd touched another's Journal and that was apparently a very serious crime. What if she was put in jail or worse? Her thoughts drifted to her parents, how scared and frightened they must've been when they had received the inevitable phone call from St. August's about her disappearance. She sat in silence, lost in her own worries for a long time, when all of sudden the ornate door reopened once more and the guard stepped out and jabbed a finger in their direction.

"Inside," he commanded solemnly.

Charity tried to read his face for a sign of their impending meeting but he gave nothing away. The two girls entered the room slowly and immediately Charity got the sensation that she had entered a very posh study. Reams of brightly coloured books lined the walls and in one corner was a majestic desk with a beige, high-backed, leather chair drawn close to it. As she moved into the centre of the room, however, she noticed that its central piece of furniture was an ornate bed adjacent to the back wall of the room; this was obviously someone's sleeping quarters. Out of nowhere, a small cough drew her attention to the centre of the large bed, where a tiny man was staring at them both with what seemed like great interest. The man was sitting up stiffly, his back propped up with several expensive looking silk cushions and Charity could see that he wore cream white pyjamas, a tri-corned white hat perched on his otherwise bare head and horn-rimmed glasses propped on the end of very long, crooked nose.

Charity and Sophie were prodded forwards towards the bed and as they moved into the light from a huge circular glass window in the ceiling above, the old man propped himself up further and leaned forward, looking expectantly at Charity and Sophie.

"Which one?" he asked in a gentle voice.

"This one, sir," said the guard from behind Charity, giving her a small nudge forwards.

"Ah, I see…" the man said, regarding Charity carefully with two very watery eyes.

Charity did not know what to say so she remained quiet. She could hear Sophie fidgeting nervously behind her.

"Finneus informs me you have *read* his Journal without permission." Charity felt her heart skip several beats and was about to explain why she had done so when the man pulled another Journal from beneath the pillow he lay on and thrust it towards her. "Show me," he commanded.

Charity hesitated, a horrible thought just occurring to her. Every time she had read a Journal until now she had been under extreme strain or pressure: horrified by the death of the old man, his Journal had opened itself to her; and angered by the treatment of Sophie and desperate to save themselves from expulsion she had found the Journal quite literally an open book. Despite her worries she knew there wasn't the same sense of urgency or despair she had felt before and she had no idea if she could do it upon command.

Her heart still beating madly, she took a step towards the end of the bed where the Journal now lay innocently on the silk sheets. The cover, she noticed, had the owner's name and year of birth in shining golden font. *'Nathaniel Perch, Year of Birth: 4049'.* Charity took a deep breath and opened the book, her heart leaping as she saw the spindly black writing scrawled over both pages. She flicked forwards, her hands moving the pages as if of their own accord, for some reason she knew that she should find the most recent pages. She looked up at the man who was now rubbing his glasses absentmindedly with a small silk handkerchief, and read:

'Who's there? *Who would call at this hour?* **Thea ease my aching**

bones, it's that wretched Finneus. *How dare he wake a Clergy of the Order.* This better be of the utmost importance. I don't believe it, spouting some nonsense story about a girl reading his Journal!? *Too long on duty!* You'll get out of my sight Finneus if you know what's good for you! *Dear me, he's Quite insistent, must mention him to the Cardinal next time I visit the capital.* If this is some sort of practical joke he'll pay dearly. He does seem certain though, very certain. How very curious. Very well, I suppose I'll acquiesce just this once.'

Charity stopped reading and looked back up at the man, and behind her Finneus looked on, a bemused, hurt expression on his face. The man in the bed had stopped cleaning his glasses now and had reapplied them to his crooked nose.

"It has happened then," he said assuredly. "It didn't take nearly as long as we surmised. A new Regalis, mere weeks after the last one passes. Most unexpected."

"Sir, I don't know why I can do this or how it helps but I'm not actually from this place," said Charity. As she was about to continue, Sophie, who had been staring dejectedly at her shoes, looked up suddenly and flashed a warning look at her.

"I need to get home…to…to…Imputtia," she said. Sophie's dire warnings that anyone else would think her mad were still residing in her head from earlier.

"Well now, dear I can help you there. The Ivory Order makes it its business to help the people of Thea." He gave Charity a wide smile, exposing a mouth of very brown looking teeth. She recoiled slightly in revulsion but the man seemed unperturbed.

"What you have my dear, Charity, was it?"

"Uh, yes," answered Charity.

"Well, Charity, what you have is a very special gift, very special, indeed."

Charity again did not respond but waited for him to continue.

"We have been waiting for you, Charity, for someone like you, for a *very* long time."

Charity opened her mouth to reply but the man started up again,

"You will be aware of the role of the Regalis within Thea, I'm sure."

Charity shook her head, Sophie had told her it was important but she no idea what a Regalis actually did.

"Oh, you don't know? My dear where *have* you been? Well it's quite simple really. A Regalis is the name given to one that can read the Journal of another, other than their own of course. Ever since the first Regalis was discovered Thea has needed their knowledge and expertise for a huge range of tasks - they can perform duties no one else can after all."

"Yes, but what sort of tasks?"

"Well…" said the old man, considering Charity, "they help us with solving criminal matters, regaining information from those who have passed, basically anything that requires the information hidden in one's Journal. For example, did you know that the Igniculus Temple in Imputtia was designed using information recovered from Ignatius Orion's own Journal?"

Charity had no clue what an Igniculus Temple was or who Ignatius Orion was and was about to question the man when Sophie interrupted her by squeaking excitedly behind her. Charity turned to face her but she averted her gaze, choosing instead to stare resolutely at her boots, her face now very red.

"The previous Regalis," continued the man as if there had been no interruption, "served the three nations of Thea and the Ivory Order very well. She did her duty without question but she lacked, like every one of her predecessors, the natural aptitude you seem to have. You see, it usually takes a great amount of concentration and effort for a Regalis to read another's Journal, and not only this but she could only read Journals of a certain age."

"Why couldn't she -" began Sophie, who had finally looked up from her feet.

"A Journal will continue to age, even after its owner has passed," answered the old man kindly. "The older the Journal, the more faded its words become, generally proving much more difficult to read. This in turn meant that any Regalis, no matter how marvellous she was in other areas, could not provide us with one particular service."

"I really don't think I'm that special," said Charity honestly.

"Oh now, stop with the false modesty!" said the man, his voice high with annoyance. "You have managed to read another's Journal without so much as breaking a sweat, something Thea has not seen for hundreds of years. My dear, I do not make habit of over-stating things and I mean every word I am about to utter. Right now *you* are the most important person in the world.

Despite her confusion Charity couldn't help blushing. "But what would you need me to do? You said it would help get me home."

"And help it will, but before I tell you any more about this fascinating task I must ensure we are quite alone. Finneus leave us and take the other one with you, please." The man shooed him from the room with an airy wave of his hand.

"No! I want Sophie to stay!" exclaimed Charity suddenly. The old man raised his eyebrows inquisitively at her. "She's been really helpful and nice and she can probably help me do whatever it is I need to do."

The man looked thoughtfully at Sophie, who attempted to meet his piercing gaze, and after a while he nodded silently in the direction of Finneus, who turned on his heels behind them and exited, shutting the door firmly as he went.

"Very well, young lady, would you be so kind as to inform an old fool of *your* name?" he asked Sophie kindly.

"Sophie," she replied. Charity could hear uncertainty in her faltering voice. Did she even want to be standing here, or had Charity just condemned her to something she had no desire to be a part of?

"Ah, Sophie, I see. Well then I address both of you. I am Nathaniel Perch, I am a Clergyman of the Ivory Order, Agua Chapter, and it has long been my job to help people like you."

The girls nodded but said nothing, so Perch continued. "Now I would like to ask you a question if I may."

"Ok," the girls chorused together.

"Ah, excellent. Now I wonder whether any of you have heard the tale of the Fateweaver."

Charity hadn't the slightest notion what a 'Fateweaver' was but Sophie had piped up shrilly behind her, an unmistakable tone of excitement in her voice.

"Oh! Yes I have…My mother used to tell me about it when I was very little. It's a really old myth about the beginning of Thea isn't it?"

"That's a very literal translation of the tale, yes. Elements of the story remain shrouded in mystery, however, destroyed by millennia of hearsay and speculation. Could I be so bold as to ask you to recount the version *you* are most familiar with?" Perch acknowledged Sophie with a kind nod and slowly she began the tale.

"Ah, right ok, I think I can remember…yes, well…Thousands and thousands of year ago, before anyone had even heard of Thea or Journals or any of that, the legend is that Thea was a really horrible place. See the Old Gods, the Gods people used to pray to, they had made the world and asked everyone to pray to them. They wanted everyone to be just and righteous and they were in the beginning, except after a while they forgot about the old Gods, they forgot about the rules they'd been given and how they were supposed to act. Soon everyone was doing whatever they liked. Years and years passed and soon Thea was a horrible, wicked place with nothing but the worst people you could imagine, but the old Gods had been watching and they weren't happy. So one day they finally decided that they'd had enough and they wiped the world clean, everyone save a tiny handful of innocent folk were suddenly struck down dead.

"But the Old Gods had a plan, they knew some people were still good, so they sent down one of their own, one of their very best,   one of fullest

110

heart in the hope that they could make a place worthy to live on. They sent a young woman, to collect information and record her detailed impressions of this strange place; the woman was only too happy to go and perform the task, for she yearned for adventure. So she descended from the heavens and scoured the lands for many years, making her notes as she went but finding no one. Just when she had all but given up hope, she came across a small settlement of men and women living on the very edge of the world. Among them was a man, a man unlike any she had ever seen. He was tall, handsome, brave and kind. The woman fell in love immediately and he with her, for she was most beautiful. The woman abandoned her mission from the Gods and chose instead the mortal life of love. The two spent many happy years together and watched as the tiny settlement blossomed under their watchful guidance, soon hundreds of settlements had spread throughout Thea. Time crept by and soon the day came she had been dreading. The woman was called back by the Old Gods who had sent her, and she left with a heavy heart, terrified she would never see her loved one again.

"The Old Gods questioned her about the world they had once sought to rekindle but soon discovered that in the raptures of love she had forgotten her task and chosen the life of a mortal. The Old Gods were furious and looked upon her with revolted eyes - she had rejected their godly gifts and chosen the path of her heart. As punishment the Gods smote the surface of Thea and broke the land up into what we know today. They abandoned her on the world once more but warned her that she would never again feel love and would never be called back to their side. The woman began searching for her love at once but found no trace of him, and stranger still, no one in her settlement seemed to remember him. She cried out to the Gods for explanation but they gave no reply. The woman travelled across all of Thea checking every cave, crevice, settlement and village but it is said she never found her love.

"On her deathbed, the woman, mad with grief and a broken heart, pulled out a tuft of her own hair and using a feather from her favourite Sun-Crane, she fashioned them together into a plume. She took a blank page and she used this plume to write down all she knew of her love and where she had searched for him, in the hope that one day someone might find him. Her love was so powerful, so intense, that when she stopped writing, too weary to continue, her feelings and thoughts continued to spread across the page. It is said that the woman knew at once that this was a great gift and using the plume she wrote that this gift should be presented to all who inhabit this world so that never again could one lose a love so pure. That is why to this day true Theans can graft to Journals," finished Sophie, softly.

"Yes, but that doesn't explain about the Fateweaver," said Charity, who had listened impatiently for information about the mysterious term.

"I'm getting to that, Charity," Sophie said, rolling her eyes. "Anyway, that plume she had used to write her first thoughts and issued her first command, it was no ordinary item. What she said actually happened. Not long after this, Theans started to see their thoughts appear on pages and eventually moved onto using Journals. That plume was actually a quill and many believe that the quill was is what we know as the Fateweaver."

"Why's the Fateweaver any different from a normal quill?"

"Well, the woman's thoughts become reality didn't they? Her writing somehow merged with her own ideas. The Fateweaver Feather is the only thing ever to have existed that has left its mark on a Journal, it is said that with it one could actually *write* in a Journal."

"So? What's so special about that?" asked Charity,

"Think about it!" Sophie chirped excitedly, "Nothing on Thea can leave a lasting impression on the pages of a Journal…If you could write in one…" Sophie trailed off looking positively giddy with excitement but Charity stared blankly back at her. She just couldn't see why you would want to write in a Journal that tracked your thoughts.

"Hmm," pondered Sophie, looking slightly crestfallen at Charity's lack of understanding. "Well, what you do and what you think gets written down in your Journal, if you could write in it, you could change what you've done, what you'll become, change your possessions, you could completely change your life!"

"Woah," said Charity suddenly catching on. "So hold on, you could change things in your past or present?"

Sophie nodded vigorously.

"Wow!" Charity whispered softly, "you could do *anything*."

"Precisely!" said Perch suddenly. "I am surprised though that your version leaves out the *name* of the woman Sophie. Surely that would seem quite pertinent to the story," Perch finished with a smile.

"I was just getting to that, there's a lot in it," pouted Sophie. "That woman, that girl, was named Thea, and she was the first person to have her thoughts recorded and because most Theans adopted Journals as their own, Thea was named after her."

"Oh don't they like worship the old Gods anymore?"

"No," said Sophie darkly, "Well I mean some people do but only real weirdos. The old Gods abandoned us when they abandoned Thea."

"Oh right," said Charity in a hushed tone. "And was she a Regalis too, like could she read Journals?"

Sophie stole a doubtful glance at Perch, "Actually there aren't any records of early Regalis until hundreds of years after Thea is said to have died. Is that right?"

"Well, as I say, a lot of Thean history is marred by subjection but we understand that about one thousand years or so passed until the first Regalis was born, although we have no record of a name, just hand-written accounts of one who could read minds and decipher thoughts hidden on 'blank' pages. The Ivory Order was founded soon after this discovery. Varium Vesium, a Thean of considerable means, saw a great potential in this gift, and he made it his life's mission to find more of these people and use them to help all of Thea."

"But wait, there's one thing I still don't get," said Charity, remembering something Gisele had told her when they had been cleaning the banquet hall. "I thought the Order gave out the Journals. Gis - eh somebody told me that Journals were made from the Ordium tree and Sophie's story doesn't mention the tree *or* the Order."

"Very perceptive Charity," said Perch who looked mildly impressed. "But like I said, the history of Thea is not without conjecture and guesswork. Many scholars, myself included, believe that the Ordium Tree was found by Thea on her travels and this is what she used to write her dying message on. Journals have been known to be made from other materials in the past but it's not nearly as effective on normal paper."

Perch readjusted his glasses, which had slipped to the very edge of his nose and continued, "Well now, we have talked for what seems like an age and I do believe it is now time I ask you a favour."

"A favour?" asked Charity, excitement bubbling up inside her.

"That's right. You see the plume that Thea used has been the subject of many literary and historical excavations, digs, explorations and discussions ever since The Order was founded. Whilst a great many details of Thea's inception are fanciful, many still believe that the feather does exist and, more importantly, that it still resides somewhere on Thea. Just consider the implications of such a tool: limitless power, limitless possibility… what good we could do for *all* of Thea." Perch sat forwards now and looked as excited as a child waking up on Christmas morning.

"The Order has funded many a journey to search for the feather but alas we are no closer than when we started over three thousand years ago. One man did however come incredibly close, closer than we've ever been. He was an explorer, I daresay you might've heard of him - his name was Charles Calville."

Perch stared down expectantly at both girls who stared back up at him, each with a look of complete non-recognition.

"Ah," said Perch, looking crestfallen. "Not heard of him. I suppose he's not a really what you would call household name, mostly Order business after all. Well Charles Calville was brought to our attention, as like us, this man had made it his life's work to find the Fateweaver feather. We have managed to collect written accounts of his prowess for exploration and his obsession with the power the feather held over the intervening years."

"Why don't you ask him then? He sounds like he would be perfect for the job," said Charity, wondering why this hadn't occurred to Perch before now.

"Oh he *was* perfect! He came close, Charity, closer than any Thean has ever been to the Fateweaver but just when he seemed certain to succeed…" Perch who had been waving his hands enthusiastically around the room, dropped them to the bed with a thump. "Nothing. Not a word from him, not a word about him, nothing spoken, nothing written, it's as if he disappeared altogether. The only thing we managed to recover of his was his Journal, found by a young Ivory Knight touring the Castlands fifty years ago. He had stopped a Laccuna near the borders to search him for stolen goods and in a dirty bag he found it. The Journal was utterly filthy and he had no idea who Charles Calville was but, thank Thea, he handed it to his Order superiors and we set to work at once trying to find out more about where he had gone."

"But you couldn't read it because it wasn't your Journal" said Charity who was beginning to see why Perch had been so interested in her unusual gift.

"Hold on, why couldn't the last Regalis read it?" asked Sophie suddenly. "She was around for ages, at least fifty years ago?"

"It was far too ancient for her, child. You see our only accounts of Charles Calville are almost two thousand years old. His Journal therefore is one of the oldest still in existence."

"Did the Last Regalis…Katherine was it?" - Perch nodded - "Did she try to read it?" asked Charity.

Perch grimaced looking as though he was trying to rid himself of a particularly painful memory.

"Oh she tried, she tried very hard indeed, nearly killed herself from the strain and effort she exerted upon herself. Truly, Katherine was a fiercely committed Regalis, *But* try as she might, she could only make out one word in the whole Journal: 'Fateweaver'. So the legend of the plume spread throughout Thea once more, as things inevitably do when you want them kept secret. Of course that wasn't the only problem with the Journal," Perch finished sadly.

"What else was wrong?" asked the two girls in unison.

"The last two pages of the Journal had been torn out. So you see even if we happened to have had a Regalis skilled enough to read the blasted thing, we'd still be quite stuck."

"So you want me to find his Journal again?" Charity said slowly.

"Oh my dear girl no, we still have his Journal. We want you to read it, read it and find out where he went on his journey. Retrace his steps so you may find what he found and then maybe with the Ivory Order behind you we'll be able to go further than he did, actually *find* the Fateweaver." Perch finished in a hushed voice and even in this small bedroom the excitement he generated was palpable.

"But what about the missing pages?"

"Well…we hope, and this is something of a long shot, but we *hope* that the pages will be somewhere Calville went on his journey across Thea. It has always been our belief and this is something I would bet my life upon, that those pages were purposefully removed."

"But who would do such a thing to a Journal?" asked Sophie in a hushed tone.

"We have suspicions, but nothing is certain - *that* is where Charity comes in." Perch turned his gaze upon her, his eyes twinkling with obvious excitement. "Charity, will you help the Order find what we seek?"

"Yes!" said Charity defiantly. Every voice and intuition in her head screamed for her to refuse, that it was dangerous, a lost cause, a fool's errand and yet Charity could not help herself. Deep down she knew that up until now there had been no plausible way she could get home but if she found this Fateweaver then she just might find her way, after all, couldn't it do *anything*? Happy images of her scribbling with a gigantic feathery pen filled her mind, followed by her running along a long corridor and jumping into her happy father's outstretched arms.

"Marvellous, just marvellous." whispered Perch and then swinging his legs round suddenly he leapt out of the bed. "Very well then, we must proceed to the banquet hall immediately. There's not one moment to lose. Finneus!" he yelled suddenly at the closed door, which opened as Finneus stuck his head round the frame.

"Yes, sir?"

"Fetch my walking robes man and for Thea's sake be quick about it!"

"Y-yes, sir!" stammered Finneus, and a couple of minutes later Sophie and Charity were following a freshly-robed Perch along a corridor and down a winding flight of stairs. They passed yet more small windows like the one Charity had looked through earlier, and although she could still see puffs of black smoke rising high into the night sky, the restrictive view meant she could not see much of whatever was happening in the town. So her mind now resolutely focused on the task in hand, and she turned her attention back to Perch who, like Sophie, didn't seem to have noticed anything unusual going on through the windows. Charity felt her heart thumping against her chest, and she found it curious that despite not knowing of Charles Calville's existence an hour ago, she was *now* positively bursting to get a look at his Journal.

They reached the banquet hall and Perch immediately strode over to behind the three long wooden tables and to a great red curtain that swept along the whole back wall of the room. He reached behind the curtain and pulled hard at something and as he did the curtain began to slide smoothly towards where he stood, its red, velvety folds flowing like water as some sort of mechanism dragged it across. At first Charity did not see anything, but upon closer inspection she saw that it was hiding a very spindly little table with a single red Journal sitting propped on a metallic stand. The Journal had been placed under a glass lid for safekeeping and Perch whispered something she couldn't make out before lifting off the glass lid and picking it up with a shaking hand.

"I've always wanted to hold this but I've never had an opportunity to do so." He beamed at them and thrust the journal towards Charity.

"What do I do with it?" Charity asked reaching out to take the Journal from Perch. "Do you want me to read it now?"

"That would be a good starting point. We can find out where Calville went first, that may lead us to the missing pages, or even the feather," said Perch excitedly, handing the Journal to Charity, who upon taking it felt again a familiar tingling sensation in the very tips of her fingers.

She turned the Journal over in her hands. It was incredibly worn, the red cover scratched and blemished with all manner of stains, the pages however looking as perfect as the brand new Journal the tiny baby had been grafted with weeks before. The Journal's cover had the same swirling golden writing which read, 'Charles Calville', his year of birth and death both so faded that the golden font was no longer legible.

"Here goes nothing," she said, pulling the book open gently and focusing hard. As she turned the first page over with a slightly trembling hand, Charity noticed that the same black spindly words were already present on the unfurled pages, "I can read it!" she shouted happily.

"Oh Praise, Thea!" Perch shouted loudly, whilst Sophie clapped her hands together, dancing on the spot.

"What does it say? Please continue," begged Perch.

Charity had just begun to read further when there was a colossal 'BANG!' outside and the door to the banquet hall was flung open. In the doorway, standing frightened and terrible looking was Gisele. Her red hair was ruffled and her cream uniform was splattered with mud, grass and something that looked horribly like blood. Gisele's eyes were wide with fear as she scanned the room in a panic. She quickly spotted the three of them huddled together near the great red curtain and bounded forwards, reaching them in six or seven massive strides.

"Charty, Soapy, what in the name of Thea d'yeh think yer doing? The Order's under attack, we gotta get outta here now!" she said hurriedly. Charity saw how her hands were trembling as she moved towards them.

"Hold on a moment, Gisele, explain yourself. What do you mean the Order's under attack? That can't possibly be -"

"Begging your pardon, sir, Clergyman Perch, sir but the Laccuna, they've scaled the water rails, set fire to parts of Upper Forfal, there's dozens of 'em, could be hundreds!"

Just then, another bang, like a gun, fired off somewhere in the distance and screams followed close after it. Perch looked at Gisele, then at Charity, still clutching the Journal. He spoke quickly and quietly to Charity so Gisele could not hear him.

"Go, quickly, don't wait for anyone, read the Journal, follow Calville's path and above all don't let anyone know you have it. All of Thea wants to get their hands on what you now possess. Now go, flee." He turned to Gisele and pointed to the floor: "You know what to do, take them, I'll be fine!"

Perch pushed Charity and Sophie towards her and indicated the door at the far end of the room. Gisele ushered Charity behind her but hesitated, glancing at the Clergyman in his soft silk gown. She paused and then suddenly made up her mind in a blur of movement.

Gisele grabbed Charity and Sophie by the hands and sprinted full pelt out of the room, and crashing through the half open door she hurtled down corridors and round corners until finally they burst out into the gardens. Charity's eyes met with a chaotic scene, women and children hurrying through the gardens, white clad Knights spreading out and down through the gates into the town whilst pillars of thick, black smoke rose ominously from the houses and shops.

Charity and Sophie were hauled through the gardens and past the open gates of Helper House, which, Charity realised with a sudden burst of fear, were bent and broken. Gisele kicked open the great door and hurried inside, slamming it behind them. She wheeled around and strode over to the nearest bed, dragging it to the door she pushed it tight against it.

"Charty, you have to get out of here, the town's full of those things, this is the only safe passage."

Charity looked around but she couldn't see what Gisele was talking about. "Gisele you've just blocked the only way out of here," she said pointedly.

"No, there's always an emergency route out of any Order Chapter, this one's right ere," said Gisele, walking towards the little platform with the golden bell suspended above it. She bent down low and began to push the platform with all her might, her legs slipped and slid on the floor as she struggled with the tiny platform but slowly, very slowly it began to shift and creep to the side. Eventually it had moved right across the floor exposing a

119

dark hole with an old ladder descending into its depths.

"I am *not* going down there!" said Sophie, looking with apprehension at the hole.

"You are if you want to keep that pretty face a yers," said Gisele angrily. "I mean it, move, NOW!" she bellowed at them. Both girls moved forwards silently and Charity climbed down onto the ladder with difficulty. It rattled as she descended and the looming, worried face of Gisele moved further and further from view. Finally when it was almost out of sight, Gisele shouted, "Just follow the path, it'll bring you out at the water rail!"

Charity made to shout her thanks but they were cut short as Gisele slid the platform back over the hole with a huge thud and they were thrown into darkness. The two girls climbed in silence, not knowing when their feet would hit ground. Up above they heard an unidentifiable scream of pain. Charity quickened her pace on the ladder, tears burning her tired eyes.

10 – ESCAPE TO THE CASTLANDS

Charity continued to climb down further and further into the darkness below, all the excitement of finding she could read Calville's Journal had evaporated in the shock and fear of the attack on the Order Chapter. She desperately wanted to know if Gisele was safe but she knew the best thing Sophie and her could do was get as far as they could from the noise and danger closing in above her head.

The two girls did not say a word to each other as they climbed, only the slapping of flesh and foot on metal could be heard in the shadows around them. Eventually, when Charity thought she could climb no more, her right foot hit flat stony ground and she clambered off the ladder. Righting herself and wordlessly helping Sophie down from above her, Charity looked around. The walls were lined with hundreds of tiny candles, stretching far off into the distance ahead of them.

"I'm sorry," Sophie said quite suddenly and very quietly. "I know you knew Gisele well."

"It's fine, just forget it. Let's just keep going."

"I wonder where we are," Sophie said, as they began walking into the distance, passing the tiny yellow candles that seemed to emanate a great deal more light than an ordinary candle would.

"Don't know, we could be miles underneath the Order Chapter by now," said Charity, staring at the high ceiling.

"Upper Forfal only goes down so far. It's suspended high into the air on four huge pillars, so if we keep going down this path, we're bound to reach one of them."

"And that'll get us far enough away?" asked Charity,

"Well I suppose we might reach the water rail."

"Yeah, what is the water rail? I heard one of the other helpers mention it once," said Charity eager to have a frame of reference. "They said it was expensive I think."

"Oh, yeah. Well it's not cheap, I know that at least. It's a huge mechanism built by the people of Agua years and years ago, it's powered by the water in the canals in Upper Forfal."

"Powered?"

"Yeah the water travels along tracks and that allows it to move."

"Why's it there?"

"Well it's the main way Theans travel up and down between upper and lower Forfal."

"There's a lower Forfal?" said Charity shocked, she had just assumed that the Upper had been a mere name, not an actual description.

"Well…yeah…but it's not err…pleasant. We really shouldn't go, I mean not if we don't have to."

Sophie looked extremely concerned but Charity was suddenly alight with curiosity at what made Lower Forfal so off-putting.

"What's wrong with Lower - ?"

"It's awful!" snapped Sophie interrupting her. "It's just terrible, everyone there's really *really* poor, and they steal and fight and riot all the time. But worst of all, they absolutely despise the Upper Forfalians, if they even heard we'd been up there for a trip…"

"Oh…well…why can't they just come up to Upper Forfal?"

Sophie stared disbelievingly at Charity, "Are you mad?! The Order would never allow it!"

"The Order? They stop people coming into Upper Forfal?"

"Well not everyone, only the Lower-Forfal folk. They just want to cause trouble, they're bitter you see!"

Privately Charity could see why but she changed the subject if only to distract Sophie who looked increasingly flustered by their current conversation.

"Sophie, what if the water rail isn't available or what if we can't find it? Is there any other way of getting down?" asked Charity,

"'Afraid not, unless you can fly that is." Sophie finished darkly.

Sophie became quiet after a while and the two walked in silence, their two sets of footsteps echoing on the cobbled floor beneath them. All of a sudden a huge bang sounded from above their heads, it sounded like something massive had crashed down upon the floor of the room above them.

Were they far enough along to have passed under the dorm where Gisele had been? Charity did not know, and the two looked at each other in alarm. Charity was still clutching the red Journal under her arm. She glanced at Sophie who stared back looking alarmed.

"What? What's wrong?" she asked panicked.

"Nothing, I was just wondering. I've never seen your Journal, where do you keep it?" said Charity trying to sound casual as she knew by now that this could be a touchy subject.

"Oh, I keep it here." Sophie answered brightly and she opened her blazer revealing a small blue Journal hanging to the lining as though it had been glued there.

"How does it stay there? Surely it falls out all the time."

"Nah, I use a clasp."

"What's a - " began Charity but Sophie had already pulled her Journal out and turned it to face Charity an understanding look on her thin face.

"It's in two bits, see?" she indicated a small metal disk that had attached itself with the back cover of the Journal, and a second disk that was clipped to her blazer pocket. "The clasps have Ordium in them, well a tiny bit, but it's enough for them to work with the Journals. They stick together so you simply attach one end to the journal and the other to where you want your Journal to stay."

When Charity continued to look perplexed Sophie pulled the clasps from her Journal and blazer and attached one to Calville's Journal and the other to Charity's hip.

"But won't it like flop around when I run?" asked Charity staring at the book now latched to her side.

"Only if you want it to, depends how you fasten them, some people like to pull their Journals out loads so they make them loose. I prefer mine secure and safe."

Charity jumped up and down and to her surprise the Journal remained quite still as though it were stitched into the fabric of her St. August's skirt.

"It's as light as a feather now!" exclaimed Charity excitedly.

"Yeah, clever eh?" replied Sophie looking amused.

Another loud bang issued from somewhere up above and the girls shared a dark look.

"We shouldn't spend any longer than necessary down here Charity." Said Sophie, "look keep that clasp, I've got a spare."

"Thanks Sophie!" said Charity gratefully, she really did not fancy lugging around the great book everywhere they went.

"I think we should put that thing to use, best to run for it." Said Sophie bracingly.

"Definitely!" agreed Charity and she set off at a run down the lit corridor, hoping to move herself as far as she could from the disturbances above.

Charity had run until her sides were splitting and sweat was dripping from her brow, and although she didn't look around to see how Sophie was but she could hear her panting close behind her. As she ran her mind raced with gruesome images of Gisele and the other helpers being tracked by dark shadows, the face of that Laccuna from the picture looming up in her mind, angry and terrible looking. She shook her head in an attempt to clear her mind. Her legs were burning and her sides ached dully. How many candles had they passed now? It must be hundreds, she thought, as her spirit began to wane. Charity was just about stop for she thought her legs were about to give way when Sophie yelled suddenly from behind her.

"Charity...look!"

Charity glanced to where Sophie was pointing off into the distance, a tiny pinprick of red light shone like a beacon ahead of them.

"It's...bound...to be...an exit!" cried Sophie through gasps of exhaustion.

"Right, not long now, c'mon head down, Sophie!" and with a great cry of motivation she pelted down the corridor on the final leg of their underground escape.

The great red orb grew larger the closer they got to it and eventually Charity could make out a small door bathed in the red light of a row of candles set just above the doorway. Charity and Sophie reached the door, panting hard.

"Shall we?" asked Charity, pushing the door open, one hand still grasping her burning sides.

Charity moved through the door and was met with an awesome sight; a colossal waterfall cascading down only a few metres from where they stood. Charity could feel the cold spray of water hit her full in the face as she hurriedly slammed the red door behind them and turned to stare in awe of the falls. They were standing on a metallic iron grid, she could feel it shudder under their weight, groaning ominously as they moved forwards.

"THAT MUST BE ONE OF THE FALLS!" yelled Sophie above the din of the crashing water.

"YEAH, BUT HOW DO WE GET DOWN FROM HERE?" Charity shouted back, craning her neck carefully over the side of the grating. Below them was an almost limitless drop down into great clouds of white mist.

One thing was for sure, she was not going to find out by jumping.

Looking around she saw that the grating wove its way down and round a corner of the building they had just exited. "DOWN HERE, THIS WAY!" Charity shouted and motioned to Sophie to follow her.

As they made their way around rogue jets of water continually sprayed them and once or twice they had to stop walking completely, scared that the shaky platform would give way. It looked very old and was dangerously rusted, possibly by the continual torrent of water all around them. Charity's wasn't sure how long it had been since someone used this emergency exit from the Order Chapter, and her apprehension was increasing with every wobble and vibration the platform made.

Eventually they made their way around the side and, to Charity's intense relief, found a large wooden platform where a small crowd had assembled. A plump, little man sat on a high stool before the crowd looking harassed. He wore a regal top hat jauntily on his balding head and Charity thought at this present moment he looked as though he would much rather be absolutely anywhere else than here. The crowd of about twenty or so people were jostling for position in front of them, all shouting and gesticulating as the little man shouted, attempting to quiet them, so far quite unsuccessfully.

"I think this is where the water rail stops," said Sophie eagerly.

"Well let's try and blend in with this lot, maybe we won't have to pay," Charity said, grinning.

"Oh but… but what if we're caught?"

"I have some Odes, remember? I grabbed a bag before we went into Upper Forfal."

"Wow you sure are organised!" Sophie said looking with admiration at Charity, who immediately felt intensely guilty. She didn't deserve anything like admiration, *she* was the one who had grabbed the Odes because it had been *her* idea to drag Sophie into town to see the sights. Had they not left that day, they wouldn't have gotten into trouble and Charity wouldn't have read the guard's Journal.

But, on the other hand, they then would've been attacked when the Laccuna came, a small voice said inside her head. In any case, whether or not it was planned, they had some Odes that, she hoped, would get them as far from Forfal as possible. So the two girls moved quickly and silently, blending seamlessly into the chattering crowd. Charity grabbed hold of Sophie's hand so she wouldn't lose her. "What d'ya mean it's late?!" a man shouted angrily from the front of the crowd.

"You said it would be here soon!" another shouted

"My children are here. What if the Laccuna have followed us, we'll be helpless," shrieked a woman from the back of the crowd. Voices erupted angrily from all over as the little man, looking increasingly flustered attempted to achieve calm.

"My good ladies and gentlymen, I was assured that the rail would be along some ago, I really was. If you'll just wait a few more -" The crowd broke out noisily again and the little man was drowned out. Just then however, a huge clacking noise sounded from high above their heads. Charity looked up in wonder as a huge bronze platform with a gigantic metal wheel on one side swung its way down towards them. The mighty wheel spun rapidly as a steady shower of water poured through it, powering it downwards to where they all stood. Then with a loud screeching sound the great, bronze platform eventually pulled level in front of them, shuddering to a complete stop.

Charity saw a man in a bright blue leather jacket and trousers, sitting at the front of the platform; he was wearing some type of goggles over his eyes and had several large levers in front of him. The tiny man in the top hat jumped excitedly down from his high stool, shouting above the now joyous chatter from the assembled crowd.

"There now see, I told you it would come. Now I think the price we discussed was fifteen Odes for an adult and -"

Another torrent of angry shouts exploded from the crowd.

"That's a disgrace!"

"No one here has that much spare!"

"You could buy a horse and cart for that!"

"Morton, you're a crook!"

"Fine fine FINE!" the little man groaned exasperated. "How's a gentlyman to make a profit I'll never know. Well…if you must I suppose three Odes for an adult, two for a child, considering the circumstances…can't see how that's my fault though."

The group piled on, apparently content with the change in price. They each handed over a collection of golden coins to Morton who deposited them into a little tin basket he had pulled from beneath his cloak.

When he came to Charity and Sophie, Morton gave them such a foul look that Charity lost all intentions to sneak on undetected. No, in the circumstances, she now thought it best to avoid angering this man.

"What *age* is an adult?" she asked, smiling kindly at Morton.

"What? Oh, um fifteen years, reckon you must be at least fifteen, girl," said Morton, warily eyeing Charity's full height.

"I'm thirteen actually," Charity replied loftily.

"Oh of *course* you are," he spat sarcastically, "Oh who even cares? I'm losing a fortune today anyways…two children is it then?" he asked, sizing up Sophie.

"I'm FIFT -" Sophie had started up angrily but Charity kicked her hard in the back of the legs. "Ow! I mean…never mind," she trailed off, rubbing her leg.

"Well four Odes then, come on, come on, cough up," said Morton rattling the increasingly full basket under their noses. They dropped the coins in and Morton sped off at once through the crowd, rattling the basket noisily as he went. When Morton was apparently content that he had received his full compensation he ambled off the water rail platform, climbed atop his high stool once more and yelled to the man in the blue leather attire, "That's your lot Charlie, get 'em outta here!"

The man named Charlie pulled one of the levers and an iron, knee-high grid snapped up around the edges of the platform, it seemed to be only precautionary, as one could easily have stepped over it, Charity thought.

"Child-gate," said Sophie, watching Charity staring at the tiny gate. "Stops little ones going over the edge. It happened a couple of times before people started saying they would stop using the water rails."

"Yeah, that reminds me, why is it called the water rail?" Charity asked. She could see no rails around her, the only thing that seemed to attach the platform to anything was the huge wheel.

"Watch and see," Sophie replied smiling.

Charlie the lever operator pulled another two levers, and the torrent of water from above began to tumble down towards the other side of the metal wheel. It hit it hard and spray bounced off, soaking the entire crowd gathered on the rig, then very slowly the wheel began to turn. As it did, Charlie eased the third and final lever slowly off and the platform, without warning, dropped. The crowd screamed as the platform jittered its way down slowly at first and then expectantly bursting into life, crashing towards the ocean below. Sometimes Charlie would wiggle one of the levers and as he did, he would send the platform swinging from one side to the other, all the while still plummeting downwards.

"THE RAIL…IS IN…THE WATER!" bellowed Sophie pointing at the huge wheel and the water cascading through it. "IT ATTACHES TO THE WHEEL AND THE WATER MAKES IT MOVE, AMAZING HUH?!" she asked very loudly.

Charity simply nodded from the ground. She had leapt to the platform's floor as soon as it had sped off, and was now clamped tightly to the child rail, her eyes almost completely shut. The whirling sound of the wheel and the crashing water were threatening to drown out all her other senses and she was struggling to even hear Sophie. She hoped desperately that the platform would stop, the falling sensation was making her feel ill. Tentatively she glanced over the side and immediately regretted it, the ground was coming towards them at an alarming rate and for the briefest of moments she was quite sure that it was here that her journey would come to a very abrupt, very wet end.

Charity shut her eyes tight once more, readying herself for the crash. Luckily, however, the water rail did not send them to their doom, and straining her ears, Charity heard the sound of crashing water ease, heard it slow and finally stop to a steady drip. She opened her eyes. The platform was settled beside a small island, and craning her neck upwards she could see a mighty pillar of stone that stretched right up to the clouds above to where she knew, was Upper Forfal.

"We were up there?" she gasped in amazement.

"Yeah and now we're down here. This is lower Forfal, and that," Sophie pointed to a long bridge just beyond a clump of tiny houses, "is the bridge across the border."

"Will that get us away from the Order?" asked Charity.

"Oh yes!" said Sophie, a grim smile across her face. "Not many cross that bridge, Charity."

"Why not?"

"Because *that* is the bridge to the Castlands."

....

The blow hit him with such force on the side of the face that he heard several teeth crack inside his jaw. The taste of blood filled his mouth, but the youth, still dressed all in black, simply stared darkly at the guard who had struck him. He twisted his lips into a thin smile and spat at the guard's feet. The blood stained the pristinely white shoes of the knight, who raised his fist once more and slammed it into the youth's stomach. *They send one man to make me speak? One man to guard me? Fools.*

Everything had happened so quickly since he had read the guard's Journal in Duradon. He had been dragged unceremoniously from the alleyway and taken to a white marble hall, 'The headquarters of the Dura Chapter of the Ivory Order', or so the gold plaque outside it had read. An old man, dressed in regal robes of white linen, had begun asking him all manner of questions. At first he was quietly spoken, calm and even pleasant. He asked the young man his name, where he was from, why he was not carrying his Journal with him; all of these were met with no response.

"Do you know what a Regalis is, young man?" the order member had asked him.

The youth had not responded. Regalis? He had heard that term used before...

"You can't stay silent forever you know, and in the long run this will be far easier for you if you just cooperate. You must know where you are, boy."

No response.

"You currently reside in a Chapter of the most powerful organisation in all of Thea, the Ivory Order. It would be most wise if you were to give up this little game and answer my questions."

Once again the youth had done nothing. He had remained quite still in his chair, his black eyes boring into the old man, who fidgeted slightly under the intensity of his gaze. *The Ivory Order, yes he had seen their Scouts patrolling the Castlands. But what did this have to do with him?*

"A Regalis," the man continued, ignoring the lack of response, "is one who can read Journals, not just their own, but any man, woman or child's who has been blessed by Thea. It is the rarest of all gifts..." The man continued to speak, but the rest of his speech fell on deaf ears.

Blessed? Any begrudging attention the young man had been paying was from that point, gone. He had been instantly consumed with a mix of uncontrollable contempt and rage. He had actually *felt* it boiling up inside him, the injustice, the spite, the hatred, all thundering through his mind. Despite the opulently white surroundings, he had felt dirty, diseased, contaminated even. Sitting in this place with these people, he had made up his mind to escape, he had to run, back to the Castlands, back to the shadows where he belonged. At that point he had known what made him so special. He would've clearly been dead a long time ago if this Ivory Order did not have a use of him; they need me, he had thought savagely. He knew he was in control; after all he was a 'Regalis' wasn't he? Straining to keep his face devoid of emotion he continued to say and do nothing.

In a last ditch effort to bring him around the robed man had given him another Journal and asked that he read it aloud. The youth had accepted the Journal without a word and sure enough when he opened it the pages burst into life, dancing black letters swirling into sentences, memories and events. This was somebody's life, etched into being in front of his eyes. The youth, however, refused to acknowledge that he had seen anything other than blank white pages in front of him. He maintained an arrogant silence and after a while shut the book with snap. The old man's face had darkened considerably, and he looked as though he had finally run out of patience with him. After this he had threatened him, warned him of the dangers of wasting the Order's time. Told him that if he were a fraud he would be stripped of his Journal and banished to the Castlands. The youth longed to laugh out loud at this threat, but, with difficulty, he remained impassive. After some final, desperate questions the old man in white had given up and ordered the head guard to take him away and help to "loosen his tongue".

Another blow came swooping down upon him, this time on the other side of this face. The noise echoed around the black tiled room, and the youth crumpled to the ground, the wooden chair he had been tied to shattering into pieces under the weight of his fall. *And now we begin.*

The youth began to sob and cried aloud, "Enough… please I've had enough, I'm ready to talk."

"Already?" laughed the large guard, his large belly protruding slightly from his glistening white armour and shaking as he sniggered at the youth's crumpled form. "Thought you might have had a bit more fight in you than that! I was just getting started. Now, on your feet!" he bellowed.

The sobbing young man was groaning, curled up with pain and writhing amongst the shattered pieces of wood. His hands clawed the ground in pain. *The sharpest piece possible, this man looks like he's made of leather.*

"I need help, please, help me up," groaned the youth, his face bruised and swollen in places.

"Pathetic," said the guard, his voice coloured with disdain. "You're not so clever now, are ya, boy?"

The guard made his way towards the youth on the ground and as he made to hoist him to his feet, agony shot through the back of his right leg. He roared with pain as he looked down to see a huge splintered piece of wood sticking out from his calf muscle, buried so deep he was sure it had struck bone. He fell to his knees and stared around wildly for the youth who had been on the floor mere seconds before, but he was nowhere to be seen. He thought he must have evaporated until he heard a calm, cool, velvety voice whisper in his ear.

"One move and I'll put another in your throat."

The youth stood behind him, holding a razor sharp piece of wood to the guards exposed neck.

"You wouldn't dare!" groaned the man, breathing sharply from the pain in his leg.

"Oh, believe me, I would. But I admit it can be a messy business."

And in a flash he had used his free hand to snipe under the guards white cloak and with a metallic click, unsheathed a gleaming leather bound book.

"What?! My Journal? How dare…" started the guard, but the youth silenced him by pulling the sharpened edge of the wooden dagger hard against the man's throat and he gagged, rasping for breath.

"You will not speak unless you are spoken to. Am I understood?" asked the youth calmly.

The guard nodded curtly. The youth thought he looked the type of man much more used to giving orders than taking them and he smiled at the irony of their current situation.

The youth opened the guard's Journal with his free hand and flicked through the pages until he found what he had been looking for. He read the page but did not vocalise it, **It is a glorious day,** *my first born,* **how beautiful he is, Tara is well, I should stay with her tonight to make sure,** *little Stefan,* **what a treasure, what a miracle you are my son. Oh Thea be praised.**

"Wonderful. Now I am going to ask you one question and if you answer me truthfully, then Tara and Stefan may well get to live."

The guard's eyes widened in fear. He could not believe it, how could the boy possibly have known?

"Now," continued the youth. "I am going to escape this place, but I do not wish to attract unnecessary attention, so you are going to tell me if there is a means of leaving undetected."

"I don't -" began the guard.

"Now, now, man, come on! There must be some form of emergency escape for the cretins that rule this place. Tell me where it is." The youth's smooth voice carried the faintest trace of a threat.

"I...I..." blundered the guard. " I don't know, I don't think there is such a thing, the only way I know is through the main entrance and it's heavily guarded."

The youth smiled a soft smile.

"I warned you to answer me truthfully,"

"I DID! I swear to you I don't know of any passage. Please, my family, don't..."

The youth cut the man off mid-sentence, reading aloud from a page somewhere near the middle of the Journal. It was the most recently written on page.

"Can't let him find the sewer, Mosia will have my head. Wish they hadn't put me in this room, of all rooms. It runs right beneath us. No wait, I cannot think about, he'll be able to read it, I must do all I can not to think about the sewer."

"What about the sewer?" asked Cassius, a twisted smile on his gaunt face. He did not need to wait for an answer. As if by magic the writing in the book scribbled what the guard was desperately trying to not think.

"The sewer runs from the throne room to near the edges of Duradon,

runs below this room"

The guard was frozen; he could not move.

"You see, man! You see what this *thing"* he waved the Journal at him, disgusted, "What this *blessing* has brought you? Betrayal, betrayed by your own self."

The man merely sat there as his own thoughts were read like a bedtime story. He felt violated and ill.

"You are strong though, so be a good man and break the tiles on the floor for me. If you fail to comply then I will plunge a spike into your Journal – that, I assume, would not have a welcome effect on your miserable life."

The man knew this was no idle threat, this boy was unhinged, deranged, his calm voice obscuring a manic sense of cruelty. The youth released the guard, who took up the hilt of his huge longsword and began pummelling at the white tiled floor. The first few blows merely scuffed the surface, but eventually thin black cracks began to appear. The cracks became more numerous and grew deeper until great chasms had appeared on the tiled surface. With a final few thundering hammer blows, the marble crumbled and fell away down a dark hole, just big enough for a person to slip into.

"Now throw your sword aside and any other weapons you have," ordered the youth, still holding the man's Journal threateningly.

He threw his great longsword towards the youth's feet, where it clattered noisily on the marble floor.

"That's all I have, I swear."

The youth perused the Journal for confirmation. "It would seem so."

The youth grabbed the rope that had been used to tie him to the chair. He ordered the man to lie face down on the floor, hands behind his back. He complied wordlessly and the youth began tying the man up. A sudden commotion from above made the boy stop; clearly the racket the guard had made opening the passage had not gone unnoticed.

"There's a good man," the youth started, throwing the Journal casually to the floor. "I'll be sure to send my regards to Tara and Stefan." He smiled coldly at the man bound on the now dusty ground.

He squeezed himself through the hole and dropped down into a wet and black passage. He hurtled down the cold, dank tunnel, his cloak billowing from out behind him, snapping and cracking like a whip in the wind that blew from the end of the passage. His footsteps crashed around his ears, bouncing off the surrounding cylindrical walls. Everything is white above the surface, below it's black as Atra wood. But this did not dismay him, for the dark was where he thrived. He ran as fast as his feet would carry him, knowing that chase would soon be given. After a while he began to see a speck of light in the distance, no greater than a pin prick. However as he ran further it grew larger and larger until eventually he could see the distant hazy outline of the Great Dura Desert. It shone a deep red and the howling wind made it feel like he was running into the mouth of a great sanguine monster.

He burst at last into the mouth of the sewer entrance, but shuddered to a stop only inches from the edge. Light burned his eyes as he tried to focus them. Sprawling for miles ahead of him was nothing but yellow sand and red rock. He gazed down below him and saw he was on the edge of a huge precipice, etched into the city walls. At least a hundred feet in the air, he was suddenly thankful for all those days spent climbing trees in the Castlands.

As he began scaling down the dusty red wall, he smiled to himself as a sudden realisation spread through his mind. The Castlands lay several days away he knew, but nothing could hinder him now. Not the great arid desert that opened up before him, not the Laccuna he would encounter deep in the forests, not all the Ivory knights from all the Chapters in all of Thea. I am Cassius, the Regalis, and soon the world will know my name.

....

"This is getting pretty ridiculous." sighed Charity wearily.

"What is?" Sophie asked brightly.

"Every time I turn a corner or walk through some passage or over a *bridge*," she stamped the long wooden bridge they had just crossed, "I'm faced with something even more astonishing. I really don't think my brain can take it anymore."

Charity and Sophie stood stock-still, their arms hanging limply at their sides as the sight of the Castlands rose up in front of them, a sweeping wasteland of swamp, forest, mountain and river exploding into their eye line.

"It's huge!" said Sophie. "I've…I've never been this close to it before." She faltered nervously.

"Do you know whereabouts the Laccuna are found in the Castlands?" asked Charity, as they moved forwards, crossing the bridge over the last of Agua water and entering the Castlands for the first time.

"No not really. I've heard right in the middle mostly but I think they're all spread out. Y'know, like in settlements and tribes and stuff."

"Hmm, that's not good. Don't suppose we'll get any warning if they're nearby?"

Sophie shook her head, a worried expression on her face.

"Well we can't do anything about that right now," said Charity resolutely. "We need to get some rest. It's nearly morning, and we'll be useless without at least some sleep."

"There's a cave over there!" pointed out Sophie and, sure enough, a tiny moss-covered hill wasn't far from where they now stood. On closer inspection the little cave was actually fairly habitable, large enough for the two girls to lie down and devoid of any threat or nasty surprises.

"We'll have to take turns keeping watch. There's shelter here, but nothing to protect us if a Laccuna does show up," said Charity wisely. "I'll go first, you get some sleep."

Sophie did not need to be told twice, she snuggled inside the cave, beside Charity, and very quickly fell fast asleep.

Charity had kept watch for as long as her weary eyes would remain open; she supposed it might have been two or three hours. In that time she had saw nothing, no people, no strange or familiar creatures, the only constant was the distant crashing of the Forfal waterfalls and the unsettling sound of silence that surrounded them. She woke Sophie, who seemed somewhat refreshed from her nap, if a little disorientated, and whilst Sophie took up the watch Charity slipped down into the cave, propping the Journal up as a makeshift pillow. Leaning against it she closed her heavy eyelids and almost at once drifted off to sleep.

When she awoke, she found Sophie snoring noisily on her outstretched arm, she pulled it hard from beneath her. "Wha's goin' on?" Sophie said sleepily.

"Nothing. We're fine, but *you* fell asleep," Charity said, agitated.

"Oh, no, I was just resting my eyes for a few…" Sophie said sleepily, then realisation dawned on her thin face, she looked suddenly guilty. "Oh dear, I'm really sorry Charity, I must've been more tired than I thought."

"It's ok, don't worry. We've both had a good rest now, we should probably set off."

"Where are we going again?" Sophie asked, rubbing her eyes with the sleeve of her red jacket.

"I - I don't know…" Charity said, realising this for the first time. During their escape from Forfal she hadn't needed to think, she had felt impulsive and brave but now the gravity of her situation had hit her hard. She had no idea where to go or how to find out.

There was a short silence as both girls contemplated the desolate situation they had found themselves in, and then out of the blue, Sophie piped up. "The Journal, you can read the Journal, it's bound to tell you!" she was wide eyed and suddenly looked completely awake.

Charity's heart leapt. In her sleep-addled mind she had completely forgotten about the Journal. She quickly the red leather book from the cave, and lying it gently on the ground in front of them she opened it carefully. She scanned each page of the now familiar black writing for a sign of any key word or phrase, 'treasure, secret, quill, Journal, feather, plume, Fateweaver.' Anything that would give her a hint to where Calville had went on his travels. Before long she had flicked her way through three quarters of the book and her heart was rapidly descending into her shoes, at almost the same rate as the water rail. What if she had escaped and gone all this way for nothing? This was something that simply had not occurred to her during her brief journey from Upper Forfal.

Charity had all but given up hope when she spotted it, a single word, all in capitals, one that caught her eye immediately: 'Fateweaver'. She ran her finger to the start of the page, which she noticed, was near the end of the Journal and read it out loud for Sophie, who sat beside her, enraptured.

'I know in my heart that the tale of the Fateweaver holds some truths. Our world was no mere accident. A hand set this wheel into motion, and I know that hand was Thea's. I believe, I need to believe, it's true, it must be true, that the FATEWEAVER is still here on Thea. *I will make my way to Duradon for there I can rest.* The surrounding desert holds more secrets than we can account for...'

Charity decided to stop and looked up at Sophie, whose mouth was hanging open, "Duradon Desert…it's huge, how in the name of Thea do we know where to start?" she asked.,

"How am *I* supposed to know?" said Charity exasperated. "I don't even know where Duradon is!"

"It's in Dura, thought that was at least obvious. Clue's in the name!" grinned Sophie. Charity shoved her playfully and she toppled out of the cave giggling.

"Hey, check where those missing pages are," said Sophie, picking herself up, her voice was high with curiosity.

Charity flicked to the end of the book and saw that indeed two pages had been torn from the book. She could see where the frayed remnants still remained bound to the spine of the Journal. She ran her fingers along the edges of the current, final page of the Journal. If what she had heard was true, then this would be close to Calville's last thoughts and actions before he disappeared. Again she read the page aloud for Sophie:

'I fear myself. Need to get away. I am so very close now, it has taken so long and taken so much from me but it is almost mine. Trust no

one, they all want it for themselves. I know this, the Fateweaver is real…IT IS REAL and …'

Charity looked up aghast. "It stops there?!" she yelled. "That's just cruel that is!"

"So we head to Duradon and check the area Calville laid out," said Sophie, ignoring Charity's frustration.

"Yeah, I guess," said Charity, glaring at the book as though I had wronged her in some way.

"Charity we really need to find those pages." Said Sophie very seriously, "Whatever happened to Calville is bound to be linked to what's happened to his Journal and remember what Perch told us, he thinks they were removed on purpose."

"Yeah, I was thinking about that, wouldn't that hurt? I mean if you're Journal's linked to you like it is, it's bound to hurt right?"

"Oh yeah!" shuddered Sophie, "Tearing a page is really hard to do, they're super strong, because of the Ordium in them. So ripping one out would've taken a huge effort."

"And it would painful?" Asked Charity tentatively.

"I read some accounts in the RD about times when it happened. It's like having a piece of your soul ripped from your body."

Charity was quiet for a long time after this. Sophie followed her lead and silently they readied their things for the journey ahead.

"Did he go anywhere else? Before the pages cut off." Asked Sophie as they began walking in what Sophie had assured them was the direction to Dura.

"O umm, wait lemme check…" answered Charity unclasping the book from her side, it slipped out as if it knew she wanted to read it.

Charity sped through the book, checking for key words again, after about fifteen minutes she snapped the book shut looking frustrated.

"What?" said Sophie, reading Charity's disgruntled look, "It's not good?"

"Well, he went to Duradon, mentions exploring. Didn't read it all, I will later though. Then he mentions Imputtia, and more exploring and something about moving stones or something, think I read something about a cliff. Sophie the thing's massive, it'll take me ages to finish and we can't stay out here until I do, I say we just go to Dura and hopefully we can fill in the gaps as we go."

"Oh," said Sophie, her face falling comically. "Well, suppose you're right. But if he went to Dura and…Imputtia was it?" - Charity nodded - "Blimey, that's a lot of travelling. We're supposed to find missing pages and we've only half the world to look for them." Sophie gave a great sigh and seemed to deflate as she did so.

"Then we best get moving!" said Charity bracingly, bouncing up and yanking Sophie to her feet.

11 – ALISTAIR GARRON

The two walked for a long time; Charity wasn't sure exactly how long. Time seemed to slip by in the Castlands as they continually passed similar looking barren hills and rock-strewn plains. Very occasionally they would come across uneven patches of grass or the odd collection of stunted looking trees but all in all Charity felt that they weren't making much progress. After a while, however, the sky began to change from a fairly bright blue, to a dull murky grey and then, quite suddenly, it was night time, the sun slipping beyond the horizon and a cold northern wind whipping them.

"It's f-f-freezing," chattered Sophie through clenched teeth. "We have to find some shelter s-s-soon."

"Yes, l-l-let's look over th – What was that?!" Charity asked suddenly, her head snapped around their immediate surroundings for a sign of movement. A low, rumbling noise had begun to emanate from somewhere, quiet at first - Charity hadn't noticed it, but now she could not ignore it. It grew in volume, louder and louder until it seemed to surround them; it sounded like the relentless purr of an engine and yet something about it was organic. Sophie and Charity were both whirling around, the cold around them forgotten, as they searched, terrified, for the source of the noise. Just then a blood-curdling scream issued from a nearby clump of trees, and before Charity could react, five wild-looking men burst forth from its midst, sprinting straight at them. The men were tall and sinewy, their ripped clothes covered in mud and moss. They continued hollering and screaming, their ear-piercing shouts drilling into Charity's head as she stumbled, disorientated, clutching at her head in pain. She heard Sophie shout a word that made her heart stop and her blood run cold.

"Laccuna!"

Of course these were Laccuna she thought to herself - nothing else could be quite as gruesome as these five figures. The Laccuna surrounded the two girls quickly. They had ceased their screaming now and Charity saw, looking up with her fingers still stuffed in her ears, that they were smiling, showing off slightly sharpened teeth.

"What 'av we 'ere then?" one of them cooed.

"Looks like travellers," another suggested.

"Crossing the Castlands, is it?" the first Laccuna cackled, showing off a set of very yellow fangs as he grinned down at them. "Well I reckon' you'll 'av to pay the toll." The surrounding Laccuna laughed coldly at these words.

"How-how much do you want? We have Odes!" Charity said, her voice shaking as she tried, in vain, to hide her fear.

The men around them cackled louder still, "Odes?!" one of them repeated in a sing-song voice, sneering horribly at them. "That there's *your* ways of paying." He spat on the ground derisively, "We got our own means of payment."

There was a murmur of agreement.

"You want to cross the Castlands, then we'll have to take out yer eyes," one of the men said, pulling a rusty looking blade from a holster on his back.

"WHAT?!" screamed Sophie as she clung tightly to Charity. "No, no…why?"

"WHY? She asks!" guffawed the yellow-toothed Laccuna, as the others continued to chuckle to one another. "Well, Miss, those fancy, little books you got strapped to yer flesh…they cause us quite a bit o' bother."

"Them's the reason we're 'ere!" bellowed a huge Laccuna, who was easily the largest of the assembled Laccuna but also looked the most dim-witted of the group.

"Tha's right Riggs, a lot o' bother they cause…so we feel it'd be better if you couldn't read 'em anymore." The first Laccuna finished logically, fingering his knife with a filthy hand.

The two girls moved closer to one another. Charity was frozen in place, she had absolutely no idea how to escape and the men were now drawing closer to them, their fangs and blades both poised and hungry-looking.

"Now, who's first?" he said, a savage grin stretched across his filthy face. "Black or white?" he said excitedly, looking between the hair on Sophie and Charity's heads.

Charity opened her mouth to scream but no words came out. Her throat was constricted with fear and she did not know how to unhinge it. Still the circle of Laccuna drew ever-closer, showing no sign of stopping. Then it happened, the tallest, most hideous-looking Laccuna leapt towards Sophie, who closed her eyes and recoiled in terror. Without thinking, Charity dove in front of her, not able to stop herself. As she did, a crash like thunder sounded out from somewhere nearby. She had expected to feel the cold metal of his blade or at least the Laccuna's weight crash into her own but instead she felt nothing but the hard ground when she landed, untouched, at Sophie's feet. Looking up she saw that the largest Laccuna now lay several feet away from them, sprawled on the ground and writhing in apparent agony. The surrounding Laccuna roared with rage, hissing and spitting at Charity and Sophie, who were now lying beside each other. Charity watched as they slowly edged forwards, seemingly daring each other to make the next move. She had no idea how the large Laccuna had missed his target by such a distance or what had made the others so angry but whatever it was had certainly unsettled their attack.

There was another crash of thunder from nearby, the heavens opening, and almost immediately a downpour of rain began lashing their heads. From out of nowhere, a strong hand pulled Charity to her feet. She turned, startled, and looked up into the impassive face of a man. At least she thought it was a man; Charity had to look twice for he was at least a foot taller than anyone she had ever met and as wide as two of the Laccuna. The man wore a great grey travelling cloak and had a wilted, black hat upon his head that concealed most of his enormous face in shadow.

He offered his hand to Sophie, who took it wordlessly; and pulling her to her feet he stepped forwards, blocking the Laccuna from their view. He bent low and removed a great wooden cane from behind his cloak, and holding it with both hands he fixed the now-hesitant Laccuna with a look of purest rage. The Laccuna stood stock still for a moment and then suddenly, without warning, they bolted, two turning on their heels and speeding off in the opposite direction, one hurtling off to the west to pick up his fallen ally who was still clutching his head. The remaining Laccuna charged straight at the stranger but upon seeing he was the sole attacker, attempted to stop before reaching his destination. It was too late, however, the stranger had leapt forwards, bringing his cane down hard upon the man's skull, which seemed to give way under the power he wielded. Charity could see a terrible cut where the stranger had struck as the Laccuna crumpled silently to the ground. The threats now dissipated and the stranger righted himself, brushing dust from his cane and cloak and turning to face Charity and Sophie, who were still standing awe-struck behind him.

"I am sorry," he said, the rain still pelting down, harder now. "I had not meant to kill, but it irks me that Laccuna would attack such innocent creatures." He spoke with a deep, booming voice, one that Charity had expected from such a hulking figure and yet she was surprised at the warmth he seemed to emanate. The man removed his travelling hat, exposing black, middle-length hair, streaked moderately with shades of grey. His eyes were a light sapphire blue and he had a large nose that looked as though it had been through its share of abuse.

"Thank you, sir!" said Sophie. She was still shaking as the rain continued to drench her, and Charity noticed the man looked taken aback by her words - perhaps he had never been referred to as 'sir' before.

He didn't respond to Sophie's thanks, instead pulling a great sheet from the inside of his cloak and throwing it to both of them.

"Here, dry yourselves off. My camp's not far from here, and you can stay the night…if you wish that is."

The prospect of an organised camp was too good to be true, thought Charity.

"That'd be most welcome," she said, putting on her most polite tone of voice. After all, she reasoned to herself, he *had* just saved their lives.

The man again said nothing, but pointed to a small bundle of items not far from where they stood which was apparently his camp. Charity had expected him to lead the way, but instead he moved towards the now lifeless body of the Laccuna and with a small 'click', removed a Journal from behind his back. He knelt slowly and placed the Journal face down beside the stricken man. The stranger's Journal had the same imprint of a tiny infant melted into the back cover. The man placed one hand over the cover, Charity noticed that his hands were so huge that they covered almost the entire book. He then placed his other hand on the man's chest, right where his heart would be and, very softly, whispered, "Thea forgive me." The man repeated this whisper wordlessly to himself at least a dozen more times and then when he was finished, very suddenly snapped up his Journal and repositioned it behind his back. He turned to see both Charity and Sophie gawking at him, his dark eyebrows raised in surprise. "Ah, the camp's over there," he said plainly.

"Oh yeah, well let's go then!" said Charity as cheerfully as she could manage, and she followed the huge stranger until they reached a small campsite, complete with a dully-burning fire and a hastily-assembled fur tent. The stranger stabbed his cane into the ground beside the fire, and setting his traveller hat and cloak on it he turned to face the two of them. With his long black cloak removed, Charity could see that he wore a blue, sleeveless jumper, white shirt, a black tie, corded brown trousers and huge black walking boots. Charity thought he looked like a very posh shepherd. She smiled at him as he met her gaze; however, he did not return her grin.

Charity moved towards him, politely stretching out her hand. "I'm Charity, by the way and this is Sophie. We'd like to know the name of the man who saved us."

The man fixed her with a piercing look.

"I am Alistair," the great man said, taking her hand in his and shaking it gently. Then, glaring at the two of them: "Tell me, what are two innocent souls like you doing out in the Castlands, alone?"

"We can't tell you," Charity said before she could stop herself. "I'm really sorry and we're really grateful to you for saving us, but we just can't."

The man raised one eyebrow in surprise. "You are a fiery one," he said, the faintest smile present on his weathered face. "You cannot tell me - very well. Have some food then. You look quite famished." And, crawling inside his tent, he returned two seconds later with a cloth sack brimming with fruits, vegetables, meats and grains. He set it down beside the fire and waved his hand, inviting them to sit. Charity bounded closer and sat down; meanwhile, Alistair looked up at Sophie, who had not moved a muscle.

"Are you alright, girl?" he asked.

"I don't – What if there are more Laccuna around?" she asked warily.

"I will watch out for them. Now eat, or you will die out here," he said flatly.

Sophie hesitated but then reluctantly moved to sit beside Charity, still glancing around the wasteland nervously.

Charity was too hungry to care, however, and as she tucked into the array of foods in front of her she savoured the feeling of protection that they were being afforded by their burly protector. For once, she thought to herself, it was safe to relax.

....

The dove pecked hungrily at the small pile of feed which had been left for it on the windowsill. Its leg bore the small clasp that allowed it to carry its master's letters across the plains of Thea. It had been a long journey and this unexpected meal was most welcome. Inside the room, two men sat around a small table, a map of Thea, the dove's letter and various pieces of parchment littered its black, Atra surface.

"Any word on the Forfal repairs, Your Eminence?" asked the first, robbed in white and bespectacled he cowered slightly under the gaze of his companion.

The other chuckled darkly, his face obscured by a large white hood he kept draped over his head, "My, my! You *did* make it out of there quickly now, didn't you Perch?"

Perch smiled nervously. "Yes, Your Eminence, I thought it best to be sure. Still, it turns out that the attack wasn't nearly as severe as first thought - only seventy three Laccuna."

"And you're quite sure you got all of them?"

"Oh yes, Your Eminence, I had the Knights sweep the city limits, no one could've gotten out without passing us."

"Ah, good. Well to answer your earlier question, Perch, the repairs are ongoing. No irreparable damage, thankfully -mostly arson."

Perch breathed a sigh of relief. "That's good. Do we have any idea how the Laccuna got into the city?"

"I have had word from Jossent that the majority used the water rail, and we have intelligence that the *imp* named Morton was being bribed into letting them travel on the rail. He has been taken in for questioning."

Perch nodded silently. He absentmindedly rubbed his hands together; something about this meeting was clearly distracting him.

"Perch, you are an experienced clergyman of the order," the hooded man said, in a dangerous tone quite clear in his velveteen voice now. "Why are you making small talk when you know full well *why* I have summoned you here to my chambers so late at night?"

Perch looked warily around the room, as if he expected something to burst out and attack him. "Your Eminence?"

"Why *have* you been called Perch?"

"The…the girl." Perch answered his voice breaking, his glasses shaking on the tip of his nose.

"The girl," the other confirmed casually. "This girl, Charity Walters was a peculiar puzzle to me, Perch – yes, even for one such as myself."

"I…I'm - " began Perch his eyes wide and terrified but the other continued and Perch snapped his mouth closed at once.

"I believe you owe one Finneus Frank a promotion. Having him send word of your actions has perhaps been the only thing that might have saved your life tonight. Although I make no promises."

"Your Eminence, I acted only in the interests of the Order, Perch blurted out. "Please…I…"he fell silent immediately as the other man raised a bony finger.

"You claim that one week ago, a small girl was brought to your attention. An thirteen year old girl who not only read another's Journal but did this instantly, without one *shred* of concentration or focus."

"Yes, Your Eminence, yes, it was quite amazing. She has far more skill than Katherine ever possessed. Or any Regalis for that matter."

Perch sounded relieved now, and his face broke into a hesitant smile as he boasted about his discovery, clearly his worries about being punished were quite premature.

"Yes, it seems she does and I can't imagine who excited you must have been *but…*" the hooded figure let the final word hang in the air between the two around the table. Perch's smile slipped off his face instantly and he suddenly looked horrified once more. "Then you went about explaining our little problem to her didn't you?" the man asked sweetly, and although his face was obscured there was no doubt that he was repressing a terrible fury beneath his hood.

"Problem?" trembled Perch.

"Yes, all that trouble we've been having with Calville's Journal, I know you remember the lengths we went to in order to assist Katherine with reading it." Cooed the other.

"I do yes Your Eminence." Simpered Perch

"Then surely you remember how highly we treasure that Journal and the secrets of its true purpose." The figure's voice was sharp and authoritative, Perch opened his mouth to reply but this seemed only to anger his master who leapt from his seat, his robes billowing out behind him and his chair crashing to the ground.

"YOU GAVE AWAY, NOT ONLY A PRICELESS ORDER ARTEFACT, BUT ONE OF THE MOST CLOSELY-GUARDED SECRETS IN IVORY ORDER HISTORY!! bellowed the man, slamming his fist onto the wooden table, so that many of parchments slid off and fell to the floor. "YOU WERE NEVER GIVEN LIBERTY TO TELL A SOUL OF OUR PLANS! YOU SHOULD HAVE CONTACTED US *BEFORE* YOU SENT THE GIRL OFF INTO THE WILDERNESS WITH THAT JOURNAL!!"

"But, but, but Your Eminence, I had planned to but the Laccuna, they attacked without warning and there was no time,I feared they would make off with the Journal." stuttered Perch. "I just -"

"ENOUGH!" shouted the man again. "I have Ivory Scouts on full alert for the girl. It would seem that she managed to escape Upper Forfal after all. We got enough out of Morton to led us to believe that she descended the water rail and headed into the Castlands." He rubbed his eyes with one hand. "She may still be alive, and if she is then both the Journal and her gift remain attainable."

Perch was still shaking convulsively and did not respond.

"Allow me to sum up our predicament then, Clergyman Perch. We, the most powerful organisation on Thea, have been in search of the Fateweaver for generations. Then, just when we find someone who might be able to finally help us, someone who gives us the tiniest glimmer of hope in our quest, you...you send her off into the desolate wastelands without a by your leave, with a readymade guide to the most dangerous and valuable artefact in Thean history," he finished in a dangerous whisper.

"But I explained the task," Perch began to explain in a fevered tone. "I explained it perfectly, told her about the plume and how she was to bring it..." He broke off as a squawking noise had started up from the windowsill. The first dove had been joined by another who was now pecking away at the small pile of seed as well. Just like the first, this new dove had a clasp around its ankle, and in this clasp was a rolled up piece of parchment.

"Get that, Perch," commanded the other man, his voice weary. Perch got to his feet and strode to the windowsill. He looked out upon the cold wastelands around him as he picked up the dove and withdrew the letter roughly from its clasp. He handed the letter to the seated man, who tore it open, scanning the page quickly.

"Well, well, well," the man said. His voice had changed now, it seemed delighted, joyous even. "It seems we have a welcome complication."

"Your Eminence?" said Perch, sitting forward expectantly.

"You may breathe freely once more Perch, you life will not end today."

The man leaned forwards, a wide grin spreading his aging face.

"It seems…the girl is not alone."

12 – SECRETS AND SUN-CRANES

The rain had been pelting the sodden ground for, what seemed like, hours; Charity could hear it outside the tent as she pulled the wiry woollen blanket tighter around herself. Alistair had been kind enough to let the girls stay the night in his tent whilst he had settled himself outside, his travelling cloak pulled around him and his wilted hat sitting low on his head. The girls had tried to turn down his offer but he had merely waved away their protests and ushered them inside with his massive hands. "Get some rest" he had commanded, "You'll need it."

Charity lay for a long time, tossing something around her mind and listening to the rain outside. An idea had occurred to her and at first it had seemed a wonderfully simple one but upon closer reflection there were a number of potential problems. She turned to Sophie who was contentedly sleeping beside her looking as though she was quite at peace with the world. Charity did not want to wake her but she needed a second opinion.

"Sophie," Charity whispered, but there was no response, "Sophie," she repeated a little louder, nudging her in the ribs. Sophie rolled over beside her and grunted sleepily to herself, "Oi!" Charity said, shaking her awake. Sophie snorted noisily and blinked wildly up at Charity, "Wha…wha's the matter?" she asked dozily.

"I need to ask you something?" said Charity,

"Oh…ok," said Sophie rubbing her eyes, "What?"

"I think we should ask Alistair to come with us, on our journey I mean. We, we're not cut out for something like this without some help, and he seems…really…"

"Big," Sophie suggested.

"Yeah, big, that's one way of putting it." Charity smiled at Sophie who did not return her grin,

"Charity, he's going to want to know where we're going *and* why!" said

Sophie frowning.

"We're just gonna have to tell him then." Charity decided self-assuredly, Sophie bit her lip in worry but Charity felt suddenly defiant. It was as if Sophie's hesitance had fuelled her own resolve and made up her mind for her. The idea to ask Alistair had taken hold of her the second he'd rescued them and now it seemed like the only choice available to them, even if it meant letting him in on her secrets. So before Sophie could utter anymore doubts she scrambled towards the flap in the tent, grabbing Calville's Journal in one hand as she made her way outside.

"Where are you going?" Sophie shouted as she poked her head out of the tent,

"To tell him everything!" said Charity confidently,

"NOW?!"

"Yes, now! It can't wait, I have to know if he'll come with us and I have to know *now!*"

Crawling out into the brisk morning air, she spotted Alistair sitting, very still beside the smouldering embers of a small fire. Charity found that his low hat covered so much of his face that she had to stare hard to make sure he was even awake, but on closer inspection she could spot a pair of pale blue eyes, which were staring intently at the dying fire with *great* concentration. Nervously, she made her way towards him, the precious Journal still tucked tightly under one arm.

"Alistair," Charity said, in a voice that betrayed her enormous sense of apprehension.

Alistair looked up at her before Charity had even finished speaking, she could his eyes see more clearly now, they really were the palest shade of light blue.

"Yes?" he answered, in a monotone voice.

"I have something to ask you, Alistair, but…but I want to tell you something first. Except you have to promise to listen to everything before you ask any questions, it's quite a long story and you'll *definitely* have questions!" said Charity her words tumbling out of her mouth in one short burst.

Alistair nodded silently and so Charity began her tale. She spoke about everything, from the very beginning in the Library right up until he had saved them from the Laccuna, she told him everything. This was the second time she'd found herself telling someone about where she had come from except this time no detail was left out as she poured her heart out to her would be companion, her abilities as a Regalis, the old man's dying message, the tale of the Fateweaver and the mission from the Order. To his credit, Alistair sat patiently through the entire story without so much as a sound and apart from raising his eyebrows at a couple of points, there had otherwise been no discernible reaction from the huge man.

"Ok, I'm finished now, that's it…all of it. Before you say it, I know that what I've told you is *unbelievable* but…well I wanted to ask you… to help us on our trip, we can only do so much on our own but you," she spoke in an admiring tone now, "You can stop anything that threatens us or puts us in danger, we'll need someone with your skills, Alistair, I've no doubt!" Charity was acutely aware that she had been talking for some time and was quite exhausted from the tension of waiting to hear Alistair's responses to both her outlandish story and her request to join them on their journey. She looked carefully at him, he was staring off into the distance, and whilst she yearned to hear his answers, she did not interrupt his thoughts instead she waited. After a couple of minutes Alistair slowly turned his head towards her, fixing her with a very serious look, he opened his mouth and finally spoke,

"You are not from here?" he asked simply,

"No, I'm from a place called England,"

"I have not heard of such a place, it is not on Thea?"

"Uh, no, no it's not."

"I see…" Alistair turned his attention back to the embers and fell silent once more. Charity stared at him, his eyes reflecting the orange licks of flame, she wondered whether she should say something but thought better of it. Alistair remained silent for a long time, Charity almost interrupted his thoughts more than once and it was only a fear of bothering the giant man that stopped her. Almost as if he had been reading her thoughts, Alistair turned from the fire to face her, his expression showed a look of mingled concern and surprise, as if he had just come to a sudden realisation. "You are not from Thea? You have no Journal?"

"Well no…and no," replied Charity quietly.

"But you are carrying one." Alistair pointed an oversized finger at the Journal Charity had tucked under her arm.

"This isn't mine, this is Charles Calville's Journal, the one the Order gave to me" and for the first time Charity noticed a flicker of interest behind Alistair's striking eyes, *these* words clearly meant something to him. Yet despite this surge of excitement behind his eyes, the face and voice remained unchanged.

"May I see it?" he asked calmly, his face was impassive and Charity could not tell *what* he was thinking.

Charity hesitated at first, but privately she reasoned that if she wanted him to trust her, she would have to trust him,

"O-ok" she said handing over the Journal.

Alistair ran his hands slowly over the thick red cover, he turned it over and flicked through the pages carefully, stopping intermittently and running a large finger over the white pages, at the very end of the book he stopped, just where the two pages were missing.

"Can…can you read it?" asked Charity, she didn't really know what had made her ask such a question, surely Alistair would be well known if he was a Regalis, but there was just something in the way he took so much time and care over each page, the way he seemed to almost caress the little book, that made Charity sure he was reading its contents the way only she could.

"No, I do not possess the gifts of a reader," he said solemnly, "You say you do though, *extraordinary*, how can one so small come to possess such a power?"

"I'm not *that* small," said Charity indignantly, "I'm tall for my age, and I'm taller than Sophie and she's older than - "

"HEY!" Sophie shouted, her head sticking out of the tent behind Charity, "I heard that!"

Charity grinned at her and then turning back to Alistair, saw he was frowning,

"I did not mean to cause offence," he said sounding concerned.

"No, that's ok, we're *both* pretty tiny, compared to you," Charity said sizing up Alistair once more.

He still looked concerned and she continued to watch him as he rummaged inside his cloak and pulled out a dark brown book that was unmistakably a Journal.

"I will require proof."

"You *want* me to read your Journal?" asked Charity astounded. It was the first time someone had willingly offered their Journal to her.

"No. But I see no alternative. Now if you would," he replied stoically.

Charity took the Journal wordlessly and creaked open the cover to a random page and stared down at the familiar swirling black writing and began to read aloud.

"It's true then, they are gone. *So alone, so scared.* I must be strong for them, they would not want me to mourn over - "

She jumped abruptly as Alistair snatched the book from her hands and snapped it shut looking suddenly horrified.

"I…I…that will suffice."

"o…k ummm sorry." She murmured.

"Do not apologise. It appears that you have been more than honest with me."

"Well, yeah of course," she replied as if this was obvious

"A reader so young, it is quite astonishing," marvelled Alistair staring down at her with renewed interest.

"So will you be travelling with us?" asked Charity

"Before I do that I must ask you one question. Would that be acceptable?" replied Alistair looking serious once more.

"Of course, anything," replied Charity brightly.

"You say you are in search of the Fateweaver feather. What do *you* wish to do with the Fateweaver if you find it?" asked Alistair, in a tone that left Charity in no doubt that this was a *very* important question.

Charity considered it for a moment and then said, "I'd use it to go home, get back to my Mother and Father."

"You do not desire wealth? Power? The feather could grant you anything you could ever wish for!" said Alistair, surprised,

"No, *that's* all I want, is to be home."

"Hmm," said Alistair, narrowing his eyes at her. Charity could not tell if he was impressed or disappointed with this response but after looking at her intently for a moment or two he stood up suddenly with great purpose.

"I will come with you."

Charity was so astonished and delighted that before she could stop herself she found that she was stretching out her arms, ready to embrace him. She realised what she was doing far too late however and retracted her arms at once. Alistair looked down at her as she slumped against his front and then immediately righted herself. Once upright and the appropriate distance from him Charity tried to pass off the awkward incident with a grin but Alistair appeared not to have noticed her strange behaviour or at least he was certainly not acknowledging it. Charity suspected that he was merely being polite and was most grateful for this.

She cleared her throat in what she hoped was a cool and casual manner,

"Well thank you Alistair, I really *really* appreciate it. We both do." she said, gesturing to the tent where at that very moment Sophie chose to pop her head from beneath the canvass.

"Alistair's staying?" she asked excitedly, reading the look on Charity's face.

"Yes!" shouted back Charity and Sophie squealed with delight as she launched herself across the tiny campsite towards Alistair. Without any hesitation she threw out her arms and latched onto Alistair's arm, swinging on it as though it were a playground swing.

"Oh thank you thank you thank you Alistair." She gabbled sounding as happier than Charity had ever heard her. Clearly Sophie had been more worried about their trip through Thea than she'd let on and having someone like Alistair was something of a safety net for her. Charity had to admit she felt the same.

Charity looked up at Alistair's awkward, uncomfortable face which had gone very red indeed. He appeared not to know what to do with Sophie and simply stared down at her, looking positively alarmed by her behaviour.

After a while Sophie mercifully released the relieved Alistair, who stumbled backwards from them and mumbled something about, "Going for a little walk." Charity and Sophie grinned at each other.

"He's fun." Said Sophie mischievously.

"Don't want to drive him away though do we?" warned Charity

"I won't, sorry I just got over excited I mean I was really ready to travel with just the two of us but I was thinking about it there when you mentioned asking him. We'd be in bits if he hadn't showed up when he did and that was just a bunch of Laccuna, who knows what we'll come across if we're following Calville.

"We better pack this stuff up," said Charity sensibly. She completely agreed with Sophie but did not want to think about any of the dangers that they might come across as it made her heart beat alarmingly fast and her head feel slightly dizzy.

They set about packing up their things, all the while Sophie hummed cheerfully to herself.

"It's great though isn't it?" she trilled after five minutes.

"What is?" asked Charity distractedly.

"Having Alistair to come along with us of course." Replied Sophie as if this was extremely obvious.

"Yeah, sure, it'll be good to have someone big to help us out!"

Sophie glared at Charity, "What do you mean by *that* indeed?"

"I mean big, like REALLY BIG! C'mon you *know* what I mean,"

Sophie fixed Charity with a disgruntled stare and then very suddenly broke out into a cheesy grin, "Yeah I do, just pulling your pages!"

Charity chuckled but threw a small, hard pillow at Sophie, who ducked, laughing to herself.

"Sorry, sorry! Couldn't resist." Said Sophie, still smiling, "But never mind about that... did Alistair believe you then?"

"About what?"

"About the whole story, how you got here and stuff?"

"Oh, I dunno actually." Said Charity, thinking about this for the first time,

"Well what did he *say?*" asked Sophie exasperated,

"He asked me to read his Journal." She explained.

"Woah, he let you read it, actually offered it to you?" said Sophie sounding awed.

"Yeah."

"And could you read it?"

Charity nodded, "I only read a line or two, he snatched it back after that."

"Oh? Was it anything important that you read?"

"Don't think so, something about someone being missing."

"Hmm, well he was convinced then?"

"Seemed to be. Well he believed I was a Regalis anyway."

"And that's all he asked?"

"No, he asked what I would do with the Fateweaver if I ever found it?"

"What did you say?" Sophie asked, her eyes alight with interest.

"I said I'd use it to go home,"

"Hmm, makes sense, I guess. But he didn't say if he believed the rest of your story or not then?"

"Nope… He must sort of believe me if he wants to come with us though, right?"

"I guess," said Sophie, looking unsure. "And he never *even* questioned you about the Order's mission?"

Charity shook her head, doubt now seeping into every crevice of her mind, why hadn't he questioned such an unusual story? Sure she'd read his Journal but what did that prove? It didn't really make sense for someone to just agree to such a task without finding out as much information as they could, she thought sensibly to herself. That's what she would've done.

Behind them the sound of something being pulled from the hard ground made them turn around, Alistair was holding his mighty cane aloft, brushing the dirt off one end. He looked up in alarm, when he saw the two girls staring at him,

"Oh um, I believe we should leave Charity, Sophie." giving each of them a curt nod as he addressed them.

With Alistair's considerable assistance the campsite was repacked in no time at all and soon they were back on their journey, back on the path to Dura. They walked in the general direction they had been going before the

Laccuna attack, with Alistair's assurances that it was indeed the correct route. Sophie and Charity both soon found that they had to quicken their pace with their new companion, as Alistair's huge strides were very difficult to keep up with.

"How…far is it…to Dura, Alastair?" puffed Sophie, struggling to match his massive steps.

"Far enough," he answered, not taking his eyes off the dusty path they were now travelling on, "Should be there in a couple of days."

Charity tried to take in as much of her surroundings as possible, far behind her she could still see the huge waterfalls of Forfal, although they looked like mere trickles now. Turning to her left and right she saw nothing but desolate wasteland, hard ground with small signs of vegetation, mounds of rocks and piles of rubble as far as she could see. Ahead of her, when she craned her neck around Alistair's massive form, she could clearly see a streak of bright yellow land, "That *must* be Dura," she whispered under her breath in amazement, the small glimpses she could catch of this foreign land showed an area that looked vastly different to the wasteland that surrounded her.

It took them about two more days of camping and travelling before they reached their destination. Sophie and Charity held off complaining for as long as they could in a bid to impress their new companion, but it had not taken long for their feet to begin to ache and their stomachs to rumble and the rough terrain did not help. Alistair had provided them with food but he only allowed them to eat twice a day as supplies were short and they had to make haste. On the third day, just as the cherry red sun reached its apex, Alistair clambered on ahead and turning to them he pointed into the distance an unusually triumphant look on his face.

The girls clambered up several increasingly tricky inclines and ascended a steep hill to reach where he stood, only then could they see what he was pointing at, it was the largest, most vibrant desert Charity had ever seen. She looked upon the swirling winds and sandy dunes of Dura for the first time and was reminded of old pictures of the Sahara she'd read about in Geography books. Books were one thing, but to see a sight like this with her own eyes, was truly magical.

On Alistair's instruction they forged ahead down the increasingly sandy slopes down into the desert below, all the while Charity continued to marvel at the scale of Dura. The sand seemed endless, stretching right across their horizon and far off into the distance. Charity squinted as she stared ahead of her, something unusual had caught her attention. Something that was glinting and sparkling in the bright afternoon sunshine, the closer they got the clearer it became until finally as they neared the bottom of the hill side she understood what she was looking at and her mouth fell open.

Here was something that made Dura's desert wildly different from that of the Sahara. Charity could hardly believe what she was seeing, sitting right in the middle of this land of burning sand was a sprawling city. Charity could see its lights and torches from where they stood, the ruby red walls shone like a beacon in the sea of sand around it.

"Is that?" asked Charity,

"That must be Duradon," said Sophie in an awed voice, "I heard, that the Durads call it 'The Ruby of Dura'."

"I can see why," said Charity, impressed, "Wait what's a Durad?" she asked realising what Sophie had said.

"Oh yeah, you wouldn't know. Uh, Durads are people from Dura, Aguish are from Agua and Imputtians are from…well Imputtia, obviously as that's the only one left." Sophie smiled encouragingly at Charity who felt slightly disappointed with herself at not working at least one of these on her own.

"Guess we better start walking. It's ages away!" she said, in an attempt to force a change of conversation.

"No," Alistair said suddenly, "The winds of Dura are fierce and changeable, by day they carry the dust and sand from the surrounding desert and conditions are rough but bearable. By night however, the wind changes, it carries the cold from the north. Cold that would come close to freezing you two where you stood."

"What?!" exclaimed Charity and Sophie together, "Well how do we reach it then?!" asked Charity, incredulously.

"Sun-Lift." said Alistair,

"What-lift?" asked Charity looking at Sophie whose face had just broken out into a wide smile,

"Is there one around here? I've heard there were Sun-Cranes in Dura, are they really used to pull them? Wow, that's incredible! Oh I really *really* wanna see one!" Sophie babbled away as Charity looked at her, intensely confused.

"I don't understand," said Charity, who was beginning to feel that she said this *so* often, that she ought to get it tattooed onto her forehead to save her the bother in the future.

"Follow me," replied Alistair, and he made his way, slowly down the side of another sandy hill. They had walked a little way along the bottom part of the dune when Charity thought she could hear voices coming from close by. The further they walked, the louder the voices became. They rounded a smaller dune and Charity could see they were heading in the direction of an enormous cave, it was cut right into the side of steep cliff face and was lined with an assortment of lamps, not unlike those in the secret passage in Forfal. Charity, Sophie and Alistair continued towards the cave, and now Charity could see the source of the voices she had heard, a small crowd of about five or six people was standing under the roof of the cave chatting happily to one another. The crowd were huddled around a small sign, squinting, Charity was just able to make out the words: 'Sun-Lift pick up point'.

The little waiting group smiled pleasantly at Charity and Sophie as they approached, then noticing Alistair they all stepped back apprehensively. One woman grabbed a small girl who was playing in the sand nearby and held her close, "Jenny, come, just come close to Mummy, the lift's almost here." Charity looked around but saw no sign of any 'lift', she supposed the woman was just unused to seeing such a huge man.

Not wanting to make an idiot of herself in front of the crowd, Charity leant in close to Sophie and whispered quietly, "What's a Sun-Lift?" Sophie did not immediately respond but grinned mischievously at her, "You'll see," she said teasingly.

Charity had just opened her mouth to argue, when the tiny girl shouted out behind her, "Mummy, Mummy, look there it is!" Charity spun round to see where the girl was pointing; looking up she saw something that could not *possibly* be real. The bright morning sky was now filled with four brightly coloured suns, but unlike Thea's red sun these suns were a brilliant, bright yellow. High, high up in the sky, the four suns moved in unison at four separate points moving away from the red sun which hung motionless above them; looking closer Charity thought she could see something indistinguishable suspended in between them. Gradually, the suns stopped moving across the sky and then began to float downwards right towards where they stood in the mouth of the cave.

The strange formation came closer and closer until it was about five hundred yards away, it was only then that Charity could see what they were. A square tablet of cast iron was being suspended in the air, not by four suns but four huge birds. Their feathers were a dazzling shade of yellow and they stuck out at odd angles all over their round bodies. As the wind rustled these feathers, Charity thought they looked exactly like licks of flame dancing round a ball of fire, from a distance each bird really did resemble a small sun. Each of the birds had a very thin neck, a small head, a long thin beak and two spectacular wings which spread out like fiery carpets on either side of them. Charity also noticed, as they drew ever closer, that they only seemed to have only one leg each, which they stuck out behind them in a very straight line as they flew.

"That's a sun-lift," said Sophie her eyes wide and awe-struck, "It's a Durad method of travel, and those things carrying it are Sun-Cranes, I used to read about them in the records office, I heard they were beautiful but…Wow!"

"They *are* beautiful, are they dangerous?" Charity whispered,

"Don't think so," said Sophie reassuringly.

"Sun-Cranes will only harm one that attempts to harm one of its flock," said Alistair softly,

"Have you seen one before?" asked Charity, turning to Alistair, eager to know more about the wonderful birds.

"I have, I tend to use the Sun-Lifts whenever I am in Dura, as it is the most inexpensive route."

The birds had slowed their flapping now and had brought the metallic platform close to where the crowd stood. They set the platform down in the sand with a soft thud and stood quite still on their single legs, grooming themselves silently. Charity thought they looked to be about twice the size of an ostrich, having seen Ostriches once, whilst on a trip to London Zoo with her mother and Father.

"How do they know where to land? I don't see a driver or anything," asked Sophie curiously,

"They know because it is all they have ever known. It is their life, their duty to Dura."

"So they're like prisoners?" asked Charity disconcerted,

Alistair considered her, "If a Thean is born into a household, and is given all he requires in exchange for a job he finds quite natural, is that prison?" he asked her,

"Well, if he can't leave then yes!" said Charity passionately,

"Why would he want to leave, it is all he has known,"

"Doesn't seem like much of a life though," Sophie said thoughtfully,

"Perhaps not, but it is a life they are comfortable with, Sun-Cranes *never* leave their route. They will fly it until they die without deviation or variation. That is the way it has always been." said Alistair sullenly, making it quite clear that that was the end of the conversation.

They boarded the platform with the other passengers and found a space on the ground to sit together. Much like the Water Rail, a tiny metallic railing ran all around the edges of the sun-lift, this was good news for the tiny girl was now rolling around the lift excitedly and Charity grimaced at the idea of her toppling over the edge whilst they were hundreds of feet in the air.

"How long will it take to get to Duradon?" Sophie asked Alistair,

"Some time, you should rest, whilst you can," he suggested,

"Does it only go to Duradon?" asked Charity,

"Yes. Now rest!" he ordered, his voice was harsh but his face was wrinkled in a kind smile. Charity smiled back, laying her head on her hands and lying up against Sophie. It was only midday but they had walked miles since the crack of dawn and the first chance to rest her legs and close her eyes was too good to pass up. Besides the gentle rocking of the sun-lift was becoming increasingly hard to ignore. Slowly Charity let her eyelids flutter, her breathing slow and gradually allowed herself to drift off into a pleasant sleep.

Charity was walking in a familiar looking village. The thundering sound of a waterfall was nearby, and she felt annoyed by this intrusion of noise. She walked a short while, until she found what she had been looking for: his house. She walked to the door, anger and revulsion coursing through her veins. Stealing herself, she kicked the door hard. *That didn't look like her leg.* The door flew open, one of the hinges snapping clean off. This room too, was familiar. It was utterly filthy, the very air swirling with dust and grime.

Where was he? She needed to find him, that much was very clear. She did not have to wait long. Spotting the old moth-eaten armchair she strode towards it and spun it round to face her. He was there, she could see him now, lying there, just lying there. Why was he just lying there? He was not waiting for him, she couldn't goad him into anger, she would never see the trembling in his limbs, the terror in his eyes, he was pathetic, useless, dead.

"You were supposed to be mine. I wanted to look into your eyes as I plunged my dagger through your Journal. I wanted to see the shock on your face…the fear you made me feel." She spoke to the lifeless body, but the voice was different from her own, this one was harsher, colder and right now betrayed her feelings of furious disappointment.

She had been robbed. Thea had taken everything from her, but in her lowest moments she had always had this one task to comfort her; the prospect of revenge. She had coveted it for so long, held it closely to her heart, it was the very reason for her existence. After all, what did she have to live for if not for retribution? The rage inside her was building to a crescendo, she slammed a fist into the man but his lack of movement only enraged her more, she struck the body again, and again, and again. Her yells echoing out around the small cabin, this was definitely not her voice, she was sure of it now, she was breathing heavily and rested a long thin hand on the chair to steady herself.

Just then, there was a small cough from behind her, she whirled around to see two men she instantly recognised as Ivory Knights, their swords drawn and pointing directly at her. She made for her knife but as she did a deep voice called out from behind the two Knights.

"Come now boy, no need for unpleasantness."

"Boy?!" she said to herself, confused.

The figure moved forwards, in between the two guards, pushing their swords down lazily as he passed. "Rendal, Alexus, leave us." The two guards dutifully left the cabin as the man spoke. "I'd like you to at least hear me out, it…could be beneficial for both of us." The man wore a long white hood over his face, obscuring it in shadow but now he raised a hand towards it pulling it up, his face was almost visible now, she could nearly see it, she leaned forward expectantly despite herself –

"CHARITY!" shouted Sophie, from far away.

Charity awoke with a start, "What, Who is it?"

Sophie looked at her, "You gone soft in the head or something? It's Sophie, we're here."

She covered her eyes to protect them from the sudden burst of sunlight but squinting through her fingers she could see that the platform had indeed come to a stop. The Sun Cranes were all perched on a nearby dock and beyond them lay a glistening wall that looked as though it was made entirely of rubies.

"Are we here?" asked Charity,

"Yup, this is Duradon." said Sophie smiling.

....

If he dropped the book and drew his dagger, in one swift dance of black fabric he could be upon the cloaked figure, his knife to his throat in a second. *The guards outside, surely there would be more of them. Hold off and see what he has to say.*

"The last person to try and sneak up on me got this dagger through his heart…" threatened Cassius in a deadly whisper, the anger that had been tearing through him moments ago was bubbling under the surface and threatening to overwhelm him.

"Well isn't it marvellous that I was waiting for you then?" answered the figure in a strangely calm voice.

Cassius could make out a wrinkled mouth barely visible in the depths of the man's hood, and to his great disbelief he could see that he was smiling.

"I'd wipe that smile off your face if I was you, before my blade does it for you." Cassius could feel his control slipping, his hand tightened on the dagger's handle. *The guards, compose yourself!*

This time, the man began to laugh. There was no hint of nerves, it was a smug, knowing sort of laugh.

Cassius' heart was pounding in his ears, a bellowing drum, playing to the beat of rage and chaos. He urged himself not to be consumed by it, his knuckles were white around the hilt of his dagger, but something in this man's voice stopped him. He had met nobody who would dare be this arrogant in light of the threats he had delivered.

"You dare laugh, have you any idea who I am?" spat Cassius.

"I might ask you the same question," replied the man quite calmly, as he raised a hand and slid the hood from off his head.

"The Cardinal of the Ivory Order here in this pitiful little shack, what have things come to?" He asked himself sarcastically.

"Ivory Order?" asked Cassius, "You're with the Order, those Journal peddlers!"

"Indeed I am, in fact *I* am not to put too fine a point on it, the head of those 'Journal peddlers' as you so diplomatically put it."

"Head of the Ivory Order?" asked Cassius incredulously.

"Yes but you may have heard me referred to as the Cardinal or perhaps the High Priest of the Ivory Order."

Cassius remained silent, he *had* heard of this man. Even in the Journal-free lands of his childhood the tales of the Ivory Order were common and if his words were true then he was a most powerful man indeed.

"I have been waiting quite some time for you, when my Scouts spotted a figure cross the border some hours ago, I had hoped that it would be you; It would seem I have not been disappointed. You have been causing quite a stir across Thea, not least in Duradon. Wounding *one* Ivory Order member is punishable by death never mind *two.*"

"I'd do it again!" Cassius spat derisively, "You Mainlanders deserve everything you get!"

"Yes indeed, but those *dogs* out there can fret about such laws, people like you and I… *We* have different concerns. We have a higher purpose in this life my boy." said the Cardinal.

"DON'T call me *boy!* I'm NOTHING like you! You don't know a thing about me!" Cassius snapped fiercely,

"Don't I? My sources inform me that you are Laccuna, raised in the Castlands, like all of your kind, you never knew your parents."

Cassius smiled wickedly, "Your sources are mistaken." He said sinisterly, *A stumble, this man was not as smart as he at first seemed.*

"They are? I highly doubt you are a Mainlander; we have no record of your grafting."

"Not about *that.* I knew my Father. I knew him better than anyone ever did for I saw what he really was. A monster and a coward!"

The Cardinal opened his mouth to speak but then closed it and instead stared beyond Cassius at the lifeless form still slumped in the chair.

"I killed my Mother you know? He told me, he always told me that, I was the reason she passed and I didn't even have a Journal to show for it. He didn't care about me, he only cared for his reputation. He kept me hidden, for years and years. I grew up in this very room. This squalid hole was my entire childhood, I used to think that life couldn't get any worse and then one day it all got too much for him. I had started to show potential you see; I started doing things, things that scared him. His fear grew more and more each day until he finally he could hold out no longer and he did what he had wanted to do all those years ago. He cast me out, he left me to die.

The Cardinal said nothing, Cassius was breathing heavily, the veins in his neck were throbbing ominously, he felt as though he was about to burst.

"I swore, *swore* I would get stronger though, I would find the traitorous wretch and make him pay for his actions. But now…" Cassius trailed off as he stared listlessly at the body that had been his Father.

"The meek have a nasty habit of stifling the mighty I have seen it many times however I do believe I can still offer you the chance to gain what you seek….vengeance!"

Cassius began to laugh, a low rumble, rising into a maniacal cackle as he rocked back and forth, his hand clenched tightly on the old armchair. The Cardinal however appeared unperturbed.

"Something amusing?" he asked,

"You offer me vengeance, Cardinal?"

"I do."

"Then you are too late…As was I." Cassius replied bitterly.

"I don't think I am actually," said the Cardinal calmly.

Cassius turned to stare incredulously at the Cardinal, "What are you talking about old man?" he was growing tired of this charade and yearned to be free of him.

"I am talking about your potential Cassius," replied the Cardinal, and for the first time Cassius could sense a burning fire behind his words.

"You know my name?"

"Of course I know your name, this may come as I surprise to you but there is little that happens on Thea that I don't know of."

Cassius was momentarily stunned but recovered swiftly, "So you know my name, you didn't know about my Father, how do I even know you *are* the Cardrinal?"

The Cardinal rubbed his eyes in frustration, "I admit that small detail managed to slip through the net but I assure you that I am the High Cardinal of the Ivory Order. I would tell you to ask anyone but my identity is a secret privy to only the most loyal members of the Ivory Order so you're unlikely to find someone able to give me a reference, especially in this squalid little hole."

"And now I know too." Smiled Cassius vindictively,

"You do."

"So what's stopping me telling every single person I meet that the Ivory Order is actually being run by - "

The Cardinal slammed a fist into a nearby wall, causing a cloud of dust to hail down upon them like rain, Cassius stopped in his tracks, his words had clearly effected the man."

"A heavy secret to bear, I agree but then you're used to holding onto such secrets are you not?…Regalis."

"Who told you?" gasped Cassius before he could stop himself.

Now it was the Cardinal's turn to laugh and laugh he did. A hollow booming laugh that was more like the rasping roar of a lion, he wiped a tear from his eyes and looked very seriously at Cassius who had remained stony faced.

"Hundreds told me. Members of the Order, tortured civilians, men, women, Laccuna, they all told me of the boy with no Journal that could read them all."

Cassius did not respond to this, he hadn't told a soul about his ability and yet somehow this man proclaiming to be the Cardinal knew of everything.

"Cassius, you want revenge? You want vengeance, yes?"

"Yes" he whispered desperately.

"Then I can help you."

 "What can you possibly do? My Father is dead, my chance is gone. I was too late," he croaked, the words tasted bitter in his mouth.

"Yes he is dead, that much is obvious but tell me have you ever heard of an item known as the Fateweaver?"

Cassius raised his eyebrows in surprise; the tale of the plume had spread throughout Thea even to the wilderness of the Castlands.

He nodded slowly.

"Ah excellent, then I do believe I have a proposition for you."

13 – A ROYAL PROPOSITION

Charity and the others stepped off the Sun-Crane and on to a dust-covered walkway that wove its way along the outskirts of the great city of Duradon. Looking along the stretch of brown wood that made up the walkway, Charity could see why the city had stood out so clearly earlier that day; the entire city seemed to be made of nothing but red clay. The houses far in the distance were distinctly visible due to their bright colour and beyond them, lay a huge structure, which looked to Charity like some sort of palace. Charity found that she couldn't see any of the buildings closest to her, due to a large wall that stretched its way ten or so feet up into the air. She craned her neck to see how far along the wall went, but after walking a few paces it seemed almost never-ending, stretching around the entire city like a great snake. Their point of entry was at least clear, as at the far end of the walkway stood a huge double door, it's dark black colour contrasting wildly with the crimson bricked wall it was set within.

"Woooaah!" said Sophie. "I wonder what they're trying to be keep out, with a wall like that."

"Or keep in," Charity added in a sinister tone.

"The wall has not been needed for many years, not since the great war," said Alistair wisely.

"The great war?" Charity asked, "There was a war on Thea?"

"Yeah, course!" said Sophie as if this was most obvious, "Everyone knows that."

Charity gave her a withering look and Sophie jumped as she realised what she had said.

"Oh right, sorry sorry sorry. I keep forgetting."

"It's ok," smiled Charity, "So there was a war then. Was Dura, were they involved in it?"

"Really involved," answered Sophie, "In fact Duradon was one of the most sought after cities in Thea for a long time during the war."

"*Really?*" asked Charity screwing up her face, "It's pretty and all that but the whole area's mostly desert, who'd want to fight for that?"

"Oh, loads of people. It's ruled by the only royal family in all of Thea, and the treasure in the royal palace alone would be worth a fortune," said Sophie excitedly.

"Sophie how do *you* know so much about Thea?" asked Charity impressed.

"I pieced it together, mostly from working in the Records Office. I didn't really get out much and if I was ever bored, I read a bit about Thea," she exclaimed proudly. Charity could easily relate to this. How many times back home had she sat and read to escape boredom or reality? And now, here she was in a different land on an incredible adventure, and deep down all she wanted was to be at home again.

"Who was fighting in this war then?" she asked, pulling her mind away from thoughts of home.

"The three main parliaments of Thea; Dura, Agua and Imputtia," said Sophie knowledgeably.

"I know Agua is where we've just come from, the place with the waterfalls, and Dura is where we are now…but where's Imputtia?"

"The north," said Alistair, before Sophie could reply, "It is the coldest and the most deadly of all the nations on Thea."

"Did *they* start the war?" asked Charity in a hushed tone.

"They did. But it is much more complicated than that. At first the leaders of Imputtia simply wanted more land, more prosperous settlements, more Odes. It is hard to raise crops and cattle on such frozen ground; however you should not absolve the other nations either. When Imputtia first attacked Dura, Agua sent support, rallying with their desert brethren, and together they fought back the Imputtian forces. In the aftermath of this battle the Durads were severely depleted and so the Aguish simply turned on Duradon, wiping out most of the Dura army and seizing it for themselves. A lot of backhand deals and collaborations were made over the course of the war. Nations changed hands numerous times and many innocent lives were lost due to nothing more than the gambling of highborn men and women.

"In the end, of course, nothing changed. Imputtia went back to the North and the leaders responsible for the war were punished severely for their crimes against Thea, though Imputtia remained mistrusted for many years after the war had subsided. In reality, it is only recently that the other nations have accepted them back into mainstream politics. It is a messy, complicated state of affairs."

"Woah, that's incredible! So people still don't really trust them?" asked Charity.

"Many do, but there remain some who feel that their crimes were too great to warrant forgiveness," answered Alistair matter-of-factly.

"Do you trust Imputtia?" she asked, curious.

"I do not," he said flatly.

Sophie gave a little squeak and managed to trip herself. She flopped onto the wooden walkway and as she was being helped to her feet by Charity, rounded upon Alistair.

"But, why not, Alistair? They've earned our trust, the peace treaty has been signed and most of the Order's highest representatives come from Imputtia these days - without *them* where would we be? Scrambling about the Castlands without Journals," she said passionately, answering her own question.

"I do not trust Imputtia, nor do I truly trust any nation on Thea."

"But that doesn't make any sense, how can you not trust *anyone*? I mean, where are *you* from?"

"That is not relevant, Sophie, the issue lies with one thing above all else…Journals!"

"What…" began Sophie but she was quickly interrupted by Alistair who towered over them, his blue eyes alight with emotion.

"I do not wish to speak of this anymore. Now come we have much to do."

He left neither Sophie or Charity in any doubt that the conversation was not just over but hat this topic was not to be mentioned ever again.

"I'm…I'm sorry, Alistair," said Sophie very quietly; she was red faced and looked as though she was about to cry. Charity put her arm around her as Alistair who had walked on several paced turned and approached her looking pained.

"Your apology is unnecessary, Sophie. I did not mean to snap," he said quietly.

He patted her gingerly on the head as if her were petting a small dog, "Please understand it is a personal issue." He added in a soft almost pleading voice.

"I understand." Sophie whispered resolutely. Alistair smiled at her and, seemingly satisfied, he straightened himself and strode on down the walkway towards the large red walls ahead of them, beckoning them to follow.

Their intense conversation at an end, the three companions walked up to the huge black door at the end of the wooden platform. Reaching it, they saw that upon closer inspection, a small window was just visible right in the centre. The window was painted the same shade of black as the door, so that even if you were staring straight at it you'd be unlikely to even notice it.

"Where's the handle?" asked Sophie feeling the door's surface with both hands,

"You must pull the bell," said Alistair indicating a piece of scraggly, rather old looking rope that was hanging from the window. "Duradon still maintains some mistrust to visitors. The Great War's casualties are not always physical," he finished mysteriously.

"Should *I* pull it?" asked Sophie, eyeing the rope warily. "Does it matter who pulls it?"

"Well if you're not going to then I will," said Charity stubbornly, "I can't wait around here forever," and she grabbed the rope tightly giving it a forceful tug.

Charity and Sophie jumped back in surprise, banging into Alistair, who had remained as still as a statue. A tremendously loud ringing sound was bursting forth from somewhere above the door; Charity staggered around looking up for the source of the commotion. At the top of the door was perched a huge black bell which was tolling to and fro, its chimes echoing out across the sandy deserts.

Out of the corner of her eye, Charity noticed that Alistair had taken a significant step to the right, so that he was no longer immediately in front of the massive door. He had also brought his traveller's hat down even further over his face, so it was now almost completely concealed in shadow. As if the bell had summoned it, the tiny window in the door opened suddenly and a man with beady eyes and a large bristly moustache poked his head through the gap.

"Who's there?" he enquired in a shrill, nasal voice.

"Umm, hello," said Charity from below the man's point of view.

"WHAT?!"

The man clearly couldn't see Charity and Sophie at first, and his head moved wildly from side to side for those responsible for pulling the bell. Seeing no one, he tutted and made to close the window.

"HEY!" Sophie yelled. "Down here!"

"ARGH!" he screamed and toppled out of sight. Charity could hear banging, clanking and scraping coming from behind the door and then he appeared again looking dishevelled and angry.

"What is wrong with you?! Coulda broke my neck!" he said. "What d'you want anyway?"

"We want to come in!" said Charity.

"In? Here? Now? Why?" he asked quickly. Charity didn't know which question to answer first, why was he so hesitant to let them in? Perhaps this wasn't the correct way to enter the city she thought suddenly.

"We're looking for a place to stay." said Sophie sounding just as unsure as Charity felt.

The man did not respond, instead he stared suspiciously at both of them for a moment and then without warning he disappeared again. They could hear him behind the door, muttering to himself, "First that Aguish tour group gets mugged and now some kids wandering the desert demand to come in. I ain't got time for this…"

He poked his head back through the window and glowered down at them, "Bog off, we don't need no more visitors, place is too full as it is."

"But…but" began Sophie desperately but the little man was already pulling the shutter down over his window.

Charity threw caution to the wind, "We've got money!" she shouted.

The man's arm that was holding up the sign paused and slowly his bushy face drifted back through the window.

"You got Odes eh?" he asked, an unmistakably glint of greed in his beady eyes, "How much you got?"

"Enough for a tour." barked Alistair from nearby, pulling the hat even further down over his face.

The effect these words had on the man was remarkable. Instantly his sour demeanour faded away as he broke out into a wide grin, his beady eyes seemed to sparkle with delight as he disappeared once more babbling excitedly to himself behind the wall.

Several loud crunches of machinery drowned out his chatter, and these noises were soon joined by the whirring of fans and clattering of metal on metal as very slowly the mighty door creaked into life. The colossal swung inwards, and as it did, it revealed a sprawling red city bursting with the hustle and bustle of life.

The small man had appeared beside them now and he waved majestically at the scene in front of them. "You're wanting a tour, well why didn't you say so then? Welcome," he said proudly, "to Duradon!"

Charity marvelled at the stunning landscape before them; the crimson-bricked buildings lined every corner and seemed to occupy nearly every space imaginable, from tiny little huts crammed into areas of shadow, to huge three-storey houses. Charity's attention, however, had been almost immediately taken up by the huge bowl-shaped lake sitting in the very centre of this arid scene, like a watery blue blotch on a fiery red campus. It would've stood out further against the violently red buildings if it were not for the structure towering over everything in sight. A magnificent imperial palace stretched right up to what seemed like the clouds themselves. This, Charity supposed, must be the palace Sophie had mentioned.

"I-I-I…" stammered Sophie.

"Quite something, isn't it?" asked the little man.

They could see his figure now. He was squat and strong, with incredibly hairy forearms and bent little legs, which made him look like some sort of tiny bull.

"There's the market," he said, pointing to a collection of men setting up wooden stalls, "That's the artificial lake," he pointed at the lake in the centre of the city, "and *that,*" he waved at the huge building in the distance, "is the imperial palace of Duradon, the highest building in all of Dura, and the home of Queen Mosia the first."

Sophie was still staring slack jawed at the beautiful scenery; it looked as though she hadn't taken in a word the man had said. Charity elbowed her in the ribs. "Thank you very much for your help, Sir," said Charity, pointedly, as she gave a little bow.

"Oh, such manners, you lot must be from Imputtia no, no, wait lemme guess, Agua it's Agua isn't it?" he said rubbing his chin thoughtfully.

"Imputtia. You were right the first time," said Charity, smiling pleasantly.

"Oh lovely!" replied the man and he imitated Charity's little bow, bending so low that his fluffy moustache brushed the yellow sand below them.

He walked into the city and Charity and Sophie followed, Charity noticed that Alistair remained a little way behind, almost as though he wanted to disassociate himself from them. Charity turned, trying to catch his eye, whilst still keeping up with Sophie, but he seemed to be avoiding her gaze. She turned back to the man who was now talking animatedly to Sophie.

"I didn't catch your name, strangers, I can't very well be calling you the Imputtians now can I?" He gave a hearty laugh, and brushed some of the dust off his moustache.

"I'm Charity and this is Sophie," said Charity. She had planned to introduce Alistair but a glance behind her made her change her mind. Alistair had fallen right back into a crowd of gabbling bystanders and although he was still following them it couldn't be plainer that he did not want any attention.

"Well nice to meet you Charity and Sophie, I am Lur. I operate the door, and as you may have already guessed, it's my job to make sure people…are…suit…a…ble," he tailed off distractedly. Charity saw that he was looking over their shoulder at where Alistair was now standing his hands in his pockets. Very slowly a look of gradual realisation spread across Lur's face.

"Oh my…what an honour," Lur said, his eyes glassy and a disbelieving smile now etched onto his face. He rushed towards Charity, his hand outstretched. Charity had thought that word might reach people about her eventually, but she had not expected it so soon. She understood that a Regalis was a rare and coveted thing in Thea but she wasn't sure she was ready for such reverie from people she had just met. Charity smiled nonetheless and offered her hand in what she thought was a modest pose. Lur proceeded to move towards her. "Please, I don't really want any special treat-" she began, but the man nudged Charity out of the way and hurried up to Alistair, who stared at him from under his hat, a suspicious glint in his light blue eyes.

"It is you, isn't it? Lur gulped excitedly, "You're…" he dropped his voice to barely audible whisper, "Alistair Garron, aren't you?" Lur finished, waiting anxiously for the reply.

Alistair moved so quickly Charity barely had time to react, in a flash of movement, he had pulled the man close so that they were almost nose to nose, he had dropped his voice too as he muttered something to the now terrified Lur. Charity had just managed to make out the words, "did…not…see…must…Mosia." Then just as suddenly, Alistair released Lur, who spluttered nervously to himself as he patted dust and sand from his clothes.

"I…I-I-I yes, well, very well then, if you insist," Lur said, his face was blotched with sweat. He was muttering incoherently as he passed right by Charity and Sophie. "Well if you're coming then," he said impatiently, turning to them and scuttling off.

Charity had no idea what Alistair had said to Lur but it appeared to have soured his mood irrevocably, as he barely spoke another word to them the whole way through the city. Leaving Sophie to walk awkwardly with the increasingly incensed Lur, she hung back to question Alistair on his unusual behaviour.

"What is *wrong* with you?" she said hotly.

"Such fire, Little Book, is not wise. Remain calm," he answered.

"What did you call me?" she asked, her frustration was apparently highly amusing to Alistair as he attempted to conceal a grin.

"I meant no offence, Charity, just a turn of phrase." He coughed, rearranging his face into a more serious expression, "You question my actions with the one called Lur?"

"Yes I *question* them!" she snapped angrily. "He was being perfectly pleasant to us and you rough him up or threaten him or something!"

"I neither threatened nor harmed him in any irreparable way." Alistair said calmly, "It is imperative that we remain as inconspicuous as possible throughout our journey and his shouting was attracting *unwanted* attention."

"So?" Charity interjected. "That's still no reason to -"

"Have you any idea," interrupted Alistair, "What someone would do, to get their hands on what you *have*?"

"The Journal? I don't know, kill me probably," said Charity dismissively. She knew this but she did not care - she had one task and that was all she needed to know.

"Yes, killing you would be a minor inconvenience for someone eager to get that Journal," Alistair replied. However it would not be wise, as you are currently the only one capable of following its instructions – or so you lead me to believe." They were now passing the great blue pool which took up the entire main square of the city of Duradon, the oppressive heat that beat upon them making its crystal clear water seem very inviting.

"We should share your gift with as few people as possible. You informing me was ill-advised, but…" he turned to smile at her once more, "I am glad you did so." Charity thought that despite his strange behaviour, he did at least seem to want to travel with them after all.

"So…you told him to keep quiet then, is that all?" she asked, her suspicions not completely quelled.

"Not all," he replied. "I asked him to take us to the palace, which is where we should seek out the one person in Dura that needs to know about your quest."

"Who?"

"Queen Mosia, the ruler of all of Dura, the only Royal left in Thea and, from what I've heard, *very* difficult to gain an audience with. However our new friend should be able to assist with *that*." Alistair smiled at the indignation on Charity's face, who for her part wondered how a lowly gate operator was supposed to get them into a royal palace. Still, Alistair had yet to let them down and so she held her tongue.

After some more walking the group reached a small stone path, which led all the way up to the doors of the colossal palace building, which Charity could now see in its entirety. The palace was an imposing sight, with a huge dome in the centre that took up most of the skyline in front of them. Beside the two on either side were two long spires, which, Charity thought, could possibly be watch towers. The central dome of the palace was decorated with huge turrets and majestic looking windows that sparkled and shone in the oppressive sunlight.

Walking up the path, Charity was impressed with just how many features they had managed to cram into the palace's design. It seemed that in Duradon, nothing was left to chance. As they reached what looked like door made of solid gold, two guards dressed in turned-up trousers and heavy combat jackets came forward. Charity could see they wore maroon-coloured berets on their heads, each with a tiny golden sun pinned to the front. She also noticed something large was flapping at their sides, and squinting, Charity realised with a jolt that it was their Journals, held in place just like Gisele's had been.

"Lur, what in the three states are you doing up 'ere?" one of the guards asked in a surly voice.

Lur strutted forwards importantly and leant close to the two guards. He whispered excitedly in hushed tones, gesticulating to Charity, Sophie and Alistair who stood waiting close by. Charity could see the disbelieving looks on the guards' faces, saw them glance up several times at them. Then one of them nodded in an approving sort of way and Lur trotted back over to them, smiling broadly.

"We are clear…follow me." he said proudly puffing out his little chest.

When they reached the great golden door Lur pushed it gently and it swung open, almost lazily, revealing a long brightly-lit hallway. A beautiful carpet lined the floor and Charity could see great stained-glass windows set high up towards the ceiling. Lur, however, did not take them very far into the room; instead he turned a corner almost immediately after entering the grand hall and pushed open a tiny black door with the words: 'Official Guests Only'.

Lur led them into a darkened room, made sure they were all inside and then shut the door behind them with a quiet click. They were standing in a room with a single torch sparking merrily on the wall, a very rickety looking train track set along the ground across one side of the small room. Glancing around, Charity could not see where the tracks went.

"This here will take you directly to the Queen. Visitors don't normally get to see this but we can't have awkward questions all the way to the throne room. Just jump in and speak into the microphone where you want to go, but be clear now because, well, we don't want you ending up in someone's bathroom." He chuckled to himself but then almost immediately became serious again. "Nah, shouldn't laugh, it's happened before, y'know? Awkward, very awkward."

"Wait I don't see anything," said Sophie, misunderstanding etched onto her thin face.

"Yeah, where do the tracks go, are we meant to walk along them or something?" asked Charity, who seemed to be sharing Sophie's confusion.

"Oh wait, hold on," said Lur absentmindedly, dismissing their worried faces with a wave. He bustled off into a corner of the room and gave a great groan as if he were pushing or pulling something very heavy into place. They heard a large bang and suddenly the room was showered in a purple glow from several dozen rows of lamps on the walls. They had burst into life just as Lur reappeared by their side. He smiled encouragingly at them as a low trundling noise started up from somewhere far off in the distance. The girls looked around the room for the source of the noise, which was steadily growing louder and louder; a screeching, rumbling sound that filled the tiny room. Lur pulled Charity and Sophie back from the little rail lines just in time. A small but beautifully-crafted cart came crashing through a dark tunnel Charity had not even noticed and stopped right before them, still and silent.

"Where did that come from?" asked Charity staring at the buggy in astonishment.

"Only the grandest buildings on Thea make use of cart travel you know." Lur explained calmly. "Her Royal Highness allows her staff and important visitors to use it to move around the palace. It's just too large for some to make it the whole way on foot."

"Ohhh, it's really pretty," said Sophie, running a finger over the edge of the silver wheel. "How does it work again?"

"Just climb in, and speak into the microphone," said Lur, indicating a long thin golden ball on the end of a stick that was protruding from the front of the buggy. "Say 'throne room', and if you're clear, the buggy'll do the rest. Now, I've got to be getting back to my post, Thea knows who could wander in." He hurried off, out of the room, slamming the door behind him.

The group climbed tentatively into the buggy and sat down. The seats were cushioned with gold trimmed velvet and studded with tiny, multi-coloured jewels. Charity thought it odd to keep such a beautiful thing out of sight most of the time. She grabbed the long microphone, which was still protruding out from the front, and clearing her throat, she spoke loudly and clearly into the golden sphere: "The THRONE ROOM!"

For a few seconds nothing happened and then with a bang like a firecracker the little cart sped off, back through the tunnel and off into darkness. As they hurtled along the track, they passed lit torches that all blurred by. Charity wondered as she hung onto one of the side handles of the buggy, just how quickly they were going. She also noticed with a jolt that made her stomach lurch unpleasantly, that there were no seatbelts in the little cart.

They had been travelling for no more than sixty seconds or so when the cart stopped, quite suddenly but surprisingly smoothly. Charity released the handle she had been grasping with extreme apprehension but to her great relief the cart remained quite still; they had apparently reached their destination. They got out, first Alistair, then Charity and finally Sophie; and as soon as Sophie's foot left the floor of the cart it sped back the way it had come.

They were in another small room, dimly lit by a collection of purple torches lining the walls, "This must be the entrance to the throne room." Alistair said, as he pointed to a small door ahead of them, the only door in the room.

Pushing the door open slowly, another astonishing room was revealed to them. This room seemed to be made entirely of gold, silver, and jewels. This dazzling collection of sparkles and colours illuminated the room and made it look like they were stuck inside a very ornate jewellery box.

"And just *who* are you?" A high-pitched voice resounded around the room and the company turned to the source of the noise. Sitting in an impressive golden chair was a woman. The young woman was dark-skinned with blonde hair which flowed from the top of her head, where an exquisite crown was placed, to her auburn coloured shoulders. She shook her head elegantly, revealing a pair of exquisitely beautiful brown eyes.

"Who is that?" whispered Charity, still gawping.

"That, is Queen Mosia!" said Alistair quietly, "She has a very high opinion of herself, even for a Queen, so speak with caution."

"I *said*, who are you!?" repeated the woman, her voice sharp with impatience.

Sophie and Charity looked at Alistair imploringly, who rolled up his sleeves and stepped towards Mosia.

"You *know* who I am." He said cooly.

Mosia's eyes widened in shock as Alistair pulled his hat from his head. She looked stunned but recovered quickly, her face falling back into a suspicious scowl.

"Bold of you Garron, to come walking in here in broad daylight. But then you never were one for following rules." She said, her elegant fingers walking the arms of her throne.

"No. As I'm sure you recall." Replied Alistair and Charity saw a hint of a smile flit across his face.

"How could I forget?" asked Mosia, "But why *are* you here? I have told you that I have no more information to give you on the Journals wherebouts, the situation has not changed, we are even now and the agreement was crystal clear."

"I am not here to discuss that. I want to discuss - " began Alisatir but Mosia cut acorss him, her demeanour shifting from warm to icy cold in the blink of an eye.

"Do not presume to demand things in my presence Garron!" she snapped fierecely.

Alistair paused for a long time, meeting Mosia's penetrating stare full on. "We have travelled far to be here today." he said finally, a steely determination behind his eyes.

The woman shrieked with derisive laughter. "You and every other travelling urchin in this city." Her voice was high and lofty but her eyes betrayed her true feelings. Charity could see how they burned with suppressed anger.

"Mosia please." Said Alistair but Charity could see that he had made a grave error. At the mention of her name Mosia's eyes widened to size of saucers, her nostrils flared and she thrust out her arm, pointing straight at them.

"YOU DARE! YOU DARE ADDRESS ME WITHOUT MY TITLE!" she shrieked wildly, her beautiful face contorted with fury.

"Your majesty!" started Sophie in a desperate attempt to save the situation but it was far too late.

"GUARDS!" the Queen bellowed, and within seconds two men in the same uniform as the ones outside advanced upon them, swords drawn.

"That…would not be wise." Alistair said quite calmly, as he pulled out his great cane from its holster on his back.

The guards stopped, clearly unsure about what to do next.

"A THREAT AGAINST THE DURAD ARMY IS PUNISHABLE BY DEATH?!" the Queen shrieked at Alistair. His face, however, remained calm and still, his cane still clutched in one hand.

"I mean you or your guards no offence, *your majesty*" he said pointedly, his eyes darting from the guards to the Queen, as if he were anticipating the one or both of them launching themselves at him. "We have been out of civilization a long time and my manners have obviously been left behind. I apologize unreservedly but we come before you on an extremely urgent matter."

"Extremely urgent, you say?" snorted the Queen, fixed Alistair with a cynical glare. "And what could be so urgent to make you risk your lives asking me a question in my own throne room?"

"We seek the Fateweaver!" croaked Alistair. Charity turned to stare at him. She was sure he could detect a note of desperation in his usual calm voice, and this, more than anything else that hand happened so far, truly terrified her. "We seek the feather and we need *your* help - this child needs *your* help."

He shoved Charity forwards in front of Mosia who glared down haughtily at her.

"Even if the feather was *not* a myth. How could a common street urchin like her have any claim to find the Fateweaver?"

"This child is no ordinary child!" said Alistair forcefully.

"What?!" she snapped. "She looks perfectly ordinary to me."

"She is a Regalis! The most gifted reader I have come across in all my life."

The Queen looked like Alistair had hit her around the head with his cane. She did not respond at once, instead she continued to stare at Charity for a long time. "And what proof do you have? Such a statement cannot go unchallenged, my Journal was not written yesterday Alistair Garron. Come, come show me your charge's remarkable abilities."

"Charity," Alistair said, "Bring the Journal to the Queen. Show her."

Charity wordlessly pulled Calville's Journal from her jacket and walked to the throne where Mosia sat, drumming her fingers on the armrest impatiently.

Charity handed the book over to Mosia and stood back, waiting. At first Mosia seemed unimpressed, she took the book from Charity and waved it at Alistair.

"Why are you giving *this* to me Alistair? I know what a Journal is, just handing me one isn't going…to…prove…any…thing." She trailed off as the reality of what she was holding seemed to sink in.

Mosia ran her hands over the Journal, reading the front cover and checking the spine. She inspected it meticulously, running her hands over the golden writing on the front with a shaking finger and flicking through the pages with an almost tender touch.

"This is…." she whispered softly. Then she looked up as if just realising Charity and the others were still there, "I- I will still need proof. Jennings!" she called out, and a nearby guard marched up from behind Alistair to where Charity now stood.

"Yes, my Queen?" he said rigidly.

"Your Journal, Jenkins," Mosia commanded sharply.

Jenkins hesitated, but after glancing at Mosia's face quickly grabbed his Journal from the clip on his side and reached it towards his Queen.

"No, no, no, give it to the girl," she said impatiently. Again Jenkins hesitated, but after the briefest of pauses he handed the large book to Charity, suspicion and apprehension etched into every line on his face.

"Well…" Mosia's voice was shaking again. "Read!" she ordered. Charity could see the fear behind her eyes now and wondered why she should be so scared.

She opened up the Journal to a random page and read:

'Mary is far too old to be acting so immature. She'll be old enough to leave before I know it. *I don't like to think of my daughter leaving me.* **She's crying now.** *I'll try and ignore her, she must learn.* **I've go work tomorrow, I must get my things ready.** *Oh Thea I miss Lola, why did she leave me, why did she leave me?* **How on Thea can I get ready with this racket?'**

Jenkins looked shell-shocked, his eyes glassy, he turned from them wiping his face gruffly with his beret. Charity had opened her mouth to utter rushed apologies to Jenkins when Mosia spoke once more.

"Well Jenkins, is she accurate?" asked Mosia, showing no concern whatsoever.

"Y-yes, my Queen," he said in a very small voice.

"I…see." Now it was Mosia's voice that cracked with emotion.

"Charity is on an important quest," said Alistair. "I assume, Your Highness, you are aware that Charles Calville was searching for the Fateweaver when he lost his Journal?" Mosia nodded silently.

Alistair then proceeded to explain how Charity had been burdened with the unenviable task of finding the missing pages and thus the Fateweaver. Mosia listened quietly throughout his tale and when he was finished she stared at Charity for a long time. Charity was going to respond to this upsurge in attention but something inside her made her remain silent.

"Well I'm afraid we've had no luck in finding those missing pages either," Mosia explained curtly. "So if that's what you're here for, you've wasted your time."

She stared around the throne room as if checking for spies and then leaned closer to them, dropping her voice to a low whisper.

"There is a way that you might be able to find them, however," she said secretively, "You see, the men and women of Dura tell of a temple built centuries ago. They claim that a great treasure was hidden inside but it was only for those of worthy heart; the heart of a Regalis to be specific."

"What kind of treasure? The feather?" asked Charity excitedly.

"I am afraid that anyone that knows that particularly secret died many years ago. I can only tell you what has been passed down through the ages, girl. The legend goes that only a true Regalis can unearth the temple; for only a Regalis can see where we cannot.

"But hold on, how come other Regalis haven't been able to find it then?" asked Sophie suddenly.

They all looked at Mosia who sighed heavily and lowered her great brown eyes. "A previous Regalis may very well have found the temple but the last recorded discovery was hundreds of years ago and subsequent recordings and records were wiped out in the Great War. Dura paid a heavy price for Thea's freedom.

"But we don't know if Calville found it then, it could be a massive waste of time, couldn't it?" said Charity,

"It is the only lead we have," Alistair said resolutely. "We won't find the pages just sitting out in the open somewhere otherwise they'd have been found eons ago, this is our best shot at finding *something*."

"But we've no idea where it could be, and the Dura Desert is humongous!" Sophie said desperately. "We'd die of starvation, or heat exhaustion or worse!"

Charity had begun pacing up and down the throne room. "Well does anyone have a rough idea of where it could be?" she asked Mosia. "I mean there's bound to be some sort of estimate…My Queen", finished Charity. Mosia's willingness to help seemed to be based on their ability to flatter her in any way they could.

"Well…" Queen Mosia shifted herself, and considered Charity appraisingly. "There is one area that my men *swear* is hallowed ground, so much so that they say it makes them feel unnerved, some even refuse to patrol this area…" Mosia let her words sink in, viewing the impact, and then said very quickly, "But I've had others scour the area up and down, and every inch has been covered at some point and we have found *nothing*."

"Well we have to at least try!" Sophie said bracingly.

"Very well I will tell you where this hallowed ground is," said Mosia her eyes narrowing, "on *one* condition."

"What do you want? I can't give you the Journal or the feather if we find it." Charity said quickly.

"The feather is nonsense, girl, far be it from me to turn you away from your fairy tale quest. The feather does not exsit, the temple on the other hand, I *know* that it did exist and I *know* it held wondrous riches. No, what I want from you is for you to find that temple and to bring me back the Durad Ruby. You'll know it when you see it, as large as a man's head and as red as his blood, it was taken from this very room almost 2000 years ago and I have long yearned for it to be returned to it's rightful owners."

"And you believe it to be in the temple?" asked Alistair.

"I am not accustomed to believing tales of whimsy or fantasy, Mr. Garron, but my ancestors have been searching for the ruby for generations; they have swept the desert and the settlements that inhabit it, and if it exists anywhere in Dura then this temple is the last remaining place it can be," she said resolutely.

"Very well," said Charity. "I'll do my best. So you'll take us to where the temple might be?"

"I will do so in the morning, now is hardly the time. You shall spend the night in the palace," she smiled as the look of shock on their faces. "Do not mistake my kindness as weakness, I merely wish people in my employ to be well rested."

She indicated a door to their immediate right. But as she did her smile slipped from her face almost at once. Queen Mosia fixed Charity with a very peculiar look and spoke softly, "Be warned, Miss Walters, many men want to find that temple. There is an old saying among the desert tribes of Dura, 'The heart of a Regalis will reveal what we seek, the heart *alone* for the flesh is weak." And with that unusual warning, she bade them goodnight.

14 – A SLEEPLESS NIGHT

To Charity and Sophie's great shock Queen Mosia had not only invited them to stay at the palace but insisted that they be offered one of the royal suites, an honour, she had said, that was usually reserved for only the most influential men and women of Thea. Initially Alistair had not been quite as accepting as the girls regarding their new quarters, but after some protest, he had agreed to take a room, as long as it was right across the hall from Charity and Sophie's. Charity supposed that he wasn't used to being offered free stays in palatial rooms and this may have been why he had protested so much, or maybe he just wanted to make sure they were to stay close to each other. In fact, Charity had noticed that on the whole, Alistair was acting increasingly peculiar once more. In general he was extremely hesitant to speak to anyone apart from Sophie and Charity and yet when anyone else joined them, to introduce themselves or exchange pleasantries, he would remove himself, his hat pulled low and his cloak high. She decided that sooner or later she would have to attempt to find out why he was acting so unusually but right now was certainly not the time.

If she was honest with herself she thought it hard to imagine a moment when they could question Alistair. They were almost always in transit when a meaningful conversation was extremely difficult due to the effort it took to keep up with Alistair and in the moments they were not moving they were either taking turns watching for threat or sleeping. Charity had been so exhausted each night that when the precious moments for rest finally came she snatched at them without hesitation, even though Sophie continually lectured her to read Calville's Journal as much as she could.

Charity could not believe her luck when she was shown into one of the regal bedrooms. It was laid out in the same carpeting as the grand hall, whilst the walls were plastered with floral wallpaper and expensive silk drapes. The room certainly lived up to its royal reputation, thought Charity, and as the last of the day's sunshine shone in through the arc window, the room was suddenly bathed in a familiar red glow. Charity and Sophie had separate beds, which they had both flopped upon, exhausted, as soon as the guard had closed the door on his way out.

"This is the first warm bed we've had in weeks," said Sophie, her face wedged into her pillow so that her words were muffled.

"What did you say?" Charity asked, turning over on her side to face Sophie's bed. "How am I supposed to understand you when you're smothering yourself?"

Sophie rolled over, with what looked like extreme difficulty, and faced Charity, resting her head on one hand. "Sorry, it's just such a relief to have a comfy bed for once. We haven't had one since the Order Chapter."

"Oh yeah, suppose that's right. Have you any idea how long we've been travelling then?" For the first time Charity checked the wristwatch on her right hand - she couldn't believe that she hadn't thought of checking it before now. The time on the little white face showed twelve minutes past ten at night, but that couldn't be right; it was only just beginning to get dark. There's no way it could be so late, she thought, looking out of the arc-shaped window at the crimson sky outside.

She glanced back down at her watch, studying it carefully. She counted out sixty seconds, then one hundred and twenty seconds, but the little black hands refused to budge. "Broken," she muttered distractedly.

"Huh?" asked Sophie, who was now rolling about her bed savouring the springy mattress and soft duvet.

"Oh, nothing. I'm gonna get some shut-eye, probably need…" Charity yawned widely, "…an early start in the morning."

"Sure…ok, but shouldn't you read the Journal maybe, so you can get some more information on the temple and stuff?"

"Morning," mumbled Charity as she snuggled under her own blankets.

"Oh alright," said Sophie.

Charity pulled the warm blankets up around her. She would read the Journal tomorrow, she thought to herself.

"Tomorrow…" she whispered sleepily.

Two men were shaking hands roughly. Charity was slouched in a familiar worn armchair; she couldn't remember how she had got here but she knew this room, that she was sure of. She tried to crane her neck to get a better look at the two men grasping hands but she found it intensely difficult to move her neck. She could just about see that both men were tall and slim, and that one had hair that was almost as white as hers. The other man was being blocked by the white haired man, who had his back to her, but Charity could still see their hands cemented together in a firm shake. The two men seemed to hold the gesture for longer than was necessary, their hands seemingly trying to crush each other. All of a sudden, they broke their hands apart and the men stepped back from one another, although, to Charity's frustration, she *still* couldn't see either man clearly. As they took their places opposite each other, Charity now noticed that the other man was actually a good bit taller than the white haired man, and she could also see that he wore a long hood that concealed his face in shadow. The only feature she could make out was a long white beard that came down past his stomach, and almost reached his knees.

"I am glad we see similar goals," the bearded man said.

"Yes, it would seem beneficial for us both," the other replied. Charity found herself shuddering at the coldness in his voice.

"You should leave at once. It is essential that we do not lose her trail, we *need* that Journal."

"Very well. I will require transportation."

"Naturally," the tall man replied smiling smugly.

"This only lasts until I can get you it, then you give me my wish and I go my own way, no ties," the white-haired men said viciously.

"No ties," the other agreed, smiling under his hood.

Looking down, Charity had suddenly noticed her legs. They were larger than normal and her trousers were smattered liberally with dust, grime and something that looked horribly like dried blood. She made to rise from her chair but to her horror she did not budge. She desperately willed her legs to move but no matter how many times she tried they would not budge an inch. Checking her arms she found that those two were immobile, her head and neck locked into place. She was completely paralyzed in this chair, at the mercy of these strangers and unable to do a thing about it. Charity felt her breath catch in her throat as she started to panic, and tried to shout out for help but no words came out.

The white haired man was approaching her chair now. Something in her head told her she shouldn't be listening to this conversation, although she didn't know how she knew that she was *not* meant to be here. There was something in the way these two men spoke to one another, so secretive and so curt - if she were discovered it couldn't be good. She struggled violently, attempting to move herself before the man was upon her but it was too late, he reached her in three strides and meanwhile she remained as immobile as ever. As he leaned over her, Charity saw the man's face clearly for the first time. His gaunt features made him look like a skeleton, with a thin razor sharp nose, high cheekbones and a wicked smile crossing his face as he drew it level with Charity's.

"I'm sorry I didn't get to say this to you," he said, with suppressed fury in every syllable. "I should have suspected you would do this. You always were a coward."

He pulled a huge sword from his belt. It looked brand new, its blade utterly spotless and the handle, a clean ivory white, shining similarly in the light.

"You deserved so much worse," he dropped his voice to a whisper so that only Charity could hear him, "but I have found a way to bring you back to me…and then…then I'll have my revenge. For now though, this will have to do," and he raised his sword in a broad arc and plunged it deep into Charity's chest.

She felt a blinding stab of agony where the blade scythed through her. Screaming in pain, she clutched at the wound and suddenly realised that she could move now, for some reason the blade had unlocked her bound limbs. Blinking hard in the dim light she fumbled all about her. She felt for the wound once more but found only her shirt, dry and free of blood. She sat up, she was lying in bed, realisation dawning quickly upon her. "It had been a dream." These were now becoming an annoying regularity, she thought. Privately she wondered whether to tell Sophie or not, but looking over to her bed, she saw it was empty.

"Sophie?" Charity called out to the room.

"AH!" came a scream from behind the drawn curtain of the huge window. "Charity?"

"Yes, it's me, what are you doing over there?" asked Charity.

Sophie pulled the curtain open, revealing herself and the dark night sky behind her. "Sorry did I wake you? I was just watching the stars, couldn't really sleep."

"No you didn't wake me," said Charity walking to the window as well.

"I always used to look up at the stars and wonder if someone like me was watching them at the exact same time. Like, maybe if we could switch lives and I could see what it was like being someone else, living someone else's life. Always been a nice thought."

Charity really didn't know what to say to this, so she kept quiet.

"Charity I don't know if I can come with you tomorrow," Sophie said suddenly.

"WHAT?" said Charity loudly. "Sophie you *have* to, I need you!"

"Why? Why do you need me? I haven't done anything for you so far, I was just thrust upon you by Gisele. I'd be a burden. Now Alistair, he's useful, you should take *him*…just, just leave me behind," she finished, looking upset.

"Shut up," Charity said abruptly, "Just shut up and listen. I'm not gonna listen to you talk nonsense like that to *me*, Regalis don't listen to things like that!" she said smiling.

Sophie's face broke out in a reluctant smile. Charity had thought this technique might work, her father had used the very same one anytime she felt scared or intimated by something at school. "I am the greatest father in the world and the greatest father does not hear complaints about how his magnificent daughter will fail her Maths exam." Then he would swan around the room, with her duvet tied around his neck like a cape, until she had laughed so much her fear or anxiety had had been forgotten.

Sophie still did not seem completely convinced, however, so she tried a different tack.

"Sophie, listen to me. I don't know anyone around here, I don't even *know* Alistair. I mean he's great and all but we don't know what he wants or why he's really helping us. Plus he's been acting a bit weird ever since we got to Duradon. Yes, you're right, he *is* useful to us, he's strong, brave and knowledgeable but I if I need help or kindness or a brief lesson on Thean history, then I know I can come to you!"

Sophie giggled, rubbing her red eyes, "Thank you Charity, I…I don't know how I can really help but if you really want me to come, then I will."

"Of course I do, now get to bed ya big idiot, you'll need all the sleep you can get." Charity pushed her onto her bed as she climbed inside her own and gradually drifted back off to sleep.

....

It had been several annoyingly long days since he had been given his mission when Cassius had arrived in Duradon. He stepped off the heavy platform, his boots touching soft sand, the morning sun shining brightly in the sky above. As he moved towards the great black gate the platform lifted off again, supported by the same four huge yellow birds. What an odd feeling it was not to have to sneak or pry, thought Cassius, as he made his way to the little slot and rang the bell hard. After some muffled rumbling, a small bull-like man opened a little window in the door. "WHAT?" he snapped impatiently, his long moustache blocking out most of his face in the small window.

Cassius lazily lifted a pin depicting an open Journal and a round orb from a pocket of his trousers and held it close to the man's face. His demeanour changed almost instantly.

"Oh! I…I…I beg your pardon, Sir," he said hurriedly. "Opening now." He dashed off to open the door, and a minute later Cassius was walking through the city of Duradon. Several days ago he would never have thought such a feat was possible, but here he was, walking with the blessing of the Ivory Order through one of the busiest cities on Thea as the whispers and rumours spread like wildfire around him.

"A Laccuna? Working with the Order?"

"Didn't he maim one of the Ivory?"

"Nah musta been someone else."

"I don't trust Laccuna, don't like this."

Cassius smiled to himself as he swept along the winding streets he had once skulked down. Odd how a piece of metal could change how one is treated. What flimsy morals they uphold, he thought scornfully.

There was the palace, where she had last been spotted. This child, this imposter. *He was the only one*, and he would prove it by bringing back the Journal and removing this girl permanently.

....

The next morning Charity followed Alistair and a much happier Sophie outside the back of the palace to a huge docking area, which housed hundreds of little bays all marked out in the sand. Charity was walking with Calville's Journal held open in front of her, and she had to keep glancing down occasionally to make sure she didn't trip and fall, for the book was taking up all her attention. Alistair had suggested that she search through the book for mention of Dura and after some hurried flicking she had found a page about three quarters of the way through the Journal, a page that more specifically told of Calville's exploits in the Dura desert. "Perfect!" she said to herself, beginning to read to both Sophie and Alistair who had stopped beside her to listen.

'I have found many clues that led me to this point. The Dura desert is truly a savagely beautiful landmark, it spreads itself throughout the great nation of Dura, making it nigh on impossible to find something as small as a feather in such a place. The natives of Duradon, *small* *but ingenious settlement nearby,* speak of a coveted temple, however they claim that only a **Regalis** can even find such a place. *This could be nonsense.* **I must search the deserts,** *I'm sure I can find it.'*

Charity kept reading, looking for a passage that told of where the desert temple would be hidden, but she could find nothing until, her heart dropping, she spotted the line: **'The temple is unreachable,** *I've walked desert for days,* **not even the native explorers of these dunes know where it is.** *I must find a Regalis."*

"He got a Regalis then?" asked Sophie. "If he found the temple then he must have found one."

"We don't know if he did find it, Sophie, he could've simply searched and gone onto the next place, which was Imputtia wasn't it?"

"Yeah, think I remember you saying that," said Sophie excitedly.

"Wait, yes wait, there's something here about Imputtia, 'blah blah, **cold lands, freezing winds, capital settlement Galcia...**blah...blah...nothing about the feather," sighed Charity, looking heartbroken.

She spotted a word on the next page, a word that for some reason leapt out at her: "**Regalis**".

"Sophie, Alistair, wait, he found a Regalis..." she paused her finger running along the pages. "He found one in Galcia."

She read: **"'Success,** *What a stroke of fortune!* **I have found a Regalis, the Ivory Order have been partly funding my trip and they have direct access to the esteemed Regalis Florence, she is new to the post,** *incidentally she is very pretty,* **she has consented to join me in my journey to the desert. The Order were very helpful, I will repay them back in kind'."**

"Florence," said Sophie, thinking slowly. "I think she was the third, no second Regalis in Thean history and that puts her around the year 2209."

"Wow...just...wow!" Charity said grinning at Sophie, "Not useful my behind!" she said quietly, so only Sophie could hear her.

"He must have returned with her then," she said loudly, so that Alistair, whose face was contemplative, could hear. "I'll keep reading!"

Sure enough, a short time later she burst out excitedly, "Got it, got it! It's here, wait I'll read:

'We have returned to the desert. *It's considerably hotter than before.* **Florence has been of great assistance in our exploration of the surrounding area. We found the place, natives claimed it was precious land but found nothing on first visit.** *Standing in the area now but* **nothing seems to be happening.............Oh my! The ground is shaking,** *have we done something wrong? I can see it, I can see it,* **the temple is here, it was here all along.'**

"Are you lot coming or not? I haven't got all day you know?" snapped a haughty looking guard from just behind them. He was dressed in the same jacket and red beret that Mosia's royal guards had worn.

She reluctantly folded over the pages she was on and closed the Journal, repositioning it inside her jacket.

They continued down a small walkway so they were adjacent to the small port markings set out in the sand. "Why do you need a docking bay if you're surrounded by sand?" Charity asked the guard. He looked at her impatiently. "They're for the Sun-Cranes!" He sighed exasperatedly as he pulled out a small whistle from a chain around his neck and gave it a sharp blast.

Almost immediately at least fifty huge sun cranes came pouring over a hill far off in the distant desert, swooping and diving through the air, barely moving their great wings as they flew. Charity marvelled as they wove their way along the desert floor just touching the sand with their feathers, as for such huge creatures they were incredibly nimble. The birds seemed to know exactly where they were going as they flew to the dock and slotted themselves neatly into each of the tiny bays available. Charity noticed that some bays remained empty yet there were no more birds in the air.

"Are some missing? Could they have got lost?" she asked the guard, who tutted impatiently again.

"Sun-cranes do not get *lost*," he said spitefully. "There are empty bays because occasionally the Sun-Cranes are preyed upon by the snakes."

"I'm sorry, what?!" asked Charity, grabbing the guards arm. "Did you say snakes? Snakes that eat *those* birds?"

"Yes snakes, mostly the adults, the children aren't big enough to take down one of these," he said casually, removing her hand from his arm and discarding it as he might a troublesome fly.

"And the adults *are* big enough? How big are these things?" she asked incredulously.

"I dunno, about this big." He held out his arms to their fullest extent, "Actually no, they're much bigger than that, but don't worry, they don't come out during the day. Dura-born snakes come out only night, always have, always will."

"Alistair did you *know* about these snakes?" asked Charity quickly.

"I did, but you have nothing to fear whilst you are with me and more importantly whilst it is daytime, so I suggest we pick a crane and get going. Manuel is going to lead us to the site his men feel is the most likely spot for the temple." He indicated to the guard, who nodded and walked up to one of the Sun-Cranes, which bent down expectantly. He hopped onto its back and turned to look at them.

"Well you heard him, let's go!" he said impatiently.

"I will take the biggest one," Alistair said and although she said nothing, Charity privately thought this quite sensible, as he was likely to crush a smaller one. "Charity, you and Sophie take one together, it will be safer."

So Charity and Sophie picked a Sun-Crane and imitating Manuel, they walked up to it and to their intense relief it bent low just as his had done. They mounted the great yellow bird and held on tightly to its feathers. "It doesn't hurt them, holding on like this?" Charity asked Sophie.

"Oh no, don't think they feel it. They're amazing, aren't they?" Sophie said lovingly, grabbing tightly onto both Charity and the bird below her.

"They sure are something," Charity responded.

Manuel had pulled out his whistle again and, pressing it to his lips, he gave it two shorter bursts this time. Charity and Sophie screamed in surprise as their sun-crane flapped its mighty wings and effortlessly soared upwards into the clear blue morning sky.

15 – THE LOST TEMPLE

Charity hung on for dear life to the huge yellow bird as it dipped and dived about the morning sky. "HOW…DO…YOU STEER!?" she yelled, at the top of her lungs, as other blurring yellow shapes spread out in the sky around her. She did not know how high Sophie and she were flying, possibly hundreds of feet - all she knew was that their sun-crane seemed to have a mind of its own. This was an extremely fortunate side effect to riding the cranes, as Charity's attention was completely taken up with hanging on to the bristly feathers underneath her, and apart from anything else, she had no idea *where* they were actually going.

One of the Sun-Cranes pulled up beside their own. It was Alistair, who sat astride the largest bird in the group, its wings seeming to spread out to twice the size of their own. Despite this difference in size, his sun-crane still looked by far the most uncomfortable, squawking loudly as Alistair struggled to hold it steady beside their own. Alistair yelled something to them above the rushing of the wind but Charity couldn't hear him. She shouted for him to repeat himself but then he was gone; his bird had dived below their own and sped off towards the ground. Charity could barely lift her head from the bird's back, such was the speed they were travelling at by now. She kept her body flush to the bird's feathers and with extreme difficulty, managed to turn to look at Sophie who was clutching tightly onto both Charity and the bird. "DO YOU KNOW…HOW TO STEER?" she yelled hoarsely.

"THEY STEER THEMSELVES!" Sophie yelled back.

"HOW DO THEY KNOW WHERE TO GO?" Asked Charity, she was worried that their bird might simply decide it wanted to visit somewhere else or even get lost among the colossal desert beneath them. "JUST DO!" Sophie yelled, as their sun-crane gave a sudden shudder and dropped several feet, Sophie screamed behind her and Charity took a peek over the side of the bird. Immediately she wished she hadn't. Her stomach lurched uncomfortably as she got the full scale of their current predicament; they were indeed *very* high up. The size of the great desert was just as unending as they had heard, and Charity began to wonder how she would find *anything* in such a place.

The sun-crane, was shifting about the sky now, rocking them back and forth. Charity thought it felt like it was searching the ground below for something. Then without warning, it dipped its head and dove straight for the ground. Charity did not have time to scream; the wind whipped her face and tears streamed from her eyes as they hurtled unrelentingly toward the sandy ground. Charity was sure that they would crash, as the ground seemed to be coming closer and closer, and the crane was doing nothing to halt their descent. But then, as if it had been waiting for Charity to think this, the bird unfurled its massive wings to their fullest extent. Immediately they began to slow down, and as they did, the Sun-Crane pulled up from its dive just in time. With one final flap it brought them to a casual floating pace. Charity glanced at Sophie, who was wide-eyed and petrified looking as the crane drifted lazily over to where Alistair and Manuel were standing beside their respective birds. The sun-crane set them down beside two other Sun-Cranes, who were now fidgeting impatiently in the hot morning sun.

After some hasty adjustments to their dust-covered clothes and wind-swept hair, Charity and Sophie glanced around their new surroundings with great interest.

"There's nothing here," she said, disappointed. She couldn't see anything different to where they now stood and the hundreds of miles of yellow desert they had just passed over. "Are you sure this is the right place?"

The guard sighed impatiently. "Yes! The sun-crane do *not* make mistakes. Many men and woman have come to *this* spot, in the hope of finding the temple."

"Has anyone ever found it?" asked Sophie.

"It has been written and 'read', that some have…"

"Oh good!" said Sophie, interrupting Manuel brightly, but he merely fixed her an icy look and continued speaking as if she had not uttered a word. "Some have been known to find and enter the Temple of Dura, but those that did could not speak of it," he said darkly.

"What do you mean?" asked Alistair,

"I *mean* that they were not seen again, their Journals were found by the desert tribes and were subsequently 'read' by past Regalis."

"No, hold on!" said Charity, realising something. "Charles Calville must have made it out. I read that he went to Imputtia after the temple."

"Then either he did brave the temple and never told another soul of this, or your Regalis skills are woefully inaccurate," said the guard loftily.

"Hey!" snapped Charity, firing up angrily. "Mosia sent me here herself! She saw what I could read!"

Manuel looked affronted by her angry tone but did not apologise; instead he gave a nasty sneer and brushed some sand from his sleeve in a distasteful fashion. "Well we've had people claiming to be *Regalis* come here before, you know. You think you're the only one Queen Mosia has ever sent?"

Charity remained silent, not knowing how to respond. Manuel continued, his voice high with derision, "Her Highness is most concerned with finding the Ruby, there have been others and just like you they've thought *they* were special!"

"I read one of her guard's Journals, she saw me read it!"

"I'm sure she thinks she did, her majesty sees what she wants to see." Manuel laughed cruelly to himself. "I'd say we get about four or five of you chosen 'Regalis' a year!"

Alistair had remained quite impassive during this speech, but Charity could see out of the corner of her eye, his hands tightening around his cane.

"Now if you don't mind I'll be off, leave to your *incredible discoveries*!" he laughed horribly again. As he moved back towards the Sun-Cranes, however, something stopped him dead in his path.

Charity was offended by what Manuel had said but a different sensation had overcome her at his words. It was a felling the like of which she'd never felt, a pure, visceral rage was filling her up from the inside, spreading through her entire body like a fire. She could not explain it and yet she knew that she had never felt so angry, her heart was beating madly as angry blood pumped through her veins to her head, making her face flushed with emotion. She continued to glare at the guard. How *dare* he be so rude? But he was not looking at her, instead he was whirling around wildly, as if searching for something. Looking around at Sophie and Alistair she saw that they were doing the same, Alistair had even withdrawn his cane from its holster, gripping it tightly in both hands. Charity could hear nothing but her heartbeat resounding in her own head… but wait, *was* that her heartbeat? It *was* very loud, too loud in fact, it was nothing like a normal heartbeat, and as she started to panic she heard the sound intensifying all around her.

She jumped back in shock as the sand shuddered beneath her feet, shaking so violently that she thought it was an earthquake. But then just as suddenly as it started it stopped and the sand fell back, quite still. Then it happened again, the sand pulsating and then falling still once more. This sequence repeated itself several more times.

"What's going on?" she asked, terrified, as the land around them continued to pulsate.

The guard turned on his heels and ran towards his sun-crane, "I don't know, just get out of here, the whole place is gonna collapse!" He bounced onto the bird and it shot off into the sky, like a bullet out of a gun.

Charity was utterly bewildered; she had absolutely no clue what was happening. The sound reverberated inside her head like a bass drum being struck, the beating getting faster now and the sand around them shaking with increased force and consistency. Soon the whole desert seemed to be vibrating wildly. Alistair had launched himself towards Charity and Sophie, pulling them close and starting to edge towards their Sun-Cranes who were squawking wildly mere feet away, clearly *very* eager to leave, but some instinct keeping them stationary.

Looking around, desperate for somewhere to flee to, Charity spotted something in the middle of the rolling sea of sand in front of her: a spire, the point of which could be seen sticking out of the sand where it had not been before. She shouted to Sophie and Alistair, gesturing wildly to it. They followed her finger to its location but both looked just as surprised as she did. The spire was getting bigger now; and she could see more of it; the spire seemed to be moving into view as the sand moved around it, and eventually an entire building's roof was visible.

"It…it's rising out of the sand!" Charity yelled.

"No, the sand is falling away," Sophie said. "The vibrations are draining everything."

She was quite right, thought Charity. As each vibration struck the area, more sand ebbed away to somewhere they could not see. It was as though someone was using a pump to suck the sand out from under them. The group continued to watch the sand drain away and very slowly, as the yellow particles trickled away before their eyes, a building had emerged from its depths. A building that was as ancient looking as the lands around them, and one that sat atop a stone platform, at the bottom of a deep pit.

Charity stared down at the building. "It's the temple, it must be, mustn't it?" she asked unsurely.

"It must," said Alistair softly, replacing his cane. The vibrations seemed to have moved to where the temple now stood and Charity felt herself relax.

Charity's heart had stopped thumping as erratically now and curiously, so had the vibrations around them, a few feeble thumps sounding out around them and the remaining sand slipping down into cracks in the hard stone floor that surrounded the temple below. They had done it; they had found something that few had ever found, and not one of them could work out how they had managed to accomplish it.

"I don't…I mean, how…what did…I don't," babbled Sophie incoherently to herself.

"It appears that the temple reacted to something, something we said or did, although I must admit I do not know what," replied Alistair honestly.

"You're sure that's the temple then?" asked Charity,

"No other temple exists in the whole Dura desert, so unless this is a *very* well hidden temple that no one else has ever found then I believe it would be safe to assume that it is indeed the Temple of Dura."

"Yeah but it was well hidden, it was under the sand for Thea's sake! How did it manage to do all that if it's thousands of years old?" Sophie asked exasperated, her tiny chest was still rising and falling rapidly as she struggled to comprehend how such an old structure had performed such a feat.

"I do not know," confessed Alistair. "It is possible that there is some form of Igniculus magic at play, but having not studied it I cannot be sure."

"Really, you think Igniculi could do something like this?" Sophie asked in a miserable attempt at a casual, uncaring voice. Charity could see that something Alistair had mentioned had greatly interested her, but she cast it from her mind, as a more pressing issue had just occurred to her.

"Hold on, even *if* that is the temple of Dura -" she said

"- which it almost certainly is." interrupted Alistair.

"Fine, fine, fine, let's just say it IS the temple, how come we practically just stumbled on top of it? There's no way other people who visited here couldn't find something so obvious, if it just pops up out of nowhere!"

Alistair hesitated, considering her question. "Well," he said slowly, "I would hazard a guess that it has something to do with what Queen Mosia said about only a 'true Regalis' being able to find it."

"No,' said Sophie suddenly. She was clearly still quite shaken but piped up shrilly behind both Alistair and Charity. "No, Mosia said that the '*heart* of a true Regalis' would be the key to finding the temple."

"Oh yeah, she did," said Charity.

"Hmm, that is true. Did you say anything unusual or do something specific before the temple revealed itself?" Alistair asked Charity looking from her to the temple far below them.

"No! Of course not!" said Charity exasperatedly, "I might not even have been something I did. I mean I was really annoyed by that guard, what was his name again? Manuel was it?"

"That's correct." Said Alistair, looking mildly interested.

"Well I mean I know it's kind of a bit weird but he was really rude to me and I got really angry all of a sudden, like I couldn't control how angry I was. My heart was beating pretty fast just now, it couldn't be that a Regalis' heart literally reveals the temple could it?"

There was a long pause as Alistair and Sophie stared at Charity.

"Woah," whispered Sophie with the air of someone being told a great revelation, "You did all this."

"I don't know if I did, it might be a coincidence." Said Charity hesitantly.

"If it is a coincidence it is a most welcome one." Replied Alistair wisely.

"Do *you* think it was me?" Charity asked, she would feel much happier if Alistair were to reassure her but he did not immediately respond, instead he paced up and down, staring around at the desert, down at the temple and across at where the Sun-Cranes had been having flown off much earlier.

"I don't know. I doubt there is anyone alive that can confirm such a theory and there's certainly no one around here now that can answer such a question."

"Oh, well it doesn't really matter now, I suppose," said Charity, who felt slightly disappointed but consoled herself with the comforting notion that despite not having any idea how they had just made a significant step along Calville's journey.

"Well…" said Sophie after a while, "How do we get to the bottom?" She was looking at the steep sandy hill that led down to the temple with great apprehension.

"Like this," Alistair said, and he shoved both Sophie and Charity down the sandy hill. Charity screamed with delight as she tumbled down the sandy dune, all her worries evaporating for a brief couple of seconds. When she came to a stop at the bottom, she looked dizzily over to Sophie, who was giggling happily. "I'm gonna kill him!" she said playfully, glaring up at Alistair who was currently skidding down the sandy decline on his backside.

The floor under their feet was made of a brownish stone. It was hard to see the exact colour as it was covered in what Charity assumed was thousands of years of sand residue. Ahead of them was a squared structure made of the same stone they stood upon, set atop a little staircase that lead up to one of its blank faces. Just beyond this was a great dome that looked to be made almost entirely of glass; Charity could see the mid-morning sun bouncing spectacularly off its surfaces. The two spires that had first poked out from the sand were present on either side of this huge dome and they rose up taller than anything else around them.

They walked along the path ahead of them until they reached a set of stone steps. At the end of this staircase was the large square building she had noticed earlier, perched at the top like a strawberry on an ice-cream sundae. Reaching it, the group circled around its circumference but they found no door, in fact they found no sign whatsoever that this was the correct entrance to the temple.

"It's a dead end," said Sophie dramatically. "There's nothing here, there's no way in."

Charity stared at one of the blank walls. Sophie was right, there was no obvious way inside the temple from where they stood. The four bare walls rose up before them, all quite impassable, and Charity had started to wonder if they had come the wrong way. She looked imploringly at the wall, for a sign, any sign of what to do, but nothing happened. In an act of desperation, she placed both hands on the wall. She looked at it expectantly and waited for something, anything to happen, however to her increasing frustration the wall remained blank and did not budge an inch.

Charity walked the entire way around the squared structure four more times, but found no way inside the temple. All four sides were as identically blank as each other, and running her hand along each did not seem to have any effect whatsoever. The group reassembled at the top of set of stairs, the heat was getting even fiercer now. They looked all around the pit but found no other possible point of entry. All in all, Charity was beginning to lose patience with the temple's twisted sense of challenge.

"Maybe you should read the Journal," suggested Sophie.

Charity rounded on Sophie. All her frustration seemed to pour out of her and before she could stop herself she was yelling at Sophie.

"It doesn't make any sense," retorted Charity. "We've found the place and now it won't even let us in! How come these things-can't-just-be-simple!"

Charity kicked the huge structure with each word. She stopped ranting and leaned on one hand on the hard surface of the wall. She felt ashamed for shouting, for losing her cool, but she couldn't help it. She turned to face Alistair and Sophie, her face red with exhaustion and embarrassment. Sophie and Alistair were both staring at her. Sophie looked scared but Alistair showed no discernible emotion under his low traveller's hat. He rubbed his face with a massive hand and pulled his hat up, revealing more of his rough face to her.

"Anger will solve nothing, Charity, he said calmly. "Focus is the key to being a Regalis and as you let anger envelop you, your focus will fade. This makes you less useful."

"Useful?!" Charity fired up, "I'm not a tool, I'm a –"

"LOOK!" Sophie shouted.

The door had begun to vibrate and Charity, momentarily distracted from her anger, turned to it. She waited for it to slide open, but after a minute or so the vibrating stopped and it became still once more, quite as impassable as before. Charity had just started to flare up again when she noticed something that hadn't been there before; a line of text scrawled along the top of the wall was now clearly visible, read: '**Prove your worth**.' Charity read it out loud, wondering if Sophie or Alistair might understand their meaning.

"What?" said Sophie. "What's that from?"

"The wall," Charity said, indicating the huge writing and wondering how they too hadn't noticed it.

"Uh, Charity, there's nothing there." Said Sophie sounding slightly concerned.

"No, there's writing on it now, look at the top." She pointed at the text but Sophie continued to stare incredulously at the wall and then at Charity.

"Perhaps only a Regalis can read the writing." said Alistair thoughtfully, "It may be another measure to ensure only a Regalis is permitted to enter the temple."

"Oh, I see. What does it say again?" asked Sophie who was apparently deeply satisfied with Alistair's explanation.

"Prove your worth." Repeated Charity, thinking hard to herself.

"Right. What do you reckon that means then?" Sophie asked, sounding bewildered.

"Prove I'm a Regalis, I guess," said Charity musing. "But how do I prove I'm a Regalis to a wall?"

As if the temple had been listening to them, another huge quake shook the area and a crunching, grinding sound issued from beyond the wall. They all watched as a small crack split the walls surface and then slowly it widened and grew until a noticeable slot was visible right in its centre. Then as if it were being blown in by the desert winds a new line of text appeared below this small gap, **Part with your past and face your future.** Charity read out the writing aloud and looked at the other two, who looked just as nonplussed as she did.

"More writing?" Sophie asked.

"Yes, you can't read it?"

"No," said Alistair, and Charity saw that he looked incredibly serious all of a sudden. "Charity...I believe I know that this means."

"What?" she did not like his tone of voice one bit.

"The temple requires the sacrifice of a Journal."

"But I don't have a Jour – oh." said Charity, her heart sinking as the realisation of what Alistair meant dawned upon her, "But, but it's our only link to the Calville's writings we might need, and what if we can't get it back?"

Alistair did not respond at once. He removed his hat completely now and rung his hands as if he was trying to clean them. "I do not know if you will get it back, we cannot be sure."

"I can't Alistair, I-I-I just can't! It's our only way of following Calville's steps."

"The temple asks for a show of faith, to demonstrate that you can find your way without a Journal. I promise, I will aid you in any way I can Charity but trust me," he gestured around the pit at the temple and sand around them, "This is the only way forward."

"But *why* does it want a Journal?"

"I cannot answer that. I only know that it wants one to allow entry and that leaves us with little choice. If a Journal is destroyed then your past and present is also destroyed, you will cease to have been and cease making memories new memories - in short you will die."

"It's way worse than that, it's like your soul dying." said Sophie looking horrified.

"Separating a Journal from its owner is probably the most foolish thing you could do so you see why Calville's must be the one."

"Alistair's right, Charity, I mean, we could put one of ours in, but if they were to get destroyed then we'd die," said Sophie rationally. "But Calville was around thousands of years ago, he's long dead, so there's less risk…y'know?"

"Less risk?!" Charity asked incredulously. "This is our *only* hope of finding the Fateweaver, what else do we have?"

"We have *you*," Alistair said simply.

Charity did not respond. She was flattered by Alistair's words but she could not think how giving up Calville's book would be a good idea. Even if it lead to the missing pages, the risk seemed just too great. For a long time she stared at the dark slot that had opened up in the wall, the slot that invited her to deposit her precious Journal. Alistair and Sophie said nothing, not trying to convince her, they simply waited for her to decide what to do. After a while, she knew that there was no alternative - this really was the only way.

There was nothing else for it - she pulled the Journal from her jacket, and with a heavy heart she slotted it into the hole in the wall. For a while nothing happened. Her heart began to thump madly inside her chest; had she just thrown away her only lifeline to getting home for nothing? Then, to her intense relief, the wall began to vibrate and shudder in place, the stone bricks began to twist and turn in place. The brown colour was draining from them and they were becoming increasingly similar to the sand that surrounded them. Charity reached out and touched one. They felt just like sand now, the structure held in place for a couple of seconds before falling away completely, into the cracks in the empty stone floor on which they stood. They were facing another set of stone steps, except this time they descended into the darkness below them. The staircase was leading them, Charity knew, into the temple itself.

Charity dropped to her knees in a panic, scrambling around the remnants of sand, searching in vain for the Journal. It was no use, however. She moved piles of sand out of the way frantically searching, but it did not seem to be there. Alistair pulled her roughly to her feet with one hand. "The Journal is not here, Little Book,"

"What does that mean? You called me that before, what's a Little Book? Is that another name for a Journal or something?" asked Charity, struggling out of Alistair's grip, impatiently.

"No…it's…I…it is unimportant. Come we must continue inside. We have no Journal to guide us now, so we must be on our guard."

Charity frowned. It seemed that Alistair wasn't in the mood for answering her questions, so she followed slowly, worry coursing through her like the blood in her veins. It was hard to explain, but she felt suddenly vulnerable, almost naked without Calville's Journal. She could not even begin to rationalise her feelings. She knew that it wasn't *her* Journal but even having it tucked close to her chest had been comforting, knowing she could have consulted it if at any time to help or guide them on their journey. Now it was as though the safety net had been removed and there was nothing to do but use her own wits, resourcefulness and bravery, something Charity, despite what she had told Sophie, was not particularly comfortable with. As they descended the steps into the near darkness, Charity thought she was beginning to understand why these books were prized so highly by their owners.

The group trudged down a long corridor, each unsure what they were about to find at the end of it. Charity noticed that at least the entrance to the temple remained open; she supposed that if they needed to they could get out the way they came and this came as some comfort to her. The hallway was, as far as Charity could tell in the dim light, made of the same stone material as the ground outside. More of the same little torches she had seen in the underground escape passage in Upper Forfal lined their way along the walls.

"Alistair how do these torches not go out?" Charity said. I mean they must've been down here for hundreds or thousands of years. And not just that - there wouldn't be any air down here once the sand covers it." She stared at one of the little torches. It was made of black wood and a bright red flame flickered at its tip, and no matter how long she looked she couldn't see any sign of the flame eating away at the wood.

"They are made from Atra," Alistair replied gruffly. He sounded agitated and was turning his head left and right, his cane clutched tightly in his right hand.

Sophie continued for him. "Atra is an incredibly strong wood you get from trees in the Castlands. It's really rare nowadays, though, because all the Laccuna used it for making weapons to kill each other with."

"And it allows things to burn really well?" Charity asked.

"Once lit the flame will not extinguish on its own. It will stay lit until someone puts it out."

"How do you put it out?"

"Water, sand, anything that stops it burning," Sophie said. "But then that would mean that the sand couldn't have gotten into the temple, well not this hallway anyways, as the torches would have gone out."

"Oh yeah, I suppose that's right," Charity said, smiling at Sophie.

"We are here," Alistair interrupted.

They were standing at another huge stone slab, but Charity noticed that this one, unlike the one at the front of the temple, had a large circular indentation in the centre. Alistair was running one hand along each side of the door, and he put his face close to the right hand side, peering hard at it. Pulling away, he turned smiling to the Sophie and Charity. "It appears that the ancients who built this temple had a primitive form of hinges."

"Hinges?" they chorused, confused.

As an answer, Alistair pushed the left hand side of the door and it swung forwards to admit them, revealing another small room with two doors on the opposite wall. Walking into the room, Alistair had taken up his cane again and was patrolling the edges of the room carefully while Charity and Sophie stood in the centre, watching him. Alistair joined them a couple of minutes later.

"Nothing," he said in a relieved voice.

"Well apart from *those*," Sophie said, pointing at the two doors.

"And the writing," Charity said, pointing at the space above the doors.

"What writing?" Sophie and Alistair said together

"The writing above...Oh it must be more Regalis writing," said Charity, understanding.

"They weren't kidding when they said a Regalis can only find the place, Sophie said happily. "We'd still be standing on sand in the middle of nowhere if it weren't for Charity. What does it say then?"

"To prove thy worth is no small ask, behind each door lies a different task.

The left demands strength beyond the skin and page, the right seeks

courage unbound by time or age. *"* read Charity.

Sophie repeated the message as she paced around Charity and Alistair, mumbling to herself thoughtfully.

"It's a trial," said Alistair.

"Like a test?" suggested Charity.

"Yes, each door requires a particular trait or ability, one door tests strength, and the other bravery and wisdom?" Alistair answered.

"How do we know which one to choose?" asked Charity,

"Hmmm," said Alistair, glancing between the door identical stone doors.

"What? What are hmming about? What do we do?" asked Charity

"It is quite plain. We have to choose a door and face the task inside."

"I knew *that*, but which one do we choose?" replied Charity, slightly exasperated.

"I don't know. None could know but Calville and - "

"And we threw him down a bottomless hole for all we know!" retorted Charity angrily.

Alistair turned his head very slowly to face her, he did not look angry thought Charity and yet she still quailed slightly under the intensity of his gaze.

"Sorry!" she said hurriedly, "I didn't mean to - " she began but Alistair snapped his head back to the doors and held a massive hand to silence her.

"I have decided." He boomed, striding to the left hand door and leaning his ear against the stone.

"Why this one?" asked Sophie as she and Charity hurried over to stand behind him.

"Strength. This suits me I think." He said flatly, closing his eyes as he craned his neck higher trying to listen.

"Can you hear anything?" asked Charity,

"What about us? We're not strong Alistair." said Sophie quietly.

Alistair sighed heavily and turned to face them. "Of course I cannot hear anything, you keep asking me questions, besides the stone is much too thick I doubt if anything on Thea could get through this." He gave the door a bang with a massive fist. "And Sophie do you really think I would leave you beh-AAARGGHH"

The door behind Alistair suddenly flung itself open and he tumbled backwards out of sight and the door slammed shut behind him.

"ALISTAIR!" screamed Charity and Sophie together as they sped towards the door and hammered it with all their might.

"ARE YOU OK?!" bellowed Sophie beside her, her tiny fists pummelled the door with such ferocity Charity was sure she would break something.

They both stopped, listening hard for a voice, even a sound would do thought Charity desperately. They had lost Calville's Journal, they could not lost Alistair too.

They waited for what Charity knew was a couple of minutes and yet it felt like a lifetime. Neither of them spoke and the only sound that emanated from the chamber or beyond was their panicked breathing as the clung to the door in the hope that it would spring open once more.

"What do we do now?!" asked Charity desperately.

"I don't, I don't know," whimpered Sophie.

"We can't leave him there but we can't get him out!" said Charity

"Isn't there anything else written on the walls? Maybe there's instructions somewhere you didn't see at first." Suggested Sophie timidly.

Charity didn't answer, she knew that she had missed nothing but despite this she whirled around the room checking every piece of wall, floor and ceiling she could see but found no new writing.

"There's nothing," she said solemnly to Sophie who looked crestfallen, "What if he's trapped there? Could Mosia's soldiers get him out? Maybe if we went back and got them to come, they could bring a battering ram or something."

"I dunno Charity, what if we leave to get them and…and the whole place just gets swallowed back up by the sand? I mean we don't even know *how* we found it and what if we can't find it again?"

Charity swallowed hard, she bit back several suggestions about Alistair's rescue and rubbed her face absentmindedly with her hands.

"Right." She said resolutely, "What would Alistair do if he were in this situation?"

"Welll I guess he would…I don't know…" Sophie started but then trailed off into silence looking disappointed with herself.

"He would be all brave and selfless I reckon, wouldn't he? He would tell us to go ahead without him. I know he would!" Charity said triumphantly.

"But we can't leave him." she said horror-struck, pacing up and down in front of Charity like a dog that wanted outside.

"We're not leaving him," explained Charity, "We have to face the other task."

Sophie had stopped her pacing and was staring from the doors to Charity and back with great concentration. "You want us to face a task…on our own?"

"Yes, why not?" said Charity trying to sound confident but she was acutely aware of how much her hands were shaking inside her jacket pockets.

"Charity we'll be killed!" said Sophie looking at Charity in disbelief.

"We'd have been killed before now if it weren't for Alistair! Sophie c'mon this is the only chance of finding him. We're not getting in, he's not getting out. He'll be pushing on I know it, and he'll be expecting us to do the same."

"But how will it save him?" asked Sophie, still gaping slightly at Charity.

"Well I don't know if it will but we can't just sit here and maybe he gets through his task and we get through ours. The doors might eventually lead back to the same path. ARRGH! If only we had the Journal we'd be able to check." She fumed, stamping her foot in frustration.

"Well I did tell you to - " started Sophie but Charity gave her a look of such fury that she changed subject at top speed, "Oh, er, never mind, right fine fine, we'll do it your way. C'mon before I change my mind."

Charity stood up straight, a steely look in her eyes. "All right, let's get through this and meet up with Alistair again. Temple can't be that big, now can it?" Sophie merely shrugged her shoulders, looking increasingly worried.

Charity approached the right hand door and banged on the hard stone surface, her hand had only just left the stone when the door swung open to reveal a long dimly lit corridor. Charity and Sophie, wary of what had happened to Alistair and eager to be segregated further hurried through as the door slammed resolutely shut behind them.

The girls set off down the long corridor, this one lined with more of the Atra torches, neither of them choosing to speak. Charity was deep in thought about Alistair, worried he would be gone and they would not only lose a valuable ally in their quest but someone who had proven to be a good friend too. Sophie was staring off into the distance, her eyes glassy and an impassive look on her thin face. At the end of the corridor was another door, which, when pushed, swung forwards easily. Clouds of steam came billowing out from the door and the two girls jumped back in alarm, flattening themselves against a side wall. The steam floated innocently up the corridor and showed no sign of harming them, but Charity could feel its intense heat on her skin as it passed by. They stuck their heads around this new door and saw that the room ahead was so full of the thick steam they could see absolutely nothing. Gradually, however, the steam cleared and, bit by bit, the room was revealed to them. The room that gradually became clearer and clearer, revealing a sight that was certainly not for the faint hearted, thought Charity. Indeed Charity and Sophie had both gasped in horror as their trial lay before them.

The most noticeable feature of the room was that it was cut in two by a deep chasm of dancing fire and molten lava, on the other side of this gaping pit was another door; the only other one in the room. Over the chasm were platforms but they were not anchored to anything, in fact, they seemed to be floating in mid-air. She noticed that the platforms were bobbing and weaving about the room, some suspended high above the lava, others dipping low so that their stone bottoms brushed the molten surface below them. It was crystal clear what they had to do. There was no other way across - they had to find their way over this pit using the unpredictable little platforms.

"I can't, Charity. We should go back, there's…there's just no way…" Sophie piped up from behind Charity, plastering herself against the back wall of the room, as far from the pit as possible.

"I…I know it seems…impossible," she said softly, looking kindly at Sophie, "but we haven't got a choice. What if Alistair's already making his way through to the other side? We can't leave now. This is a trial, a test, we have to show we have courage, besides Alistair is counting on us."

Sophie's eyes darted from Charity's face to the open pit and back again. Charity put a hand on Sophie's small shoulders.

"Soph, my Dad used to tell me, 'True courage is not a choice we can accept or decline, true courage is acting when it is thrust upon you. Going against every fibre of your being and not lying down.' C'mon, we *have* to show be brave if we want to find Alistair again, if we want to find the pages, if we want to find the Fateweaver!"

Sophie seemed to be struggling with something in her head, wrestling with her own sense of outright terror and loyalty to Charity and Alistair. Charity smiled to herself. She could tell from the look in her eyes, before Sophie answered, what her response would be. In the relatively short space of time she had known her, Charity had always got the distinct impression that Sophie would *always* do what she could to help.

"Ok," she answered, in such a small voice that Charity barely heard her over the bubbling of the pit far below.

Both girls stood at the edge of the precipice, watching the swinging platforms with increasing terror. "How do they stay in the air?" asked Charity.

"I have no idea and I really don't care." said Sophie, who sounded as if she might be sick. "I think we should just take the next one, before I change my mind. You're sure they'll hold us?"

"I'm not sure of anything! But there doesn't seem to be any other route across, so they must do, mustn't they?"

Sophie did not respond. She looked even paler than usual and Charity could see she was rubbing her fingers together nervously as they stared across the chasm at the independently moving platforms.

"Ok," said Charity watching a particularly big one float closer to their side. "Do you have *your* Journal somewhere safe?"

"What? Oh yeah, here." Sophie opened her red jacket, showing a little blue book that was clipped to a chest strap around her middle. "Safe as it can be, considering the situation," she said ominously.

The platform was now only a couple of feet from them. "Alright, hold my hand, we jump together," said Charity, grasping Sophie's hand tightly. It was icy cold.

They both took a couple of steps back. The platform was now exactly level with them. Both girls suddenly sprang forwards and jumped into the air.

. . . .

Alistair stepped forwards. The girls were alone and there was not a thing he could do about it. He had been careless, he knew that. The stubborn door bore only minor scratches and scrapes and yet he had charged it time and time again, given it everything he had. He must trust them to do the right thing, to venture forwards and hope they meet along the path, it was the only way.

He was standing in a circular room that was remarkably similar to the room he had just left. The floor was made from the same brown stone and apart from the door behind him, the room itself appeared to be lacking an exit. He began walking the edge of the room, searching for something that might allow him to proceed further into the temple. As he did so he tapped his cane on the walls and floor, in the hope that he might trigger something significant. He walked the full length of the room but had no success. Just as he started his second circumference, he noticed a small pebble in the middle of the room. It couldn't have been bigger than one of his fingers and yet its odd colour had made it stand out. Alistair did not think it had been there before, as surely he would've noticed it.

He walked over to the stone and picked it up, turning it over in his hands. It was smooth to the touch and a beautiful shade of jet black, quite beautiful, he thought to himself. Alistair turned and made to throw the stone back to the ground but as he glanced around he saw another one, another stone clearly sitting near the edge of the room. He stared, perplexed, at the little stone sitting innocently against the wall. This one *definitely* hadn't been there a couple of seconds ago, he thought seriously. Clutching the first rock in his hand, he made his way to this second one and examined it with increasing concentration; however, it was exactly the same. He had bent down low, choosing to view this one where it had sprung from. This was most worrying. He straightened up and turned to face the room, and as he did, jumped back in alarm. The ground behind him was now littered with the same tiny black stones. They weren't just on the floor, they were swarming the floor beneath his feet, popping up from the ground like little round plants. Soon there was no place he could stand that wasn't awash with the black stones, and he could hear them crunching and sliding over one another as they sprung up from below.

Alistair looked around the exit but there was no escape, he readied his cane but what could he do against a collection of self-raising stones? Just as this thought occurred to him, the scraping noises stopped, and the stones seemed to stop sprouting and remained quite still. Then the little stone in Alistair's hand began to vibrate, began to squirm and twist in his hand. He let go in shock and as he did the stone whizzed across the room right into the centre and hung there, motionless. With a cracking noise it was joined by a second stone, the clash of stone on stone echoing, like a whip, around the otherwise empty room. All of a sudden the room was filled with flying stones, hurtling towards their brothers, firing through the air and cracking beside the others. Alistair whipped his cloak over himself and dove onto the ground, his hands over his head. The cracking noises around him were almost deafening and seemed to be never-ending: crash, after crash they came, one after the other. After a while the crashes slowed and eventually stopped altogether, it was only then that Alistair felt it safe to peek out from his cloak. Looking up, he saw a great stone arm above his head come crashing down upon him. He rolled out of the way just in time and saw the stone arm collide horribly with the floor, cracking the dust covered tiles cleanly in two. He straightened up and got a look at the thing that had just attacked him. The stones had completely gone from the tiled floor beneath his feet now, and in their place was something that certainly had not been there before, a golem stood tall and mighty in the centre of the room. The golem roared to the ceiling as it raised its colossal arms into the air and slammed them into the tiles below, Alistair felt the tiles quivering beneath him as he lay transfixed by the best.

It's stones glistening black, its hands and feet round and misshapen, its head squat with just two empty eye sockets set within it. It stood up to its fullest height and Alistair saw how its head brushed the tall ceiling above. He gritted his teeth and pulled out his cane, unfurled his cloak onto the floor and prepared for battle.

....

Charity and Sophie slammed onto the platform, which shuddered ominously below them, Charity gripped Sophie's hand tighter still and pulled herself to her feet, her knees shaking as the platform wobbled.

"This is, I can't, I just…" babbled Sophie.

"Just, just don't look down!" commanded Charity. She was sweeping the room for the other platforms. She counted seven in all, including the one they were currently residing on. The other six were gliding about the room, hovering over the bubbling pit below. Despite herself Charity snuck a look beneath them and immediately wished she hadn't. The orange surface bubbled and belched viciously, the rising smell of sulphur and heat of the steam an unwelcome distraction. Looking around she saw that the other platforms were much smaller than their own, and a horrible thought occurred to her. They were going to have to use different platforms. This one would not simply float the two of them to the other side. They would need to split up.

Sophie seemed to have spotted this too. She turned to Charity, her knees bending and convulsing as the platform teetered: "This is easily the biggest platform, Charity, does that mean we're going to -"

"Yes," Charity said. "I know, but there's no other way, just, look there's one coming close and another not far behind it, we'll take those two."

She was right, two smaller platforms were moving close to their own, if the platforms continued on the same path then they would pass quite close to one another. You take the first one," Charity said. "It should be closer."

Sophie did not respond, but took two laboured breaths and a resolute step back. She waited until the first platform had swung just close enough to their own and jumped forwards, her arms outstretched like a cat. She collided with the side of the platform. Charity screamed, as she was sure that she would slip off and into the molten depths but she hung on tightly, clambering her way upon the platform, breathing very fast. Now it was Charity's turn. She took a step back just as Sophie had done and waited for the second platform to swing by. She saw it move ever closer, made her decision and leapt forwards but just as she did the little platform veered off course slightly, away from Charity's outstretched hands. She felt her hands pass through the air where the platform should have been and she hurtled towards the pit. She could hear Sophie screaming, then WHAM! She hit hard stone, and felt something wobble beneath her impact. Another little platform had apparently made its way around the room and found Charity's falling body just in the nick of time.

"CHARITY! CHARITY!!!" Sophie screamed from somewhere up above. Charity could hear her anguished yells and could tell she was sobbing.

"SOPHIE, I'M FINE! I'M DOWN HERE, ANOTHER PLATFORM!" she yelled upwards. Charity's platform moved up to where Sophie was kneeling and Charity managed a few words to her before the platform swooped back down again.

"Sophie, go to the other side…I'll try and make it there too…"

Sophie locked eyes with her, she looked utterly petrified but nodded determinedly nonetheless.

"Go, just be sure to hang on tight," said Charity, and she turned on her own platform and readied herself for the final leg across the pit. She did not have to wait long. She spotted a platform close to hers almost immediately and dove at it. She had decided that she was not going to wait for the platforms to make up their own minds, she must be the one in control. To her surprise, she easily found the next platform and hauled herself up, delighted with herself. She turned to look for Sophie but her platform was empty, she scanned the room quickly but saw no sign of her.

"Sophie? SOPHIE?!" she shouted. "WHERE ARE YOU?"

"HERE!" A voice came from just below her, a tiny platform with Sophie riding upon it swept below her own and moved around the room, close to where the other side was.

"You're close now, jump, JUMP!" Charity said, but she needn't have shouted. Sophie had already bounded to her feet, taken two steps forward and hurtled towards the comforting safety of the other side. She hit the ground, rolled hard but stopped, safe and sound. Beaming from ear to ear, she turned to Charity.

"YOUR TURN!" she shouted happily.

It was not quite as simple for Charity, however. Her current platform did not seem to want to move closer to the other side, and it kept moving around the same area, too far for her to jump. Looking around, she noticed a small portion of stone that jutted out from where Sophie was, just big enough for her to grab onto, if she could only get a little bit closer. She waited patiently as her platform swung around the room, frustratingly far away from her destination. Then all of a sudden it took a slight dip and turned off its course, towards the other side. She still wasn't close enough yet, but she might be able to reach the protruding portion. Charity willed the little platform on, moving closer and closer to her jump. All of a sudden it seemed to change its mind again once more, turning slowly in the opposite direction. This was it, she thought, it was now or never. She leapt at the stone without thinking, feeling the air whip past her as she flew towards the other side. Her heart leapt into her moth as once again she felt her hands slip agonisingly past her target. She flapped desperately and managed to grab onto something hard, something that was not stone, but felt worn and waxy, something with the distinct imprint of a human hand embedded into its surface.

Sophie gave a great groan from somewhere above her and Charity felt herself being pulled upwards, away from the steam and the sulphur and away from the burning pit below. She reached out and grabbed onto the stone when she could, hauling herself up see what she had grabbed onto. Sophie lay puffing and panting on the ground, her leather bound Journal at her feet.

"Did you…?" Charity asked disbelievingly.

"Just…glad…safe." Sophie panted.

Charity ran up to Sophie and pulled her very close, hugging her tightly. "Thank you Sophie!"

"'S no problem," Sophie said, embarrassed. Her face had gone very red again and Charity released her, looking across the great chasm they had just crossed, pride swelling up inside her like a great balloon. They had just done something she would've thought quite impossible an hour ago. They had crossed a lake of fire and come out unscathed, and most unbelievably of all, they had done this without the Journal, without Calville and without Alistair Garron.

16 – CASSIUS VICTORIOUS

Alistair leapt aside, narrowly avoiding another huge blow from the golem. He lunged forwards, his great cane held aloft, and slammed it against the beast's side but it barely left a scratch. Certainly there was no reaction from the golem; in fact the only thing Alistair could be sure of was that his hands were now throbbing from the vibrations of the blow. He fell back as the golem lumbered its way towards him once more. There seemed to be no way of physically harming it; he would have to think of a different plan. Alistair could see that the golem was slow, that was clear, the way it dragged its heaving form across the floor towards him showed as much. It raised its eyeless head in his direction and slouched forwards once more, swinging its arms wildly. There was no doubt, thought Alistair, that a single blow from one of those fists and he would be done for. He would have to tread carefully.

The golem was so large that it took up most of the floor, which left Alistair very little room for manoeuvring around the great beast as it continued to silently lurch towards him, smashing its huge fists into the ground whenever it got close. The room was soon filled with the sounds of stone crashing upon stone, and Alistair's grunts as he desperately dived to dodge the incoming blows. Alistair would make darting movements towards the golem as he leapt, jabbing and scything with his cane, picking off various points for weaknesses. He continued this tactic for some time, slamming his cane hard into the stone crevices and cracks within the giant stone torso but to no avail. The golem appeared completely unperturbed by his attacks.

Another colossal blow landed inches from where Alistair had been standing just a couple of seconds ago. The Golem reared its head and slammed another fist towards him. Alistair had not been expecting this. He jumped backwards nimbly, but not before being caught on the side with a glancing blow from the golem's flailing arm. He rolled over on the floor, grimacing in pain. The monster strode towards him triumphantly as Alistair got gingerly to his feet, still gripping his cane. Checking his side quickly he saw no sign of blood but that had been too close for comfort. This was useless;

the golem was simply going to wear him down until he was nothing but bone at this rate - he must try a different tack.

No sooner had this thought entered his head, when he spotted something: a glint, a spark, something twinkling inside the Golem's skull. Alistair couldn't quite make out what it was but it seemed to be the only area of the Golem that was not made of impenetrable rock, meaning it was his only viable attack point. He charged forward, but just as he did, the golem let fly with a huge collection of stones from its torso. They flew off its body like bullets, peppering the walls and narrowly missing Alistair, who slid along the ground to avoid them. He righted himself with extraordinary speed and hurtled towards his stone quarry, leaping into the air and parrying a huge blow from the golem. Holding his great cane aloft he plunged it deep into the eye socket with as much force as he could muster. It lodged hard within its head but the golem did not yield. As Alistair fell back hitting the hard ground, he saw two fists come down hard from above, and he rolled to the side dodging one, then the other. He smiled to himself: the beast was slow, too slow, but his joy was short-lived as a heavy stone foot stomped hard onto his spine causing him to howl out in pain. How had he not anticipated this? He inwardly cursed his hubris, as the golem pressed down harder upon his back and Alistair heard several cracking sounds reverberate around the room. He looked up, the pain almost blinding him. Lying just in front of him was one of the fallen stones, and he reached for it, trying to find anything that might pull him from under the beast's weight. Picking up the stone, he tried in vain to wriggle from beneath the golem's vice-like grip. He could still move his hands and feet, so his back was not broken, but he had no idea how long his spine would last under such strain.

Looking up, he saw his cane, perhaps his only means of defeating the behemoth, still lodged in the golem's head from before. From the ground he spotted something that he had not been able to see before. Now he knew why the cane hadn't stopped him: the reddish glint was coming from the golem's right eye and the cane was lodged firmly in the left. Alistair knew he could not reach it from his current position but staring at the stone in his right hand, he was struck by one last desperate idea to free himself and destroy the golem. Alistair waited for the golem to turn his head to just the right angle. He could feel his spine bending now under the pressure from the golem's foot - if he didn't act now he would surely break him completely in half.

All of a sudden he saw his chance. The golem turned his head just enough to allow Alistair a shot at the cane still sticking out from its face. He thrust the rock hard at the cane, barely able to look such was his agony, but miraculously it struck the end of cane hard and Alistair saw it shift violently to the side. The portion of the cane that was already jammed inside the skull of the golem smashed to the left and collided with the shining object Alistair had spotted earlier. There was a blinding flash of red light and the golem staggered backwards off Alistair. He felt the great stone foot release mercifully and in that moment he knew he had succeeded. He turned just in time to see a huge pile of black stones collapse into an innocent heap on the floor. There was a sliding sound and another door opened up at the other end of the room. Alistair got gingerly to his feet, battered and bruised but thankful that he could still move his legs. He picked up his cane from the pile and, using it for support, he walked through the door, his travelling cloak clasped tightly in his free hand.

....

Cassius brushed the sand over the dead man with his boot, thinking that on the whole, he had been most unhelpful. He casually covered up the last of the body so that none would find him for some time. Why had the fool been so petulant? He had initially made his way to the back of the Dura palace, where several citizens had been 'persuaded' into informing him that a young girl had spent the night in the royal palace but left for the desert with a palace guard this very morning. He had dutifully made his way to the back of the palace and found a guard brushing down one of the Sun-Cranes. The guard had been sarcastic, unhelpful and did not seem eager to give information about the Queen's business to just anyone. Cassius had flashed the Ivory badge, as he had been told to do, but there seemed to be no pleasing this man. "I work for Queen Mosia, not the Order," he had stated boldly. His death had been unnecessary but he could not pretend he hadn't enjoyed it. His new blade, courtesy of the Order, was incredibly effective. Why hadn't he got one this fine sooner?

Cassius knew of an ancient temple hidden deep within the Dura desert. The Laccuna of his old tribe had talked of it as a place of worship for Mainlanders. How he hated both of them, Mainlanders, Laccuna, he was the only fit Thean left on this paltry rock and once he had the feather he'd show all of them exactly how he felt. He approached the mighty bird, which bent down obediently and allowed him to climb up. These creatures at least knew their place, he thought, as he pulled the feathers roughly. The sun-crane gave a loud squawk and shot off into the sky.

Cassius looked down upon the great city of Duradon and the surrounding desert as he passed above it all atop the sun-crane. He flew further into the desert in the hope of finding something, anything out of the ordinary. He did not have to wait long; some way out was a huge stone building, which looked quite out of the ordinary in a land like this. He leaned forwards and the sun-crane responded by swooping low and landing him at the bottom of a set of stone steps.

....

Charity and Sophie pushed open the door and moved into the dimly lit room ahead of them. Across from them they could see another door that lead into the chamber they had just entered. This would lead to where Alistair was, she was sure of it. She ran to it but there was nothing to grab onto, so she tried pushing. "Sophie, come help!" she said, struggling against the stone. Both girls pushed and puffed against the stone door but it did not move an inch. Exhausted, they sat down.

"Do we wait?" asked Sophie tentatively,

"Yeah, course, we *need* Alistair. He'd wait for us," said Charity, resolutely.

"What if he didn't wait? He could've gone on ahead," Sophie replied, quietly.

"Don't talk like that," snapped Charity. "He'll find us. He has to… Oh…I wish I had the Journal, at least to see what was coming next."

She looked up ahead at the other door in the room. This was smaller than the rest and Charity could see an ornate golden handle in the centre of it. Sophie was watching her carefully. "We could at least go and have a look at the door," she said, correctly guessing what Charity had been looking at.

"Ok, but we wait for Alistair," she said and they set off towards the tiny door. However no sooner had they walked a couple of steps then a scraping sound came from the door behind them. They whirled around to see the door creak open and Alistair stagger through. He was covered in cuts and scrapes and he walked limply into the room, his cane propping his great frame upright.

"Alistair! Oh Thea, what happened?" asked Sophie, rushing towards him.

"Alistair, what...?" said Charity, who felt as though she was about to faint.

Alistair shrugged Sophie off gently. "Please Sophie, I am fine."

"What happened?!" asked both girls at once, and Alistair smiled at the look of shock on their small faces.

"Golem."

"What?" asked Charity, but Sophie had clapped her hands over her mouth in terror.

"Alistair, no! How did you get past it?"

So Alistair told them of his fight with the stone creature and how he had just managed to escape. Charity and Sophie marvelled at his tale and not for the first time Charity thought he seemed to grow in size as the story unfurled inside her mind.

"What happened to you two?" he asked, concerned, noticing their filthy hands and knees.

"Oh it wasn't that bad. A little too hot maybe," said Charity, grinning at Sophie, and they in turn told him about their perilous route across the lava pit.

"I see," said Alistair, sounding most impressed. "Well it is over now, not many would still be standing here and since we have the limited choice of one door this time around, I suggest we take it." He smiled pleasantly at them, indicating the golden handle ahead with a wave of his massive hands.

The three walked up to the little door and Charity studied the handle carefully. It looked quite out of place in the ancient temple. In fact it looked like something she would've found back home, perhaps in an old mansion or posh building of some sort. "It's not booby trapped or anything is it?" she asked warily.

"After those trials, I doubt it," said Alistair. "Come, let us enter."

Charity turned the handle, which rotated smoothly under her grip and, with a sharp click, the door swung forwards. Sophie and Alistair gasped behind her but Charity stayed quite silent. She was utterly dumbstruck, and for a split second she thought she was home once more. The room ahead of her was a room completely identical to the huge library she had found herself in at St. August's. The long corridor with the tall bookcases piled high up to the ceiling, the only thing different was that in place of the small pedestal was a winding staircase that seemed to lead all the way up to a floor above. Her heart sank as she realised, that although similar, she was not looking at a way home.

"What's a library doing in a place like this?" asked Sophie, sounding enthralled.

"It is most unusual." Said Alistair, glancing about at the hundreds of stacked books with great interest.

"Well maybe Calville's Journal is on one of these shelves?" suggested Sophie.

"Are you kidding? It would take far too long to check all of these," said Charity, exasperatedly. "We'd die of starvation before we found it."

"There is a set of stairs near the back," said Alistair. I believe that what we seek will likely be out in the open."

"How do you know though?" asked Sophie slightly sulkily, "It *might* be hidden in one of the books, that would be a great place to hide it."

"I don't know Sophie but the temple asked us to prove our worth and I personally feel that I've proven my worth and then some don't you?" he asked smiling slightly,

"Well yeah," said Sophie sheepishly,

"Exactly! No I think if we are to find the Journal again, it'll be in a more obvious setting than this." He gestured around at the library.

"Where then?" asked Charity.

"The stairs," replied Alistair, pointing to the winding staircase at the far end of the library, positioned precisely in the place the pedestal would've been back at St. August's.

Charity was most confused, she had no idea why the library here resembled the one she'd been in before but knew that the link could not be a coincidence. She pushed the intriguing mystery to the back of her mind and followed Sophie.

They both followed Alistair up the winding set of stone steps at the far end of the library and into another room. This one was not dimly lit by the light torches but flooded with reassuring daylight. Great glass windows were set into the domed roof all the way along so that they were cast into bright sun light and could see the blue sky above them. She realised that this was the huge domed room she had seen from the outside of the temple. How long ago had that been? Charity thought it must've been only a couple of hours and yet it felt like a different life altogether.

"Charity, look!" Sophie said excitedly, pointing to something in the centre of the room.

Charity saw what she was pointing at - a tiny pedestal, eerily similar to the one from the library at St. August's, stood in the middle of the room. On its stone surface lay a book, its golden writing shining and glistening in the light coming from all around them. Even from a distance Charity could recognise its familiar slanting writing: 'Charles Calville'.

She ran forwards and seized the book. "But how did it get here?" she asked.

"This place is full of many old tricks and ancient magic, it could have got here a number of ways," said Alistair warily. "None of which I am able to explain."

Charity noticed that the book felt different. She checked its front and back cover but there was no difference. She flicked through the book and as she did, something fell onto the ground at her feet, a, single, solitary page.

....

Cassius could almost sense her now, she was close. He swept along the passage and through the door at the end of the hall. He was standing in a room with an inscription scrawled on the wall above two separate doors. He read it carefully. 'To prove thy worth is no small ask, behind each door lies a different task. The left demands strength beyond the skin and page, the right seeks courage unbound by time or age. Both doors looked quite identical to him but if it was a show of strength the temple wanted, then it is what it would get. He clutched his blade tightly and strode to the left hand door, slamming it open.

Inside, he found a circular room with a collection of black rocks piled high in one corner of the room. There was an open door at the far end and nothing more of interest to him. They have been through here, the trial is over, he thought, disappointed. He pressed on, the Journal was close, something inside of him could sense it now. Walking through the dimly lit corridor, he spied yet another door, which led to a long library. He did not have time to read. There was no sign of them here, so they must be above. They must have used the staircase. He eyed it, hungrily, his blade still clutched in his hand.

....

Charity bent low and picked up the page that had fallen from the book; it was covered in the same black writing. Her first thought was that a page had ripped from the Journal as it had made its way from the temple door to the pedestal but upon closer inspection she saw that the page was discoloured and moth-eaten at the edges, as if it had spent years in the bright sunlight. It simply couldn't be the from Calville's Journal, its pages pristinely white and totally unmarked.

She opened the Journal to the back. She couldn't explain it, but somehow she just knew what to do. Instinctively and without uttering a word to Sophie or Alistair, she picked up the page and fitted it back into where the first of the pages had been torn out. She aligned it with the torn remnants in the Journal and watched as the book emitted a blinding flash of light,

Sophie squealing in shock behind her. Charity couldn't see the Journal, but once the light had subsided, she saw that the missing page was there, just like new, as beautifully white as the rest of its brothers.

"Well done, Charity! How did you know that would work?" asked Sophie exasperated.

"I dunno. I, I just knew."

"Little Book," said Alistair softly, practically grinning at Charity.

"Huh?"

"Little Book. You asked me earlier what it meant. It -"

Alistair was suddenly lifted off the ground as something smashed into his side. It happened too quickly for Charity to do anything. Alistair hit the dust-strewn ground with a great *crash* and rolled over, staring at his attacker. Charity gawped at the man, the Journal still clutched tightly in her hands. She knew him from somewhere, from a dream she had once had. He was tall, with white hair; his gaunt face was cut by a savage grin and his dark eyes showed nothing but a look of cold emptiness.

Alistair had righted himself and whipped his cane out from behind his back. He bellowed with fury at the man, who looked almost lazily back at him. Alistair charged forwards like an elephant but stopped abruptly, a look of outright terror on his face; the man was holding his blade aloft, the top of it pointed directly at Charity's neck. She hadn't had any chance to react; the man had been so quick it was as if he had materialised right beside her.

"I think we'll stop right there," he said in a dangerous whisper. "If you move another muscle, oaf, I'll kill her."

. . . .

Around the great table nine men sat rigid and impatient. They fidgeted in their starchy white robes and drummed impatiently upon the ivory surface. One man, taller than the rest, spoke loudly above the others and their inane conversations of land, profit and power, "Gentlemen, I would like to thank you on behalf of His Eminence for coming today."

"Yeah and where *is* the Cardinal? It would've been nice for him to join us. I've travelled a long way to be here," one said, his surly expression and sentiments were echoed around the rest of the men.

"Believe me, gentlemen, he would be here if he could. Urgent business of the highest priority, I assure you," said the man apologetically. "Now as you are all aware, the Order has had a recent, unforeseen breakthrough in the quest for the item known as the 'Fateweaver'." There was another round of murmuring, many faces showing sceptical looks. "Well we *have* had a breakthrough - a young girl was discovered in Upper Forfal several weeks ago, and was brought to the attention of the Order as a supremely skilled Regalis."

The man paused, letting the impact of this sink in around the table.

"Our trusted brother and friend, clergyman Perch here, is the man responsible for this miraculous breakthrough." He acknowledged the man sitting to his left with a wave of the hand.

"The Order would, *if consulted*, have sought to find out more about this girl, however. We would have *liked* to understand her gift more comprehensively so we could use her in our quest for the feather. A couple of days after this discovery we got the extraordinary news that *another* Regalis had been seized by the Order in Duradon. This one, a young man, managed to escape, but we were fortunate enough to catch up with him in Lower Forfal.

"This is a meeting of the Ivory Council, Solstis, as well you know. We have heard this tale told hundreds of times from The Imp the Edge of the World they talk of nothing but the two readers. Now we all came to hear from the Cardinal which one he has given his blessing to follow."

There was a murmur of agreement and nods among the rest of the seated men and women, Solstis flushed red but continued as if he was reading a statement from a piece of paper.

"It is the feeling of the council that one among our ranks -" he shot clergyman Perch a disgusted look, "- has made rash decisions and in light of these new discoveries His Eminence feels it would be best to place our faith, principally, in the boy and remove the girl from such a perilous journey."

"How can you be sure they are both genuine Regalis?" asked a portly man from around the table. "I mean I've heard the tales of course but I've seen no proof."

"They have each given a number of flawless readings. We are certain," answered Solstis concisely. "His Eminence is more than satisfied."

"So what are you going to do with the girl? Wouldn't it be better to have two Regalis than one?"

"Well, we are not completely discounting the girl; however, His Eminence believes that the boy seems to be more, ahem, suited to our way of operating."

Knowing nods broke out from all around the table.

"I heard that she has Calville's Journal, is that right?" said another man, standing up.

The tall man sighed heavily. "Regrettably, that is correct." Again he glared at Perch, who averted his gaze. "The Journal was gifted to them, something that greatly hinders our plans; however, all is not lost. As I speak, the boy has, on our orders, tracked down the girl and should by now be extracting the Journal from her. In any case, whatever the outcome. *Our* hands should remain quite clean."

17 – THE FALL OF ALISTAIR GARRON

Charity's breathing was erratic, her chest was convulsing alarmingly and she could not tear eyes away from the young man standing straight in front of her. The sharp point of the man's blade was inches from her throat and yet it was not this that had caused Charity to stop dead in her tracks. It was his eyes, his cold, black eyes that seemed to bore right through her, flitting from her terrified face to that of Alistair's who stood frozen in fear, mere feet away.

"One move, and…" he dragged a long finger across his neck in a cutting motion. Charity noticed that his skeleton like face split into a grin as he mimed her murder to Alistair.

"Now drop your weapon!" He issued the command with force and an air of one who expected to be obeyed. Alistair took one last desperate look at Charity and reluctantly complied, setting his cane on the ground in front of him. Charity saw him screw up his face in pain as he righted himself once more.

"Unfortunately, my hand has been forced into a show of *mercy*," he spat out the word as if it were a horrible obscenity, "if you give me what I want, then I can continue on without any unnecessary *distractions*." His black eyes were still flicking between Charity and Alistair, whilst Sophie, Charity found, was suddenly nowhere to be seen. Charity surreptitiously glanced around the room, looking for her but desperately trying not to catch the man's eye and draw attention to her absence.

"What do you want?" asked Charity. She had to concentrate to keep her voice calm and steady, but she could feel her heart hammering hard inside her chest.

"I want *that*," he pointed a long white finger at the Journal. "And you *will* relinquish it or I'm afraid things will get…unpleasant for you, and your large friend."

"But but why?" she asked trembling slightly,

"That needn't concern you, girl. The contents of that Journal are worth more than your measly lives.

Alistair had started to laugh coldly, "And what use would that be to you? A blank book."

"Blank?" and now it was the youths turn to laugh, a wicked callous hiss of a laugh, "No Journal is blank to a Regalis."

Charity gasped out loud and Alistair almost dropped his cane as he gaped at the youth who smiled wider still.

"Come, come now, you didn't think *you* were the only Regalis on Thea now did you?"

"I...I..." muttered Charity, dumbfounded.

"I must say my skills would've been most useful in navigating this temple, 'Proving my worth' was embarrassingly easy after you'd done all the work Charity."

"You could read the writing?"

"Of course, it was written for a Regalis' eyes only."

"But I thought..."

"Thought you were special, well isn't life unfair? I'm afraid though I don't have anymore time to fritter away on idle chit-chat so, the Journal...*now!*"

There was a long pause as Charity stood, too stunned to speak let alone move and then Alistair spoke out from across the room. "Do it Charity, just..."

Charity heard him tail off. She had opened her mouth to argue back - she would not give up the Journal, not again, but she had just spotted what had made Alistair stop his speech. Sophie was emerging slowly from the shadows at the back of the room. She looked out of breath and was clearly struggling with something in her arms. She came pelting out from where the staircase had been, her arms laden with heavy leather books, and without any warning, she began firing them at the man with all her might.

The first one flopped pathetically at his feet. He looked up, a sneer spreading across his thin face, just in time to see the second hit him right on the side of the head. She threw a third and a fourth, one hitting him in the gut, the other narrowly missing his back leg, but the man had his blade pointed in the direction of Sophie now, and he whirled spectacularly, twirling the sword like a piece of silver ribbon. Sophie stumbled backwards in fear. She hurled the final two books straight at the man, but he was more than a match for them. Several exquisite slices and the books were cut into confetti before their eyes.

"You *dare* attack me, girl?!" he asked, his cool demeanour shattering. The man sped straight towards her, fury emanating from him with every stride he took.

"I am Cassius, the most gifted Regalis in Thean history, and I will not be treated like a common dog." He struck Sophie with his free hand and she went flailing across the floor, whimpering in pain. "Get up, GET UP!" he bellowed at her, pointing his sword at her chest. "You have spurned your one chance at mercy you little - ARGH!" Alistair had taken his chance and leapt across the room so quickly Charity had barely had time to register he had moved. He had slammed this man, this 'Cassius', with such a bone-crunching tackle that he was actually lifted off his feet and had flown into the air, his sword still clenched in his hand. Charity watched as he crashed into a nearby wall; dust and stones falling as the vibrations shook the entire observatory.

Charity ran to where Sophie still lay, clutching her face. "Sophie, are you alright?" she asked hurriedly, her eyes still on Alistair and Cassius.

"I'm fine," said Sophie rubbing her cheek. "Are you - Oh Thea, LOOK OUT ALISTAIR!" she yelled suddenly and Charity spun around to see Alistair sprawled on the ground, Cassius towering over him and his sword slicing through the air towards him. With what looked like a massive effort, Alistair managed to pull his cane up and block the incoming blow. Rolling out of the way of another blow, he jumped to his feet and swung his cane at Cassius, who dodged it almost casually, jabbing and weaving at Alistair in return.

Once or twice Charity or Sophie made to move forward to help him but each time they did Alistair growled his disapproval and met their eyes with the briefest of meaningful looks.

So the two men duelled to and fro throughout the great observatory and try as she might, Charity could not look away. She knew Alistair was monumentally strong; to her, he seemed almost invincible, but Cassius seemed almost bored by his efforts to defend them from him. For someone so thin he was a phenomenal warrior, his sword technique was almost spellbinding, and the way he managed to elude every one of Alistair's attacks was extraordinary. All this was nothing when compared to his speed, it seemed, to Charity, like a white blur was darting around Alistair, scything in and out with his long blade. All the while, Alistair was showing clear signs of struggling to keep up with such an opponent. It looked like it was all he could do to block the incoming attacks; he could not get an opening for even one meaningful attack of his own, and Charity knew that sooner or later he would make a mistake and then what would happen?

Charity felt helpless, she knew that she could do nothing but watch on. Alistair was by far the most powerful man she'd ever met and here he was, resigned to flailing around desperately, as Cassius lazily dodged and dived about him, a twisted smile just visible on his gaunt face. She gasped in horror as Alistair tripped and fell to the ground, his cane just out of reach; Charity made to move for it but Cassius landed a leather boot on top of it and flicked it sharply to the other end of the room. He booted Alistair hard in the ribs, Charity heard a terrible cracking sound as Alistair fell back coughing and spluttering in agony. The man pointed his blade at Alistair and with one last malicious look at Charity, plunged his sword forwards.

It happened so fast she did not know what she had done or how she could stop it. She had screamed as the blade was driven straight towards Alistair's exposed chest, screamed as loudly as she had done in the library when she had first touched the mysterious book that had thrown her into this world, as loudly as she had done when she saw the body of the old man in the shack, shrivelled and helpless. Her screams surrounded her. Stranger still, a bright light seemed to have erupted from somewhere very close to her. She closed her eyes, momentarily blinded, but even with her eyes shut tight she could not rid herself of the piercing brightness that had enveloped her all of a sudden.

She could still hear screaming but it wasn't her voice anymore, it sounded like Sophie's. Mingled voices joined this shriek, the noise almost deafening her.

"WHAT'S HAPPENING?!"

"CHARITY, WHAT ARE YOU DOING?! CHARITY?!"

Gradually the light dimmed, and through half clenched eyes, she could just see that she was still in the observatory. Looking down, she almost fell over with shock. The Journal in her outstretched hands was emanating an intense blast of bright white light, like an incredibly powerful torch. It was pointing straight at Cassius, who was no longer smiling. His sword was lying at his feet and he was caught in the beam's light, struggling and writhing in agony. Something in her head told Charity to keep doing this, to keep Cassius locked in place, and she held the book out straighter and the beam seemed to get brighter. Cassius was still struggling, his face grimacing in pain and his arms seemingly glued to his side.

"Alistair, what's happening?" yelled Charity, unable to see where he was through the light.

"I'm not sure! Just keep doing whatever you're doing!" Alistair yelled back.

"I don't *know* whatever it is I'm doing!" bellowed Charity, starting to panic.

"Charity, just…just keep him still, I have to think, I -"

Alistair stopped speaking and whipped around, staring where Cassius was being pinned. He had seen something, Charity could not tell what but she had heard something, a tinkling of metal, as if someone had dropped something small and metallic onto the tiled floor. Alistair screamed from the ground, "NO! What have you done, you fool!" Charity had no idea what had happened but she could see Cassius twist his face into a smile.

"Alistair, what's going on?" cried Sophie from beside Charity.

Alistair emerged from the light, limping towards Sophie and Charity, terror etched onto his bloodied face.

"We have to go NOW!"

"Alistair, what?" asked Sophie.

"Just come on, this way!" he commanded, pointing to a side door. They scrambled through the door, the beam still locked onto Cassius, who followed Charity with his eyes the whole way out of the observatory. She could still make out his wicked grin. As soon as they whipped round the door frame, she felt the Journal shudder and become still once more, and Charity knew that at that moment Cassius would be free of whatever hold the Journal had had on him. She couldn't explain how or why she knew, but something deep down inside her made her sure that Cassius was free to come after them once more.

They sprinted for their lives across a narrow bridge that stretched ahead of them. They ran as fast as they could away from the observatory, away from Cassius and away from the thing that had terrified Alistair so much. They had just crossed the half way point on the bridge when something behind them exploded. They heard it before they saw anything happen, a great "BANG" echoing into the sky, but they did not stop to look back. The bridge had shuddered ominously as the explosion vibrated all around them and Charity felt the stone give way beneath their feet as they ran. The bridge crumbled astonishingly quickly and they were lifted into the air from the force of something behind them. Charity felt herself hurtle like a stone across the chasm, the huge bridge cascading down into the depths below. She struck the hard sand and felt herself losing consciousness, a hail of glass and masonry was raining down all around them. She tried to right herself, to pick herself up but her arms gave away and she fell to the ground, darkness enveloping her.

When Charity awoke it was early morning. At least she thought it was, the red moon was slipping away over the horizon and the sun beginning to peek out from the other side. Despite the presence of the sun it was bitterly cold. A chill wind was whipping her face and arms with alarming ferocity and Charity cursed herself for not bringing something warmer. She sat up and looked around her. The ground was littered with pieces of stone, bits of shattered glass and burnt pages. Turning her head, she saw the observatory behind her was now gone and in its place nothing but the same yellow sand that was ever-present in the Dura desert. The temple had been swallowed up by the desert once more. She wondered desperately if everyone had made it out of there in time.

"SOPHIE!" she called out to the winds, "ALISTAIR!"

No answer came, instead only the rustling of the pages in the wind made any sound. Charity checked herself for the Journal but it was not in her jacket, panicking she stared around at the strewn desert searching for it. To her intense relief spotted it a couple of feet from where she had landed, dashing over to it and clutching it to her chest she saw that it seemed to be quite unaffected by the fall. She looked around but the area appeared to be deserted, and the only thing Charity could see of interest was a tiny blot of red just over the horizon. This could only be one thing, she thought - the city of Duradon.

Charity had just began to walk when she tripped over something hard and sharp sticking out of the sand below her feet; another Journal. She picked up the brown book, brushing the sand off the front cover and read: 'Alistair Garron, Year of birth: 4080'. If this was Alistair's then he must be nearby, she thought. Her heart momentarily leapt, but as she ran her hands along the Journal she felt something that made the smile slip from her face and her blood turn to ice. She turned the Journal over and stared at it, a huge crack in the spine, right along the middle, was separating the leather cover into two distinct portions. Charity's hands shook with fear, and she felt suddenly sick. Did this mean what she thought it meant?

Fortunately it did not take her long to find Alistair. She had ascended a small hill nearby and spotted a large shape lying quite still, a hundred metres from her. She hurtled towards him as fast as she could go, and as she got closer she spotted a small figure kneeling beside Alistair - Sophie. Alistair was lying flat on his back and Sophie had her face buried in her hands. When Charity was close, Sophie looked up, startled. Recognition dawned on her face and she ran towards her, tears now streaming down her face.

"Oh Charity, you're ok, thank Thea!" she said, hugging her. "But Charity, Alistair, Oh Charity!" She began sobbing into her shoulder uncontrollably. Charity could do nothing but pat her on the back as she stared ashen-faced, at Alistair. He was almost completely still, his breathing very slow, his eyes bloodshot and tired.

Charity moved towards him, shrugging off Sophie with another pat on the back. She knelt down beside his face and taking one of his great hands in hers, she placed his Journal in it, closing his fingers around it tightly.

"I found it. It's here," she said, in a hoarse whisper,

"Little Book," he spoke softly to her.

"Yes, what does it mean? Can it help you?" she asked desperately, angry tears now burning her eyes.

He shook his head resolutely.

"Little Book!" he said again, more forcefully. "Old Saying…Ancient Meaning."

Charity blinked and rubbed away tears, her heart pumping fast in her chest. She gripped his hands now, as tightly as she could.

"In the darkest night," said Alistair, his breathing ragged, "A Little Book will show us the way."

"Alistair…I don't…" she said pathetically, furious at herself for not knowing what to do or say.

"Charity Walters…our Little Book," he said and a faint smile broke out across his face. Then very quietly he shut his eyes and was still.

Sophie burst into anguished sobs behind her but Charity barely heard her. She was numb. She raised a trembling hand to his neck and gripped it softly, her hand barely wrapping around half of it. The sun had begun to emit its warm glow now and the sun-crane could be heard squawking and swooping above their heads as they moved towards the city.

"Oh Thea, Charity, is he, is he?" asked Sophie, emotion echoing through her crackling voice.

"No," breathed Charity, relief coursing through her. "Not yet."

....

Charity and Sophie had been standing around Alistair's limp form for some time, both silent, simply watching him breathing in and out. Charity so was terrified his great chest would stop moving she could barely tear her eyes from him but she knew that if they waited long enough the night would come again. They had to act now she thought resolutely.

"C'mon we have to get him to Duradon," she said, speaking softly to Sophie.

"What…how?" Sophie asked, her eyes were wide with shock and now quite swollen from crying.

"We carry him, or drag him or anything, it doesn't matter how!" she said, determination flaring up inside her. She tried to pull his limp form to his feet but he did not wake and the sheer size of Alistair meant she could barely get his arm up off the sand.

"Sophie…" Charity said, struggling with Alistair's weight. She ran over and attempted to help haul him upwards but even with their combined efforts they barely moved him an inch. They set his head back down in the sand, their brows furrowed with worry and sweat. The morning sun had now made its way into the sky and with no wind cutting through them, the heat was becoming oppressively fierce.

Flopping down beside Alistair, she looked across the dessert at the little blotch of red on their horizon, where she knew they had to be, Duradon. "One of us is going to have to walk," Charity said quietly. "There's no other way, we can't move him and if we don't find some help…" she trailed off, not wanting to finish her own sentence.

"I'll go," said Sophie standing up. "You stay with him, you'll be better at fighting off anything that comes near him."

"What makes you think that? I can't fight things!" said Charity desperately,

"But you did that Journal thing with Cassius earlier, you -" began Sophie but Charity cut her off.

"You think I knew what I was doing?!" she asked madly. "I hadn't a clue what was happening, I couldn't see anything and then all of a sudden the Journal was acting all weird. I just…I've no idea what that was or how I did it, Sophie!"

"Oh," said Sophie, looking crestfallen. "I just thought…"

"I'm not magic, Sophie, I can't just do whatever I want. If I could…" She looked down at Alistair.

"Charity, guard!" Sophie said quickly,

"I think, on the whole, you'd be just as good at guarding Alistair as me. Besides I got us into this situation, so it should be *me* that crosses the desert. *You* guard him," said Charity. She had made her mind up and didn't really appreciate being ordered around by Sophie like this.

"NO! *Guard!*" shouted Sophie pointedly, gesticulating to something a mile or so away from them.

Charity looked at where she was pointing. A little troop of red figures were sweeping their way along the dessert towards them. Their distinctive berets perched atop their heads they marched in unison along a nearby dune, their sheathed swords glinting in the sunlight. Both Sophie and herself waved and yelled at them from afar and within minutes the guards were upon them.

The first man that reached Charity called back to his comrades, "I found 'em, they're 'ere!" The rest had soon followed and Charity was quickly swamped with questions about Alistair's condition and how it had happened. She attempted to give as much information as she could without giving away any details that might reveal her to be a Regalis. With an unpleasant jolt of guilt she remembered what Alistair had said to her: "Do you have any idea what some people would do to get their hands on what you have?"

With great difficulty the troop of fourteen men managed to carry the still comatose form of Alistair on their shoulders like a coffin. They walked slowly but resolutely towards Duradon, Sophie and Charity following close behind.

"Will he be alright?" Charity asked one of the guards closest to her.

"I do not know, little one," he said sadly. "His Journal is severely damaged, but we will take him to Nadia."

"Who's Nadia?" asked Charity,

"She is our city's foremost healer. If there is one in all of Dura that can help him then it is she. If she cannot…" he bowed his head. Charity's eyes widened in fear but she quickly changed the subject, eager to talk of something that wasn't so dark and depressing. Sophie, who had seemed increasingly fragile since the incident, was listening beside her and Charity felt it best to try and keep her spirits up.

"Why were you out here?" she asked the guard. "You don't usually patrol the desert, do you?"

"No we don't. In truth, we were looking for you two. Queen Mosia needs to see you on an urgent matter."

"What is it? What's wrong?"

"I cannot say. Her majesty has requested an audience with you, as soon as you were found," the man replied curtly.

"I'm *not* leaving Alistair!" Charity said hotly.

"Me neither!" Sophie said quickly.

"Please, girls, we will have him in the care of the best healer in the city. The Queen has been quite aggrieved that she has not been able to question you herself," he said imploringly.

"Question us? Why would she be questioning us? We haven't done anything!" Charity said, her temper rising dramatically.

"Please. I just bring the orders, I do not make them," the man said apologetically. "I will take your friend to see the healer first, and perhaps that can convince you to meet with the Queen and then you can return to him."

Charity considered this for a while. "Very well," she said, sighing heavily.

So they travelled onwards, the great red city moving closer and closer to them. Charity had fallen back to walk just behind the group carrying Alistair and Sophie hung back with her.

"What do you think she wants?" Sophie whispered, close beside her.

"No idea. It's not going to be good though is it?" she replied, as Sophie shook her head.

"Well I'm not even gonna think about it until Alistair is safe," Charity decided.

They walked until Charity's feet ached. The sand under her feet felt like it was drawing her down, and she slipped and slid as she clambered up and down dunes and over long stretches of uneven terrain. Sophie was struggling terribly to keep up with the group. More than once Charity had to support her weight as she walked, which slowed them down even more but still the guards walked on seemingly unencumbered by the massive body supported between them.

Eventually, just when Charity thought she could walk no more, they reached a familiar looking walkway with a black door at the end of it. The guards walked towards the entrance to Duradon and hammered on the little black window. Lur peeped out and then seeing the odd ensemble of people dashed back into the shadows to open the door. They entered the city and Charity and Sophie followed the group down the main street and up a side passage. People stared at them as they walked, stopped their conversations, dropped their shopping, one little girl even shouting out, "is that man dead, Mummy?" as her mother shielded her eyes. But Charity didn't care; she just wanted to get Alistair to someone who could help him.

The guards lowered Alistair to their side and squeezed down another side street, his arm flopping pathetically down and trailing along the sandy ground as they shimmied awkwardly along the cobbled street. The passage was so crowded with people that Charity and Sophie could barely see in front of them. On one side the great snake-like wall towered up beside them and on the other, a row of hastily-built houses seemed to be have sprung up, as if from nowhere. One of the guards broke away from the group that was carrying Alistair and stopped at a small wooden door outside one of the houses. He knocked on the door softly and two minutes later it opened, although Charity couldn't see its inhabitants such was the darkness inside the house. The guard was speaking softly to someone, nodding and shaking his head intermittently. He turned to face the group.

"Bring him in here!" he said forcefully. "She will take him." He made his way over to Charity. "Your friend will be in the safest of hands, but I'm afraid I must insist that you come with me," he said, in a resigned voice. "Queen Mosia will wait no longer, and she will've been alerted to our return to Duradon."

Charity nodded silently. She did not have the effort to argue anymore as the long journey had sapped her of fight. She and Sophie followed diligently as the guard led them out of the passageway once more, into the bright sunlight and up to the palace. They swept through the palatial entrance and through the main hallway, this time not travelling using the speed-track but walking up several long winding staircases and through a set of double doors, where they arrived in a familiar looking room with an ornate golden throne at the far end.

Queen Mosia watched them beadily the entire way up the hall, yet she waited until they had been brought right up to the little stand her throne was placed upon, before she spoke to them.

"So," Mosia sneered at them. "You thought you could just ride off into the sunset and escape what you had coming, did you?" She eyed them suspiciously, as though they were about to make a run for one of the doors and Charity recognised the smug sense of satisfaction in her lofty voice.

"I don't understand," said Charity, honestly.

Mosia gave a nasty laugh. "Oh you don't *understand*? Let me enlighten you, shall I?!" Her voice was suddenly sharp and shrill. "You two, and that giant, managed to convince Jenkins to pretend you could read his Journal. All so you could *steal* a pair of sun-crane, Thea knows how much they'd fetch on the open market! Then when one of my most loyal guards found out your little scheme and tried to stop you, you murdered him in cold blood!" Queen Mosia's eyes popped and her veins were bulging at the side of her neck. She looked utterly mad with rage, and even her crown had slipped to the side of her head during her rant. She corrected it angrily. "Before I cart you two off to rot in the dungeons, do you have any last words?"

Charity was completely dumbstruck; she had no idea where the Queen had gotten this information. She rubbed her temples as her brain felt like it was leaking out of her head.

"Your Majesty, I have no idea what you're talking about!" Charity said imploringly. "We took the Sun-Cranes like *you* instructed."

"LIES!" she bellowed at Charity. "You *knew* you could sell them! Who put you up to it? Was it that crook Foy? Or maybe one of those blasted Nikko brothers?"

"We've no idea what you're talking about!" retorted Charity defiantly.

"You were convincing, I must admit," sneered Mosia, a savage grin spread across her face. She clearly wasn't listening to a word Charity was saying. "How much did you plan on splitting with Jenkins? He must've wanted quite a share in return for lying to his Queen!"

"Jenkins?" Charity was confused.

"Yes, Jenkins, the man whose Journal you 'read' so expertly," Mosia spat.

"I DID read his Journal!" shouted Charity, now losing her temper with Mosia.

"And I told you *all* about the hidden temple. That was highly sensitive information. Too bad you'll not be able to tell another soul about it!" said Mosia, talking loudly to herself more than anyone else.

"But we *found* the ancient temple, and we got what we needed!" bellowed Charity, her face flushed and angry.

All of a sudden Mosia's manner changed, the anger and smugness evaporating so quickly that it took Charity completely by surprise. "You did?! You brought me the Ruby then? Where is it? Give it to me!" She spoke in a rush, a savage greed now very clearly present on her beautiful face.

Charity thought her heart had stopped permanently, and she suddenly felt as terrified as she had done when the man named Cassius had threatened her at sword point. The ruby, *the ruby,* in all the adventure, excitement and danger they had completely forgotten about the ruby of the desert that Mosia had asked them to procure. They hadn't even tried to look for it. How could she have been so stupid? Hadn't it been part of the bargain that she told them where the temple would be? She looked up at Mosia, who seemed to read her look of dismay, her brown eyes narrowing dangerously.

"You…did…not…bring it here," she said, repressed rage behind every syllable.

"We were attacked, Your Majesty. We had every intention of finding it but, but…" Charity faltered, unsure of what to say next. She *was* lying now, she had completely forgotten about the ruby up until now.

"The attacker stole it!" Sophie shouted suddenly. Charity turned to stare at her in surprise, then catching herself, turned back to the Queen. "Yes, Your Majesty, the thief took it. He blindsided us and took it, then he blew up part of the temple as we tried to get away."

Mosia considered them both. "I have no proof of your innocence regarding the murder of my guard nor of this supposed discovery of yours. Once again, this could be nothing but childish tales of fantasy, made up to fool a kind hearted Queen."

Just then something occurred to Charity, something that might be able to prove their innocence after all.

"His Journal, bring me his Journal," she said quickly, "If we didn't murder him then I should be able to tell you *who* murdered him and *when* it happened."

"That would be quite a show, however it would only require you to switch your name with another's and you would seem completely guilt-free, wouldn't you?" Mosia asked cleverly. Her face was sweet and saccharine but her eyes, still bore into Charity. "However, if you can tell me something about the man that you couldn't otherwise know, then I might be more convinced."

"Fine, fine, I'll do it, just please give us that chance?" pleaded Charity.

Mosia gave no answer but clicked her fingers and a nearby guard rushed off. He returned some time later carrying a yellow leather book which, upon Mosia's request, he handed to Charity. With a jolt Charity noticed the words: 'Peter Dwindle, Year of birth 4070, *Year of death 4102*' inscribed in golden writing along the front cover. She opened the book to the last couple of pages and read.

'Brushing down Ophelia, she is easily the best flyer of the crew, *I love when she lets me brush her,* **her feathers are beautiful. Someone coming this way, if I don't look at him, he'll leave me alone, he'll think I'm too busy. He is tall and thin with white hair.** *He's talking about that girl, Charity, the one the Queen sent to find the feather.* **He wants to know where she went, it's none of his business, I shan't tell him anything. He's flashing an Ivory Order badge in my face now, my wretched older brother was in the order,** *he always thought he was better than me,* **well I don't work for the Order, I work for Queen Mosia! Good line that,** *I feel proud.* **He's unsheathing a sword, looks like Ivory Order metal, I must get to my whistle, must warn someone, I can't get back. I can feel the blade, feel the hot sand,** *feel life draining away,* **so much blood. I cannot speak, too painful, it is hard to breathe! I love you Maria. I cannot move at all now, face being covered with sand, everything going dark.** *I'm scared.***'**

"That's the last of it," said Charity soberly, resolutely snapping the Journal shut. "This man was murdered but not by us."

"That, that can't be, Peter said his attacker had an Ivory Order badge, the Order don't get involved in things like this they…they *must* remain impartial, it's their sacred duty," said Mosia quietly. She looked as though her very world had crumpled about her.

"Then he stole it from an Ivory Knight, or a Guard, it doesn't matter! The fact is, I told you *exactly* how he died, I told you that he clearly loved someone named Maria and that he was found buried beneath sand, is *any* of that incorrect?!" Charity finished, suddenly furious. She was fed up standing here, having to prove her innocence for a crime that Cassius had committed. All the while, one of his victims, her friend, her protector on so many occasions, lay dying in a bed somewhere in the city.

Mosia did not speak immediately; her previously smug face now white with terror and revulsion, "I am not as blind as I may seem, girl. I was told once of a reader of unparalleled ability. I am ashamed to say that I did not believe but now…now things are becoming clearer, events are falling into place."

"I don't care what you've heard, I just want to see my friend!" Charity replied angrily. She no longer cared if she showed disrespect, Mosia was a fool and her actions were stopping her from getting to Alistair.

"You are right. Peter went to his death to protect you for some reason, he swore his loyalty to me as well. His death shall not be in vain. Go, please go and find your friend. If you ever need any assistance I will be at your beck and call…Charity Walters." It was the first time Mosia had addressed her by name and also the first time, Charity thought possibly ever, that she had shown an attitude of humility and a willingness to help someone other than herself.

"I…thank you, Your Majesty," said Charity, bowing low as Sophie imitated her.

They turned on their heels and sped from the throne room, down the stairs, out into the city and through the winding sand-covered streets until finally they arrived at a little wooden door. Charity hammered on the door and after some tinkling and the sound of muffled footsteps from beyond, it opened with a creak. An exotic woman, who wore the same grey robe as most of the Durads she had seen, stood at the door holding a bouquet of lilies, her dark brown hair tied into a bun and her features were slightly obscured by a shawl she had wrapped around her mouth.

"Yes?" she asked expectantly, her eye brows raised in surprise.

"Alistair," Charity said, puffing and panting, the run having exhausted what little energy she had.

"I beg your pardon?" the woman said, removing the shawl and showing a mouth of glistening, white teeth. "Who is - ? Oh, you must mean the man!" Realisation dawned on her face.

"Yeah, is he, is he ok?" Sophie said from under Charity's arm. She was resting her hand on the frame of the door for support.

"Please do come in," she said, standing aside and offering them into her home. "You are family of his?"

"Friends," Charity said. "We were travelling together and he had an accident. His Journal was, well I found his Journal all…cracked."

The woman had shown them into a very small house with a low ceiling and only one room. It was unlike any house Charity had ever visited; firstly it was incredibly cramped with an odd collection of furniture haphazardly placed in various places all around the room. Charity looked around. There were great glass jars full of different coloured liquids, some of which bubbled and sparked, there was a large black pot on a stove in one corner of the room and beside this a small table with a very slimy looking knife stabbed into it. In the corner, she spotted him. Alistair was lying flat on his back on top of a bed that was much too small for him. The room itself was incredibly dark, with only a few candles set sporadically around the room lighting up the otherwise dingy scene.

"Mosia's men mentioned an explosion, how did this occur?" the woman asked curiously. She had shown them to three small chairs, one of which she sat on, watching them closely.

"It was -" Sophie started up.

"It was an accident. We're not sure what happened!" interrupted Charity. She thought it prudent not to share too much of their task with this stranger. "We were travelling through the desert and someone must've mistaken us for Laccuna and BOOM!" she made an exploding sign with her hands. "We escaped unhurt, but Alistair, Alistair wasn't so lucky."

"I see," the woman said cynically. "Well I've had a look at his Journal…" She unveiled Alistair's Journal from a pocket of her dress. "…and well…" she hesitated, her face worried.

Charity felt her lip quiver but bit back any tears. She tried to ask for more information but found she couldn't speak.

"It's certainly not good."

"Not good?" squeaked Sophie, "You mean he's…he's…"

"I wouldn't go that far. It's more than I can do to predict his recovery but currently I don't have the sufficient ingredients for an antidote."

"Can you get the stuff? It doesn't matter what it costs we'll pay, we have Odes!" said Charity finding her voice suddenly and looking desperately at Nadia.

"Oh child, don't fret about *that*. I'm getting a delivery any day now, so we can attempt a proper fix then."

"So, so he's going to be alright?" Charity asked hoarsely, ignoring Sophie who was now positively vibrating from shaking so much.

"I do not wish you to dwell on false promises, so I will give you none. I have given him extract of Desert Lily and once fresh supplies are in I'll be able to supply him with some venom from the fang of a Dura snake. This should prove most helpful," she said sagely, indicating the bundle of white flowers now lying on the table beside the knife.

"Venom?!" Charity asked horrified.

"Just a touch, a snip, a drop, it has healing properties you see. Too much though…" she tutted dramatically, "…not good news." She laughed to herself and then seeing their concerned faces, changed her own to that of similar concern.

"Will his Journal ever get better?" asked Charity. "Will he be able to walk again?"

"Again it will depend. It is risky but this is the one and only cure for a broken Journal. If his body takes to the venom, his book should heal itself. They have been known to do this in the past, why I've seen whole covers grow back and pages magically reappearing after being ripped out."

"What if his body rejects the venom?" asked Sophie in a tiny voice.

"Then he may not wake up at all. As I said, it is a risk."

Charity held Sophie close and they both looked at the still figure on the tiny bed. At that moment Charity decided to halt her expedition for the feather. It would just have to wait, she told herself. Alistair had been there for her many times on their short trip and it was time for her to return the favour.

....

Charity had intended to find the nearest inn for she would not beg Mosia for a place to stay even if her attitude had improved slightly. However to her great surprise Nadia had offered them both sanctuary for as long Alistair was with her. Both girls had offered as much money as they could but Nadia had waved them away, asking only that they performed a little housework to earn their keep.

Throughout the day many men and women would come to Nadia, complaining of all manner of injuries and illnesses, her door never seemed to close for more than few minutes before another desperate stranger was hammering upon it looking for help. During their stay Nadia had tried to reassure Charity and Sophie that she was doing all she could for their friend and all the while Charity kept a very close eye on Alistair. His cane, traveller's hat and cloak she had hung up on the back of the door, wondering if he'd ever get to use them again.

One of Charity's jobs was to make sure Alistair did not lose too much heat. Something Charity thought most unlikely in the stiflingly hot little hut but she obeyed nonetheless covering and adjusting his blankets to that they covered as much of his massive body as possible. It was only when she attempted to lift one of Alistair's hands off the blanket to better position it that she understood the importance of her job. Alistair's skin was icy cold. His forehead, face, every area of skin on show felt like it had been in a freezer and had his chest not been rising and falling in front of her she would've been sure he was dead.

On the ninth day of their stay, Charity asked Nadia for a piece of parchment and a quill and sat down purposefully to write a letter. The letter was to be sent to the Ivory Order in Agua, to Clergyman Perch, and it would explain how she had managed to get the first missing page of Calville's Journal and why she was abstaining from her task for a short time. It did not take her long. When she had finished, she set down her quill and looked at what she had written. She had explained how they had been attacked by a man claiming to work for the Order and gave as best a description of him as she could recall. She had underlined that she was still going to go after the Fateweaver, but in the meantime she needed to wait for Alistair to get better. She signed the letter and rolled it up carefully, just as Sophie entered the hut from outside.

"Hey what you doing?" Sophie asked, eyeing the rolled up parchment suspiciously.

"Sending a letter," said Charity, standing up.

"A letter, to who?"

"To the Order, I need to tell them I'll be delayed on my trip, just whilst Alistair is getting better."

"Yeah, I thought you might do that. We can't really go without him, can we?"

"No, we can't," said Charity. She was glad Sophie shared her feelings on the matter as she didn't feel like arguing at the moment.

"But hold on," said Sophie. "Do you know *how* to send a letter?"

"Of course, you just give it to…the…post…man." Charity trailed off, as a wide grin gradually spread across Sophie's face.

"What's a post…man?" she laughed. "A man made of signposts or something!?"

Charity elbowed her in the ribs. "Well tell me *how* to send a letter, then!" she said, smiling despite her annoyance.

"You use a dove, don't you?"

"A dove?"

"Yes, a dove," Sophie said, grabbing the letter off Charity and running back out into the street. Charity followed her at a run. She led her back out into the main square where Sophie had stopped outside another red brick building. It had a rickety wooden sign hanging over the door which read: 'Letters, Parchments, and Packages: Serving the community of Dura since year 3560'. Charity frowned as Sophie went inside and dragged her in behind her. She walked up to the old man at the desk. Charity could see hundreds of doves behind him all swooping about into different little holes and crevices etched into the walls around him. Under each hole was a number.

"Hello. We would like to send this parchment." Sophie rolled up Charity's letter and set it on the desk. "To the Ivory Order Chapter in Upper Forfal, please."

"Who may I say is your recipient?" asked the man in a bored voice, without looking at them.

"Clergyman Perch of the Order," said Sophie without any hesitation. The man looked at them suspiciously, then after running his hands over the parchment he said, "You're serious?"

"Of course," said Sophie,

"Oh Thea, well then you'll be wanting it there quick?" he said excitedly.

"Naturally," replied Sophie cooly.

"NUMBER EIGHTEEN!" he yelled to the back of the shop and a small white dove came pelting out of one of the holes behind him and landed spectacularly on the desk in front of them.

"How does it know when to come?" asked Charity, and the man looked at her as if she had gone quite mad

"Just does, love."

"That'll be two Odes," he said, thrusting a grubby hand at Sophie.

"Blimey, that's not cheap!" Sophie said indignantly,

"That's the price for quick delivery, love. This is the fastest dove I've got. Your parchment'll be there before sunrise tomorrow!" he said proudly.

"Oh fine, fine," said Sophie, slamming two gold coins on the counter. The man grabbed them greedily, picked up her parchment and folded it intricately, so intricately that it seemed to almost shrink in size as he folded. Eventually, Charity's parchment was no bigger than a postage stamp. She stared in awe at the fat little square of white paper in his hand. He clipped the folded piece of parchment to the dove's leg, in which a strap had been placed, and then tapped the little bird on the head with one finger. It whizzed off out a side window and off towards the sun.

"A pleasure, ladies," he said happily, dropping the coins into a little bag behind the desk.

They turned to face the door but found it blocked. Nadia was panting in the doorway, her eyes popping excitedly.

"Girls," she said breathlessly, "he's awake."

18 – A KNIGHT'S TALE

Charity and Sophie burst into Nadia's little hut two minutes later, out of breath but buzzing with anticipation. Alistair was going to be fine, she knew it! Scanning the room, she quickly spotted Alistair propped up awaiting them, his huge back against the headboard and a pained smile upon his face.

Charity and Sophie bounded over to him and wrapped their arms around his mighty waist.

"Oh!" he grimaced in pain. "Careful, girls!"

"Sorry," said Sophie as they both backed away, smiling broadly at him.

"We thought you might be…," said Charity softly but she was unable to finish the sentence and instead changed the topic. "What happened to you anyway? How did *you* get so badly hurt?"

"I am not sure. The last thing I remember is throwing you two across as the bridge collapsed. I was lifted into the air from the blast and then nothing," said Alistair slowly, his brow furrowed in thought.

"Why did everything explode? What did Cassius do?" asked Charity who had been thinking of little else all week.

"He dropped an O.D.D, I saw it land just before we made our escape."

"O.D.D?" said Charity, looking over at Sophie who was looking as though she were deep in thought.

"Order Dynamo Device. It is a widely used and highly effective explosive used only by the members of the Ivory Order. I saw him slip a hand inside his pocket and drop it just as you had him trapped.

"Hold on, hold on, go back a second. You *threw* us across the gap?" Sophie asked,

"I thought the force of the explosion lifted us across the gap," said Charity.

"It most likely did some if not most of the work, my job however was to protect you two from harm, and my intention was to get you both as far from the explosion as possible," he said flatly. "I managed to get you just off the ground and away from the bridge as we were all caught in, what I assume, was the blast radius. I –"

Charity punched him hard on the arm.

"Ow!" he said reproachfully. "Why did – "

"You idiot! You nearly died trying to act like a big hero!" she yelled angrily at him.

"I'm sorry, Charity, I only meant to help," he said looking bashful.

"Oh don't apologise," said Charity exasperatedly. "That makes it worse! Just, just don't be so noble all the time!"

Alistair seemed to not know how to respond to this, so he remained quiet, passively staring at both Charity and Sophie. Sophie was looking torn and was glancing between Charity's conflicted face and Alistair's blank one, apparently unsure who to align herself with.

The tiny room was soon filled with the impenetrable sound of silence as Charity continued to glare at Alistair, who for his part looked at the ceiling, averting his gaze from her own. Sophie gave a little cough and then broke the silence in a very quiet voice.

"Well, we're just glad you're safe."

"Yes, just don't do anything like that again, not for us!" Charity said in a warning tone, her eyes narrowed dangerously.

"Very well," said Alistair, and although Charity knew that he was just placating her, she pushed the thought from her mind. She was far too eager to finally talk with him after such a long time.

"Well how long was I sleeping?" he asked casually.

"Sleeping?! You were out cold Alistair, your Journal, *your spine,* was cracked!" said Charity.

"Well Miss Nadia seems to think I will make a full recovery," he said simply.

"She wasn't always so sure, when we first brought you in…" Sophie tailed off.

"I know it can't have been easy for you, both of you," Alistair said placing a massive hand over theirs. "Thank you for helping me."

"Of course we helped you, we couldn't have just…well you know." said Sophie.

"I know. You show a bravery far beyond your meagre years and I thank Thea that I travel with such worthy companions," said Alistair.

"Does that mean you're going to travel with us some more?" asked Charity eagerly.

"It does, if I am able," he responded. "It should not be longer than a couple more days of rest and whatever that dreadful concoction Miss Nadia seems to have been giving me."

"That concoction saved your life!" a voice called from the doorway. Nadia had re-entered the hut, holding a tray of smouldering cups that belched and bubbled as she set it on a nearby table. She leaned against the frame of an old cabinet, her arms crossed and a broad smirk across her face.

"I, I, I apologise Miss Nadia, I meant no offence, it's…" Alistair stammered looking flushed. Charity had never seen this side of him before and grinned at seeing him squirm like this.

"Oh stop your stuttering, ya big lug, I'm just pulling your pages. Everyone and his sand snake knows that Lillium tastes wretched but we don't use it for its delicious flavour now do we?" she said, looking at the little scene gathered around the bed.

"Oh don't you three look a sight?" she laughed. "These two never left your side, Alistair, right dedicated little madams you've got yourself."

Alistair beamed at Charity and Sophie who retuned his smile; just then Sophie gave a squeak, as if she had trodden on something sharp.

"Oh Charity, tell Alistair – tell him about Mosia?" she said, shrilly.

"Oh yeah…" said Charity slowly. She had completely forgotten about the interrogation they had received when they had brought Alistair back from the desert. It seemed like a lifetime ago. "Well, when we brought you in, or when the Durad guards brought you in, one of them insisted we visit Mosia. She had summoned us, see…"

So Charity recounted to Alistair the story of how Sophie and herself had been dragged to the Royal Palace and accused of the murder of the Sun-Crane handler, named Peter, how they had managed to prove their innocence by reading his Journal and how the man named Cassius had been the real perpetrator of the murder. Alistair listened carefully and then when she finished, he stared into space for a moment of two, apparently turning over her words inside his head.

"Cassius," he said, after some time,

"Do you really think he's a Regalis?" asked Charity, voicing something that been plaguing her thoughts her since she'd met the man.

"I do not know. He correctly translated the message outside the temple when Sophie nor I could even see it."

"Maybe he was following us, he could've been eavesdropping." suggested Sophie helpfully.

"Not unless he owns an invisibility cloak." Said Alistair assuredly, "We saw the area from atop the Sun-Cranes and there wasn't another soul for miles where we landed."

"Maybe he came afterwards, when we were trying to work out how to get in and was hiding behind a pillar or something." said Charity.

"I have yet to meet the man or beast that can remain undetected in my presence." said Alistair, making it quite clear that this option was a dead end.

FATEWEAVER

"I am sure of one thing however: his presence in the temple was no coincidence, he *knew* we would be there."

"How do you know *that?*" asked Sophie,

"Think about it. He just *happened* to find that temple in the middle of an expanse of desert. He was in the *exact* location of a temple that has not been unearthed for hundreds of years. That's too convenient, far too convenient. Never mind that he was able to walk straight through to us without so much as breaking a sweat, we were careless definitely, we let our guard down I know that now but he *knew* what to do and where to find us, that's why he was there."

"It could just be a coincidence." suggested Sophie quietly.

"Not a chance!" boomed Alistair. "No, he knew. Someone told him where we were heading, maybe even what we were searching for. Someone sent him; the question is, who?"

"The Sun-Crane handler could've… Cassius clearly threatened him, maybe he gave away our location?" Sophie suggested.

"No, remember, I read his Journal. He didn't give us up, he…he died to protect our whereabouts," Charity said sadly.

"Then, he died like a hero," said Alistair proudly. "No it must've been somebody else."

"Maybe Mosia," said Charity, remembering her obsession for treasure and riches.

"I very much doubt that, Charity. Queen Mosia is a head of state, and is one of the three most powerful figures in all of Thea. NOT only that – " he raised his deep voice, as Charity had opened her mouth to interrupt, "But she claimed to know nothing of Cassius and you tell me she showed a sincere grief upon hearing of Peter's death."

"Well she could've been lying to protect him – Cassius, I mean," said Charity.

"Do *you* think she was lying?" asked Alistair,

267

"Um...no, no I think she was being honest," Charity said. "But who could've told him? We didn't tell anyone else about our task."

There is one who would know of your task and also of your whereabouts, one that has the means of tracking your progress and informing Cassius," said Alistair, a stony look in his dark eyes.

"Who?" chorused Charity and Sophie eagerly.

Alistair glanced at the door and then at Nadia. He nodded silently and she rushed to it, closing it tightly and turning a key in the lock. She then moved to the window and drew the curtains closed so that no one could see or hear what they were discussing inside the tiny hut. Nadia moved swiftly and silently, as if she been given this instruction before. She took her seat once more at the rickety little table and looked at Alistair, who smiled kindly at her.

"I am about to tell you something that I have never told anyone else. You two have more than earned my trust and I have Miss Nadia to thank for repairing my Journal and bringing me back to full health. She has consented to stay and listen as well."

"You're a long way from full health, love," said Nadia.

"I am well enough to speak and give you my thanks. If you are to stay and listen you all must promise not to tell another soul of what I am about to tell you," Alistair finished seriously.

All three nodded and gave their individual promises and Alistair stared intensely at them as they did. Charity was tingling with anticipation of what she thought was sure to be a ground-breaking revelation. Alistair waited a while. He seemed to taking great care over his words but finally, after what seemed like an eternity of silence, he spoke.

....

The snake slithered along the hot sand, savouring its last meal. The tiny bird had been unsuspecting and the darkness of the night had provided adequate cover for such an assault. It weaved its way down a dune, stopping suddenly as a noise from nearby had startled something. The snake watched as a small rabbit sped across the sandy surface and into the dark horizon beyond. Darting its tongue out, tasting the fresh night air, it could smell something, something that was not usually present in the desert. The snake turned its head as the smell grew stronger, it could feel the vibrations of something hurtling along the sand at tremendous speed. The night was too dark, the snake could see nothing, it turned its head desperately back and forth, spiking out its forked tongue to sense for the source of commotion. All of a sudden a tall two legged creature reared out from the darkness a shining metal blade raised high above its head. The snake hissed in fear and rage but this strange creature was upon him before he could bare a single fang. Cassius' sword sliced through the cold night air and cut cleanly through the snake's flesh in one go. Its head rolled down the sandy bank and came to a stop at the bottom, its forked tongue lolling from its mouth onto the sand below.

Cassius sheathed his blade, the snake's oily blood dripping from his sword and down his trouser leg. He did not care; it had been a long time since he had eaten and the snake, properly prepared, would provide necessary nourishment. He picked up the carcass and carried it to a nearby campfire; regrettably he had been forced to destroy his bow to make a suitable fire. He had withstood for many hours, the cold wind beating him fiercely until finally he had yielded to the temptation of a warm flame. So, with a heavy heart, he had snapped it into several pieces and quickly forged a roaring fire. The Atra wood easily resisted the strong winds, burning merrily away as soon as he had managed to light it. It was greatly regrettable but this sacrifice had provided him with the warmth he needed to survive the long, cold nights in the Dura desert.

He had been wandering this wasteland for two days now. Foraging was not something he found difficult, in fact his years in the Castlands had prepared him well for such an endeavour, however the whole experience was made more difficult by his incessantly nagging conscience. He felt tortured by his failure, his failure to extract the Journal from the girl. When she had managed to trap him in that excruciating white light, he had been forced to change tactics. His only option was to take out the observatory, a regrettable but sound move on his part, but the girl, what had she done with that Journal? He seethed at the thought of her face. She was worthless, cowardly and yet she had forced him to experience something he had not since his childhood: horrible, unimaginable pain.

In his mind he watched himself charge out the observatory door and across the bridge. He had been just inches from them when the oaf had thrown the girls out of his reach and the Order explosive had gone off behind him. The blast had been suitably intense, a useful toy, he thought, and he made a mental note to retrieve more when he next met the Order representatives, who seemed so eager to recruit his services. He recalled how he had awoken in this sandy wasteland, dazed and bruised but otherwise unhurt. He had frantically searched for them, for her, for the Journal, for any clue to their whereabouts but all he had found were pieces of broken glass and burning pages, and even the temple seemed to have receded back into the sand.

Cassius roasted the snake over the roaring fire until it was crisp. Biting into it, he narrowed his eyes. Something had alerted his senses on the line of the horizon, a light. The little orange dot was burning brightly in the distance, and was easily reachable by foot, he thought. It was far too small to be Duradon. Was it a village? Was it a place where he could find shelter? In any case it was likely to be better than where he was now. He finished the snake quickly; savouring the feeling of food in his stomach. He gave one last look at the fire, the flames voraciously licking his once proud bow, and swept a heap of sand over it with his boot, extinguishing it immediately.

He moved as silently as the snake he had been tracking, travelling over the dunes and across the sandy plains with consummate ease. His speed had clearly not been affected by the blast but had his swordplay? He should find some practice in this nearby settlement, he thought hungrily. As he reached the glowing orange light he could see that it was, in fact, another roaring fire, almost three times as big as his own had been. Surrounding the fire were several tiny huts constructed out of animal skins and wooden sticks. The settlement looked relatively new and Cassius noticed with a jolt of excitement that they had two huge boars roasting atop the fire. He took another step into the village but was immediately alert. Someone had stirred in the tent nearest to him. In a flash he dashed behind a particularly large rock placed nearby and watched silently.

The man crawled out of the tent and straightened up, creaking his back in an arch and complaining loudly as he plodded his way to the flames and poked them impatiently with a large stick he had picked up from the ground. This man would prove no challenge; he would not even waste his time on such a pathetic –

An ear-splitting scream broke his thoughts. A small girl had appeared right beside where he had been kneeling. She had spotted his silver blade dripping with blood and let out a truly awful shriek. The little settlement was suddenly alive with noise and motion as the inhabitants of the tents spilled out towards the fire and towards the screaming. Cassius bounded to his feet, his sword drawn. The little girl had fled to what was clearly her mother, who stood beside the fire with the rest of the settlement. One man took a step forwards, he was crooked, with gnarled yellow teeth and beady bloodshot eyes.

"Stranger, you'd best be moving on, this ain't no place for unwelcomes," he said, hostility echoing in every syllable of his foreign tongue.

"Give me all your food and I may spare your young ones," Cassius commanded quietly.

"WHAT'S THAT?!" yelled the old man, smiling wickedly. "Son, you clearly don't know where you've stumbled into. Now just leave before I'm forced to hand out a lesson to you."

Cassius was beginning to lose his control, his hand shaking with repressed rage. How *dare* such scum speak to him in this way, he thought savagely. He had been stopped in his task of retrieving the Journal by a freak accident, he had been stranded in this paltry land for days and now this common desert rat was threatening him, *him*. He drew his sword, his mind set, his voice resolute, "I do not ask twice," he whispered.

Not far from the small settlement, two Duradon guards sat atop the great wall, keeping a watchful eye over their city.

"You hear that?" one of them said, "Sounds like, like screaming coming from the desert."

"Probably the settlements fighting again, they're always killing each other over whose piece of the dirt is theirs, or what tribe killed the most snakes," the other replied distastefully.

"Yeah, but shouldn't we check it out, make sure they aren't coming to the city?"

The second guard sighed in a bored sort of way, "One they *never* come to the city and *two* I've been doing this job near my whole life and the best thing I've learnt is that *you* do *not* want to go out into that desert, at night."

The screams and clashes of metal stopped suddenly. "There see, it's all over," said the second guard in a satisfied tone.

Back at the settlement Cassius wiped his blade on the sand, purging it of the unfit blood that stained its surface. He had just put it back into its holster when a deep voice spoke from the shadows behind him.

"Quite a display," it said, as he wheeled around to face it, his sword redrawn, his breath sharp in his chest.

"Put it away, boy!" the familiar voice commanded reproachfully, as a hooded man stepped out and into the moonlight. He was tall, bearded and dressed all in ivory white, his spotlessly clean robes looked quite out of place among the blood-strewn scene that surrounded him.

He tutted distastefully at the pile of bodies lying around the settlement. "Messy. Very messy. *You* lost control," he said.

"I don't need lectures from you!" spat Cassius. "Do you know what I've just been through?"

"I know enough. Firstly that you did not retrieve the Journal and secondly that not only did the girl manage to escape your clutches but as a result of this you are now suspected of murder in Duradon."

"I, no I took care of –" started Cassius.

"You took care of *nothing!*" barked the man angrily. "I expected more from you, Cassius. Now the Order is under scrutiny from those in Thea. They suspect we may have a hand in these misdemeanours and this simply cannot be tolerated!"

The figure thrust out a thin hand towards Cassius. "Your badge?" he commanded. "It will be safer if you remain as disconnected from us as possible."

Cassius threw the silver pin depicting a white Journal and red moon to the man, who caught and pocketed it quickly.

"Fortunately despite your *failures,*" he placed great emphasis on the final word, his lip curling at Cassius' flushed face, "The girl does not suspect us yet. This is most surprising but not unwelcome news. Clearly she trusts far too easily and we can certainly use that to *our* advantage."

"How?" asked Cassius, his mouth tight and frustration etched onto his gaunt face.

"By following her. She is walking Calville's path. She clearly knows how to reach the missing pages. She has already found one and is now likely to go after the second."

"How do you know all of this?" demanded Cassius.

"The Ivory Order has an eye on everything in Thea. We know because it is our duty to know."

"Well do we know where she is going?" asked Cassius, eager to change the subject.

"Of *course* we know!" snapped the figure angrily. "We know almost everything that occurs in Thea. We understand that Calville visited several places in search for the Fateweaver, we know that the girl is following his route. He went to Agua; however the place has been almost torn apart over the years in search for a clue, and nothing has been found. We always surmised that something was in Dura, and we appear to have been correct in our assumptions. This leaves one place for the girl to travel to, a place where, thankfully, we are more than prepared to…*welcome* her."

"Imputtia?" asked Cassius.

"Precisely!" said the figure, his eyes alight behind his dark hood.

"You want me to track her, when I could simply take the Journal from her now and follow the path for myself?" asked Cassius scornfully.

"Well you had your chance to take the Journal and you failed," the man snapped.

"The girl, she, she did something, something with Calville's Journal," said Cassius desperately, and he told the man about the mysterious beam of light that had caused him such pain.

"Yes, I heard as much. A side effect of reading such an ancient Journal, no doubt. It is not uncommon for some Regalis to perform such feats when overexposed to a such a Journal. She will certainly not be able to rely on such a thing," he said casually, flicking sand off his long white sleeve. "But it would be wise to anticipate such an event for the next time you meet Cassius. Just in case."

"She is weakened. I could get the Journal now that I know, now that I'm prepared."

"You should have been prepared from the start, boy! You truly underestimate the repercussions of your actions. The Order is now suspected of foul play, our spotless reputation has been tarnished and it's all because *you* let your guard down! If we put so much as another page out of line then all of Thea will be onto our plan and that is quite simple, unacceptable."

Cassius looked as though he wanted to continue arguing but seemed to think better of it, and breathing very deeply he looked up at the figure, his face calm and restrained.

"Very well. Where should I start?"

"Come with me, I have a Sun-crane nearby. We've been looking for you for some time and all that commotion," he waved his hand lazily at the pile of bodies scattered around them, "led us straight to you. I daresay Charity will make her way North soon and it's there we'll intercept her. When this is all over, one of you *will* lead us to the Fateweaver, and Cassius?" he turned to stare deep into Cassius black eyes, "You better hope it's you."

Cassius followed the man into the shadows whence he had come. His heart was beating like a drum and his hand was wrapped so tightly around the handle of his blade he thought he might snap it clean off.

....

Charity sat in awed silence as Alistair began his tale. She felt honoured and intensely excited to be trusted with what was obviously a very closely guarded secret.

"My story begins fifteen years ago. I was seventeen and had just left my parents' home to try and make it on my own," Alistair had just started but Charity interrupted.

"Seventeen? Wait," she counted on her fingers, "you're only thirty-two!?" she asked, exasperatedly.

"Yes, I am thirty-two," said Alistair looking at them as if he wondered why this was a problem.

"But you look *way* older than that," said Sophie. Alistair stared at her silently. "And uhhh way *wiser*!" she added nervously.

"I am aware that I look older than I am; however Garrons have always looked older than our true age, *wiser* too." He added slyly smirking at Sophie who grinned apologetically. "It is a fortunate coincidence that has helped me on many occasions and I shall not complain about it. This is an incidental detail, however, so if we are finished with discussing my aesthetics, may I continue?" he asked quite calmly.

"Yes. Go ahead, sorry," said Sophie.

"Well, I was seventeen and I needed a career, something that befitted my size, for I was already quite large and a formidable opponent, if I do say so myself. I looked all over Thea and found nothing that exercised my need for adventure and excitement, so I took work in a tavern just to keep myself in food and drink. It was my job to keep the peace when things got slightly out of hand. I used to throw out men that caused trouble and make sure all the paying patrons were looked after. I was well paid for my services but it was not what I truly wanted to do with my life.

"Then one night, I overhead a customer talking about something that greatly interested me. He was explaining how his friend had gotten into the Ivory Order as a Knight. He spoke of incredible adventures all over Thea and the terrific battles he had been involved in as a result. Well I was convinced that this was the path my life should take. I marched to the nearest Order chapter the very next day and asked for the possibility of work. They recognised that my size would be an advantage and were only too happy to have someone like myself aboard. They signed me up there and then and began my training almost immediately.

"It took a short while, only fifty-seven days, as I recall, but soon I had received enough training to be given the title of Ivory Order Knight. I believe I still hold the record for quickest Ivory Knighthood in Imputtia. The training was nothing I wasn't used to, you see – my Father used to put me through trials ten times as gruelling as the ones in the Order. He was a great man, a great…but oh, I apologise, I am getting off topic. Well, after fifty-seven days I was finally given the title of Ivory Order Knight. I was given my official Ivory armour on that day too and I remember, the Order instructors said, that they'd never seen such a gifted warrior; it was the proudest day of my life.

"I greatly enjoyed my time at the Order, helping innocent civilians, sorting out problems and looking for those in Thea capable of reading Journals, for that is part of the Order's purpose to help bring about the next generation of Regalis. One day, however, I stumbled upon something that changed my feelings about the Ivory Order and everything they claimed to stand for. I had been posted to the Order Chapter in Upper Forfal for a standard scouting mission, looking for Laccuna and handing out an emergency shipment of blank Journals. On my second day there I happened to leave my quarters for a midnight stroll, a favourite pastime of mine, when I overheard an argument outside the main hall of the Order Chapter. Two men, both shrouded in the shadows, were having a heated debate about what I later realised was a young girl."

Charity listened to Alistair's account, trying to imagine what the scene had looked like. She could almost see the two speakers in her head, acting out the scene as it was dictated to them.

"I told you, she's not ready, she shows promise I cannot deny that, but to send her out on her own would be tantamount to murder!" said one man.

"It is not your decision to make. Clergyman. She is the only ray of hope we have had in our quest for some time. She will leave in the morning," said the other.

"I haven't even asked her yet, how can I inform her family of such a thing? We aren't even sure the feather *exists!* I…I…don't know if I can do this!" said the first.

"You will hold your tongue, Clergyman, or I can arrange for it to be removed," the second said, in what Charity imagined was a dangerous whisper.

"I didn't want to be heard," Alistair continued and Charity's mind refocused on his tale. "I had no idea what had happened or what they were talking about so I snuck back to my bed and tried to forget about it." Alistair looked darkly at his own hands. "I was a coward, and did not act when I should have. When morning came, we received news that a young girl, aged about fourteen years had been abducted from her bed whilst she slept. Her family had babbled about men in white cloaks taking her from the house. Some thought them simply mad with grief, that the girl had obviously just run away from home, but most folk felt that *they* had been the ones guilty of her disappearance. Eventually enough public pressure grew on the Order and they were forced to do something about them," Alistair finished solemnly.

"Do something about them?" enquired Charity,

"I watched them being carted off to the dungeons myself. I saw the panic and fear in their eyes, heard their screams as they protested their innocence." Said Alistair looking disgusted with himself.

"What, what happened to them then?" asked Sophie in a hushed whisper.

"The men and women of Upper Forfal were happy to see *justice* being done. They believed the couple were imprisoned for the remainder of their lives but that was not the case."

"What?" asked Sophie but Alistair interrupted her.

"They were put to death, destruction of Journals…a punishment enforced *by* the Ivory Order."

"WHAT?!" Charity exploded. "It was the Order! Men in white, you said, clergymen arguing, it was obviously the Order, they were taking her away and they framed her parents!"

"I came to the same conclusion. I felt strongly that the Order was hiding something, that they had something to do with the girl's disappearance and had eliminated the parents so none could make such a claim against them. Something else concerned me, however. I felt that all of this had something to do with the Fateweaver."

"They said, that girl would help them find it, that she could read," said Sophie. "Alistair, you don't think - ?"

"It's my belief that the girl possessed some Regalis abilities and that the Order sent her out to look for the Fateweaver," said Alistair, correctly interrupting Charity's implication, his great brow furrowed in thought

"They sent her out alone?" Charity asked concerned.

"She was not spotted with anyone else so yes, she was most likely alone. The Order revealed itself to me that night as an organisation obsessed with one thing above all else – power, the power that the Fateweaver holds. I could not be a part of it any longer. I resigned from my post the very next day but it was not that simple. Few simply walk away from the Ivory Order. They came for me whilst I slept, three senior Ivory Knights. I just managed to fight them off and escape Forfal but I lost everything that night. From then on I have been roaming Thea, attempting to undo the wrongs I am implicated with. The Order would still very much like to take me in, very much indeed." he finished pointedly.

"Wow!" said Sophie. "So you're like on the run?"

"I suppose that is one way of putting it. I do prefer to keep a low profile and up until now I have been able to keep myself relatively unnoticed but current company," he gave a nod to Charity, "makes that slightly more problematic."

"But wait," said Charity, who had had been rolling things over and over in her mind, "there's one thing I don't understand. They must've given that girl Calville's Journal, if they wanted her to find the Fateweaver, that is.

That doesn't work out though," Charity said thoughtfully. "Remember Clergyman Perch gave it to *me,* so she couldn't have taken it and just disappeared."

"Oh, she did not disappear for long. Few in Upper Forfal were privileged to such information but she showed up not two days after she was reported missing," he said darkly.

"She showed up?! Where?" asked Sophie eagerly.

"In a ditch in the Castlands. She had been dead for some time when Ivory scouts found her. Nearby they accosted a Laccuna with some of her possessions, including…"

"The Journal!" said Charity suddenly. "But why didn't Perch tell me any of this when he asked to find the Fateweaver?"

"He didn't mention any of this?" asked Alistair his mouth tight.

"No! Why though, why wouldn't he warn me?!" asked Charity desperately, she felt suddenly embarrassed at how easily she had trusted Perch and how quickly she'd agreed to help the Order.

Alistair fixed her with a firm stare, and pulled himself up in bed. Even whilst sitting he still towered over everyone in the tiny hut.

"He didn't warn you for the same reason that they sent an defenceless girl out into the wilderness all those years ago. They thought it might lead them to the Fateweaver," he said coldly.

Charity heard Sophie gasp in horror beside her.

"Charity, Sophie, I meant to teach you of the true intentions of the Ivory Order by telling you my tale but what I have seen and heard of this man Cassius troubles me greatly. I have never faced anyone like him in all my years, his strength and speed are quite extraordinary. Not to mention the fact that he claimed to be a Regalis as well."

"Oh yeah, he did!" said Charity, remembering Cassius' words properly for the first time, "He couldn't be a Regalis though could he?"

"The ability to read small portions of Journal text is not uncommon but to read entire Journals with the turning of a page is quite rare." said Alistair logically.

"Two Regalis on Thea at once, that's never happened though, not ever." said Sophie sounding awed.

"It is possible that he was lying but I do not see what benefit this would be to him." replied Alistair, "Regardless of this though I still believe that he is a very real threat to your mission Charity."

"You mean he wants to kill me?!" gasped Charity,

"Perhaps but I get the impression from our meeting that above all he means to procure that Journal...and if you stand in his way..."

"We didn't seem him in the wreckage though, he could've died couldn't he?" asked Sophie hopefully.

Alistair fixed her with a long and thoughtful stare before addressing all of them, "This man will not be so easily gotten rid of, that is something I am sure of. Just as I am sure that the Order means him to find the feather for them. That is something we cannot allow to happen."

"But, hold on, if the Order wanted to hire *him* to find the Fateweaver why did they give it to me?" asked Charity.

"I regret that I do not know." answered Alistair, looking troubled.

Charity and the others sat in silence, stunned by what she had heard.

"But wait! I just sent a letter explaining what we'd done to Clergyman Perch, at the Order Chapter in Forfal!" she said panicking. "Now they know where we are!"

"That is regrettable." said Alistair slowly.

"Oh Charity," whispered Sophie, biting her lip in concern.

"There is little point in worrying over spilt ink girls, what's done is done." Alistair said sagely.

"But I told them about finding the page and everything." Said Charity hurriedly.

"Doesn't matter, we cannot get the letter back now so what's the point in worrying?" answered Alistair kindly.

"That reminds me," squeaked Sophie excitedly. "You should read the missing page. We've never really got a chance to, since, well since…"

"Since I almost died," said Alistair quite happily.

"Yeah, that," said Sophie awkwardly. "Well it's bound to tell us where to go next."

"Hmm," said Charity distractedly. She was still thinking of the poor girl that was sent out on the very quest she was now upon and her insides swelled with sudden appreciation for her two friends.

"Charity, the Journal!" said Sophie loudly, as Charity snapped back to reality. "Can you read the missing page for us, it could help."

"Oh yeah, sure…."

She extracted the leather Journal from her jacket and laid it flat on her knees, opening it to where the page had fused with the spine. She took a deep breath and read:

'I fear myself. *Need to get away.* I am very close now, it has taken so long and taken so much from me but it is almost mine. *Trust no one, they all want it for themselves.* I know this, the Fateweaver is real, I know it resides deep where no one else would dare tread. When I find it, I can do what she begged me to do, *she did so much for us, I will not fail!* I will hide these last two pages in places where only those worthy can reach. The Dura Desert and Imputtia Plains will prove a suitable challenge for anyone who wants the feather for themselves and then I will hide the feather somewhere even I do not know yet, it must be impregnable, it must be a true test of heart. It must be a test worthy of *her*."

19 – A LINE IN THE SNOW

Despite Alistair's self-diagnosis that he was absolutely fine, Nadia was quite insistent that he was still a little way off being back to full health, and certainly not ready for travelling just yet. She had even been kind enough to allow all three of them to continue to stay for as long as was necessary, which Charity was eternally grateful for. In the short time Charity had known her Nadia had turned out to be one of the kindest people she had ever met. She seemed to nearly always have a string of appointments throughout each day and Charity supposed that in Thea, she acted very much the way a doctor would back home. Theans would come to her little house at appointed times and bring their Journals with them, some with minor problems, such as torn pages or scratched covers. Occasionally one or two of the visitors had problems similar to Alistair's, whole sections torn or burnt from their books. One frantic woman was beside herself with worry about her husband, whose cover had completely been ripped off by a gang of raiders in the desert. Nadia had left the house immediately to visit the man, and had returned some time later, splattered with what looked like blood and shaking her head ruefully. Charity had not questioned her any further on the topic, dreading to think what the man's appearance had been like.

On the whole Charity had greatly enjoyed her stay with Nadia. It had been a truly eye opening experience and one that had taught her a valuable lesson about keeping Journals very safe indeed. After six more days, Alistair seemed fit and well enough to not only get up and walk about the small house, but also to run around Duradon on myriad different errands that Nadia insisted he help her with.

"It'll give you a bit of exercise, plus I could do with the help!" she had smiled happily at him as she'd pushed him out the door for the past two mornings.

So they had packed up their belongings, Charity stowing the bag of Odes, which she reminded herself to count the next time they were on their own, and Calville's Journal into her jacket and then helped Sophie check she had not left anything behind in Nadia's hut. Alistair, too, had packed up his things and stored them in the many compartments of his huge traveller's cloak.

With one last look at the tiny room that had been their home for the past two weeks, they all filed out into the morning sunlight and towards the great black door that led to the desert of Dura. Nadia had spoken to Alistair, Charity and Sophie about the tale that Alistair had shared with them in great detail. She, like Charity, had been fascinated by the accusations it levelled at the Ivory Order, a group that seemed, to Charity at least, to control Thea entirely, no matter what anyone else said. Nadia had of course promised not to repeat this tale, for not only could it land *her* in serious bother, but it may lead to the Order to tracking them down, something that Charity did not see as particularly desirable.

"I've no family so no one to tell," Nadia had said heartily, her eyes closed and hand on her heart so she looked like she was swearing an oath, "But I promise all of you, that not one soul shall hear your troubled story, Alistair. I mean it, may Thea strike me down if I utter so much of a syllable of it!"

They had reached the door now and heard the clanking of metal and gears that usually signalled it was about to swing open, when Charity had a sudden idea.

"Why don't you come with us?" she asked Nadia excitedly. "C'mon, it'd be great to have another set of hands to help us, plus you clearly know an awful lot about Journals. We might need you again – I mean, I hope we don't but you never know!" Charity couldn't believe it hadn't occurred to her before now. Nadia was bright, cheerful and extraordinarily knowledgeable about healing Journals, which was bound to come in handy at some point.

Nadia considered her with kind eyes, she looked Charity up and down, an unreadable look on her face.

"My dear Charity, I would love nothing more than to join you on your quest. Adventure is something I have long craved, but I am afraid I have a duty here to the people of Duradon. Without me, there is no one who can provide vital aid for those whose Journals are damaged or in need of repair.”

“Oh yeah, never thought of it like that,” Charity said, her spirits dropping slightly.

“Don’t lose heart, Charity. Once we lose that, there can be no going back,” said Nadia mysteriously, giving Charity a meaningful look.

“Well, thank you!” Sophie said, ignoring Nadia’s strange comment and giving her a hug, which Nadia returned, smiling at her.

“Sophie, dear, be safe.”

“I’ll try,” grinned Sophie, as Nadia ruffled her hair affectionately.

“My pages, I’ll miss you girls. Quite a change to have some company here.”

“Then -” began Charity, who was about to ask her to come along once more. But Nadia shook her head, and smirked at Charity who fell silent, correctly interpreting her signal.

Alistair approached Nadia and awkwardly held out a huge hand in her direction. “Um, thank you Miss Nadia,” he said gruffly. “I would not be standing here if it weren’t for your expertise.”

Before Alistair could react, Nadia had pulled him into a bone crushing hug, laughing happily as she did.

“You, Alistair Garron, are a big softy! I thought you were meant to be a tough nut, but you’re all bark no bite!”

Charity and Sophie fell about laughing at the intensely awkward Alistair, who could only stutter and mumble through this unexpected embrace. When Nadia finally released him, he simply nodded silently, tipping his hat in her direction and falling back in line with Charity, his big face as red as the buildings that surrounded him.

“Oh Thea, I almost forgot,” said Nadia suddenly. “Take this.” She handed Alistair a small copper vial with a cork plugged in the top.

"Thank you. Is it more elixir?"

"It is. You shouldn't need much more but any pain or discomfort just take a few gulps, should be enough in that vial to last you five or six days," said Nadia comprehensively.

"Thank you for everything," said Charity, walking up to Nadia and hugging her tightly.

"Oh Sophie, dear, I almost forgot," said Nadia, peeping over Charity's head, "Could you grab one of the old maps on my table, it should give you some useful information on the routes around Imputtia. Alistair, love, show her where they are."

Alistair and Sophie bustled back into the city to get the map, leaving Nadia and Charity quite alone, Charity had released her from the hug and, looking into her face she saw that Nadia suddenly seemed deathly serious.

"Charity I am glad you have confided in me these past days and Alistair's tale has given me a great deal to ponder but I must ask you something before you leave. Something of the utmost importance."

"Ok," said Charity, panicking slightly over what she was about to be asked. She was suddenly acutely aware that she had not officially told Nadia where she had come from. Should she have told her? Nadia was definitely trustworthy; what if she had worked out that Charity had no Journal and in the eyes of many on Thea would be considered an outcast, a Laccuna. Would she resent or even fear Charity? Hundreds of questions and theories exploded into Charity's head, as she waited for Nadia to continue with baited breath.

"Are you quite sure that Sophie and Alistair are trustworthy?" asked Nadia, her dark eyes staring fixedly into Charity's.

Charity opened her mouth reproachfully. She had never even considered the idea that her friends might betray her trust, and continued to look into Nadia's brown eyes, unsure of how to respond in a way that did not come across as rude.

"I mean you or them no offence, I just, I just need to know," said Nadia kindly, her forehead crinkled in worry.

"Nadia, I trust them both with my life," said Charity defiantly. "If there is one thing in all of Thea that I am sure of, it is that those two would never let me down!"

Nadia stared into Charity's pale blue eyes for a long time and then hearing the black door behind them scrape open, she said in a hurried whisper so that only she could hear her, "I had to know that *you* were sure."

"We couldn't find the maps, where did you say they are?" asked Sophie, emerging from behind the black door.

"Oh, I just remembered, I must've left them with Queen Mosia. I was giving her advice on an expedition some days ago. Never mind, you shouldn't need them, not with such a warrior as Alistair with you!" She winked at Alistair, who went very red again and averted his gaze. Charity and Sophie laughed as they waved goodbye to Nadia and made their way from the great crimson city and towards the Sun-Lift platform at the far end of the long wooden walkway.

Their plan was to find a Sun-Lift that would take them to the Northern border of Dura. This would be as close as they could go by bird, the rest of the way having to be on foot, or so Alistair had told them the night before. They had arrived at the landing dock at the front of Duradon and Alistair had quickly found a bay that seemed sufficient. Charity thought it looked almost identical to the other four bays, the only difference she could spot was a small sign that read, 'Northern route'.

"This is us," he had said gruffly and they had waited only a couple of minutes when sure enough a flock of four more Sun-Cranes came swooping towards them carrying one of the heavy platforms.

Charity marvelled at how the birds had known they were waiting. Alistair had not given any signal of their arrival, but she surmised it was just one of those things in Thea that nobody questioned. The birds seemed to know their own route, as whenever the group had made their way onto the platform they took off quite suddenly and without any provocation from Alistair.

Charity must've been staring at the birds because Sophie leant in beside her and whispered into her ear, "The birds travel one route, back and forth. These birds must go North and then back to Duradon, that's how they know where to go."

Charity smiled thankfully at Sophie who looked sufficiently pleased with herself. As the rattling platform made its steady away across the morning sky, the group soon realised that they were quite alone and talk soon turned to the last extract from Calville's Journal, something they had not had a chance to speak of due to the severity of Alistair's injuries. Nadia had previously banned all talk of adventure and excitement, claiming that Alistair needed to relax. Privately, Charity had agreed.

Charity repeated a single line from Calville out loud to the group: "**I will hide these last two pages in places where only those worthy can reach. The Dura Desert and Imputtia Plains will prove a suitable challenge for anyone who wants the feather for themselves and then I will hide the feather somewhere even I do not know yet.**"

"That whole thing about hiding the feather, d'ya think he actually went back and hid the pages in these specific places and then the feather just so someone would be able to *prove themselves?*" she asked exasperatedly.

"Well, we know very little about Charles Calville. All the official records of Thea show are that he was an intrepid explorer who was constantly searching for the Fateweaver feather," said Sophie knowledgably. "His whole life seemed obsessed by it, and he never married or even settled in one place."

"But that makes even less sense," Charity said, frustrated. "Why would someone spend his whole life looking for something and then hide it in a new place as soon as he finds it?"

"It is an odd thing to do with such a powerful item, if it does indeed exist," Alistair said thoughtfully.

"You don't think it exists?" asked Sophie,

"I did not say that, I just mean that we have no categorical proof, only Calville's thoughts and assumptions."

"But the first page *was* in the Dura Temple!" said Charity heatedly.

"Yes," smiled Alistair, "I admit that does suggest that he was leaving a trail for someone, which would lead one to feel that he is telling the truth." He was leaning on his cane and grimacing somewhat as the great platform shook and rolled about the morning sky.

Charity was thinking of the last reading, turning over Calville's penultimate thoughts in her head. **'When I find it I can do it for her, *she did this for us, I will not fail!* I will hide the feather somewhere even I don't know yet, it must be impregnable, it must be a true test of heart. It must be a test worthy of *her.'***

"Who's 'her'?" she asked Sophie and Alistair out loud. They looked at her blankly so she repeated the quote from Calville's Journal. "Her – a woman, or a girl or someone, who do you think she was?"

"No idea. Like I said, Calville never married or had children but we don't keep records on the people we fall in love with so it could be anyone, an old flame maybe?" Sophie suggested.

"No it's more than that, he's willing to go to the ends of the world for this woman. There's something more to this I'm sure of it." Charity whispered, to herself more than anyone else.

"You are worrying about an inconsequential detail, Charity," Alistair said, "Whomever the woman was she has long passed on, so it is no longer relative."

"Of course it is! I mean it could be! What if he left the feather somewhere relating to her, like her grave stone or her old house or something?" said Charity excitedly.

Alistair looked mildly impressed. "I suppose that would be useful but it matters not, we have absolutely *no* way of knowing the identity of the woman or where she came from, so I suggest we continue on with our original plan and head to Imputtia."

"Fine, but I'm gonna check the Journal for her," said Charity sulkily. She flopped the Journal onto the platform, which gave another shake, and rifled through the pages searching for a record of a woman, a girl or anything that could help them. However after over an hour of searching she had found nothing relevant. The one thing that did catch Charity's attention was that Calville's Journal did not go from his thoughts at birth to his dying day, as she had assumed all Journals did; She decided to voice these concerns to Alistair and Sophie.

"Guys, Calville's Journal doesn't start when he was born, it begins with him at twenty seven, when he's just starting his expedition for the feather. Is that normal?" she asked.

"No, it is not normal," said Alistair. "However it is not unheard of. At times people can lose their Journals and very occasionally if they are skilled in the art of concentration and focus they can graft with another, although I must stress that the link between this *new* Journal will not be nearly as strong as the original."

"So you think this was his second Journal?" asked Sophie excitedly.

"Yes that seems very likely, but if it is, the old one will have crumbled into nothingness by now. With no memories to record it becomes another lifeless book and with time succumbs to decades of decay," said Alistair wisely.

"Journals decay after their owner dies?" asked Charity.

"No, not when they die, when they graft with another Journal. It's incredibly rare for it to happen though. If a person dies of natural causes or in a way that leaves their Journal quite unaffected then it simply remains there, although to all intents and purposes it may as well be an empty book, as none will be able to read it – well, except a Regalis. Do you understand?" asked Alistair.

"Yeah, I think so, but Clergyman Perch mentioned that Journals get harder to read as they get older, is that right?"

"That is also true. The longer a Journal remains unread and untouched, the more difficult it will be to decipher, at least that *was* the theory. However you seem to be the exception, Charity." Alistair smiled at her kindly and she grinned back up at him then snapped the Journal shut.

"There's nothing in here about this woman." She said sadly.

"Not to worry Charity, we will forge ahead." replied Alistair

"Yes, well then, onto the Northern border it is!" Sophie boomed in a startlingly accurate impersonation of Alistair.

Charity guffawed with laughter as Alistair narrowed his eyes in Sophie's direction.

"Very amusing," he said quietly, and although he sounded frosty the corners of his mouth did twitch slightly.

"Are we near to Imputtia?" asked Charity,

"Near enough." Replied Alistair stomping along the platform to stare over the side.

"What's Imputtia like Alistair? I've never been. Is it *very* cold?" asked Sophie, sounding suddenly concerned..

"It is cold, yes, but like Dura, the conditions are more manageable as the sun shines. At nightfall however it is nearly impossible to survive the chilly winds and icy rain that batter the continent and that's without even considering the various beasts that roam the ice plains."

"Beasts?" asked Sophie, looking petrified. "What beasts?"

"All sorts, Sloaks, Wolves, even the powder rats grow to alarming sizes up there. It's not a great place for a trip, that much should be clear, but try not to worry. I will do my utmost to protect you both," he said, giving Sophie what he must've thought was a reassuring little shake but seemed to disorientate her so much so that she was forced to sit down beside Charity.

"Ok, so that's a thumbs down on the location, but how do we at least get there? Do we just walk into it? You know like Dura." asked Charity.

"No, no, no," Alistair said shaking his great head, "Imputtia has only one major city, Galcia. That is where we are headed now. The Sun-Lift should drop us at the border and we can board one of those new-fangled steam engines I've heard so much about. That should deliver us right into the heart of the city."

"Isn't there a way of walking? I'd prefer to stay as clear of the Order's influence as possible."

"As would I, but Imputtia is nothing but ice, snow and death. It is a land where nothing grows and only fearsome predators tread. There are no paths in the Ice Plains and we'd be lost as soon as the first snow storm hit. The only routes in and out of the cities and settlements are by steam engine or Ivory-drawn carriage."

"Ivory-drawn carriage?"

"Yes, hmm how to explain…well a carriage is like a box on wheel-"

"I know what a carriage is!" Charity said exasperatedly, "What do you mean *Ivory-drawn* carriage?" In her mind she could see a little wooden carriage being pulled by a huge ivory tusk that floated weightlessly above the ground.

"The Ivory Elephants, they are one of the few beasts of Imputtia that are not hostile to Theans."

"And they're like elephants that are made of Ivory are they?"

"No, they are elephants that bear the stripe of Ivory that runs from their distinctive tusks across their head and back. They are truly phenomenal workers, and can pull a carriage across the Ice Plains in a matter of days."

"Then why not get one of those? It'd be more personal?" asked Charity, who would've very much liked to see such creatures in action.

"Because they are the property of the Ivory Order," said Alistair simply. "Part of their success across Thea in their early years was down to being able to utilise the Ivory elephants. Any elephant used has to be driven be an Ivory official, and they're surely on the lookout for me, especially since I'm with *you*!" Alistair sat down heavily, making the platform drop several feet as he did so, the Sun-Cranes squawked indignantly at the vibration but kept flying north nonetheless.

....

"Alright my lovelies, that'll be all today. So off you pop back to Helper House and I'll make sure you know when dinner is ready. Any questions, by the way?"

"When will the bell be fixed, Gisele?"

"Well now I don't rightly know, we were told to take it outta commission soon after the attack. I reckon they just want to make sure nothing else goes wrong. Keeping a low profile the Order is, see and with less people visiting the chapter there's less cleaning to do and that means less reasons for you lot to stray too far, so just stay close to Helper House and if I really need yer I'll find yer."

"Alright," the group of children chorused.

"Do you still want *our* bells?" asked a tall boy with very black hair.

"Erm, yes s'pose so, not much use in you havin' 'em *now*, is there?"

The group lined up and one by one they dropped their tiny silver bells into a velvet green sack Gisele had pulled from a pocket and opened in front of them.

"Twelve, Thirteen, Fourteen, Fif - Oh is that our lot?"

The group glanced around at each other. "Has anyone not handed in their bell?" asked Gisele loudly to the assembled crowd.

The group shook their collective heads.

"Hmm, should be fifteen, we're missing one."

....

The Sun-Lift rattled on through the clear, mid-afternoon sky and Charity leaned over the little barrier to see what was found on the ground below. They were passing over yet more deserts, the wind-swept sand hundreds of miles below them was just the same as they had found back at Duradon. Thinking privately that she'd rather jump off one of the Forfal waterfalls than see another grain of sand, she sat back down.

"How long till we get there?" she asked Alistair and Sophie, who were both sitting on the floor of the Sun-Lift, Alistair with his back to the barrier and his traveller's hat pulled over his face and Sophie doodling absent-mindedly in the dust with her fingers. When Charity had spoken they had both looked up at her in surprise. Her question had broken their own personal thoughts and Charity wondered: if she had their Journals would she be able to find out exactly what they had been thinking about?

"It will not be long. The sun is at its highest point and we will reach the border before it falls beyond the horizon," Alistair said, not removing his hat from his face.

Charity leant on the barrier, watching yet more desert below. She was impatient and felt frustrated at not being able to find out who this mystery woman Calville seemed obsessed with. She was just considering revisiting the Journal for a third time that journey when something on the ground far below her caught her eye, a sudden change in colour. The bright yellow desert had surrounded them for miles, nothing but yellow with the occasional red or black rock. Now, however, the ground was suddenly spattered with speckles and spots of grey and white; indeed they had exploded into the scene below them so suddenly that Charity had to keep checking and rechecking their surroundings to make sure she wasn't imagining it. The four birds flapped onwards and as they did the the white became even more pronounced, taking up more of the scenery until finally after about ten minutes the entire ground was a sea of white powder.

"SNOW! THERE'S, THERE'S SNOW!!" yelled Charity pointing excitedly at the ground below them. Sophie scrambled to her feet and bolted over to the barrier leaning over, but Alistair remained where he was, seeming quite content on dozing.

"Woah!" said Sophie softly. "I can't believe it, I never thought I'd see the Ice Plains…" She tailed off, gazing in wonder at the glistening scene below.

"This *is not* the ice plains," Alistair said quietly from the floor.

"What? Why not, there's ice *and* snow!" said Sophie.

"We are travelling into Imputtia now. The border should be very close but the Plains are more than a mere smattering of snow upon the ground. They are almost untraversable and never ending, warped with gales and torrential blankets of snow that fall thick upon the ground and in front of your face. You'd be lucky if you could see your hand in front of your face up there."

"I don't understand," said Chairty, confused. "Are the Ice Plains not in Imputtia?"

"They are. Imputtia is the name for the continent, the huge mass of land we're *about* to enter. However, the Ice Plains are the expanse of truly awful land that takes up most of Imputtia." said Alistair patiently.

"Oh, I understand, sort of." said Charity sheepishly.

Alistair sighed deeply and lifted up his hat, better to look at them. "Look," he said pointing to the sky above them. "The sun is still shining, and we can see it in the clear blue sky. You will see soon enough that the sun does not shine on the Plains, or at least it is not truly visible behind the dark storm clouds that forever hang over the land like a shadow of doom."

"Why are you telling us this, Alistair?" asked Sophie, sounding concerned.

"Why? Because Calville clearly made it to the Plains and traversed them at least once, so it is looking increasingly likely that we will also have to venture out into them. The last thing in all of Thea that I want is for you two to underestimate the difficulty of the task ahead. If you do, then I promise that it *will* be the last thing you ever do." Alistair finished talking and tugged his hat down further over his face, crossing his arms.

Charity and Sophie stood staring at him. They had not expected such a dire warning and Charity could see that Sophie, already easily worried, was now white with terror. She couldn't think what to say to her, however, having never experienced the Plains herself, so she decided just to stay quiet and wait for the Sun-Lift to land.

She did not have to wait long. As it turned out Alistair was eerily accurate with his prediction and the Sun-Crane began to descend slowly after a couple of minutes. Thankfully there were none of the harsh winds or snow storms in the air and the sky was a cheery light blue, with even the sun seeming to shine brightly above their heads. The birds took a little change of direction and began swooping down towards a circle which seemed to be some sort of landing port for the lift. Moving down, Charity could see a huge wall stretching all the way along the horizon. It was pure white and must've been at least fifteen feet high. It reminded Charity of the wall that encompassed Duradon, although this wall was possibly even larger and stretched the whole way along the horizon, as far as she could see.

"What's that?' she asked, pointing into the distance at the wall.

"What's what? Oh the wall," said Sophie distractedly. "I think…that's the Ivory wall, well I mean it must be. I've only ever read about it, never actually seen it before."

"Yup," said Alistair still lying down.

"How did -" began Charity but Sophie had already launched into an explanation.

"Yeah, well it was built around the time of the Great War, just before it ended actually. Imputtia wanted to make sure no one could get to their capital city so they sacrificed nearly all of their pieces of ivory armour and weapons and used it to build a huge wall. Bit of a risky move, I reckon."

"Does it go the whole way across the border?" asked Charity, eyeing the wall with even more amazement.

"Yup, stretches all the way around Imputtia, or at least all the lands that they own. I guess they thought keeping everyone out was the best policy to win the war!"

"Did it work?"

"Well…no, it stopped anyone getting in but it meant they couldn't get out. Eventually the Imputtians had to venture from beyond the wall when they ran out of food but by then Aguish and Duran forces were camped out waiting for them. Imputtia surrendered and thus ended the war," finished Sophie astutely.

"Waste of time," mumbled Alistair curtly,

"The wall?" asked Charity as Alistair nodded mutely.

"Why?" she asked, curious.

"Because they don't need a wall, not with the Plains in between Galcia and everything else. It's only now that people can even get to Galcia without Ivory Elephants and they're bloody expensive."

"Why did they build it then?"

"They were desperate," said Alistair unhappily. "Most of Thea were against them at this point. It was the last act of dying movement, and not a wise one at that."

"Oh, I see," said Charity. "What's Galcia, by the way?"

"I told you, it's the capital of Imputtia, the only city in the whole continent and quite a status symbol for Thea's richest," said Sophie informatively.

"Galcia's the capital, ok got it…just about. And it's where all the rich people live?" Charity said, trying to digest these new facts as best she could. There was so much to remember, she wasn't sure she'd be able to process everything.

"Oh yeah the richest!" said Sophie, clearly excited to have the opportunity to impart yet more information to Charity. "I've read that Galcia's the wealthiest place on Thea! It used to be that only people with hundreds of Odes or really brave explorers could even travel there."

The little group chatted animatedly for a long time, as the great white wall came closer and closer. Soon they were descending upon the landing port and as the Sun-Lift landed with a soft thud onto the platform. Charity got up and stretched lazily. Looking back she could still see the yellow blur in the distance that she knew was the land of Dura. She felt a swell of pride in having travelled so far and yet her pride was extinguished almost at once by a nagging reminder in her head that she was still no one near finding her way home.

As usual the four Sun-Cranes sat for a short time grooming themselves with their long, thin beaks but once Charity, Sophie and Alistair had vacated the platform and Alistair had closed the barrier gate, the birds took off again, back in the direction they had come.

The group ventured onto the metallic walkway and Charity stared up at the great wall which loomed over them, casting a dark shadow across their path. Alistair led them down several flights of metal stairs, which they descended in silence. Charity was lost in her own thoughts about the Great War and how the Imputtians had managed to build such a structure. Breaking from her reverie, Charity realised they were actually heading underground. She could just about see the white wall above them now, bobbing out of sight as they walked. The sun was still shining high in the sky but it was becoming less visible the more they descended and soon it became too dark for even the sun's rays to penetrate. Thankfully, however, the wall to their right was lined with many Atra torches, so they were still able to see as they wove their way deeper underground.

The group filed off the final staircase and onto a cobbled footpath that was also lined with a row of burning torches. The roof above them was carved into the rock above and stretched far into the into the darkness in both directions. If she was honest, it looked to Charity like they had arrived in a huge underground tunnel. Charity could just hear the sound of something rather large in the distance. A combination of various noises, bangs, scrapes, whistles and voices, all mingling together into an unintelligible wave of sound that was just too far off to identify.

They began walking along the platform, towards the source of the noise. On one side of them was the wall, which stretched down from high above and on the other a seemingly limitless drop into the darkness, or at least it looked that way to her. Charity even leaned over tentatively to peek down into the gap but Sophie pulled her back.

"What are you doing? You might fall!" she warned reproachfully.

"I'm fine," she said dismissively. "Alistair, what's down there?"

"Tracks."

"Tracks?" asked Charity

"Ooooooo!" cooed Sophie excitedly, "we must be close to the engine then!"

Charity was about to question him further when her proposed question was answered for her. As they turned around a tight corner a most unexpected sight met her eyes: a sparkling white train positioned outside what looked like a huge platform a couple of feet from where they stood. The train was twice the size of any train Charity had ever seen, its surface seeming to be made entirely of white metal and connected to a large collection of similarly sized carriages. The first ten or twelve were the same majestic white as the head of the train but the others were slightly more modest looking, though just as large. These were plastered with advertisements and made of a dull grey iron or stone.

"That," said Alistair, jabbing a thumb in the direction of the train, "is the Imputtian Line, runs all the way from here to Galcia and all over Thea. Means people can finally get to Galcia if they want to, only opened a couple of years ago too."

"How did they get to Galcia before the line?"

"Had to brave the Plains didn't they? Wasn't an option for most," said Alistair ruefully.

"What are all those other carriages attached to the back?" asked Sophie.

"Goods and merchant ones mostly. Galcia is rich-pickings for salesmen these days, and plenty want their stock moved there."

"Is it really expensive Alistair? I mean I've only got…" Charity ruffled about in her jacket pocket, "ten, no eleven Odes left."

"It is not cheap. I believe nine Odes is the price of a one way to Galcia."

"NINE? For a ONE WAY!?" Charity spluttered. "I'll have barely anything left! How are we gonna get back?"

"Do not fret, I have a plan. Sophie do you have enough for yourself?"

"Um, yes, yes I think so," Sophie squeaked from behind Charity. She was fumbling in one of her pockets, and Charity could hear the rattling of the fat little coins in her hands.

"Very well, let us board. I would prefer if we didn't take the main carriage. The last white one will be sufficient."

Charity had just begun to wonder why Alistair had chosen *this* compartment, until she spotted three burly guards standing at the door to the first couple of carriages. The guards were dressed all in white, their shining cloaks and metallic helmets clashing violently with the white of the train behind them.

"Ivory Order guards!" she whispered, gesticulating towards them.

"They are Knights," said Alistair. "I want to remain quite inconspicuous, so I suggest we board the train now and pay on the way. The Knights will be sweeping the station soon."

They made their way through the bustling crowds, Alistair leading the way, his knees bent low to avoid detection. It was hardly a perfect plan, Charity thought, as she followed in his wake. His massive size still drew stares from others and some even openly pointed at him. Charity kept shooting glances over at the three Knights to see if they were aware of their presence but luckily they were all deep in conversation with one another, one miming a sword fight whilst the others nodded knowingly.

Soon they had reached one of the white carriages and Alistair lead them inside into one of the oddest rooms Charity had even been in. It was nothing like the trains she used to frequent back home. The compartments were almost completely empty except for eight silver poles that stood on either side. Charity at least recognised these as the poles people held onto when the train moved. Alistair turned to them and looking extremely relieved said, "Don't think they noticed us. We'd best use the upper floor though, no Order folk'll be patrolling through there, much too important."

Charity thought she had misheard him. "Upper floor?" she asked, staring at the low ceiling panelled in expensive looking oak slabs that looked very solid.

"Yes, upper floor. Just copy what I do," said Alistair. He walked up to one of the silver poles and, grasping it tightly with both hands, he stamped one mighty foot on the floor of the carriage. The floor around his feet seemed to lift into the air, the pole had begun to vibrate wildly and Alistair headed up and straight towards the ceiling. Charity closed her eyes, ready for the crashing sound as he tumbled from the platform and back to the floor but it never came. She opened her eyes and saw a large hole in the ceiling where Alistair had to have passed through. A yell came from above.

"Come on, hurry up!" he shouted as the platform passed back down through the hole and it closed up tight again as if nothing out of the ordinary had happened.

Sophie went next as Charity felt that she would need another demonstration of how these floating platforms seemed to work. Sophie gripped the platform with both hands, stamped her foot and again the little platform lifted off the floor, Charity now noticing that the piece of floor seemed to be sliding up the vibrating pole. The hole in the ceiling opened once more and swallowed Sophie through, closing again once the platform, now empty, had made its way back down to the floor where Charity still stood. Nervously she stepped forwards. People had started to flow into their compartment now and were either settling themselves on the floor or grabbing poles and moving upwards. She grabbed onto the nearest pole with both hands. It was icy cold, she thought, and wondered if her hands would even come away when she let go. She stamped her foot resolutely and for a horrible moment nothing happened. Panic beginning to swell up inside her and she made to let go but just as she did, the pole began to vibrate just as the others had done, and she felt herself drifting upwards. Even though she'd seen Sophie and Alistair go through the hole she couldn't stop herself bending low and bracing herself for a bump as she neared the oak ceiling, but no such collision came and as she passed through the hole she got her first view of the upper floor of the Imputtian Line compartment.

The ceiling was high and curved and the side windows stretched all the way along the compartment, which looked almost twice as big as the one below. It was laden with white chairs and tables, all strewn randomly about the room and a crystal chandelier with burning candles swung from the centre of the room bathing them all in a pleasant glow.

"We shall be much safer here," said Alistair in a hushed tone.

The compartment was busy but not full so they managed to gather three seats together in the far corner near one of the windows, as Charity had insisted on being able to see their surroundings. Sophie had said she was feeling tired and decided to catch up on some sleep and after Alistair had assured them that it would be quite a while until they reached Galcia, Charity had also closed her eyes and attempted to get some much needed rest.

20 – SPARKS FLY

"Charity! Charity, wake up! Charity!" a voice was calling her, bidding her to wake from her slumber.

"Wha, hmm, later," mumbled Charity sleepily.

"Charity you don't wanna miss this, c'mon!" moaned a familiar voice. She realised that it belonged to Sophie, who was tugging forcibly at her arm, jostling her awake. Unable to slip back into sleep, Charity sighed heavily and very reluctantly opened her eyes. The dim light of the chandelier above was just pleasantly dull enough to allow her eyes to adjust to the carriage. She could see that nothing had changed in the carriage, it was still the same as it had been when she had drifted off to sleep, but outside the great windows, the scene was something else entirely.

The huge windows that stretched all along each side of the compartment looked out upon a blanket of white seemingly enveloping the entire Imputtian line. Charity stared through the window but it was like staring at a blank canvas. There wasn't a dot of colour present, nor was there any scenery, sky or ground, she could see nothing but unending, impenetrable white.

"Is that the snow? I don't understand, why isn't it stopping the train?" she asked, deeply confused.

"The steam engine runs along a track protected by a glass tunnel, it runs the whole way along the border and up to Galcia. It really was the only way the people of Imputtia could guarantee getting the line to run smoothly through such conditions." said Alistair.

"So that outside, that's the snow *on* the glass?"

"Correct. The snow storms on the Plains are almost unending, so the view from the line is almost always," he waved a huge hand at the window, "rather bland."

"Are the Plains just in one place?" asked Sophie,

"They are not, like I explained earlier, they are the name given for any part of land on Imputtia that is not populated. There aren't many places habitable for Theans, so that makes them quite expansive. Really there only a few small settlements scattered across the continent, and of course the capital city, Galcia."

"Are we near there now?" asked Charity, eager to know more.

"It is very hard to tell, but considering the time we have been on the line I would estimate that it won't be too much longer."

The scenery outside did not change from the relentless stream of white and after a while Charity began to get the feeling that she was stuck inside a giant snow globe. Fortunately, however the carriage was comfortable, warm and fairly spacious so she, Sophie and Alistair were able to spend the remainder of the journey chatting animatedly about where the next page would be and what obstacles they may have to overcome.

"I think it'll have something to do with Igniculi," said Sophie, her eyes alight with enthusiasm.

"What's an Ig-nuck-a-lie?" asked Charity, sounding out the word with difficulty. She felt as though Sophie had mentioned this word before but couldn't quite recall when.

"Wow!" said Sophie slowly. "It's weird to think that someone doesn't know about them. Suppose you wouldn't know about the temple either then?"

For a response Charity simply looked blankly at Sophie, who seemed to understand. Alistair meanwhile had opted to stare out of the window and not be involved in the conversation.

"Well, ok, this is kind of difficult to explain but in Imputtia there's, well it's a bit like a church, sort of, I mean it's nothing to do with the old Gods or Thea but ummm…" Sophie was clearly struggling with her explanation; she screwed up her face in concentration, thinking hard, then an idea seemed to hit her. "Ah! Right, well, it's more of a school actually. Yeah, a school, where you can go and learn all about Igniculi and how to become one."

"Ok…" said Charity slowly, "But what *is* an Ig-nicer-li?"

"*Ig-nick-uh-lie,*" Sophie said patiently, smiling at Charity's frustration. "They are special Theans who can use the elements to their advantage. Igniculi can create fires, make water move and even freeze things, and most of the more complex machinery on Thea is powered by Igniculus magic, like the water rail. But not everyone can do things on a big scale. Only the most gifted can do stuff like that."

"Have you ever tried it?"

"Oh Thea no! There's no book on the topic, no instructional ones anyways, besides it's very difficult to explain *how,* think it's just something you can or can't do. There's only the one temple in all of Thea that teach it and it's in Imputtia, so I've never had a chance to even visit." Sophie was suddenly acting very peculiarly. "We could…maybe…go?" her face was light and casual but Charity saw the glint of desperation in her green eyes.

"I dunno," said Charity sarcastically, Sophie's face fell comically. "Not sure if we'd have the time, we're *sooooo* busy you see."

"But, but…"

"What d'you think Alistair?"

"Very well. We should just have time to see the Sparks," said Alistair distractedly, still staring out of the carriage window, lost in thought.

"Oh, you mean it! Oh Thea, that's wonderful news!" said Sophie excitedly.

"Wait, Sparks? What do you mean: 'see the Sparks?" asked Charity. But before could even turn from the snow outside, Sophie answered for him.

"That's what they call Igniculi: Sparks," said Sophie. "Something to do with sparking up fires I think, like I said, I've only read *about* them, never actually met one before."

Just then a man dressed all in white swept into the carriage through a door at the far end, and for a heart-stopping second Charity thought he was an Order member and made to push Alistair out of sight. As he walked towards them, however, she saw thin red stripes upon his white jacket and an unfamiliar logo emblazoned on one of the breast pockets. The logo, which had been stitched to the jacket, depicted a snow flake surrounded by a circle of train tracks with the letters I.L.C woven below in navy blue lettering. Sophie had spotted the man now too and had begun rummaging in the insides of her jacket.

"What are you doing?" asked Charity looking at Sophie, whose tongue was sticking out of her mouth in concentration as she reached for something in one of her inside pockets.

"Getting Odes. We need to pay before we arrive."

"Pay? Is that the ticket master then?"

"Yeah, that's him. Fancy uniform eh?" smiled Sophie, removing a handful of golden coins and dropping them onto the empty seat beside her.

"What does I.L.C stand for?" asked Charity, imitating Sophie and pulling out her own bag of Odes, pouring them out onto her lap.

"Imputtian Line Company, I think."

"Oh, yeah, shoulda guessed that I suppose." said Charity, absentmindedly. "Do you have enough?"

"Yea, how much did you say, Alistair?" asked Sophie distractedly counting the golden coins.

"Nine."

"Yeah, I've enough, just," Sophie said, looking with concern at the tiny pile of Odes on the seat beside her.

The ticket master had almost drawn level with them now. There were only two other people in the compartment, a squat little woman whom the ticket master had to shake until she awoke and a bald man with a great top hat perched upon his head, who had thrust a handful of coins at the ticket master before he had had time to even open his mouth.

"Single or return?" the ticket master said in a weary voice as he reached them.

"Three singles please," Sophie said, smiling warmly at him. He did not return her smile but instead withdrew a long sleeve of paper tickets from a pocket and tore off one for each of them.

"You paying separate?" he asked curtly.

"That's right," said Sophie bracingly, continuing to smile at the man. Charity admired her perseverance but thought it most unlikely to change the man's mood.

"Nine Odes each," he said, still unsmiling.

"Here," said Alistair, handing a fistful of coins to him. The ticket master poured the coins into his other pocket and handed one of the tickets to him. Charity and Sophie imitated him and were both handed a ticket by the surly ticket master in return. Charity sat, examining her ticket with great interest. It was lightly stamped with the same logo that embroidered the ticket master's uniform and the word 'single' was imprinted on the back in black, block lettering.

The train was beginning to slow now, and Charity could hear the rumbling of the engine quieten slightly and the high pitched brakes intermittently screech into life. The carriage suddenly gave a great shunt forwards and Charity was thrown towards the chair in front of her. Alistair caught her with one outstretched hand just before she hit the ground. The ticket master had stumbled too but managed to grab a hold of their seats.

Steadying himself, he muttered, "Wilson, don't be so hard on the brakes! Thea help us, we'll be killed one of these days."

He sidled carefully out of the carriage the way he had come as the train rolled to a much smoother stop.

Alistair stood up, fixing his traveller's cloak about him as he did so. He walked to one of the silver poles and looked over at Charity and Sophie, a determined glint in his eyes. "Come," he commanded, and the two girls obeyed quickly.

Placing her hands on the pole once more, Charity gave another stamp and sailed downwards, this time descending into the lower compartment below which was now full of bustling people. There was a great commotion as the platform moved closer to the ground and the people jostled to get out of the way. Eventually her little platform thudded against the ground of the carriage below and Charity hopped off into the crowd of people making their way towards the exit.

Following Alistair, with Sophie close behind her, Charity made her way out of the carriage and through a bustling tunnel much like the one the train had passed through on their journey. The walls and ceiling were plastered with white from the snow outside and the torches on the ceiling seemed to illuminate the snow so it shone all around them. Alistair turned, making sure they were still following him. "This way," he said loudly, walking up a flight of stairs and out into the midst of a vibrant city. Great walls of cobbled stone rose up all around them. The city seemed to comprise mostly classical buildings. Charity spotted what she thought were old churches and a grand hotel nearby. The sky was just as snow white as the tunnel had been and Charity, looking carefully, could see that the whole city was in fact enclosed in a gigantic dome of its own.

Galcia was easily the most magnificent city Charity had seen on Thea. It dwarfed both Upper Forfal and Duradon and Charity could instantly see why the wealthy were attracted to such a place. The people spilling out from the staircase flowed into the city like ants, scuttling away down the many side streets and avenues that littered the place. Charity could see shops and stalls that sold all manner of things, including potions, weapons, books, Journal accessories and much more. She tried to take in everything but the bustling city was bursting with such unusual sights, sounds and smells that she found herself simply staring, slack jawed around at everything. Alistair stood beside her and Sophie beside him. He looked proudly around at the city, breathing in the sights and smells for himself, while Sophie looked just as awestruck as Charity.

"Well," he said bracingly, "I did promise you a visit to the Sparks," and he purposefully set off down one of the busy side streets.

"We're going now!?" asked Sophie, running to catch up with him and looking as if she was about to explode with excitement.

"Yes, now," said Alistair, smiling at her.

"Shouldn't we be going after the other page? Surely, we need to get to the Ice Plains!" said Charity who felt that as amusing as Sophie's reaction was, they surely needed to prioritise Calville's journey.

"We have time for a small de-tour." Said Alistair, "Beside we have to prepare."

"Prepare, can't we just get going?" said Charity impatiently. The encouragement of the discovery in Dura had made home seem slightly close than it had ever been on Thea and the longer they spent wondering about with Sparks, the longer she would take to get there.

Alistair looked at her seriously. "You saw outside the train, did you not?" She nodded mutely. "Well I have a vey strong feeling that we shall soon face those same elements. Do you think we are prepared to venture into the Plains without proper planning?"

Charity suddenly felt very stupid indeed. "No," she said in a small voice.

"Do not feel bad, you are eager, there is nothing wrong with that. But *this*," he waved around at Galcia, "Is all part of your journey, and learning to plan your moves *before* you make them is a sure strategy for victory!"

"I know, it's just…" Charity began.

"It's just you wish to get started. I understand, perhaps more than *you* will ever know. I feel that we all could do with a little rest before such a dangerous trip. I would also like to get some supplies, which we will most certainly need if we are to remain alive whilst out on the Plains – which as any explorer worth his ink will tell you, is most unheard of," finished Alistair darkly.

Charity's eyes widened at this, and she looked at Sophie, expecting to see a similar reaction but she was no longer walking beside her. Instead she had bounded forwards and was hurrying along in front of them, her eyes fixed on something large and majestic some way down the cobbled side street.

"There it is, there it is!" she shouted happily, bouncing up and down and pointing down the street at a very old, but very regal looking building with a large sign outside it. Squinting, Charity could just make out the words:

'Temple of the Igniculus'. She could see why Sophie had thought this organisation was a bit like a church. At first glance she thought it *was* a church, it even had the same spires and stained glass windows that Charity associated with one from back home.

"That's the Spark place, right?" Charity asked Alistair, as Sophie hurtled towards the building like a small child running into a sweet shop.

"That's it, but don't call it that inside, these types get very uppity about their practices. Just say Igniculi or Temple of the Igniculus," said Alistair in a whisper, then seeing the perplexed look on Charity's face he added. "I know it's a mouthful all right, just try your best and if you can't pronounce it, then...just don't say anything, don't want to offend them. We may need them."

When they reached the grand double doors of the Temple of the Igniculus, Sophie was waiting for them, fidgeting impatiently and bobbing up and down like a rabbit as her hand hovered over the door.

"Should we go in?" she said, her high pitched voice barely concealing her obvious excitement.

Charity smiled to herself and pushed the doors open with Sophie. Looking over, she saw a broad grin now stretched across her thin face.

The temple was hardly spectacular, she thought. It certainly didn't live up to the hype Sophie had surrounded it with. They had stepped into a huge hall that was, as far as Charity could see, almost empty except for several long benches that were lined up against the walls. The walls themselves were laden with burning candles and long emerald green drapes, each of which had a symbol Charity had never seen before emblazoned on them. At first she had thought she'd been seeing things but looking closer she saw that the symbol was that of a severed human hand with three of its fingers pushed together and a bright orange flame set behind it.

At the far end of the room was large set of double doors, which partly concealed two sets of staircases, and in the centre a small, square platform that was just visible amongst a group of people who were currently on top of it. There were five people in all, four of them sitting cross legged on the little square, each with their backs to them. One particular figure stood out from the rest as he was standing before the other four, rocking back and forth in a very unusual manner. His head was bent low and his hands clasped together, as if in prayer. Charity had no idea what he was doing but Sophie seemed almost giddy having spotted him.

Charity and the others walked forwards into the temple, their footsteps echoing around the room. The seated figures turned to face them, some curious, others agitated.

"Oh my! That's…that's…" babbled Sophie.

Charity did not find out who the man was, as at that very moment one of the seated figures got to his feet and hurried towards them. He looked intensely annoyed at the interruption into what was obviously a very private gathering.

"Yes, yes, yes? What is it?" he snapped.

"Um," said Charity awkwardly. She looked helplessly at both Sophie and Alistair, she had no idea *why* they were here and had no clue what to tell the man.

"Um?" he retorted. "Are you to take away the broken pew?" He indicated a bench that had been smashed clean in two.

"We're here to watch, please Sir, we've travelled a long way and I've *always* wanted to see the Igniculi at work. Could we maybe stay and watch just for a little bit?" Sophie pleaded, positively quivering with excitement. The man was thin with grey hair and wore spindly black rimmed spectacles; Charity thought he looked like an old librarian. He was clearly greatly agitated by their presence but seemed distracted by something in the centre of the room; he kept glancing quickly back to the square platform and then at Sophie who was still staring imploringly up at him.

"Fine, fine, just sit down over there, and whatever you do *don't interrupt!*" he said in a worried whisper, cajoling them to one of the little benches at the side of the room and bustling back to his place on the square platform. Charity and Sophie sat down and Alistair did so too, lowering himself apprehensively onto the fragile looking bench, which creaked under his considerable frame. Charity watched on curiously, smiling at Sophie, who was now sat so far forwards that she was almost off the bench entirely.

For about two minutes absolutely nothing happened. The man standing on the square remained quite silent, still rocking his head back and forth as his audience sat in similar silence, staring up in awe at the mysterious figure. From their seats, Charity could finally get a good look at the man now. He had flowing black hair that was almost as long as Sophie's, a portion of which he had tied back into a neat ponytail. The remainder of his hair fell down his back, where it clashed with the dark cloak he wore around his shoulders. His face was partly concealed by a wispy, black goatee and Charity saw that he had, unusually, placed his purple Journal on the outside of his clothes, much like the Ivory Order Knights tended to do.

The black clad man had begun chanting something in a low whisper, his mouth barely opening, and yet Charity could hear a low rumbling of speech from his direction, and very soon the little ensemble had begun to imitate him. They grew in volume until Charity could just make out what they were chanting, "Little Spark, small and lonely, Little Spark, we tend and grow. Little Spark, locked inside us, Little Spark, whose power we know." Charity glanced at Sophie, who looked confused but no less enraptured by the unusual chants, and then at Alistair who was nodding knowingly beside her. He seemed to understand these words. She opened her mouth to ask him what they meant, but no sooner had she begun to speak than he turned to face her, shaking his head disapprovingly. Hugely confused by the events, Charity closed her mouth.

The chanting was now reverberating about the entire chamber and Charity could see the bearded man begin to straighten up. He had stopped his own chanting now and had reached out his arms to the ceiling, his eyes remaining closed and the look on his face triumphant. With a small gesture he elegantly raised one hand into the air, his thumb, forefinger and middle finger raised; the little group had raised their voices to a shout by now but at this action they fell silent almost at once. He waited a whole minute before moving and Charity had to admit that this did create a sufficiently tense atmosphere in the chamber; she waited excitedly to see what would happen next.

The man opened his eyes, revealing dark brown eyes and spoke – not only to the group in front of him but to the entire room – in a crackling voice, that sounded far too old to be his own.

"Ladies, Gentleman, thank you for coming." He paused again, savouring the attention he was receiving. "I feel that considering the worrying rumours that have been riding on the winds, we should be discussing what the Temple of Igniculus' position is regarding these 'tensions'." He stopped suddenly, staring down at his audience. "Ah, but I cannot continue one second more, until I address *this*...We have a new face here." He gestured to one of the seated figures who shuffled back on his bottom nervously. "Now, now brother, please do not show fear. I can see from your lack of a badge that you have not been initiated – would that be correct?"

The figure, who turned out to be a boy that looked to be in his mid-teens, answered in a petrified voice, "Y-y-yes Master Ruven."

"Ah superlative! I do love new recruits, it gives me a chance to..." he flashed a toothy smile at the other three on the floor, "get *warmed* up..."

The rest of the seated figures laughed, however Charity did not understand the joke, if indeed it was meant to be one. The bearded man had pulled the new recruit to his feet with surprising ease. "Now stand up straight, man, c'mon, yes, just like that," he said, pulling the man's legs apart. "Shoulder-width, yes, almost there!"

"That's Ruven," whispered Sophie in a barely audible whisper. "He's the most gifted Igniculi in all of Thea."

Charity looked at the man named Ruven. He certainly looked mystical, she thought, with his long thin frame and jet black hair he looked just like what she thought an ancient fortune teller would look like. Ruven was weaving around the man in the centre of the square now, darting in and adjusting his body shape and then jumping back to take in the full image. He continued this practice for some time, shaking his head and tutting to himself, "There's something just not..." he said distractedly. "I know, left foot forwards, just a bit, ah, theeeere we go, perfect!"

The man now stood, looking increasingly awkward in the centre of the square. In fact Charity thought he looked as though he might collapse in a heap any moment now. Ruven, however, looked more than satisfied and he copied the man's stance beside him, so that the pair of them closely resembled two very odd looking statues. "You will have no doubt been recommended by someone?" he asked the man.

"My, my brother Richard," the man answered shakily.

"Richard, ah yes, a gifted Igniculi. Then there are some considerable expectations of you…" he left the statement hanging, waiting for the man to provide his name but the man remained quite silent, his face frozen in fear.

"Your name, my good man, what is your name?" said Ruven smiling.

"Thomas. It's Thomas, my name I mean."

"A fine name. Well then, Thomas just watch me and listen carefully. As I'm sure you are aware, Igniculi are those who prize one thing above all else: focus. To truly focus is to talk to one's soul, tap into potential, syphon away distractions and unnecessary thoughts and be left with your pure emotions. There are many variations of Igniculus magic and some take years to master but fortunately we have a very concise way of gauging *your* ability immediately."

Charity listened intently. Ruven certainly knew how to captivate an audience; he spoke eloquently and quietly and yet she caught every word. Despite his mystical appearance he gave the impression that he was very comfortable addressing a crowd. Thomas, on the other hand looked like he was going to be sick, his face very green as he wobbled ominously and attempted to remain in his awkward standing position.

"Close your eyes," Ruven commanded and Charity watched Thomas close his eyes. She looked over at Sophie, who to her surprise had also closed her eyes. Alistair too had leant back and closed his eyes in concentration – or he could simply be taking a nap, she wasn't sure. Despite feeling rather foolish, she too closed her eyes and listened to Ruven. "Empty all thoughts from your mind. Your Journal should be blank, unreadable, a page without ink, a mind without thoughts. Once you have achieved this state – and it *will* take time, do not rush – once you have reached this state raise your strong hand into the air," His voice was smooth and relaxing.

Charity wondered what her strong hand was and supposed that it must be

313

the one she wrote with. She raised her right hand. Her mind didn't seem particularly empty but she ventured on nonetheless.

"Now you must withdraw the three weapons necessary for an Igniculi; your thumb, your forefinger and your middle finger." Ruven said dramatically.

"Bring them together and focus your mind once more, focus on a fire, a little fire, flames licking and embers dancing, try to picture the fire inside your head. When you have that image etched onto your very Journal then bring your instruments together once more and click, spark the fire yourself, make…it…happen." Charity heard Ruven click his fingers together but kept her eyes shut tight. She clicked her own fingers but did not feel any different. She slowly opened her eyes and nearly fell off her seat in shock. Ruven was standing quite casually where he had been, but in his left hand was a tongue of fire, flickering and wavering on the end of his thumb.

Ruven turned to Thomas who was looking increasingly frustrated. "I don't think I can do it," Thomas said sadly, clicking his fingers madly, his still eyes shut tight. Ruven clicked his own fingers once more and the fire disappeared into nothingness. He turned to Thomas, a consoling look on his face.

"Do not worry, you have sufficient abilities Thomas. It is very rare to see an uninitiated perform such a feat on their first attempt, but if we can get a spark we will have hope." He manoeuvred Thomas' fingers together, slipping his thumb into a more prominent position. "Now click." Thomas closed his eyes and clicked his fingers but again nothing happened.

"No, no! Open your eyes now man. Your mind is clear and focused, I can feel it. Just click!" Thomas clicked and clicked, snapping his fingers together so much that Charity thought the friction alone would set them alight. Then very suddenly, a tiny blue spark issued from one of his click-fevered finger snaps.

"There, there, did you see it?" Thomas said happily. "I did it!"

"You did my man. Congratulations, a fine start!" said Ruven, heartily slapping Thomas on the back. Thomas was staring in awe at his own fingers. He clicked them again and another blue spark danced from his thumb.

"Excellent! Well Thomas, one of the Igniculi will take your details and you will hear from us in due time. I dear say you will want to tell your dear brother yourself."

Thomas nodded happily and Ruven motioned for him to retake his seat on the platform. "Well, before we get down to business, it seems a waste to not flex one's fingers. Shall I give you a demonstration of what young Thomas will be able to do when he has been adequately trained?" Thomas looked delighted, his youthful face shining with joy as he and the rest of the little group murmured their approval of Ruven's offer.

Ruven held aloft both his hands and clicked his fingers in the same characteristic manner as before. All of a sudden a thin line appeared between both his hands, a line that appeared to be made of fire, giving off wafts of smoke as it lay suspended between his two hands. Ruven clicked away from the line and it remained there, levitating precisely where he had left it. He clicked three more times and as he did Charity noticed two shapes coming into existence in front of her eyes, shapes that smoked and sparked just like the line. She tilted her head trying to make out what Ruven was conjuring, as he continued to click the air, like a gifted painter adding finishing touches to his masterpiece. She could see two needles now, one large and magnified, its eye large enough for them to see right through and the other thin and miniscule, just visible beside Ruven's left ear. Both of these majestic creations flickered and burned in the air and Charity was sure that they too were made of burning fire.

Charity watched, open-mouthed, as Ruven clicked dramatically in the air in the direction of the little needle. He waved his hand majestically and the needle followed it, soaring through the air towards the thin line. Charity and Sophie both gasped out loud as the small needle picked up the string as it flew past, Ruven motioned as it wove its way towards the eye of the larger needle, and with amazing accuracy, it looped through the eye and tied the string in a perfect bow around the head.

Ruven clapped his hands together and the objects disappeared suddenly in a cloud of black smoke. He clicked again and this time a bird Charity instantly recognised as a Sun-Crane appeared above his head. He clicked as the bird soared all around him, leaving a twisting trail of smoke in its wake. He placed his hand out flat and the fiery bird landed delicately on his palm. Charity saw how it did not seem to cause him pain, although some of the hairs on his hand gave off faint spirals of smoke as they were singed by the little firebird's wings. Ruven smiled at the tiny Sun-Crane. He clicked once more and the bird gave a little squawk and disappeared into the air with puff of smoke.

The figures on the floor whooped and clapped as Ruven bowed low to the floor, smiling serenely. "Brothers, thank you, thank you, I -" He stopped short. Something had just caught his eye, something very close to where Charity, Sophie and Alistair were sitting. "What's this now?" he said, his eyes narrowed suspiciously.

Charity watched him hop off the square platform and stride purposefully towards them, his black cloak billowing out behind him as he walked. Charity glanced at Alistair in alarm but he looked just as nonplussed as she did. Sophie too looked bewildered and Charity saw how she was staring at Ruven, something like disbelief on her face, her hands cupped together as if she were begging forgiveness. Ruven stood before the bench and addressed all three of them.

"You are new initiates?" he asked expectantly.

"No," said Alistair, who had pulled his hat down low over his face. "Pardon our intrusion but one of our party greatly wanted to see some Spar- some Igniculi displays." He corrected himself quickly and indicated Sophie with a massive hand.

"Not at all! I welcome any interested to come and find out as much about the temple as possible. I always say, 'misinformation means malicious mumblings'." He smiled at them with a mouth full of glistening white teeth and then turned his full attention to Sophie.

"But *you* my dear, you are something different. Interested is one thing but, ahhh!" He breathed out softly, pulling away one of Sophie's hands gently and revealing a protruding orange flame which was burning merrily away on the end of her thumb.

"Your name, my dear?"

"Sophie, Sophie Pierce." she said quietly, her eyes flicking between his face and the little flame on the end of her thumb.

"Well Sophie, if you want to put that out," he clapped his hands together with a loud, "SNAP!" and Sophie reluctantly imitated him, the flame was extinguished immediately, leaving nothing but a wisp of smoke and the faint smell of burning.

"Whom may I ask initiated you, my dear?" asked Ruven, a tangible sense of excitement in his wheezy voice,

"I, well I um, I haven't really *been* initiated." Muttered Sophie, reddening under Ruven's intense stare.

Ruven did not respon immediately, he mouthed something Charity could not hear and then glanced furtively at Charity and Alistair.

"You're not seriously telling me you've never tried to achieve the Little Spark before now, are you?"

"Well, I mean, I've *tried* but I've never managed more than a little bit of a blue before now."

"My dear," began Ruven sounding awed, "Such a feat, and you could not be more than sixteen years."

"Fifteen." Replied Sophie softly.

"Fifteen…." whispered Ruven, his eyes widening in surprise.

Charity looked from Ruven who was staring down at Sophie as though she were a child of his own, she looked at Sophie whose eyes were flitting between Ruven and her still outstretched hand. Noone moved or spoke for what seemed like a long time and then without warning, Ruven clapped his hands together once more making them all jump.

"Sophie," said Ruven enthusiastically. You know we're always on the lookout for new recruits."

"I, I, Oh Thea, I don't know, I just…"

Sophie looked desperately from Charity to Ruven for some time before bursting out, "I can't! I'm sorry, Ruven, sir, I just I made a promise to Charity that I'd help her and I have to see it through but I promise when I'm done I'll come back."

Ruven looked a little shocked at having seen his invitation rejected but composed himself quickly. "My dear, whatever the heart wishes is the right path. You may return whenever you like but I can sense great things in your future and you may not be the same little girl that stands before me now."

Alistair stood up suddenly.

"We really should be going now," he said solemnly and without another word to Ruven he made his way to the exit. Charity followed soon after with Sophie, who had issued further apologies and hurried promises to Ruven that she would indeed return. He had nodded in an understanding way and bade them goodbye quite cheerfully but something about him made Charity uneasy. Despite all his attention being on Sophie she could not shake the feeling that he was intensely aware of *her* presence.

When they reached the door leading out of the Igniculus temple it swung open without them touching it and a figure entered, sweeping his way inside and shutting the door tightly behind him. The figure was a tall, bald man with a long white beard that almost reached his knees. He was dressed completely in a white gown and Charity saw, fear bubbling in the pit of her stomach, the flash of a silver brooch attached to his lapel. She looked closely at it but realised with immense relief that it was not an Ivory Order badge, but had a small snowflake on it, not unlike the Imputtian line logo. She turned to acknowledge this with Alistair but realised that he was almost completely out of sight. He had taken two swift steps into the corner of the room, his hat bent low and his cloak about his face. Charity and Sophie, however, hadn't reacted quickly enough and the man had entered the chamber stopping purposefully right in front of them.

The man was very tall, almost as tall as Alistair, but much thinner and his light blue eyes, although surrounded by a lined and wrinkled face showed a keen intellect. When he spoke, it was with a deep, commanding voice that Charity had not expected. Neither had Sophie, apparently, as she gripped Charity's arm in shock when he first addressed them.

"Ah, Charity. Charity Walters, isn't it?"

Charity's mind began to race. How did he know who she was? She looked up into his eyes. They were the palest shade of light grey, and she could almost have mistaken them for white in the right light; for some reason those eyes made her feel very nervous.

"Yes, yes that's me." Charity said, trying to sound confident, she had briefly considered lying but something about those eyes made her think that this man was not to be fooled.

"Oh, how fascinating. I've been simply dying to meet you my dear!" He dropped his voice to a whisper. "You know, there have been all sorts of funny rumours flying about. You two are quite the talk of the town up here."

"Oh, well I'm not sure about –" started Charity edging towards the door.

"My dear, you can't go – I've barely introduced myself!" said the man jovially, sticking out a long thin arm to block Charity and Sophie's escape. "I am Euphestus, although here I suppose you would call me Chancellor," he said in a lofty voice. "I am the man charged with the unenviable task of running this entire city."

"That's great!" said Charity, slowly edging around Euphestus' outstretched arm as Sophe continued to cling on to her own arm with a vice-like grip.

"Oh and this must be Sophie. Fantastic to meet you my dear, truly it is a wonder to see you both here." He furrowed his brow in what Charity assumed was mock confusion, "Tell me what *are* you doing up here so far north?"

"We're looking for something," said Charity flatly.

"You *are*?" said Euphestus with great interest. "My, my, what a mystery, I don't suppose you would tell the Chancellor of Imputtia what you were looking *for* now would you?"

"I don't think we can…sir," said Charity apologetically, and Euphestus' face fell as he clasped his hands together dramatically.

"No, no I quite understand, don't worry. I've heard the tales, I am very well acquainted with the Cardinal. Such *interesting* reports but," he tapped his long nose secretively, "my lips are sealed."

"Thank you, Sir. Could, could we perhaps be going now?" said Charity, indicating the doors behind him.

"Oh my, of course, why off you go, but -" he grabbed Charity's arm as she passed, "- I must insist that you come visit the palace. It's up *past* the Ivory Order Chapter. That's the big white building so you shan't miss it."

Euphestus released her arm and she sped out of the room at as casual a pace as she thought was necessary and turned to see Alistair slink through the door a couple of seconds later. He kept a normal pace until he reached them.

"Move, now!" he whispered softly, passing them by at a very brisk walk. She followed diligently until they had walked what felt like the full length of the city, when Alistair stopped outside a tall, thin house of the same cobbled, discoloured stone as the ground.

"I thought that was an Ivory Order member!" said Sophie.

"Me too, the badge, I nearly died!" said Charity.

"Likewise," added Alistair. "However it is not an unreasonable assumption to make. Imputtia is home to the largest Order Chapter in all of Thea. Most of the Order's control comes from Imputtia, and for many years its solitude was key to the Order's secrecy and power."

"So he's chancellor of Imputtia?"

"Yes, Euphestus, He controls Imputtia in the same way Queen Mosia controls Dura. He's the figure head of the nation."

"Should we visit Euphestus?" asked Sophie. "He might be able to help us with the quest."

"I do not know. I am aware that he has a lot of power and this would doubtless make him a valuable ally, but I have also heard disconcerting rumours about him. I do not believe he is as jovial as he seems," said

Alistair, furrowing his brow. "For now I suggest we get a night's rest, we have travelled long and far."

Charity looked up and saw that the building they were standing beside did in fact have a small sign nailed to the door: 'Rapier's Inn: all welcome'. Alistair had already moved to the door and opened it, and as he did so a little bell chimed above his head. Charity watched as he sidled up to a large wooden desk and after a brief conversation, paid a young girl several Odes in exchange for two large iron keys. He then he lead them up a very crooked flight of stairs to a hallway containing half a dozen red doors.

"Two rooms. One for me," he said indicating a door which he opened. "That one should be yours. The girl said it'd be open." Alistair bade them goodnight and entered his room, shutting the door behind him. Charity and Sophie did the same. Their room was surprisingly pleasant, modestly furnished with two large comfortable looking beds against the far wall.

Before they retired for the night, Charity and Sophie sat up whilst Charity read aloud from Calville's Journal. Sophie greatly enjoyed listening to the tales of Calville and Charity felt it was prudent to read as much about the trip he had been on as possible. This way they would be adequately prepared.

One passage in particular caught Charity's eye:

'My first trip to the Ice Plains, they are as rugged and impassable as was written, *Florence and I are becoming closer, merely as friends of course.* **She was instrumental in crossing the pit within the Dura temple and I doubt I would be standing here if it wasn't for her constant support. Our plan is to circle the mountains until the weather dies down and search for a safe route up, if reports are correct then the Haven should be somewhere in the midst of the mountain range.** *Florence suggested we fly,* **quite out of the question, no creature on Thea could withstand the winds and rains of Imputtia.'**

The two discussed these events deep into the night and Sophie delighted Charity by lighting up her thumb and extinguishing it. She had been practicing continually since they left the temple of Igniculus and was now quite proficient at it. Eventually they both succumbed to sleep, however, and the last thing Charity saw before she nodded off was Sophie's thin face illuminated by the faint light of her own thumb as she held it close to her face.

21 – INTO THE STORM

The next morning Charity rose early. Over the course of her journey she had become quite used to doing so and was now fully accustomed to washing and dressing herself in the light of the red morning sun. After making sure Calville's Journal was safely stored in her jacket, she readjusted her hair in a long mirror and followed Sophie downstairs. When they reached the reception area Alistair was already waiting for them beside the check-in desk. Charity felt refreshed from her comfortable stay at the inn and was now more eager than ever to accomplish more of her quest. Even the potential trip to the Ice Plains couldn't dampen her spirits. As they left Rapier's Inn, Charity noticed that it was pleasantly warm in Galcia, although she supposed that this was mostly due to the fact that they were living inside a giant snow globe, sheltered from the winds and snow outside. She wondered how people were able to breathe inside the dome but she supposed that like everything in Thea there would be an explanation that she was expected to already know, nod along to and then blithely accept. In any case, she *could* breathe and was therefore perfectly happy to wait until later on to find out how this was possible.

Something whizzed past them as they left the tiny inn, just brushing past Charity's nose as she stepped into the high street. It moved much too fast for Charity to get a proper look at it but whatever it was flew on, a little white blur hurtling into the distance, over people's heads and round buildings and lampposts.

"Argh!" yelled Charity. "What was that?"

"A dove," said Alistair calmly. "It's on its way to the Ivory Order Chapter."

Charity watched as the little bird, now more recognisable, soared high into the sky and then shot forwards towards the Ivory Order Chapter, which resembled what she could only describe as a castle, a castle that clashed spectacularly with the snow covering the great dome around them. Its colour was purest white and even from a distance Charity could tell that it was almost twice the size of the Order Chapter in Forfal where she had once resided.

"And that beside it," Alistair said pointing over to the right of the white castle, "is the Imputtian Royal Palace . Of course there's no royal family anymore, just the High Chancellor."

"The High Chancellor? That was the guy that we met yesterday wasn't it?" asked Charity.

"Yes, High Chancellor Euphestus." answered Alistair, readjusting his cloak around his massive shoulders.

"You said yesterday he was like a ruler, does he make laws and things in Imputtia?" asked Charity.

"Essentially yes, he is well known for his tough stance on crime. But he is also quite famed for his sharp intellect and is apparently one of the wisest men in all of Thea. Many send doves seeking his counsel and advice, which is why he was voted to head of the Imputtian government."

Charity glanced around the street. She hadn't had time to really take in all the various things that stood out to her the day before but now she could see just how busy Galcia was. People poured from the shops and houses and throughout the many winding streets ahead of them, the shops themselves were covered in advertisements, some similar to ones she had seen in Upper Forfal. As she looked stalls were just now being set up outside some of the windows, each displaying a huge arrangement of objects most of which Charity didn't recognise.

"Alistair, where are we going?" moaned Sophie, who stretched lazily and leant against Charity as they walked.

"We are going to Silvus' Supplies. It's the only place we'll get what we need."

"What *do* we need?" asked Charity inquisitively.

"Hiking boots, food, liquids, a map," he eyes the girls' skirts, "A change of clothes is crucial, we cannot venture into the plains wearing a skirt."

"I didn't know you were wearing one," said Charity grinning.

"I meant that you two, your skirts, I - " started Alistair but stopped as Charity and Sophie fell about laughing at him.

"Imagine Alistair, in a dress!" said Sophie, falling against Charity, tears leaking from her eyes.

"Yeah! I think he'd look *beautiful!*" said Charity in a mock serious tone.

"Girls!" said Alistair suddenly sternly, snapping the girls from their amusement at once. They both stared up at him reproachfully, Charity immediately began to worry that they had gone too far in making fun of him.

"You must act properly. We are in the epicentre of the Order's territory and two out of three of us are unlikely to gain a welcome reception from Order officials should they encounter us," he said sounding most serious.

Both girls looked suitably chastised and they followed Alistair down the street, Charity walking in what she hoped was a 'sensible' manner behind Alistair's massive strides. She had got rather good at following him by now, and she would skip every couple of steps to make up the extra ground which kept her at roughly the same pace. She and Sophie followed Alistair, craning their necks upwards as they did to see the full height of the many houses and shops that surrounded them. Some were bent and misshapen, others looked squished together as if they had tried to fit too many houses into an otherwise tight space. It gave Charity the unpleasant feeling of being constantly surrounded and she felt that, despite her good mood and optimism, she would be glad to leave Galcia in exchange for the wide-open spaces of the Plains, regardless of what they had in store for her.

"Um, Alistair," said Charity after waiting, what she hoped, was a sufficient amount of time for him to calm down. "Why do we need all that stuff? I mean I know we're going out into the plains but do we know *where* in the plains?"

"I believe we do." Said Alistair, who sounded slightly happier now.

"I told him about what you read," said Sophie matter-of-factly.

"What? When did you tell him that, you've been with me the whole time," said Charity.

"No, I couldn't really sleep last night, you were out like a light though." She clicked her fingers and a blue spark rose into the air and disappeared, "I went for a wander about the inn and found Alistair downstairs."

"What were *you* doing?" asked Charity, slightly upset that she hadn't been invited to this unofficial meeting.

"Having a night cap, Rapier's is famous for it's Frost-Whiskey, I rarely get the chance to - "

"So what were you talking about during your *special little meeting*?" asked Charity, frowning at the pair of them.

"Oh Charity, don't crease your pages, it was just a coincidence. I went down and spotted Alistair at the bar and we had a quick chat about where we were going tomorrow. I mentioned what you'd read and Alistair seemed most interested." explained Sophie calmly.

"Most interested indeed." Confirmed Alistair, "You mentioned something of great importance in your reading Charity, I doubt thought you would've understood the significance."

"Well…" said Charity impatiently, "What was it?"

"The Haven of the North." replied Alistair,

"I didn't read about that, oh no wait I did, **The Haven**, Calville wanted to reach **the Haven** he said."

"He did, and I believe that it is there that we shall find the second page." said Alistair triumphantly.

Alistair had brought them to another large building. This one had an ornate golden sign on a pole outside it, which read: 'Silvus' Supplies'. The shop had large stone steps which led up to a red coloured door with a large silver handle and door knocker. Another sign, this one etched in wood and hanging on the door, read: 'OPEN'. Alistair seemed to take heed of this as he ignored the knocker and entered Silvus' Supplies without any hesitation.

Charity and Sophie followed silently behind him.

Charity's first impression of Silvus' Supplies was that it was deceptively large, which was a good thing, as it clearly sold a baffling array of different products. Among the clutter Charity saw clothes, book holsters, jars of funny coloured liquids, and things that looked worryingly like human skulls packed onto the cramped shelves. Each item was labelled with a paper price tag that had been stuck either on the item or on the shelf below it, and looking at them Charity could see, for the first time, the symbol Theans seemed to use for Odes. She thought it looked a little bit like the letter 'O' but it had two curved lines running through its centre, Charity made a mental note to memorise it, in case she saw it somewhere else.

There were more shelves the further she walked into the shop, and each of these shelves seemed to hold more and more items, some so jam-packed with goods that they looked like they would collapse under the strain. Charity thought this surely couldn't be helpful when customers wanted to find a specific item. There must be a more organised way of housing such an array of things but to her surprise, the customers in the shop didn't seem to mind. They were all chatting animatedly to one another, some pulled out objects and examined them carefully, others baulked at the price tags whilst a couple of patrons could be seen carrying an armful of things over to a low wooden counter, where a tall man with slicked back silver hair stood wearing a grubby apron.

Alistair glanced carefully around two or three of the shelves before turning to them and shaking his head in a frustrated sort of way. "No, it's too cluttered, we shall have to ask Silvus," he said, indicating the desk at the back of the shop.

"That's Silvus?" asked Sophie.

"It is." Answered Alistair.

"He owns the place then?" asked Charity,

"He does, he's quite the success story actually. Began with nothing many years ago and now he has a supply shop in each of the major cities on Thea."

"Is he rich then?" asked Sophie,

"Exceedingly."

"He doesn't look too rich!" said Charity, staring at Silvus, who was now handing a woman her change from a wooden box behind the counter.

"And what does a rich man look like?" asked Alistair,

"Y'know, like a top hat and cane…and…stuff."

Sophie laughed and Alistair smiled at Charity. "You must not set too much on appearance. Look at you two, a reader and a spark, I wager that none in this store would guess *that* from first impressions."

She smiled at Alistair but as she did a question popped into her head, a question that had occurred to her a long time ago that she obviously forgotten to ask him.

"Yeah, you're right. Um, Alistair…back in Dura when you were… you know.

"Dying." Said Alistair flatly,

"Uh, yeah, dying. Well you called me 'Little Book' you said something about 'A Little Book lighting the darkness' or something like that. I just wondered what it meant, I mean it's ok if you don't want tot talk about it."

"No no, I will talk about it. It was not the demented last words of a dying man if that's what you think Charity."

Charity, who privately had thought that this might've been the case went very red and Alistair smiled pleasantly at her.

"I can understand how you might think that but no. That phrase is merely an old tongue phrase, for one whom you believe in; you are likely to hear it from the older families on Thea."

"You believe in me?" asked Charity, slightly stunned.

"Of course, look at what you have accomplished. Look at what you can do."

328

Charity was conflicted. She did not feel particularly special, the unexpected gifts that she had adopted were, if she was honest, a mystery to her and although she was gaining in confidence within her own abilities she still saw herself as a thin, thirteen-year old girl who was rather lost. She smiled, however, and put on a brave face for Alistair who was looking at her with an unusual look in his blue eyes. Was it pride?

"Ahem!" coughed Sophie loudly, breaking Alistair and Charity from their thoughts. Charity continued to feel conflicted and Alistair made quickly for the desk, looking distinctly ruffled. When he had reached it, Silvus greeted him warmly, his arms outstretched and a broad smile on his lined face, "Alistair, old friend, how does Thea keep you?" he said happily.

"She keeps me well Silvus. We're here for some items that should remain *between us*," he said, whispering the last two words to Silvus, who looked suddenly concerned.

"Anything the matter? Anything I can help you with?"

"Only supplies. We should manage from then on our own, thanks."

"Well alright then, just a moment, I'll get the front desk covered so we can chat. Thomas!" he yelled suddenly to the store at large, as a young man came scuttling out from behind one of the shelves his arms laden with a variety of items, one of which was spinning madly.

Charity recognised him at once, as the apprentice from Ruven's demonstration. He wobbled ominously where he stood, attempted to right himself and then toppled over completely, the heap of items he had been carrying crashing down around him. The spinning item he had been carrying, which turned out to be a pretend throwing star, bounced away of its own accord whilst Thomas attempted to pick up the rest of the fallen goods, all the while spluttering his apologies.

"I - I'm so sorry Uncle, just got distracted, I'll put them all back, I couldn't remember which shelf was the cloaks and which was the Journalmarks."

Charity and Sophie jogged over to help him pick up the rest of his items and together they soon collected everything, Thomas was still mumbling to himself, but having crammed the last of the items back into his increasingly full arms he managed to finally look at them.

"Thanks, thanks… HEY! I know you!" he said, waggling a free finger at Sophie with great difficulty. "Yeah, you were at the Igniculus Temple. You're a Spark too!"

"Yeah, I guess I am," said Sophie and Charity could see her swell with pride at these words. Charity rolled her eyes and turned away, trying to conceal her amusement.

"Thanks. We can just put this stuff up at the counter and I'll put it back later," said Thomas, making a shaky path towards the counter where Alistair and Silvus were chatting contentedly.

"Is Silvus your Uncle?" asked Sophie.

"Yeah, on my Mam's side, he got me the job here, just until I can get into the Temple mind, then I'm gonna become a full time Spark!" he said proudly.

"What *does* a spark do?" asked Charity curiously.

"Oh loadsa stuff" said Thomas dumping the goods on the ground. "They help people, think up new inventions, some *even* go on adventures. Can you imagine? A real life adventure, like, like in a story book!"

"Yeah, sounds too good to be true." said Charity quietly, as Sophie grinned beside her.

"When you're *ready*, Thomas!" said Silvus sarcastically from the other side of the counter, "I'm not paying you to chit-chat, am I? Now man the counter, I have to show an old friend some stuff in the back room. Any problems give me a wail!"

"Yes, sorry, no problem, Uncle Silvus!"

Silvus was still chatting to Alistair as Charity, Sophie and Alistair were whisked into a dingy back room just behind the counter.

"You hear 'bout Turner?" asked Silvus, grinning mischievously.

"Turner Foy?" replied Alistair.

"Aye!"

"No, what did the fool do now?"

"Only went and bought himself a flock of six Sun-cranes. I mean how in Thea are they meant to get all the way out there to him when they won't go near water!?"

Alistair and Silvus laughed together. "Odes never were a substitute for sense," said Alistair, shaking his head disbelievingly.

Charity looked around the little room. Like the rest of the shop, this room was also lined with packed shelves, except these were covered in several layers of dust and cobwebs. Clearly the items that resided here were rarely used. The room's centrepiece was a wooden dining table that had six solid oak chairs set around it.

"Sit, SIT!" shouted Silvus, taking one of the seats himself. Alistair sat, and Charity and Sophie followed suit. "So what secret task are you embarking on *this* time?" he said wearily to Alistair, a slight smirk on his face and a knowing twinkle in his brown eyes.

Alistair removed his hat and stared long and hard at Silvus, who withdrew a little under the intensity of the look Alistair fixed him with.

"We are going to find the Haven," Alistair said finally.

Charity noticed there was no air of grandeur or boasting in his words, this was a fact, a true statement and nothing more.

Silvus looked as though Alistair had punched him around the face. "You're mad," he said softly.

"No I am not. We cannot explain why but we have to make it there, and it has to be soon. Tonight if possible."

"You'll die, you fool!" said Silvus angrily.

"I may do," Alistair said flatly. "But it is my job to see that these two do not, and that is why I require your assistance."

"You don't mean… You can't mean… That, that, you're not taking these two *with you?*"

"They are following a course that I believe will lead them to the Haven. They have consented to follow me advice and venture into the plains, is this correct?" He turned to Charity and Sophie. Charity tried to give her most resolute nod and look sufficiently determined but Silvus was far from convinced.

"Alistair, my friend, please see reason. This is a fool's errand. The Haven has only ever been found by a handful of people."

"Including me," Alistair interrupted. "I found it when I was seventeen and I will find it again. Silvus, *please* I am not asking you to come along, all I want is some equipment to help us on our way. You know I can trust no one else."

Silvus looked desperately back at Alistair. "I couldn't, I can't, the young ones, Alistair, *PLEASE!*" he pleaded desperately.

"Your mind is set?" asked Alistair darkly. Silvus did not reply but continued to stare imploringly at Alistair, all the while glancing between Charity and Sophie, and agitatedly running his hands through his greasy hair.

"Then we must go elsewhere. Girls, come," said Alistair, getting to his feet.

"NO! Oh Thea, oh…" Silvus looked from Sophie to Charity once more and then to Alistair. Charity knew he would see three tired but determined faces staring back at him, and it may have been this, she thought, that seemed to make his mind up. Silvus sighed very heavily. "Very well," he croaked weakly. "I will help you." He got up and left the room, shutting the door behind them. Alistair took his seat once more, a relieved smile just visible on his face. Charity could hear Silvus outside the tiny room, yelling commands to Thomas, who could be heard banging about the shop in response.

Silvus returned five minutes later carrying a similar sized bundle to the one Thomas has been fumbling with earlier. He slammed the contents onto the table, standing over it with a peculiar look on his face.

"Snow shoes, those'll help you on ice and snow *obviously*, winter cloaks, fur-lined hat, trousers, gloves, heavy duty Journal clasp, that's very useful actually and a book on the geography of the Plains, although most of it unrecorded guesswork, so that I'll throw in for free."

"Why is it mostly unrecorded?" asked Charity.

"Because when you're out *there*, the last thing on your Journal is jotting down the scenery, girl!" Silvus said darkly. "Let's see, three of each of these, minus the book, hmmm that'll come to twenty eight Odes. Do you a discount, old times an all that."

"I should have enough," said Alistair. He reached into the pocket of his cloak and pulled out a black bag with golden string tied around one end, he untied the string, fished inside it, and poured the contents onto the table. It was suddenly littered with dozens of the golden coins. He counted out twenty eight and slid them over to Silvus, who did not pick them up.

"We will need three backpacks," Alistair said, "for transportation."

Silvus nodded and disappeared wordlessly back into his shop. He returned a couple of minutes later carrying three heavy brown backpacks, each lined with what looked like goat fur.

"No charge," said Silvus quietly, throwing the backpacks onto the pile on the table.

The three packed up their individual items into their bags and hitched them onto their backs. Charity decided she would take the book on the geography of the Plains as she was eager to find out more about this strange place prior to their expedition. When filled, all three of their bags were a lot heavier but as Alistair had rightly pointed out. "We'll be wearing most of this stuff when we leave Galcia, which means a lot less weight to carry."

Sophie in particular looked immensely awkward, her large bag and slight figure meaning she resembled an upright tortoise as she waddled her way out of the room. Charity saw Alistair fall behind as she left. He embraced Silvus and they both whispered something inaudible into each other's ears.

When they had both spoken Silvus paused, his eyes widening in shock, and then he seemed to compose himself. He stared at Alistair, his eyes flicking to where Sophie and Charity stood at the door of the shop. Silvus nodded wearily and Alistair seemed to take this as his signal to leave. He bade Silvus a genial farewell and moved towards Charity and Sophie, ushering them from the shop and back out into the bustling street.

Alistair turned to Charity and Sophie, looking more serious than they had ever seen him. "I have to ask you both something and I need you to truly think before you answer."

"Yes, anything Alistair, what is it?" asked Charity. She was worried. Something was wrong, she felt it, and if she had had a Journal of her own then it would surely be scribbling away those feelings right now.

"Do you trust me?" asked Alistair.

"Yes, of *course* we trust you!" chorused both girls, as if this was a very stupid question to ask of them.

"Do you? Do you trust me with everything?"

"Yes," they both answered.

"Your lives? Even those?" he asked, grasping their shoulders.

"YES!" Charity and Sophie both stated boldly.

"I need you to remember that girls, because there will come a point, very soon, when you may forget. Promise me that you'll remember that you trust me, can you do that for me?"

"We trust you Alistair," said Charity honestly. "We always will."

Alistair stared into their eyes as if he was looking for something inside them, and seemingly satisfied, he straightened himself to his full height. "Very well, then we leave *now*. It is still dawn and the winds will be at their least fierce for a couple more hours."

"We're going NOW?" asked Sophie exasperated, but Alistair had already begun walking down the winding street and they had to run to catch up.

"We have to leave now or the winds will change. It will be too late and we will have to wait until tomorrow."

"What's wrong with waiting another day?" asked Charity,

"Silvus told me something in there before I left. He told me the Order know I am here. Someone has told them."

"Oh my!" said Sophie, clapping a hand to her mouth.

"They also know I am with *you,* Charity," he said, turning to look at her whilst he walked. "And I will not risk your capture whilst in this city. We leave now whilst we can."

Neither Sophie or Charity could think of an argument to this so they simply nodded, both choosing to walk the rest of the way in stunned silence, weaving in and out of the people hurrying past them and ignoring offers and shouts from the stalls and shops they passed. After a great deal of walking they had made their way to the very edge of the city. The houses were less crooked here and yet they looked somehow more dishevelled, their bricks worn and covered in grime and dust. Alistair had led them to a huge glass door. Charity wouldn't have even noticed it *was* a door unless she was standing in front of it. The curved door was cut into the glass dome that surrounded the city of Galcia and it lead outside to another smaller dome. This one looked just big enough for a group of people to stand inside. Alistair pushed open the door and held it open for them. They entered the tiny dome hesitantly and Alistair slammed the glass door shut once they were all safely inside.

"This is the safety dome. It'll let us properly prepare for our exit, you see once we open that door," he indicated a new door opposite the one they had just used, "there really is no going back. Get your things out, and just put your new clothes on over your old ones. You'll need all the warmth you can get."

They complied without question, pulling on their new clothes with great difficulty. Charity felt very exposed in the transparent dome despite only removing her tie, which she felt might constrict her breathing under all the layers of warm clothes. It took them longer than expected but eventually they had managed to apply their new garments to every exposed area of their bodies. In their new finery Charity was stiflingly hot. The clothes certainly did their job and she pulled the fur cloak about her more tightly as she stared at the white blizzard now engulfing the little dome. Her new fur hat had ear flaps and she pulled it tightly onto her head, smiling at Sophie who was struggling to tuck her long hair into her own hat. Charity helped her tie it up and crammed the hat on top roughly. Alistair meanwhile had made about tying a heavy rope around his waist. He let out the line a bit and then tied around Sophie and then finally Charity.

"This is to make sure we don't lose each other," he said, answering their unasked question.

When he had finished his preparations Alistair turned to look at them, a steely glint in his sapphire blue eyes.

"I only know that we head North for a mile or so, then we should find our own way."

"Our own way?" asked Charity, alarmed. "Isn't there a path or something?"

Alistair smiled grimly at her. "You will see," he said and turning to the door he yanked it open.

A roar of sound and snow enveloped Charity, and blistering, unrelenting snow suddenly blinded her eyes. She covered her face with her hand and attempted to see through the snow but it was impossible. She felt the rope around her waist tug her and she obeyed it, moving forwards out of the little glass pod and onto the surface of the Ice Plains. Her feet crunched in the deep snow below. It was almost up to her knees and she could feel it seep into any parts of her legs that were even slightly uncovered by the layers of clothes she wore.

Charity kept walking. She could hear only the roar and whistle of the winds, and every now and then she would feel a little tug on her rope and would keep up her pace. She looked around her, squinting through the slits in her gloved hand which was still covering her raw eyes, she thought she could make it blurred shapes ahead of them, huge forms that towered above even Alistair but when she tried to get a better look at them they had gone. The wind rocked her from side to side and only the rope and her heavy snow shoes kept her on both feet.

After they had walked for an age Charity felt the rope tug violently off in a different direction, this time tugging to the right. Charity followed the instructions quickly and as she did she felt that the ground beneath her gradually getting steeper. The snow was just as thick but it was now becoming dangerously slippery. She bent her head low to protect her eyes and grasped the rope with both hands for support. It seemed to Charity that they were now climbing up and around a large incline but she could not be completely sure. She tried to imagine where they were or how high they had gone but it was all pointless, the hellish conditions made it impossible to have even the faintest idea of her surroundings.

Charity continued to trudge forwards when without warning she felt a sharp tug, this one harder than any of the others, then suddenly the rope lurched forwards violently, pulling her off her feet. She crashed to the snowy ground, her body sinking into icy, wet, snow. The rope was straining and yanking around her waist, she thought that it was going to tear her in half, she screamed in pain as she fumbled with the knot but it was too tight. Digging her fingers into the rope she attempted to tear it off, the pain almost unbearable now. She screamed out but the wind was so fierce that she could barely hear her own voice. Then she heard something, a cry, a cry of anguish that echoed out louder than the wind and rain around them. The rope gave another mighty tug, pulling her across the snow and then, just as suddenly, it fell slack once more. Charity had no idea what was going on but she decided that the best thing to do would be to find Sophie and Alistair, so staying low to the ground she crawled along the rope to where she thought Sophie should be. After some difficult groping she found her laying on the ground, her knees to her chest and her hands covering her face. For several heart-stopping moments she thought she was dead but when she got up close she saw that she was shivering and shaking convulsively.

Charity turned her over to look at her. Her face was raw red and her eyes were hazy with tears, and she seemed barely able to communicate. Then she noticed Charity looking over her and began shouting something at the top of her lungs. Charity couldn't make out what she was saying over the roaring of the winds, Sophie was still shouting, her eyes popped and tears cascaded down her face as the winds howled around her louder still. Charity shook her head indicating that she could not hear her and Sophie held up something in response, a severed line of rope. Slowly, very slowly, Charity understood what Sophie was showing her. The realisation hit her like a blow to the stomach, and she fell back against the snow, almost paralysed with shock. She felt the cold winds burning her face once more but did not shield it this time. She could not move, she would not move, the northern winds had won, Alistair was gone.

22 – PAGES FROM THE PAST

The butler set down the final piece of cutlery on the intricately decorated dining table just as the front door slammed somewhere down below. Hurrying off to greet his master he fixed his black tie and straightened his perfectly ironed white shirt, as he had done almost every day of his life. He had only just reached the door to the dining room when a man with long black hair swept into the room and greeted him genially.

"Spencer! How splendid to see you. I trust you had a productive day,"

"Yes Master Ruven, sir." the butler answered stiffly.

"Spencer for the last time, please don't call me 'sir'. I know you've worked for the Ruvens all your life but I don't require such formalities. Ezekiel would do just fine."

"Sir…" muttered Spencer, "I do not feel that would be appropriate for a man of my post." As he spoke, straight backed and monotone, Ruven rolled his eyes dramatically. "Thea! Fine, fine do what you will. Have we at least got something delicious for dinner?" he asked, seating himself at the ornate dining table.

"Poached snow quail with a side of moltenberry compote and mixed vegetables," said Spencer loftily, lifting up a silver cloche that covered up the steaming plate of food.

Ruven's eyes flashed hungrily at the sight of the meal.

"You really are a marvellous butler Spencer, I probably should be paying you more," he said, jabbing a fork into a piece of quail and popping it delicately into his mouth. He savoured the flavour for a couple of seconds, his eyes closed, then he looked admiringly at Spencer who met his gaze reluctantly.

"Perfection, Spencer!" he said, contentedly. "Well any doves for me today?"

"Yes sir, just one from your brother in Forfal. He is having a function in three days' time and politely requests your presence."

"Launching another invention is he? Oh very well, tell him I'll be there, but, oh! I've just remembered. You'll never guess what happened today," he said, his mouth full of food. "I had ol' Euphestus pay me a visit."

"Really sir? Anything important?" asked Spencer, unable to hide a flicker curiosity in his voice.

"As a matter of fact, yes," Ruven gave a huge swallow and then continued. "Wanted to know what I'd heard about that palace murder in Duradon. You heard about that I take it?"

"Yes sir, a palace official murdered within the grounds," answered Spencer without a trace of compassion in his voice now.

"Precisely, in brightest daylight and no one saw who did it. Well I told him what I'd heard, same as everybody else, no doubt but then he starts asking me about this whole Regalis rumour."

Ruven looked at Spencer, who did not respond. "You heard about *that* one?" he asked, pointing a forked piece of quail at him.

"No, Sir, I have not," said Spencer calmly.

"*Really*? Thought everyone had. Well, the rumour on the wind is that a new Regalis has been found already! Some folk are saying it's this girl, an amazingly young thing, whilst others swear on their Journal that they saw a young lad, about seventeen or eighteen years, read an Ivory guard's Journal in Duradon. Course it could all be nonsense…nonetheless Euphestus wanted to know if I'd seen anyone resembling any of these rumours. I told him that I'd heard too many rumours, that I hadn't a clue if they even existed never mind spotting them walking down the street!"

Spencer nodded, indicating that he understood Ruven's story and Ruven continued, his fork still dangling in the air, the food on it now forgotten.

"Then you'll never guess what he said." Ruven did not wait for Spencer to reply, but ploughed on. "He said, that all the ruddy rumours are *true!* That

340

there are *two* new Regalis on Thea and that one is working for the Order as we speak. He's a grand lad apparently, showed startling abilities, even at such a young age. Euphestus told me that the Cardinal himself had informed him of the boy and spoke very highly of him. Now there's a ringing endorsement, eh?"

Spencer looked suitably impressed and Ruven smiled seeing the impact of his story.

"What about the other, sir?" asked Spencer.

Ruven drew breath excitedly, tutting as he waved the fork about and shook his head ruefully. "Now that is a different Journal altogether. Well the other, Euphestus said, was a scoundrel of a girl, she's about thirteen years I think. Possesses promising abilities but apparently she rejected the Order and made off with a valuable artefact to boot. It turns out that it was she and her cronies that killed that palace worker in Duradon. Well I was a bit sceptical, and asked him how a girl could kill a fully grown man but he told me she had this huge warrior helping her. He said that she had recruited…Alistair Garron."

Spencer raised an eyebrow at this and Ruven gave a hearty laugh. "Ah so that's intrigued you has it? Tell me, what've you heard about Alistair Garron lately?"

"Only that he has been helping the citizens of Thea for many years now."

"Exactly, *helping,* not hindering. He only ever had a problem with the Order, Thea knows why but he never so much as layed a finger on regular folk. I asked Euphestus why a good fella like that would go so bad. He just kept shaking his head, he told me that Alistair Garron had finally snapped, that the death of his parents had gotten to him. Said he's been bewitched by this girl, this other Regalis and together they were terrorising Thea one nation at a time. It wasn't just them either. They had another with them. He described them all just in case I saw them, told me I should tell all the Temple staff and workers to be on their guard."

"Was this third man dangerous also?" asked Spencer, who looked suddenly alarmed.

"No that's the oddity of it all Spencer. The third was just another young girl; a particularly tiny one at that. Old Euphestus was very detailed in his descriptions. This one has black hair…pale skin…and….green…eyes…" Something was just dawning on Ruven's bearded face. His eyes looked suddenly terrified and he dropped his fork to the plate, which clattered noisily.

"Sir whatever is the matter?"

"They, they were here, in the temple, they were in the temple with *me, today!*" he said in a panic.

"Who, sir?"

"The group, that girl, he did tell me she had white hair, I hadn't been thinking, it's not that unusual anyways. But Alistair Garron, well I haven't seen him in years, not since he was a boy, only the Order sketches they occasionally put up around the city but still, how could I not recognise him? That girl though, Sophie, Sophie Pierce, she was travelling with them, Spencer!"

"Sir?" questioned Spencer, looking positively alarmed at his master who was babbling away to himself.

"Spencer that girl, Sophie, she produced a fully formed flame on her first attempt, not even I…"

Ruven rubbed his black moustache clearly deep in thought.

"Would you like me to contact Chancellor Euphestus?" asked Spencer obediently.

Ruven didn't answer immediately; he seemed to be toiling with something, whilst Spencer stood waiting patiently. Then without warning, he seemed to come to his decision. Before Spencer could so much as move, Ruven had gotten to his feet and walked to the door. "No, I'll see him myself, Spencer, something isn't right here."

....

Charity could feel the cold envelop her, she felt herself sinking deeper and deeper into the snow, the pummelling rains and winds splashing and bouncing off her face but she remained quite still. She could feel it now, she was close, her eyes were almost certainly frozen shut but even if she could open them the white of the snow above would be all she could see. Suddenly she felt something nudge her, was it a man or a beast? She didn't care, she began to roll, to tumble down the incline she had just ascended, felt her body flail pathetically on the ground, over ice, stone and snow and finally after descending what felt like the entire mountain side she came to a stop. It was there she lay in a mangled heap, the cold clamping her limbs to her side so that even if her heart desired it, she could not move a muscle.

She wondered how long it took someone to die of hypothermia or exhaustion; did the person feel a lot of pain? She supposed not, the numbness in her muscles would surely stop most of the discomfort. Her mind wandered to Sophie. Had she been pulled down the hill with her? What about Alistair? What had cut him away from them so cruelly? Questions tumbled about her head as she lay staring into the darkness of her own eyelids. She was no longer cold, she suddenly realised, perhaps the numbness taking effect.

This was taking too long. How long did it take someone to die? The lack of cold was at least some comfort to her now. In fact now that she really considered it, she felt quite warm, this was obviously another side effect of the hypothermia, she surmised. She heard something stirring beside her and realised that for the first time since they had ventured onto the Plains that the winds were quietened. She could still them howling but now they sounded like they were coming from a distance. Had her ears been frozen too?

Charity opened her eyes with great difficulty, as her eyelids felt like they were made of lead. She blinked a couple of times. The winds had subsided, the icy rain had stopped and the snow was no longer falling; she was not outside anymore, she was lying on a hard stone floor and looking up at a rocky roof. The warmth she had felt was coming from a little fire burning happily beside her. She creaked her neck an inch or so to her left and right and saw that she was inside a small cave. She could just make out just something behind the fire, - a little bundle of fur that could only be one thing. Sophie.

Charity tried to sit up but found she couldn't. She opened her mouth to speak but her throat was dry and no words issued forth. She managed to rock from side to side just a little bit at first and then using the momentum more and more. She rocked herself like this and then with one huge effort she rolled herself over so that she faced the comforting flames of the little fire in between her and Sophie. She knew that she would need to warm her limbs before she moved. She wondered how they had reached the little cave, if they had just rolled into it by sheer luck or if someone had dragged them there. She thought of Alistair bravely charging through the snow, dragging their bodies behind him but Alistair would be here if this was the case and currently he was nowhere to be seen.

After several hours Charity felt the feeling return to her lower body, the pins and needles she experienced were incredibly unpleasant but that was a sign she had been hoping for, the fire had done its job. She wiggled her feet happily as she lay prostrate on the ground, her fur cloak wrapped tightly around her. With difficulty Charity finally managed to sit up, her arms working too now. She clambered gingerly to her feet and felt her knees buckle beneath her weight. She would have to move slowly as she got her bearings, she thought to herself.

Charity moved to the mouth of the cave and looked out. It was as usual nearly impossible to tell where they were; however, she could at least guess from the roaring winds that they were still high up. Perhaps they had not fallen as far as she first thought. Just then, something caught her eye, a footprint marked out in the snow, a footprint that was far too big to be hers. She reached out to touch it but as she did, a sudden gust swept through the cave forcing her to stumble backwards and grab the cave wall for support. When she looked again the print was gone.

Stumbling over to where Sophie lay, she shook her awake. It took her a long time to get Sophie to a point where she could both sit up and speak fluently but with the fire's help Charity eventually managed it.

"Where's Alistair?" Sophie said hurriedly, looking finally lucid, her eyes wide and terrified.

"I don't know," answered Charity honestly, her own heart sinking as she said it aloud for the first time and the reality of their situation came crashing down upon her shoulders.

"The rope, the rope was cut, someone snapped it right off, I felt it!" Sophie rambled looking suddenly maniacal. "Then the winds, they were so strong I just, I must've blacked out!"

"We can't do anything about that now! If we can make it to the Haven we might find Alistair when we get there, or maybe he'll find us on our way back to Galcia."

"You still want to go to the Haven?" asked Sophie incredulously. "But Alistair…"

"Alistair could have died to get us to the Haven, something happened to him that didn't happen to us. We collapsed outside and then we both woke up here wrapped in our cloaks with a roaring fire burning. Something is going on Sophie and I intend to find out what!"

Sophie stayed very quiet. She looked as though she were about to break into tears. Charity felt appalled at herself for snapping at her. She had only been trying to help but the strain of the journey was now getting to her.

"Look Sophie…"

"It's alright," she said softly. She got up and started wringing out her wet clothes and drying them over the fire. Charity imitated her. Her outer clothes were soaked through but thankfully her school uniform had survived much of the moisture. So they both worked away in silence, hovering their garments over the flames only occasionally glancing at one another across the embers.

Both girls continued to work closely even though no more talk had been shared. Charity had no idea what to say that would comfort Sophie and Sophie looked as though she were constantly on the verge of breaking down in tears. They had just managed to fix a meal of some sort of pale silver fish and a glass bottle of a fizzy, purple liquid that Alistair had packed in their bags for them. Charity had cooked the fish over the fire using a flat rock they had found nearby, she thought sadly that if it weren't for Alistair they wouldn't be sitting here eating. The fish was delicious and the liquid had seemed to give her a brief sensation of renewed energy but she could tell from the sky outside which grew steadily darker that nightfall was upon them so she had privately decided that they should leave the rest of their journey to the morning. Charity lay close to Sophie, both huddled together for warmth. She desperately wanted Sophie to speak but no words came. Charity closed her eyes and let sleep envelop her once more.

A chill wind brushed at the bare skin on her face. Charity opened her eyes and saw with a stab of horror that the fire had gone out. She sat bolt upright and began fumbling with bits of stick and rock, poking and prodding the fire, desperately trying to find some embers amongst the black soot but she found none. She was now dangerously cold. She pulled her cloak tightly around herself and rocked Sophie awake.

"Sophie, Sophie, the fire!"

"What 'bout it?" Sophie said sleepily.

"It's out, we have to find something for fuel before we freeze."

"But there's nothing here but rocks," said Sophie standing up, bleary eyed and pacing the cave.

"There has to be something, anything… wait, Sophie, use your Spark!" It had just occurred to her that they had a readymade source of heat at her fingertips and she looked encouragingly at Sophie who removed her hand from a her fur lined glove and held it out in front of herself in the now familiar starting position. She clicked her fingers together in the characteristic manner Charity had seen her do hundreds of times since her first Spark but this time nothing happened. Sophie looked frustrated and clicked again, nothing happened once more, she clicked and clicked, again and again, but the only thing she could muster was the tinniest of flickers that jumped from her protruding thumb every now and again.

"It's not working. I don't understand, I can't," she clicked her fingers madly, her eyes narrowed and teeth bared in frustration. "I can't do it!"

Charity put her hand over hers. "Look, don't worry we'll find something else. If we can just get some wood I can make a fire using stones…I think." Charity assumed she could make a fire by rubbing together two stones but in truth it was something she had never managed to do, she'd seen plenty of people on television do it, read about fearless explorers doing it but she'd never needed to perform the task herself. Sophie and Charity continued to search the little cave and to their great relief they managed to find a couple of pieces of bark, some twigs and a bundle of dry moss that'd covered some large boulders near the back of the cave. Putting the items on top of the soot where the old fire had once burned, Charity took two sharp stones and struck them hard against one another. This had no effect, so she tried hitting different parts of the rocks in the hope it would change the outcome but it did not. Growing weary of failure Charity looked around the cave at Sophie who was now aimlessly kicking tiny pebbles about the ground.

"You know you *could* help," snapped Charity annoyed. Sophie looked up. Her face was dark and mutinous but she approached the fire nonetheless, giving one of the pebbles a final frustrated kick with her right foot. Charity watched the stone bounce off the side of the small cave and hit the boulders at the back, falling in between one of their many cracks. She had just opened her mouth to issue an angry retort to Sophie's bad attitude when a sound made them both stop, their ill feelings evaporating in an instant. A small 'plop' had issued from somewhere at the back of the cave. It sounded like something had dropped into a pool of deep water. Charity bounced to her feet, following Sophie, who had already moved to the boulders where the sound had come from. Together they heaved and pulled one of them aside. Had they not heard a sound Charity would have never assumed there was anything of interest behind a couple of moss strewn rocks. The top one slid off quite easily and just behind it they could see a small hole. The bottom two boulders were still in the way so the two girls pulled and pushed them to the side of the cave and bent low, peering inside this new avenue.

"Can you see anything?" asked Sophie.

"Yeah I can. There's some light shining in from the roof, must be some cracks."

"Is there water? Is that what the noise was?"

"Yeah, think so," said Charity, moving closer into the passage. "Looks like a little lake in one corner. I'm going in ok?"

"Ok, but…be careful."

"Course!" Charity turned smiling to Sophie who returned her look, their anger at each other forgotten in the mystery of this unexpected discovery.

Charity crawled through the passage. It was also covered in the same furry moss, and she could feel it under her fingers as she crawled through the little hole, just big enough for her and Sophie. Once inside this new cavern she took a look around. The walls were indeed cracked and the roof had several intricate slits cut deep into the rock. This meant that light was able to pour in through the crevices but that no snow or rain cascaded down upon them. The lake in the corner was a deep blue and the water, if indeed this was water, looked clean and drinkable, another bonus she thought to herself. "Sophie c'mon through it's, it's perfect!" she yelled through the hole.

Sophie joined her a couple of minutes later. She had to throw her large backpack through first as it would not fit whilst on her back. For added safety, Charity rolled another small boulder in front of the hole, cutting off any danger from the outside world and silencing the wind once and for all. The two girls stood in the dim light of the cave savouring the sound of silence; it seemed like a million years since they had heard it.

"This is amazing but we'll still need a fire for when night falls." said Sophie sensibly.

"You're right. Ok there's some moss here and more sticks but that wasn't really lighting all too well. Hey what are these?" asked Charity. She had just stepped on something that subsequently stuck to her heavy snow shoe, and peeling it off she realised it was a page.

"It's paper. There's loads of them over there, look!" said Sophie animatedly, pointing to a small pile of torn and dishevelled pages scattered about the far corner of the cavern. Sophie rushed towards them and picked up a bundle, carrying them back over to a spot for their makeshift fire. "These will definitely burn!" she said happily.

Charity didn't respond, she was staring at the page in her hand, her eyes scanning its surface in disbelief.

She heard a small click and Sophie said excitedly, "I can get a pretty decent Spark now, must've been the cold or something earlier, this'll be enough to light these pages though." She clicked madly and then came away a small ember burning on the page. Charity heard her whoops of joy, but did not look up from her page, had she done so she would've witnessed Sophie staring avidly at the little flames that were just beginning to lick their way up the collection of other pages she had carefully assembled.

"Now we just have to blow on it," Sophie said, leaning close to the pile but Charity, suddenly alert, dove forward, knocking her out of the way and stamping out the fire with her heavy shoes.

"Hey! What's the matter with you!" said Sophie angrily.

"These aren't just pages!"

"Of course they are, they're -"

"They're Journal pages," Charity said in an excited whisper. "I can read them. This one," she waved the one in her hand, "talks about finding this cave."

"What?" asked Sophie, astonished. "But how?"

Charity didn't answer, instead she fished up the pages from the soot, brushed them off laid them on the floor. Sophie looked at her, perplexed.

"Charity what on Thea are on doing?"

"It's the Haven, Sophie, I think we might be close to it. I think these pages can help us find it."

"Wait, wait, what *exactly* does that page say?" asked Sophie.

Charity stopped searching the pile of pages and read the page still clutched in her hand.

'It is the 24th day of our foolish expedition. I am so cold, *Thea has abandoned us, I am sure of it!* Donnelly keeps talking in his sleep, keeps screaming about Sloaks, *no sign of them so far.* We have managed to dig some more of the way inside the caverns it seems

that they all interconnect in some way. *Wait, Smyth shouting*, Smyth has found something! The excitement, the tension, I wonder what he's found. He has made it through to the other side, *please let it be a route home.* Oh blast it all, it's just another cavern, well at least it has fresh water. We can rest here for now."

"Then he goes on about making his camp, it's not till the very last part," said Charity and she continued reading a little way down the page:

"Donnelly has finally found a way out, he found it whilst we slept, *escape is so close now I can taste it.* At long last we can finally make it to the Haven! All these years of work and research will – What was that noise?' and it cuts off there," said Charity, looking intensely frustrated.

"Whoever owned this Journal, he was close to the Haven? You think he found it?" asked Sophie excitedly,

"I dunno, do I?" asked Charity exasperatedly, "But this is only part of his journal, if we can find the next pages we can see where he went or what he did."

"Well if that's the twenty fourth day then that limits our search slightly," said Sophie wisely and she too began rifling through the pages, handing them to Charity who scanned them quickly and responded with a "nope" or a shake of the head. Soon they had created a very large pile of rejected pages and yet the unread pile still looked insurmountable. Charity's eyes ached as she read through reams of pages, filling in unwanted details about this man's life and why he had decided to enter the Ice Plains. Once or twice she thought she caught the word, **'Fateweaver'** but she was skimming through the pages so fast that she barely paid it any attention. When the pile in front of them was severely depleted and Charity felt that she would rather go back outside than read another page they finally made a breakthrough. Sophie had shoved yet another page in front of Charity's eyes, and she had responded with a shake of the head almost before reading. But a word then caught her eye, and she read the entire page hastily, grabbing hold of it from Sophie, her eyes widening excitedly the more she deciphered.

"Is it?" asked Sophie,

"YES!" Charity yelled, so loud that some dust and debris fell from the cracks in the ceiling above.

"Read it, read it!" said Sophie and Charity complied.

'It is 25th Day of our Journey and we are going to make it to the Haven this moon! Going to follow Donnelly now to the lake, he said that there's a short passage that leads out of the mountain range and right into Haven itself. *Oh my! What excitement!* **Wait! There's that noise again, it's louder this time. Something is coming, something is breaking through the wall, it's a Sloak, a Sloak, I'm running, scrambling trying to reach the lake, Oh Thea it's got me, something's grabbed me, the claws I can see the claws,** *the horror, the terror,* **I can't breathe, I'm being pulled apa…'**

"Um it, uh, it ends there." said Charity quietly; her heart was beating extraordinarily fast.

"Sloaks, they…they exist then?" asked Sophie just as quietly, her face displaying a look of outright terror.

"I'm almost afraid to ask," said Charity.

"They're these huge bear-like creatures that are meant to live in the Ice Plains, I wasn't sure they even existed. People have only seen glimpses of them and most people that have gone in search of them never really came back to tell anyone about it."

"Ok so they're *very* bad news, got it. Well considering all of *that,*" she gestured to the piece of paper in her hand, "I think it would be best if we just follow this guy's lead and use the lake," said Charity sensibly,

"You think he meant this?" asked Sophie pointing to the small pool of water at the back of the cave.

"Must be, there's no other water here or anywhere near here." Said Charity, glancing around as if expecting to see a huge body of water hiding in one of the other corners.

"Not much of a lake though is it?" asked Sophie, looking sceptical.

Charity peered down into dark blue water, "Maybe it's deeper than it looks. You'd never think to dive into it."

"Guess there's no harm in taking a small dip." said Sophie resolutely.

"No suppose not, can you swim by the way?" asked Charity curiously, she wasn't sure if people on Thea ever learnt such a thing.

"Yeah of course, you?"

"Yeah, I was actually quite good, well I won a certificate in school," said Charity proudly.

"A what?"

"Oh never mind," she smiled. "Look, I'll go first, just follow me straight away, I don't want to get separated." She made sure her heavy cloak and boots were stuffed into her backpack stopping momentarily when she felt the Journal, "Wait, hold on, Sophie can Journals get wet, I mean do they get damaged if they're soaked?"

"Nah, they're pretty sturdy, the Ordium is pretty much waterproof, it just slips straight off the surface of the Journal. Course it can still be damaged in other ways, fire, stabbed, torn apart."

"Torn apart?" asked Charity, staring around at the individual pages with renewed horror, "Sophie, you don't think…"

"I don't want to think about, can we just go? It's starting to feel a bit creepy in here."

Having had her temporary concerns lifted Charity made sure everything else was tightly packed away. She tucked in her shirt and after making sure Sophie was ready she dove into the pool. The water was icy cold and the shock took her breath away at first, she could feel her limbs ache with pain as she swam slowly down into the depths, her heavy backpack weighing her down and making her strokes laboured and awkward. Opening her eyes, she saw that she could see clearly enough in front of her. Willing herself on, Charity swam down until she could go no further. She paddled hard and eventually reached a small incline, she could feel her lungs ache in protest now as they begged for air, she had maybe a minute or two left or she was likely to pass out. Kicking her legs as fast as she could she swam upwards. She could see a light up ahead now and charged for it with all her strength, the light coming closer and closer until with a crash she broke through the surface of the water and into sweet, delicious air. A couple of seconds later Sophie burst into view beside her, coughing and spluttering up mouthfuls of pool water.

Charity looked up to the sky and a beautiful sight met her tired eyes. She could see the red sun now. It burned down upon them, a solitary dot on an otherwise blue canvas of pleasant sky. Sophie too had looked up, bobbing up and down in the water.

"Look at that!" she said pointing skywards. "The snow and winds seem to pass around this part of the Plains."

Charity looked more carefully and saw that she was indeed right, the sky just above them wouldn't have looked out of place in the deserts of Dura and yet about a mile or so from where they now resided the harsh weather of the Plains was clearly visible, beating down relentlessly.

"The Haven," said Charity, as Sophie nodded silently beside her.

They climbed out of the little pool and found they were now in a leafy alcove, just below them a small drop lead to a forest path with all manner of trees and plants. The leaves on the path had been trampled and showed signs of breakage; clearly someone of something lived here. Beyond the path, a magnificent forest lay ahead of them, bursting with vibrant colour, starkly contrasting the icy white cliff faces that encompassed it.

Despite their success both girls were soaking wet and it was quickly decided that before they ventured any further they should dry off first. The two girls set about making another fire which Sophie sparked into life with renewed confidence. They worked for a long time, drying their clothes and unpacking their backpacks to properly dry their snow gear. When they were finished, the red sun had begun to dip down towards the horizon and Sophie yawned loudly, flopping down onto a particularly spongy bit of earth.

"Could we rest for just a little bit do you think?" she asked, stretching out and shutting her eyes.

With a pang Charity imagined what Alistair would've said, 'No time for rest, move now.' But Alistair was gone, for all she knew they might never see him again.

"Yeah, sure, guess we could do with it." She replied, positioning herself onto the ground and leaning back, her eyes fluttering shut as sleep enveloped her once more.

Charity had not slept long, and she still felt totally drained when she awoke to a sudden noise from nearby. Sophie had awoken before her and Charity could see her glancing around warily looking for the source of the strange interruption. The fire was still burning away, the embers sparked and danced in the little pit they had dug. Charity could hear the noise louder now. Something was sniffing just beyond them in the shadows of the alcove. The sniffing grew louder until she could just see a shadowy outline stir amongst the undergrowth. She saw it move slowly from the darkness, saw its huge head move into view, its fur black and mangled, saw the huge fangs bared, its body arched and volatile as it snarled and shook. The enormous wolf emerged into the light and stared at them with its yellow eyes, she had barely time to think when the wolf was joined by others, all emerging from the shadows beside it, three, four, five enormous wolves standing snarling and grinning terribly at them.

Sophie stammered with terror and Charity felt her cold hands grip her own. She glanced quickly over to the small drop and then back at the advancing pack. She gave Sophie's hand a squeeze, felt for her backpack which only held Calville's Journal and the Imputtian Geography book, their snow clothes were still drying in the sun near to the fire. They would have to come back for them, if they survived, she thought to herself. Charity took one last desperate look at the Wolves and then pushed Sophie roughly off onto the path below. Jumping down after her, she heard the pack burst into life behind them, pounding on the soft ground with their mighty paws. Charity hauled Sophie to her feet and ran for her life.

23 – THE LAST WORDS OF CHARLES CALVILLE

Charity pelted forwards through the thick undergrowth. She could hear the wolves snapping their powerful jaws behind her, feel their presence edging ever closer to her and Sophie. They scrambled over a fallen log, Charity pulling Sophie hard so she kept pace with her, Sophie gripping her hand so tightly they seemed almost locked together. They kept running, their lungs aching dully from the strain of their efforts. Soon both girls burst from the grassy undergrowth and found themselves hurtling along an indistinct path that had been cut into the ground, the path was sodden with dirt and mud but Charity didn't care, she barely looked up from her feet, focusing instead on moving her legs as fast she could.

They sprinted down a sharp incline, stumbling a little as they did. Charity felt something claw at her back leg and urged herself forwards, fear and doubt tumbling over in her mind. She couldn't think, she couldn't speak, she could only flee. Charity looked up from the uneven path, just as something came into view that almost stopped her dead in her tracks. Ahead of them, just at the bottom of the hill, the path came to a sudden stop and in its place a yawning chasm stretched out into apparent darkness as far as she could see. A hundred desperate thoughts burst into Charity's head, and she briefly considered jumping but she knew that chasm would be much too wide – deep down she knew that no matter what she did, this was a dead end. Reaching the bottom of the hill, Charity and Sophie managed to stop themselves just in time, their heels brushing the edge of the black chasm below. Both girls turned to see the five fully grown wolves stalking towards them, their eyes flashing mercilessly, clearly aware that their prey was quite helpless now.

Charity pulled Sophie close to her. The huge wolves were closing in on them now, their white teeth bared. Charity checked the chasm behind them but whatever was down there was enveloped in impenetrable darkness. It looked fathoms deep, and jumping it was surely suicide, but if they stayed here, then what? Suddenly a desperate idea hit Charity like a thunderbolt.

"Sophie, use your spark!" she shouted.

"I'm trying!" Sophie yelled back, and Charity saw that Sophie was indeed clicking her fingers madly but only producing a harmless blue glint, her eyes were still fixed on the wolves that were now stalking towards them, their shoulders hunched, ready for the attack.

"Don't look at them!" Charity yelled. She knew that Sophie had to concentrate, knew that her fear was affecting her abilities. She took a resolute step forwards, shielding the wolves from her view. She knew exactly what she had to do. "Clear your mind Sophie. Do it, *NOW!*" and she held her arms aloft offering herself up to the hungry wolves.

"Charity, NO!" Sophie yelled in protest, but Charity did not listen. She could see the wolves, now mere feet from her, see their yellow eyes, their teeth dripping with saliva.

"Just…click!" yelled Charity, trying with immense difficulty to remain stationary as the wolves bounded towards her.

"I'M TRYING! CHARITY!" She heard Sophie's yells mingled with the incessant clicking, saw one the biggest wolves leap high into the air in front of her, and she closed her eyes and waited for the impact. To her surprise though, no impact came. Instead a sound like a hot air balloon lifting off issued from behind her, from where she knew Sophie had been cowering. Charity opened her eyes and saw the wolf standing warily inches from her, its yellow eyes wide and terrified. The others had followed suit, flinching as a bright light emitted from behind her, and she turned to see Sophie holding her hand aloft, a bright red flame the size of her head burning like a beacon on the end of her thumb.

Sophie moved forwards, warily at first as if she thought the flame might go out if she moved it, then gradually with increasing confidence she bounded towards the pack, jabbing her flame at the wolves who flinched back in terror. Fire was clearly not something they were accustomed to. Sophie waved the flame like a torch above her head and swept her hand towards the wolves, who were now considering her warily. She screwed up her face and clicked with her left hand. A similar sized ball of flame erupted onto her other thumb and she ran at the wolves like she had been possessed.

Charity made to call out in warning but there was no need, the wolves turned on their great heels and ran off back into the undergrowth, yelping in fear. Sophie returned panting, she clapped her hands together loudly and the flames extinguished immediately.

"There, piece of cake," she said breathing hard.

"That…was…amazing!" said Charity, awestruck by her friend.

"I dunno, I just, I can't explain it, I just knew I could do it that time, knew I could do it just like Ruven did."

"I reckon those were bigger than his one," said Charity smiling, "But I'm taking marks off because you didn't show the wolves a needle or a sun-crane."

Sophie laughed and Charity for the first time in a long time, laughed with her, the two girls sitting on the edge of the cliff-face laughing until their cheeks ached. Charity lay back, exhausted, and looked up at the split sky above and around them, "What next?" she asked.

Just then, a huge hand grabbed her by the scruff of the neck and yanked her back from the cliff's edge. She tumbled backwards and looked up in surprise, as a large shadow loomed over her.

"What were you thinking going so close to the edge? You'll be killed!" a familiar voice boomed angrily.

"ALISTAIR!" yelled Sophie and Charity, jumping to their feet and launching themselves at Alistair Garron, who stood before them, battered, bruised but otherwise quite well.

"Girls, don't go near that ledge. Someone could've just wandered by and pushed you both to you deaths!" he said again agitated.

Charity ignored his worrying and exploded with questions about where he had been and how he had reached them whilst Alistair leant on his cane, patiently listening to her rambling. When she had finished, he rubbed his eyes and spoke with an air of someone who had travelled a very long journey in a short space of time.

"On the mountain, I don't know about you but I couldn't see a thing." The girls nodded in agreement, "I knew from my last visit that we headed north and up the Imp Mountain, an ironic name for the largest incline in all of Thea," he said with a wry smile.

"I thought we were up a mountain!" said Charity, "But I didn't know it was called that, why's it called Imp Mount - ?" began Charity but she stopped herself quickly. "No wait, Imputtia, got it!" Sophie smirked beside her and muttered so that only Charity could hear her. "Not your proudest moment!"

"Shuddup!" whispered Charity, grinning despite her embarrassment.

"Yes, quite," said Alistair distractedly. He kept looking around their surroundings, but continued his story nonetheless, "Well we climbed the majority of the mountain, got quite near the summit as it happens. However I managed to venture onto a portion of thin ice. Part of the land must have fallen away because I crashed straight through sheets of the stuff, must've fallen about ten feet. I knew you two were still on the mountain though, I could feel you both hanging on. The rope was taut and straining to pull you down with me, and I had to at least give *you* a chance of finding the Haven…so I cut *myself* loose."

Sophie clapped a hand to her mouth in shock whilst Charity just looked stunned.

"I was exceptionally lucky. I fell only a short distance, tumbled down a mountain side and then finally dropped twenty feet maybe but I managed to land in a tree, which cushioned the fall substantially. The weather above me had changed noticeably, the snow storms had gone and I could see my surroundings quite clearly. I had been here before and I knew at once that I was in the Haven of the North. If I had known where I was going to fall I would have pulled you two with me. I even tried to climb back the way I came to get to where I'd left you but it was not possible. I am sorry for leaving you both." he finished solemnly.

"I am running out of ways to thank you for risking your life for us, Alistair Garron." said Charity going very red and thumping him on the arm.

"But wait," said Sophie suddenly. "You *didn't* come back for us?"

"Alas no, I could not ascend the mountain, the incline made it quite impossible. I wondered around making shelter in trees to avoid the wolves, I lost count of the days that I spent here if I am honest but a short time ago I heard shouting and yelling and I was sure that it was you two. I followed the noises straight to you."

"You didn't save us then?" asked Charity confused,

"Save you, what do you mean?"

Sophie and Charity told Alistair how they had collapsed and woken up in the little cave, how they had used the fallen Journal pages to find the passage into the Haven and eventually found him.

"You woke up in the cave *after* losing consciousness?" asked Alistair quietly.

"Yes." said Charity,

"Could you have rolled there, down the hill I mean?"

"I suppose," said Charity slowly. "But it's a million to one shot isn't it?"

"It is indeed, and you saw no one else?"

Charity hesitated for a moment, thinking about the fleeting footprint she had seen in the snow. Had it been her imagination or something real?

"We didn't see anyone!" said Sophie, seriously. "Not a soul!"

"Puzzling…" said Alistair, now deep in thought. "Well it seems Thea is shining down upon us, so we should push on whilst she still shows fortune."

"Do you know where we are?" asked Charity. Pushing the footprint out of her head and changing the subject.

"I do. We are in the Haven of the North, as I have said, but more specifically we are a very short distance from where I believe Charles Calville will have placed his last missing page."

"Where? How do you know that?" asked Charity eagerly, staring avidly around their surroundings. However apart from the gigantic chasm behind her she could see nothing of interest, certainly nothing that looked linked to Calville or the Fateweaver..

As a response Alistair bent low and picked up a handful of rocks, and walking along the edge of the cliff he scattered them out over the chasm. Each one fell straight into the darkness below. He picked up another handful and threw these out in another direction. He continued this for some time, ignoring their requests for further information until at last he pointed out into the middle of the chasm, a triumphant look on his face.

"What? What is it?" asked Charity,

"The stone, it's there, right…there!" he said, pointing excitedly into the chasm.

"I don't see, oh my!" said Sophie shocked. Charity could now see the little stone, it was suspended motionless in mid-air, right in the centre of the chasm.

"This is the bridge of faith. Legend has it that the bridge was a gift from the Old Gods to Thea upon her first arrival. The Haven is where she ascended into the Heavens and as such it had to remain almost impossible to access. Only Thea knew of the bridge's existence and so only she was able to make it across."

"How do you know all this?" asked Sophie, awestruck by Alistair's breadth of knowledge.

"Well it is a common story where I grew up. My Mother and Father used to tell it to me when I was a boy," he said gruffly, averting his gaze from their own. "They used to, erm, study this sort of thing."

"Really?" asked Charity, eager to know more about Alistair. "What did they do? What were their jobs I mean?"

"That is unimportant, Charity. We have little time, and we must press on."

"Oh, ok then," said Charity, slightly crestfallen.

"As I was saying, when I first visited the Haven, our party discovered the bridge completely by accident. We'd all heard the story but not one of us dared put such a tale of whimsy to the test. We argued for hours about what to do or how to cross the chasm, tensions were high and tempers frayed. Two of us got into a brawl as a result, and one of our number fell off the cliff after being shoved aside in the melee. But instead of falling to his death, he rolled a couple of feet out into the chasm. Of course we thought we had all gone mad when we first saw it but after further tests," he shook one of the rocks, "we were convinced and we used it to cross to the other side."

"That is incredible. How on Thea is that even possible?" Sophie wondered aloud.

"Remember what I asked you in Galcia," said Alistair, ignoring Sophie's question, " 'Do you trust me?' Now I need you to remember what you told me."

Charity and Sophie both nodded resolutely and Alistair smiled in return.

"Very well, follow me and be careful; you *must* mimic my exact movements whilst on the bridge."

He led them out into the chasm. Charity felt sick as she stepped out on what appeared to be thin air, however placing one foot down first she could feel something hard under her feet. No matter what her eyes were telling her, there was definitely something there. They did not spend long on the bridge as Alistair was eager to cross as briskly as possible. Charity kept glancing down to see the bottom of the chasm, for she was sure if she didn't, her feet would slip into the abyss below. Soon they reached the other side, where a similar looking forest sprawled out around them and Alistair moved forwards with more purpose now looking more excited than she had ever seen. He gestured to them and then broke into a jog, travelling along a similar dirt path to the one they had left on the other side. Charity and Sophie ran to keep up with his huge strides.

"Alistair, why were you here before? What were you looking for?" asked Charity, puffing and panting as she ran. She'd been most curious about this since he mentioned his previous visit to the Haven back at Silvus'.

"That is not important, Charity, rest assured it was nothing to do with what you were searching for."

Charity fell silent once more. He was being awfully secretive, she thought to herself, if she didn't trust him so implicitly so would've been worried about what his true motives were but Alistair had so far never let her down.

"It is here, just up here," he panted.

"The page?" asked Charity but Alistair did not respond. Instead he wordlessly pointed at something just off in the distance. It was a small puddle cut into the ground, no bigger than a child's paddling pool and just as shallow. Charity approached it and saw that in the centre of the pool was a stone pedestal, its presence was for some reason was no surprise to her. In fact, something inside her had expected it to be there. Charity stepped forwards eagerly, as Alistair and Sophie, both beaming, moved aside for her to approach the pool. She could see what lay atop the pedestal now, and as she spotted it her heart began to thump and her spirits rose, it was a solitary white page. She had made it, she had found the last page, now she would finally see what Calville had done with the Fateweaver.

She dropped her backpack beside the small pool and grabbed the Journal from inside it, then she pulled it back on and slipped into the water. It barely came up to her ankles which meant that thanks to her boots, her feet remained mercifully dry. Opening the book to the torn edge she had ran her fingers along many a night, she picked up the page and slotted it neatly into place. It happened instantly, just as it had done before, the book gave a little rumble and then issued a blinding flash of white light. Shielding her eyes, Charity peeked out as the light died away and the book became still once more. She checked its contents with baited breath. The dirt covered page was now pristinely white, mirroring its brethren in every possible way. A golden line had fused the page along its torn seam and then with a flash disappeared, leaving the entire Journal quite still. Charity's hands shook a little as she stared down at the object in her hand, savouring the enormity of what she had accomplished. After all this time, after all these hardships, Charles Calville's Journal lay complete, ready for her to finish.

Charity wasted no time. She would not be deterred by anything. She jumped from the pool and yanked the book open to the back page where she had last read. Alistair and Sophie stood motionless, utterly engrossed, just waiting for her to speak. The last page was only filled with a single paragraph of writing. Charity's heart fell when she saw its meagre length, however she did not scan ahead like she usually did. She simply opened her mouth and read to her friends:

'These will be my final thoughts before I go. I found it, found it in the very heart of the Imputtian plains, the Haven of the North but here it must not remain. *How very appropriate.* I will use it now as she instructed; I can use it to do everything, use it to hide the pages and to ensure the feather does not fall into wrong hands. *She was right, she was always right. It is the only way.* This final page I will leave where the feather once lay, the first will lie in the Durad Temple. *Both suitable challenges for any worthy Thean.* As for the feather, the plume known as the Fateweaver, it will be hidden where true power resides and revealed to her equal only.

Writing something in my Journal with the feather now, hands shaking, trembling. It feels incredible, pages ripping, joy turing to pain, blinding pain! Journal closing, Journal disappearing… I did it I did it, *I am coming my love.*'

'That's it?" said Charity looking devastated. "That doesn't tell us anything! What a waste of time! Great, we know that the Fateweaver *was* here and he *moved* it!"

"You truly are a fool," said a cold, casual voice from behind them. Whirling around they stood face to face with Cassius, his great blade shining red with blood and a thick black cloak tied around his shoulders.

"I really doubted that this plan would actually work you know. To think that mere children and their oaf could make it to the Haven of the north is quite something, but to rely on them piecing together the last of Calville's Journal, now that, that takes *true faith!*" Cassius said vindictively.

Alistair had quietly pulled out his cane, but Cassius flashed a look at him, his calm demeanour momentarily gone. "If you move again, I *will* kill you. I'm afraid that I'm going to kill you all anyway but it will distinctly more uncomfortable for *all* of you if you don't drop that cane." His voice was low and dangerous, a savage whisper uttered through shining teeth.

Alistair did not move but he did not drop his cane, "Do you really want another exhibition of my power Garron? If it wasn't for *lady luck* here," he stabbed his sword in the direction of Charity, "you'd be dead and I'd have already found this wretched thing and well, you don't need to know the rest of the plan now do you?"

Still Alistair's grip remained tight on his cane. Cassius sighed wearily, "Very well," and in a flash of movement he charged at Alistair. Stooping low to the ground, he swept up an underlying branch and slammed it into Alistair's chest, pinning him against a nearby tree. Alistair fell back, his head slamming hard against the trunk. Charity watched in horror as his head drooped forward and slumped to the ground.

"Next we have the quiet one," Cassius said with relish. He turned to look at Sophie who had started to click her fingers almost uncontrollably. Cassius stepped towards her. She looked up at his tall slim figure and into his dark eyes. Charity could not move. Everything happened so quickly. Before she could so much as utter a cry of shock, Sophie was slammed into the hard dirt, her Journal spilled out onto the ground from her jacket and she lay there, quite still.

He picked up the little blue Journal and casually flicked to a random page, reading aloud to Charity a euphoric look on his skeletal face.

"Scared, *I cannot sleep*. Charity talking in her sleep again. *She does this an awful lot, maybe she's worried*. Tomorrow is fast approaching and I know I'm going to ruin things for everyone. Charity is a Regalis and Alistair is a famed warrior but what am I? *Just a stupid little girl without a family, that's what*."

Cassius stopped reading and tossed the book aside like he were tossing away a piece mouldy food. "Well put Sophie, it's good to see some refreshing honesty now and again."

Charity felt white-hot tears burn her face as she stood helplessly clutching Calville's Journal in the shallow pool.

"Well then," said Cassius emphatically. "No more interruptions. You see I wanted us to have a conversation before I kill you. Oh yes," he said, his eyes flashing mercilessly. "I am going to kill you." He laughed to himself, correctly interpreting the look of fear etched onto Charity's face.

"I'm not going to offer you a bargain, or ask for the book in exchange. I'm going to kill you, slice you in two as it happens. Do not worry you will not feel *much* pain; it will be a quick, clean death. Before I do that, however, I *would* like to ask you a question." He paused as if he was waiting for her to respond, and Charity nodded silently.

"Ah, good. Tell me then, have you worked out how I keep finding you yet?"

"You're working for the Order, and they sent you out to find the Journal just like me!"

"Oh bravo!" Cassius said dramatically clapping his hands. "How long did it take you to work things out?"

Charity did not immediately respond. She felt sick being toyed with like this. She could not pull her eyes from Sophie and Alistair's lifeless forms. She tried to answer but her words felt constricted in her throat.

"ANSWER ME!" screamed Cassius, suddenly ferocious, Charity jumped back in shock, but then before she could so much as utter a word in reply, his mood was once more composed, clam and saccharine. "Oh, you see how I get when people don't respond to my questions. Tell me, how long did it take you to work out I was assisting the Order?"

"Soon after we left the Duradon Temple," said Charity in a quivering voice, "Alistair told us the Order's obsession with finding the Fateweaver."

"Indeed, they are quite incessant on finding the thing. Old habits die hard, I suppose. Well this is all very impressive, I must say. It is comforting to know I will not be ending a *totally* worthless life today. But Charity, if you will indulge me, one last question, my dear: do you know *why* you are standing here holding that Journal?"

Charity turned over the question in her mind, but she had no idea what Cassius was alluding to. "No," she said, meeting his gaze for the first time.

"You stand there, defiant in the face of almost certain death because I allow it Charity. *I* was chosen by the Order to find the Journal over you; they saw my greatness and your normality and they chose me! They let me follow you, track you, find you, I *let* you slip through my fingers at Duradon, I saw you ascending the Imp Mountain and I let you proceed because I *knew, KNEW* that you would bring the book straight to where I needed it, ready for the reading. You're nothing but a toy, my dear, a plaything used to move forward in a game that's so much bigger than you can ever know. When this is all over *I* will be the one to rule the Fateweaver and it will be me that writes my name in the annuals of history: Cassius, the last of the Regalis."

"NO!" shouted Charity. She was breathing very fast, her chest rising and falling so much that she almost dropped the Journal. "*I* did this, *I* found the pages!" she shouted at him. "I accomplished things with more than just power or brute strength. I used my wits, I used my heart, and I didn't do it alone either, I had help…help from my friends!"

"Yes, and very useful they look too," said Cassius sarcastically as he surveyed her two companions sprawled on the ground before them. "All very amusing, I must admit, such fight from such a little thing. Well time's up, I'm afraid," Cassius said casually, and without warning, he charged at Charity. But she was ready for him, and she dove out of the way just in time so he clattered into the little pedestal, which smashed noisily into the pool below. Charity knew this would only slow him down, so without thinking, she pelted off into the undergrowth, into the unknown. She knew that this would draw Cassius away from Sophie and Alistair, she knew that he would always come after her, he would *always* come after the Journal.

24 – A SWORDS AND A SLOAK

Charity hurtled down the mossy side of an embankment and splashed into a shallow river below. She could hear Cassius puffing behind him, his sword tinkling lightly at his side.

"You cannot run from me Charity, there's no place to go!" he screamed maniacally through the trees.

Charity sped down a small path, trampling the wet grass and leaves as she went. She had no idea where she was or where she was going but she knew that she could not stop running. Vines and branches whipped her face and arms as she scrambled through thickets and over puddles of rainwater that had pooled in the dirt. Emerging from a particularly thick patch of forest, Charity spotted a cave just off in the distance. She could see no other alternative so she pelted forwards once more, turning her head to see Cassius leap through the last of the undergrowth and out onto the path behind her.

She entered the cavern at a run, not stopping to check where it led or what might dwell within, her footsteps echoing about the dank surroundings as she turned round corners and slid through thin gaps in the rocks. Cassius was following her every step. She could still hear still his footsteps as they slowed to a casual walk, and his voice crackled with barely-suppressed rage as it bounced off the walls and reverberated inside her head.

"Your punishment for running will be severe, Charity," he said casually. "I was going to make this quick but now, oh no! Now I'm going to take my *sweet time*. Then when I'm done, Charity, I'm going to bring your body back to your friends, let them get a glimpse of what I've done before I do the same to them."

Charity tried to ignore him, tried not to listen to his taunts and threats but it was growing increasingly difficult. The further she ventured into the dark cave, the grimmer her situation felt and the more fear and doubt clouded her judgment. Once or twice she considered going back, begging Cassius to let her friends go in exchange for the Journal, but she shook her head violently in a bid to expel such thoughts.

Suddenly a huge 'BANG' went off behind her. Part of the wall beside her crumbled away and acrid dust enveloped her. Charity coughed and spluttered, groping her way through the cloud, trying to find her bearings. She could hear a tapping, like the striking of something hard on stone. The tapping grew louder and louder; whatever it was, was making its way towards her. The cloud of dust had begun to clear now, and as it did Charity could see what the noise had been. Cassius was strolling towards her, haphazardly striking his blade against the stone walls around him. She locked eyes with him and a triumphant look spread across his gaunt face.

"This ends, now!" he said, sternly.

Charity had only one way to run. She hurried away from the dust and down a dark incline, just behind her. The vestiges of sunlight that had managed to penetrate the cave had all but disappeared as she descended deeper into the cave. She was forced to feel along the walls for support as she pelted down, away from Cassius, who was calling to her again.

"Charity, oh Charity." He sang to her, taunting her, tormenting her.

Charity could hear something else now besides the delighted mutterings of Cassius, a low growling noise coming from further down into the cavern. She just could make out a dim light at the very bottom of the incline she currently travelling down. Was there someone who could rescue her? Perhaps it was a way out of this maze and a way to safety! Renewed hope bubbling up inside her, she sprinted forwards towards the light.

As she got closer, Charity realised that the light was in fact coming from the remnants of a small fire, its flames extinguished but the embers still smouldering brightly. The hill had come to stop and ground become more even. Charity looked behind, checking for Cassius, but he was nowhere to be seen. She ceased her running and crept forwards towards the burning embers, and the rumbling sound had started up once more, louder than before. Charity hesitated. What if it was another wolf that was making the noise? Or what if she had inadvertently stumbled into its lair? She edged closer the fire. She was standing at the mouth of a shallow pit, the dying fire right in the centre. As Charity moved warily over the threshold of the pit, she saw something, two creatures unlike anything she had ever seen before. Not in any book, or even on Thea had Charity ever seen such a monstrous sight.

She dropped Calville's Journal to the hard ground as she clapped both hands over her mouth to stop herself from screaming. She slammed herself against the wall of the cavern unable to tear her eyes from the two creatures. They were humungous, at least the height of a Sun-Crane and as wide as a bear, they had dirty, matted fur that covered their entire bodies except their heads which remained quite bald. Charity could see the pink flesh on their heads underneath several layers of filth and grime, their eyes bright slits that glowed red in the light of the embers. They had very crooked, snout-like noses too, and the whole effect made them look like a grotesque hybrid of a bear and a wolf.

One of the creatures yawned lazily, exposing a huge mouth packed with jagged, misshapen teeth. She noticed with a wave of dread that there were several bones protruding from in between these fangs. The beasts' hands and feet were also covered in fur, but Charity could see huge claws extending out from their ends, claws that looked razor sharp and were at least the length of her entire arm. Charity had known immediately when she first laid eyes on them that these creatures were Sloaks. Nothing this terrifying could have gone undiscovered in any place, no matter how remote. One of the Sloaks was picking its teeth with a clawed hand. It seemed to be having immense difficulty, as suddenly it slammed a fist into the dirt and stood up, its bald head brushing the stone ceiling.

Another noise echoed out from behind Charity, making her whirl around. Cassius' footsteps were getting louder – he was drawing ever closer to her. What if he had grown bored of taunting her? She knew that he would not hesitate in killing her where she stood, but she had reached a dead end, and she couldn't possibly go any further, not with those *things* prowling so close by. With a grim sense of realisation, Charity knew she was going to have to choose between two equally gruesome ends; there was no other way out. She picked up the Journal once more, praying for an idea to come to her rescue. Almost as though it had been waiting for Charity to ask for it, an image popped into her mind, fully formed, an image of a white-haired youth squaring off against two ferocious Sloaks. That was it, she thought excitedly; if she could just lure Cassius into the pit of Sloaks, then it might just give her enough time to escape. Charity set about with her backpack, quickly fumbling with the contents and the Journal. She straightened up, resolutely facing the shadows and waited for him to come. She had one shot at this, and she had to do it right.

Cassius emerged slowly from the darkness. His smile was most evident and he looked positively delighted with himself as he strode to where she now stood, bathed in the distant light of the embers.

Cassius walked nonchalantly towards her, his sword still outstretched, and he waved it through the air, as if planning where to strike first.

"No more talk," he said, his voice impassive.

Charity pulled something from her cloak and held it aloft, just out of sight of Cassius, dangling it tantalisingly in the shadows in front of her.

"Fine with me! You want *this* don't you?!" she whispered viciously. "You've maimed, killed and who knows what else, *all for this!*"

"You attempt to bargain with me, Charity," he said his lips curling. "My dear, you have absolutely nothing to offer me. Very soon I am going to kill you and then take the Journal from you, or take it now and then kill you, the schematics are inconsequential. You've lost, so face your fate with a modicum of dignity, girl."

"And if I destroy it?" Charity asked, matching Cassius' cold voice.

For the first time since she had encountered Cassius, Charity saw something in his eyes, something that was suddenly much more pronounced than the greed, or callousness that he usually emitted. Cassius was fearful.

"Oh you wouldn't like that then?" said Charity, reading his face and imitating his casual tone. "If I say, throw this Journal into the fire?" She indicated the embers behind her. Charity's face was cool and collected but her mind raced with worries. Could Cassius see the two Sloaks standing just out of sight beyond the light? One of the Sloaks shifted, moving towards the mouth of the pit. Charity was sure he would see the beast but Cassius had eyes only for the Journal. He followed the book like a moth to a flame, as she waved it about in front of him, teasing him, testing him.

"Give it to me, *now!*" spat Cassius viciously.

"Fine! Go and get it," whispered Charity and turning she threw it with all her might at the little fire. It hit the ground just short of it and slid into the flames. Even from a distance Charity could see the light grow as flames began to lick and dance on the surface of the book.

"NO!" screamed Cassius, leaping forwards in terror.

He shoved Charity out of the way, his eyes locked on the now gradually burning book. Charity saw him slide to the ground, grabbing at the book desperately and patting it down with his heavy cloak. She did not wait to see what happened. She took her one chance and turning on her heels sprinted back up the incline and out the way she had come. She had just reached where Cassius had blasted through part of the cave, when she heard a scream of pain and a roar of fury from far below her and instantly she knew her plan had worked. The Sloaks had realised his presence but that did not mean she was free – she needed to escape the caverns and find Sophie and Alistair. Retracing her steps, she eventually found her way to the mouth of the cave. The sunlight split the rocks and Charity could finally see properly again. She clambered her way out of the cave and into the blinding sunlight, as two familiar figures burst out from a large patch of trees nearby.

"Alistair, Sophie!" she yelled happily to them, relief washing over her. "You're ok?!"

"We're fine. A little sore," said Sophie, rubbing her head. "Oh Charity! When we saw you had gone, we were so worried but... Cassius... how did you...?"

"No time to explain," said Charity in a rush, bounding towards them and pulling them away from the cave. "We have to go now!"

. . . .

Cassius thumped the Journal hard on the ground, managing to douse the remainder of the flames with his heavy cloak. He tentatively brushed the ash and soot from the cover and inspected his prize, his heart beating excitedly. The light from the embers of the little fire illuminated the writing on the front of book, but it was not the same golden font he had expected. Cassius read the writing, fury bubbling up inside him as he understood gradually what had just happened. '*A Geographical Survey of Imputtia and the Ice Plains, by Timothy Dembling*'. How could he have let the girl get the better of him once again? He sprang to his feet, roaring with rage. He would find her now, he would find her and there would be no more idle taunting, no more talk, he was going to tear her limb from limb. Just then a colossal shadow danced across the wall. Cassius heard the swish of an object come flailing in his direction and a great clawed fist smashed into the ground, inches from where he had been lying. He leapt back in shock as two huge creatures lurched forwards from the surrounding darkness, their red eyes flashing hungrily. Cassius instantly recognised the beasts as two fully-grown Sloaks. Their eyes popped and they snorted with primal rage as they swung their great claws and gnashed their many fangs in his direction.

Unfurling his blade, he unclipped his heavy cloak and without abandon, threw himself at one of the monsters which reared up angrily snapping its great jaws at him. He dodged one mighty bite and scythed his blade into the beast's side, and pulling it free, he watched as ink-black blood spilled noisily to the floor. The beast cried out in agony and crumpled to the floor, his great head smashing hard on the stone. Cassius turned to the other but the Sloak was ready for him. A huge claw came hurtling through the air and caught him full on the side of the head, and he spun to the ground, his sword still clasped tightly in his hand. Cassius put a hand swiftly to his temple where the beast had struck. He could feel hot blood trickling down his cheeks and onto his neck.

He had no time for self-pity however. As the Sloak bounded towards him, its mouth frothing, its hair raised, Cassius attempted to side-step the Sloak, but its arms were so wide that it managed to grab a hold of him with one outstretched paw, pinning him roughly to the ground. Cassius drew back his head till it hit the stone as the beast snapped and lunged its fangs towards his throat and face. Cassius strained with all his might. He was just managing to hold it off, his feet and arms straining under the weight of the beast as it scrambled its claws in the dirt beside him, attempting to force its way closer to his head. One bite and he knew he would be finished. Cassius summoned all his strength and with one almighty push, he kicked his legs upwards. The beast flew from him and hit the back wall with a devastating crash. Several large rocks fell from the ceiling above and the beast looked up dizzily to see Cassius charging towards him, his face and blade wet with blood and his eyes alight with fury.

Cassius finished the beast with two intricate slices to its neck. The fight, although short, had taken its toll on him, and again he gingerly felt where the beast had struck him, finding two long scratches just below his ear. He did not dwell in the cave. He had one motive, one purpose now, and he would find her, find her and finish this obscene chase once and for all.

....

"Did you hear that?" asked Sophie. "That sounded way bigger than a wolf! Alistair you don't think there's Sloaks up…" she tailed off, giving Alistair a look of outright terror.

Charity however knew what had made the noise and it filled her with more fear than she dared mention. Cassius was coming for them.

Alistair had started to reassure Sophie but Charity interrupted him. "It doesn't matter, we have to go, *right now!* Alistair how do you get out of the Haven, how do we get back?"

"There is one way, but…" Alistair hesitated, looking quickly between Charity's petrified face and the depths below, and then he seemed to come to a sudden decision. "Very well, follow me."

He hurtled off along the cliff side that ran parallel with the chasm. Charity and Sophie followed at a run. Charity kept glancing down into the darkness beside them; she truly hoped that whatever Alistair had in mind it didn't involve going down *there.* They ran until the forest had begun to show less greenery and more signs of the barren wasteland Charity now associated with the Plains. The lush innards of the Haven were fast becoming a distant memory and Charity thought that they must be getting closer to where the Haven ended and the Ice Plains began. The group struggled to manoeuvre themselves along the cliff's path, which was becoming exceedingly narrow as they moved forwards towards their unknown destination. They had even begun to move in single file so they could accommodate Alistair who was leading, with Sophie and then Charity following from the rear. Charity stumbled, bumping into Sophie, who teetered perilously over the edge. Charity grabbed her roughly and pulled her level

"Sorry!" Charity panted apologetically.

Sophie nodded in an understanding way and continued along the path, which was becoming increasingly dilapidated the further they travelled. Charity was starting to wonder if Alistair knew where he was going.

As they travelled, Charity breathlessly told them about Cassius' attack, his reading of Sophie's Journal and his confirmation of his work with the Order. Alistair grimaced at this revelation but remained silent. Charity thought that perhaps he was still sore from being disarmed by Cassius so easily – it couldn't have happened very often. She told them about how she had tricked him into using the Geography book and left him alone with the Sloaks. Sophie looked mightily impressed. She was gawping at Charity so much that she momentarily took her eyes off the path and almost tripped over a stray root that was languishing at her feet. She managed to hop over it just time but kept her eyes firmly glued on where she was going from then on.

Finally, however, Alistair seemed to decide they had travelled far enough and he brought the group to an abrupt stop. Sophie and Charity almost ran into him but managed, at the last second, to steady themselves. It was a good thing Alistair had stopped, she thought, glancing around, as they had come to the end of the path and the end of the cliff. Looking into the distance, Charity could see the snow and rain of the Plains, pelting down mercilessly just a couple of miles from their idyllic viewpoint. But it was what she saw when she looked down that caused her the most concern. Glancing just below her was a sheer drop into darkness, a drop that looked to Charity like certain death. She looked around confused, unable to see why Alistair had led them here. Had he taken a wrong turn? Was he lost?

"Alistair, you're not expecting us to –"

A scream from behind them interrupted Charity and caused them all to turn, her question now forgotten. Cassius was there, charging towards them along the cliff's edge, his sword drawn and his black eyes burning with a terrible fury. Charity had never seen anyone look like this: he looked deranged, almost insane, his hair matted with dirt and soot whilst his usually pale skin was smothered in soot and blood. Terrified, Charity backed up against Alistair, who grabbed her and Sophie close to him.

"Alistair, what are you - ?" asked Charity.

"Charity, Sophie..." said Alistair, his voice shaking. "Do...you...*trust*...me?"

Cassius screamed with fury, slashing his sword from side to side as he rushed towards them.

"What...I...YES!" they both faltered.

He was feet from them now. Charity, Sophie and Alistair had backed up to the very end of the path, and Charity saw Alistair's foot slip and slide over the dwindling ground.

"Good!" Alistair bellowed to both girls, and holding them tight he jumped backwards, off the cliff and into the darkness of the crevice below. Charity screamed in terror as the edge they had been standing on, now far above them, got smaller and smaller as they fell. She could just make out Cassius bellowing to the heavens, his bloody face taut with rage.

They were falling extraordinarily quickly. Charity didn't even have time to think, she could only watch as they fell through the impenetrable darkness, towards certain death. She had her eyes wide open but could see nothing. She could feel leaves brushing her as she whipped by, and then suddenly she burst through the darkness and sunlight flooded her eyes once more. Glancing down, Charity saw a wonderful, marvellous sight, a sight that made the last few seconds of her descent almost euphoric with relief; it was a river of crystal clear, blue water.

They were heading straight for this tumbling river. She saw the water moving closer and closer and then finally, she braced herself for the impact. With a colossal splash all three of them hit the water hard, Alistair still with them clasped to his huge chest so they sunk, like a strange anchor, down into its depths. Deeper and deeper they drifted. Charity thought they were bound to hit the bottom but they never did, instead coming to a gradual stop, floating calmly in the crystal clear water. Alistair released both Charity and Sophie and turning them towards him with a massive hand, pointed a huge finger to the sky above and began swimming upwards.

Charity followed him, breaking the surface of the water minutes later and turning to look at Sophie and Alistair, her face sopping wet but a feeling of incredible relief washing over her entire body.

"Thank you for trusting me," said Alistair.

"STOP BEING SO NOBLE!" yelled Charity as she dove at Alistair, punching and kicking him with her legs under the water, which made things noticeably more difficult.

"ARGH, I cannot, ARGH, CHARITY, STOP!" he shouted, as Charity snapped and swung just as ferociously as one of the Sloaks.

"You keep…on…risking your…life…to save…us." she panted, finally allowing Sophie to subdue her.

"You do, Alistair, she's right," said Sophie smiling at him. "We really do appreciate it, it's just I think Charity is worried you might get yourself hurt."

"AGAIN!" added Charity moodily. "I just…" she sighed very heavily, "thank you, for the millionth time!"

"It is my job, Charity, I swore I would protect you and a Garron never gives up on a promise." he said proudly.

"Oh forget it!" said Charity as Alistair continued to stare at her, a concerned look in his eyes.

Charity realised that she sounded upset, and she couldn't pretend she wasn't annoyed with him, but deep down she knew that no matter what she said, Alistair would stop at nothing to help her and Sophie. It was an unusual feeling, she thought, to have someone so dedicated to keeping her safe, someone she could call a true 'friend'.

She was conflicted by recent events, however; it gave her a feeling of immense security to have Alistair with her but she couldn't shake the nagging voice inside her head that kept warning her, 'He'll get hurt with you, just send him away'. This little voice had been growing louder and louder ever since he had damaged his Journal in Dura and right now, despite the euphoria of their incredible escape, it was bellowing inside her head. Charity pushed the worries to the back of her mind.

"Never mind. I'm sorry Alistair, I am grateful you know?"

"I do," he said calmly.

Sophie looked content that the disagreement had subsided and turned to Alistair. "Where do we go now?" she asked, looking up and down the river.

"We swim towards the Plains," said Alistair, pointing towards the huge sheet of ice and snow in the distance. "The current changes dramatically as soon as you cross over. The river will carry us out of Imputtia and we should be able to ground ourselves somewhere in the Castlands…at least that's how I managed to get out."

"We're swimming? That'll take weeks won't it?" asked Sophie, aghast at the suggestion.

"No, the current will do most of the work. You will see soon enough," said Alistair, an unmistakable tone of warning present in his deep voice.

"Why aren't we going to Galcia though? Why the Castlands? Surely it's way too dangerous?" remarked Sophie, looking increasingly concerned.

"Sophie, right now it is the safest place on Thea!"

Charity and Sophie both looked at him, shock and confusion on their faces.

"The Order will know of your success soon. They will be more desperate than ever to find you and that Journal. Don't forget you have seen a side of the Ivory Order that no ordinary Thean was ever meant to see."

"But but I didn't ask –" started Charity angrily.

"Charity you *must* understand that the Order is an institution thousands of years old and the trusted right hand of every ruler on Thea. You cannot simply walk into Galcia unnoticed anymore."

"Yeah, but what if we went to Euphestus or Mosia about it?" said Charity, a little taken aback.

"Go to Euphestus…Mosia?" repeated Alistair in disbelief. "Charity, haven't you been listening? You will be wanted by every Ivory Order, guard, knight and scout on Thea, and won't be able to set foot in any settlement under Order rule without being spotted. We *can't* just go barging into cities, demanding the Order be brought to justice, so please don't treat this like some sort of a game!"

Charity fell silent, red-faced and angry with herself for being so naïve. She let Alistair's words sink in, and as they did the impossibility of her task was greater than ever before. Still something in his speech had begun to resonate inside her head. "Game…game," she said to herself thoughtfully. Alistair's words had reminded her of something that Cassius had said to her earlier, something that she thought Alistair and Sophie ought to know.

"Alistair, Cassius told me that this whole feather thing..."

"Fateweaver thing."

"Yes, yes, *Fateweaver* thing," said Charity impatiently, "that it was all part of a bigger game, something bigger than all of us. Do you have any idea what he meant?"

Alistair looked off thoughtfully. He paddled forwards towards the Ice Plains someway and then turned to her.

"I'm afraid I do not." he said flatly.

Charity felt disappointed. This was yet another mystery she had been tasked with working out showing no sign of being solved anytime soon. She felt a heavy weight inside her chest expand a little as she digested this new information. There were so many things she had to do, it was a wonder that the weight wasn't dragging her beneath the surface.

"What's this river called again?" asked Sophie, who looked as though she'd rather not discuss serious matters anymore.

"Koben, it is the River Koben," said Alistair.

"Oooh, I know that name. Koben is the river that runs right through Thea. I didn't know it went all the way through the Haven of the north," said Sophie excitedly.

"Yes, it does, quite a happy coincidence for us."

"But then how come people don't just swim up it to the Haven, you know instead of going through the Plains?" asked Charity, remembering with a shudder the dreadful conditions they had experienced and staring apprehensively at the white sheet of cold that was hammering onto the distant parts of the river.

"Well, two reasons. Firstly, the current is incredibly strong, as you are about to find out and secondly there is no way of climbing up from where we fell. That cliff face is completely vertical, there's not a Thean alive who could scale it," Alistair said wisely.

"Ah, I see. Oh…Um the Plains are coming up, should we duck under the water?" asked Charity, a worried look across her face.

"That would be very wise," said Alistair. "The current will do the pulling, just stay afloat and keep bobbing up for air and it should not take us too long. Oh and keep your arms moving or they're likely to drop off."

Sophie smiled at this last warning but Alistair did not return her smile instead whispering quietly: "I have seen it happen, keep…them…moving."

Sophie gulped as they moved under the huge white curtain and once more into the windswept land of ice and snow. Alistair had not been exaggerating. The water's temperature plummeted the second they floated out of the Haven's safety. The river seemed to change around them, the current, once lazy and weak was suddenly ferociously strong. Charity was yanked and pulled downstream with surprising force and it was all she could do to keep herself the right side up. She just managed to swim to the surface and gasp in air when she needed it, but as soon as she broke the surface of the river, her face and arms were bombarded with heavy raindrops and huge globules of frost. Very quickly, she came to the decision that it was actually warmer under the water and so it was here she spent most of her journey, swimming along with the current and keeping the blood flowing in her arms and legs. Alistair had been doing this also but Charity noticed that he only needed to come up for air every five minutes or so, perhaps one of the advantages of having lungs as large as his, she thought to herself.

Charity, Sophie and Alistair sped down the River Koben. Charity felt like she was on a very cold, very dangerous water slide. The speed they must be travelling was quite unbelievable. After a long time swimming, what seemed like thirty or maybe forty minutes, Charity felt someone pulling at her hair. She screamed in protest as a large bubble emitted from her mouth and sailed towards the sky, and turning she saw Sophie pointing up towards Alistair who was bobbing on the surface, his great arms paddling hard against the current. She swam upwards with difficulty and Alistair grabbed her arm tightly.

"Hold on," he said. "Head towards the bank."

He indicated a sandy bank just to their left, the river was certainly deep but luckily it wasn't too wide and it only took them a little while to ground themselves once more on dry land. They fell back against the ground, Charity panting and exhausted but utterly triumphant. She had made it, they had made it – they had braved the Ice Plains and won.

....

The white Knights flowed into the cities and towns across Thea, visiting tiny settlements, showing up at the temples and giving long drawn out speeches to packed halls crowded with people. All over Thea, a very clear message was being delivered to the people, and as the Order Knights trooped out of the Chapter in Upper Forfal on a fine morning, a great crowd had assembled in the gardens to hear for themselves this urgent news. Order workers, citizens, tourists and onlookers all craned their necks curiously to see, as a small man with a crooked nose and black-rimmed spectacles took several nervous steps towards the crowd. He unfurled a letter and after pausing hesitantly, read:

"The Ivory Order would like to formally issue a decree for the arrest of one Charity Walters, one Sophie Pierce and one Alistair Garron. These three have been accused of the murder of an unnamed Dura official and the theft of a highly valuable Order artefact from this very Order Chapter. If anyone comes into contact with any of these individuals please do not approach them but contact a member of the Ivory Order immediately. Thank you."

The man folded the letter with trembling hands, and turned and wordlessly crept back into the Chapter behind him as the crowd murmured in reaction to his words. He had just made it to the door, when a voice bellowed from somewhere in the midst of the onlookers, "LIES!"

Clergyman Perch stopped in his tracks and turned to face the crowd. The Knights turned their heads frantically, searching for the one who had spoken out, the one bold enough to challenge the Order. A large woman, with flaming red hair stood forwards, her huge frame blocking out at least two of the people behind her. She stood before the crowd now, an imposing figure, bristling with shock and anger.

"I don' believe what I'm hearin'! Look," she said hotly, "I know this girl, Charty, I know Soapy too and a pair of nicer girls you've never met, I tell yer. Now granted, I only met Soapy a short while but Charty she's no criminal, she's just a gurl!"

"Hold your tongue Gisele," said one of the Knights brandishing a blade at her. "This is an official decree from the Cardinal himself, which means it's law!"

"You just try takin' me in whitey, just you try it. I'm speaking the truth, and the people of Thea know the truth when they hear it! Charty Waters is an honest gurl, she ain't responsible for such a crime, there's no way! I won't let her good name be tarnished by these cowards!" she bellowed passionately. People in the crowd had started clapping now, some even cheered her on tentatively as she spoke.

"Sir?" said one of the Knights turning to Clergyman Perch, who had remained silent throughout the exchange. Very slowly Perch nodded and then made his way inside, shutting the door.

Nathaniel Perch did not see the ambush but he could hear it, could hear Gisele's screams of fury, quickly followed by those of pain and then the terrible silence he had expected. There were some more murmurings and shouts from the crowd but these were soon doused by the troop. As he climbed the great staircase Perch glanced outside, despite himself. Three figures in white were dragging a woman's body away, dragging her, he knew, to the dungeons.

....

"She's dead Charity, she's dead!" screamed Alistair as he cradled Sophie's lifeless form in his massive arms. "Why? Why didn't you just *leave?!*"

"Alistair I don't know... What happened?"

"All you do is ask questions!" he spat savagely. "You don't give one Ode for other people, the people that took care of you whilst you floated your way around your *wonderful land of adventure!*"

"I'm sorry, Alistair!"

Tears streamed down her face. She wanted to run, to look away from his terrible face, so full of hate and Sophie's cold, limp form.

"SORRY?! You're SORRY!? Sophie is DEAD Charity, and it's because of *you!*"

Charity sobbed uncontrollably. Her legs were stuck to the ground like glue, and darkness was surrounding Alistair and Sophie now. She wanted to warn them but her anguished sobs were constricting her words, and no matter how hard she tried, she couldn't stop crying.

"But you knew, didn't you?" asked Alistair in a vicious whisper. "You knew it would be dangerous and yet you still dragged us along to protect you, all so *you* could get home!"

Charity saw the figure rear up from the shadows, its eyes flashing red, a dripping blade in an outstretched hand. It cleaved the blade down through Alistair, who fell silently to the floor. Sophie falling from his arms to the ground beside him. Charity was drawn to his face, which seemed frozen, frozen with that look of intense hatred he had fixed her with. Charity could barely see from the tears stinging her eyes. She could bear it no longer, she wrenched with all her might and finally pulled herself free. She turned on her heels and ran from the harrowing scene but she wasn't travelling fast enough, the shadows were closing in now, enveloping *her*. She swiped her hands ferociously but she couldn't rid herself of them. It was no use; nothing could stop them and they were almost upon her now. The same terrible black figure rose up in front of her, its red eyes shining like the Moon, and as it swiped its mighty blade down upon her she screamed in pain!

Charity sat up suddenly, her brow soaked with sweat. She was panting just as heavily as she had done when they had first reached the little embankment of the River Koben.

She shook herself. "A dream, it had been a dream," she told herself again and again, and yet something would not let go of her, some tiny infestation of guilt had grabbed a hold of her thoughts and begun to grow inside her mind. She looked over at the sleeping forms of Alistair and Sophie, who were both lying spread-eagled under the starry sky, their travelling cloaks wrapped over them. They looked blissful, unburdened by her or her task, which was how they should be, she thought.

"If I leave now, they can remain just as happy forever," she said to herself. She had made up her mind; she would not burden her friends any longer with *her* task. She packed up her belongings, made sure the Journal was still safely tucked inside her backpack and set off at a brisk walk. She glanced at her friends as she left. She desperately wanted to say goodbye but knew they would not consent to her going. It was incredibly difficult but it was this way or... she shuddered, again remembering the horrible image of her two friends, her only friends, lying lifeless on the dark ground.

Charity had only travelled a short way, when a shout from behind her caused her to turn around. Alistair and Sophie were running towards her, terrified looks on both their faces.

"Charity, what are you doing? Where are you going?" asked Sophie.

"I'm leaving," Charity said solemnly. "We've come too close to death too many times and I *know* that Cassius and the Order will come for me now, harder than before. I can't let you put yourself in that sort of danger."

To her immense surprise, Alistair was smiling broadly. "I wondered how long it would be before you would do this," he said, his smile widening at the incredulous look on her face.

"What do you mean?"

"You're leaving to 'protect' us, are you?" he asked. As Charity nodded in reply, he said, "Charity, we know full well what we're doing. We aren't here because we want the Fateweaver, we aren't here because we owe a debt to you. We are here because we're your friends."

"Yeah, we've stuck by you this far and I *know* you'd do the same for us," added Sophie defiantly.

Charity felt like someone had clobbered her around the face with a Journal. 'Friends' they had said. Her heart swelled suddenly inside her chest, knocking the huge weight she had felt earlier, down into her boots.

"Yes but –" she started, but was immediately interrupted, this time by Sophie, who looked upset but resolute.

"Before I met you, I was lost. All I had was my job at the Records Office and when that went, well I had no idea where I would go or what I would do."

"I am a fugitive, wanted in every nation on Thea, I have no family and had no companions to speak of," said Alistair solemnly.

"You took us into your group, made us part of your journey, Charity. Can't you see how wonderful that was for us?" asked Sophie excitedly.

"But I was lost too! I had no idea where I was going or how *anything* worked on Thea, and I still don't!" said Charity flabbergasted.

"We were just as lost. Don't you see all of this is so much bigger than any of *us*," said Alistair.

"Yeah," agreed Sophie.

Her two friends looked at her, a burning fire of determination behind their eyes. Charity returned their gazes but still felt completely conflicted. They stared at one another for a long time under the stars and then slowly, very slowly, something dawned on Charity, something more important than anything she had read in any Journal. These friends, her first friends, her best friends would always stand by her, whether she wanted them to or not. She made to speak but could only mumble, her lip trembling, she fought back the tears but they broke over her like a wave upon the shore. She attempted to brush them away but they kept coming. Sophie rushed forwards, embracing her in a kindly hug, and she spoke words of reassurance as Alistair approached from behind and grabbed them both very close. They stayed in this embrace until finally Charity felt she was ready to continue. She struggled free and the three friends made their way wordlessly back to the campsite.

"Thanks," whispered Charity, as they finally reached the spot beside the River Koben. She felt somewhat foolish but was ultimately glad to know how they felt.

"Don't be so noble," grinned Alistair and the night sky was soon filled with flying insults and gales of laughter emanating from the tiny campsite. Inside her head, Charity was still terrified, she was confused, she was still very much lost in this utterly bewildering world but she knew that here in this wasteland under the star-strewn sky with Alistair and Sophie, she had never felt more at home.

25 – DARION OF THE CASTLANDS

Cassius wiped his face roughly with his cloak. The red stain it left on fabric sickened him to his stomach. How could he have been made to suffer so much by one little girl? He spat bitterly into the thick snow that surrounded him and continued to trudge onwards, ignoring the bitter winds and icy sleet hammering his exposed face. He no longer cared; pain was for the weak and he would not show an ounce of it, not anymore. It was almost impossible to see anything in the torrent of frost that was the Plains, but fortunately his eyesight was keener than most and he just could make out a sparkle of glistening light on his horizon: Galcia. Steeling himself, he pushed on harder, breaking out into a run, his feet crunching in the snow and speckles of blood dotting its surface as he whipped across the Plains like a black spectre, hurtling towards the icy dome. When he finally reached the safety of the dome he slammed the door open and collapsed inside, exhausted. He did not stop, however. He wrenched off his outer attire, leaving it in a heap on the ground and stepped into the city of Galcia.

People gawked and pointed at him as he stalked through the bustling streets. He could still feel the patches of dry blood that had stuck to his face and with his dirt-spattered white hair and bloody sword at his side, he imagined he must've looked quite terrifying.

"Worthless cretins!" he whispered, through clenched teeth as he glowered at them all.

He crossed the bridge that lead to the Order Chapter and didn't even acknowledge the shining, white Knights that stood guard at the door. No one stopped him, however, which could only mean one thing: they had been expecting him, and his stomach twisted slightly at the thought of what he was about to endure.

He strode across the many hallways of the Chapter in the direction of a small room that he knew was located near the back of the building, hidden away from prying eyes and those unworthy. It was a room he had visited only on one other occasion: to plan his assault on the Haven with *him*. Cassius stopped at the Ivory white door, which resembled every other door in the Chapter but with one miniscule difference. He ignored the silver handle and felt along the opposite edge of the door, just where the hinges were found. He groped for something, his hand clasping something that, to the naked eye, wasn't even there. Cassius rotated the rogue handle as he had been instructed.

He had told him, "If anyone tries to enter this room uninvited they will find no obvious solution. Thean nature is to use what is laid out in front of us, Cassius. However *we* must look beyond the ordinary, beyond what is handed to us, and only then can we access what is rightfully ours."

Cassius heard a lock slide open and he pushed the door open and entered the room. It was exactly as it had been on his first visit: an intricately decorated study, housing a large globe of Thea, several high bookshelves and an obsidian-black desk, behind which a leather armchair lay empty. The only thing that was any different was that, this time, someone was already present, someone who had been waiting for him. The man was sitting in a high-backed chair, facing a fire that was roaring merrily in the grate. He did not turn around when Cassius entered, but Cassius had known instantly that it was *him*.

The seated figure spoke quite confidently as Cassius drifted further into the room. "Cassius, at last…shut the door." Cassius complied wordlessly. "You have been gone sometime, I had wondered if perhaps…well never mind, you are here now…bring *it* to me."

Cassius remained silent, shame and revulsion spreading through his veins like a poison. The man spoke again, this time more coldly. "Am I to take from your silence that you have once again, failed to retrieve it?" he asked, barely-repressed fury present behind every syllable.

"Yes," said Cassius solemnly, his eyes on his boots.

The man got up from his chair and approached Cassius, his white hood drawn over his face once more. Cassius thought he looked taller than before, or perhaps that was just the light of the fire playing tricks with him. He placed a hand delicately on the two bloody scars Cassius had received from the Sloak attack, and Cassius felt a sudden surge of pain crackle through him as his fingers brushed the open wound.

"Hmm, this looks most uncomfortable." he said pityingly, and just as Cassius opened his mouth to reply, the man cracked his hand across Cassius' face and he fell to the tiled floor. He could feel the burning on his face and a roaring fire erupt in his heart.

Quick as a flash, Cassius withdrew his blade, no longer caring what happened to him, or what repercussions his actions yielded. However he had barely pulled his sword fully from its holster when dozen or so white knights stepped forwards from the surrounding shadows. Silently they surrounded Cassius, pointing their own identical blades straight at his throat. This had been planned, thought Cassius bitterly. The man had known he had failed, known he would lose his temper and lash out.

"Not smart, boy," the hooded man snapped angrily. "How *dare* you attack the Cardinal of the Ivory Order? I should have your head removed for the thought even entering your Journal…if you had one that is!" he sneered savagely.

The man pulled off his hood, revealing a very old, lined face, a bald head and a very long white beard.

"High Cardinal Euphestus, we await your orders?" asked one of the Knights, his sword shaking a little as he struggled to keep it steady in front of Cassius' exposed jugular.

"Leave him!" said Euphestus, "I want to hear exactly what happened in the Plains, and I want to know," he leaned in close to Cassius, "How you managed to squander *another* opportunity to relinquish the Journal from that girl."

Cassius remained silent. He knew he was in no condition to fight his way out of this situation. The journey had greatly weakened him and he was woefully outnumbered by these Knights. He would have to comply.

"I reached the girl and her friends as they left Galcia, followed their path up the Imp, I knew Garron had found the Haven before, he *knew* his way round the Plains a little too well, didn't even use a map." He croaked, "Near the summit he got separated from the others, he fell straight into the Haven. Sheer luck but it allowed me to sneak in afterwards and head straight for the page. I waited for them, just bided my time until they found their way to me. I knew they would come and she would make the Journal whole once more and I was right."

"I see," said Euphestus, who sounded most intrigued by Cassius' tale. "Go on."

"She did the same bonding thing she did in the temple of Dura. The page fused into the book and she was able to translate it. I heard her read the last passage to her pathetic friends and it was then I attacked, took out the oaf and the other girl easily but she ran. She led me into a winding cavern and when I cornered her she threatened to throw the Journal into a fire. She threw something and I leapt to save it, but…she tricked me."

Cassius heard his voice echo around the room now, and shame flushed his face so that it matched the colour of the dried blood pooling around his ear.

"She threw another book, used the shadows I, I couldn't see it properly. She ran and just as I was about to give chase, two Sloaks attacked me. I managed to destroy the brutes and gave chase. I caught up with the three of them near the edge of the Haven but they dove off a cliff. They chose death rather than face me. So it was all for naught, and the Journal is much likely lost, destroyed, along with *her*."

"A *fascinating* tale," the man said sarcastically. "But you have miscalculated the girl's capacity for escape too many times already. They were not jumping to their deaths, they were jumping into the River Koben. Unfortunately for us, the River Koben leads directly out of Imputtia and down through Thea. Quite ingenious on their part, I must say."

"I…they're alive?!" said Cassius exasperatedly.

"I would think so, unless the fall killed them. However they do have an annoying habit of surviving such feats, wouldn't you say?" He glanced at the cut along Cassius' head. "Tell me: you said that you heard the contents of the final page. What did Calville write?"

Cassius told him what he had heard whilst Euphestus paced up and down the room, deep in thought.

"Hmm, puzzling. Calville really did like his little riddles, didn't he? I will have to take considerable time to explore our options. In the meantime I want you to go into the city. I have issued a warrant for their arrests on behalf of the Order so she will have likely fled to the Castlands by now but she is bound to have friends, accomplices, well-wishers, so search every house, every side street, anywhere that you think of, only return to me when you have a link to her. Is that clear, Cassius?"

"Yes," said Cassius tensely.

"Oh good. And Cassius," the knights had retreated back into the shadows and Cassius turned to look at Euphestus as he headed for the door, "if you raise your sword against me again, I *will* kill you, Regalis or not."

Cassius nodded silently and left the room, his face taut with suppressed fury.

'In time, all in good time,' he thought savagely.

....

"My Queen, you summoned me?" said a startlingly thin man bowing low before a great golden throne.

"Yes Zachary, I did. I require a royal letter to be sent to Chancellor Jossent of Agua."

"The head of Agua? My Queen, it would be an honour!" gushed Zachary, unfurling a huge rolled up carpet he was holding under one arm. As if by magic the carpet lay draped on top of a spindly little table that hadn't been there seconds before. He bent his knees to sit and two long thin sticks sprang out from behind his legs, propping him up in the air as a wooden plank which was affixed to his rear slotted neatly on top of the poles, making a perfectly formed chair. The whole process took only a couple of seconds but it left him sitting quite comfortable in front of his work table, almost ready to begin. He rustled in his waistcoat for something, sticking his tongue out in concentration; Queen Mosia drummed her fingers impatiently on the arm of her winged throne. At last Zachary pulled out a long white quill, several pots of swirling black ink and a roll of spotlessly white parchment.

"Can we begin?" asked Mosia impatiently.

"Yes, of course, my Queen!" he said hurriedly, bending over the page. He dipped his quill in the ink and waited for her to speak.

Mosia cleared her throat regally and began,

"From the throne of Queen Mosia Zahar of Dura. Dear Chancellor Jossent it has come to my attention that a decree has been passed by the Ivory Order and that an arrest warrant has been issued for a Charity Walters, Sophie Pierce and Alistair Garron. I would like to officially declare my own personal objections to this. I was not consulted on this very serious matter and considering one of the supposed crimes occurred in *my* own city I feel that it would have been prudent to find out *the truth*. Furthermore, having met the figures in question I find it highly dubious that they have been charged with any crimes against Thea. I write to you, Jossent, to ask you to sort out this travesty. My sources inform me that the Order has begun encroaching upon people's homes in search for the girl and her companions. If *we* do not act now then it will be too late. We may be mere figure heads but we must speak for the people and must stand up to this inequality. Please write back soon with your response.

P.S. I am also writing to Euphestus to see how Imputtia is dealing with this mess. I understand that he will be most closely connected as this likely came from the Cardinal himself, perhaps Euphestus, as a more experienced Chancellor can make the Cardinal see reason."

Mosia finished speaking and Zachary stopped his writing. Looking up at her he said, "You wish me to write a letter to Chancellor Euphestus, Your Majesty?"

"I do," said Mosia, and she read out another prepared letter as Zachary scribbled away madly. This letter was almost identical to the one she wrote for Jossent.

"Thank you Zachary. Now please send them immediately, using the royal doves. It is imperative that both letters reach them in time, before it is too late."

....

Despite her late night wanderings, Charity rose early the next morning. She had awoken feeling surprisingly refreshed and once more optimistic about their task. Whilst she was only too aware that they still had no idea where they were going, they had at least managed to find Calville's missing pages and had twice escaped the clutches of Cassius and the Order. Alistair had managed to save some of the food he had brought with him from Silvus' Supplies and so after a breakfast of fish and dried fruit they had set off once more, their camp packed and their spirits high.

"Where are we going again?" asked Sophie as they walked alongside the River Koben,

"Into the Castlands. We must travel as far from the Order as possible. Scouts and Knights patrol the outer edges so we'll be safer in the centre."

"The centre? But Alistair what about the Laccuna?"

"You are with me, do not worry."

"C'mon Sophie, it'll be alright," said Charity reassuringly, but Sophie continued to look concerned. She decided to change the subject to take her mind off such things.

"What about the last page then," she asked bracingly. "What do you think it means? '**As for the feather, the plume, the Fateweaver, it will be hidden where true power resides'.**"

"Power. The word *power* could mean more than one thing. It could mean *anything* quite frankly!" said Alistair wisely.

"Yeah but it said *true* power. What's true power mean?" asked Charity.

"Well the Fateweaver would be the closest thing to true power, the ability to control your destiny, do anything you wanted."

"Can it *really* do anything?" asked Sophie curiously.

"That depends…"

"On what?"

"Whether it exists or not."

"You're not sure it exists?" asked Charity.

"I'm not rightly sure. I just know that there are no documented sightings of the feather – it's all based on myth and hearsay. Depending on where you go, different areas in Thea will provide different answers. I have heard from some that the Fateweaver's power is limitless, that it could move mountains, turn back time, whereas others say it's limited by the imagination of the user. There only appears to be one thing that everyone manages to agree upon."

"What?" asked Charity breathlessly,

"Death. The Feather has no effect on it." said Alistair darkly,

"You mean it can't like bring someone back to life?" asked Charity,

"That is what is claimed."

"But that still doesn't tell us what *true* power is or where we'll find it on Thea, does it?" asked Sophie exasperatedly.

"You know what? I don't think he wanted anyone to find it," said Charity, flaring up. "Not if he went to all this trouble to be so bloody vague about it."

"It's certainly not helpful," said Alistair rubbing his stubble-covered chin. "Perhaps Calville was referring to something more than the usual definition of power."

"Like magical power! Hey! Maybe it's in the Igniculus temple!" said Sophie, looking delighted with herself.

"Perhaps, but then wouldn't Ruven have found it some time ago, a man like that doesn't miss much." Replied Alistair sensibly.

"Oh yeah, s'pose." said Sophie dejectedly.

The three continued to chat away animatedly as they walked, sharing theories, asking questions and trying desperately to understand what Calville had meant by his cryptic suggestion. They had been in such deep conversation that Charity didn't even notice the small group of people who had assembled on the horizon and was now watching them closely. She had just started discussing the best places to hide an object you wished never to be found, when she bumped straight into Alistair, who had stopped walking, his body rigid and tense. Sophie and Charity had just opened their mouths to question him, when he held a huge hand up, silencing them.

"Shhh!" he hissed at Sophie, who had looked like she was about to speak. "Someone is watching us."

He pointed just beyond them to a little ridge in the distance, where a group of four or five men were standing quite still. Even from afar Charity could see their ragged clothes and dirt-covered skin.

Sophie gripped her arm tightly. "Alistair," she whispered, "are those…?"

"Yes, they are Laccuna," said Alistair. "Strange though, they have not yet attacked. Our guard was down and they had ample opportunities. I wonder why…" he trailed off into silence, his blue eyes fixed on the lone group on their horizon.

The little group had begun walking towards them now, quite calmly and with no hint of malice or threat. Alistair imitated them, moving forwards himself now as Sophie burst into whispered objections.

"Alistair, wait, stop! It could be a trick or a trap, wait, *please!*" She pleaded but he was not listening.

Sophie clung onto Charity as she too walked forwards, just beside Alistair, and together the group crossed the barren ground towards this new party of onlookers.

As Charity drew closer to the group she could make out the figures more clearly. Five men strolled briskly towards them, all well-built, dressed in ragged but protective clothing and completely covered in dust and dirt. Their faces were inscrutable and Charity wondered, like Alistair, why they had yet to attack. They finally reached the Laccuna and as both parties stopped just short of each other, Charity felt the atmosphere crackle with tension. Neither group spoke at first and Charity noticed that Alistair was gripping his cane very tightly in one hand as he eyed the Laccuna suspiciously. After a while, one of the Laccuna, a small man with a surprisingly elegant side parting, took an uneasy step forwards, he was eyeing Alistair's cane warily but he spoke loudly and confidently nonetheless.

"We mean you no harm, travellers, please do not worry."

"Oh, we're not worried," said Alistair coolly.

"Ah, alright then," faltered the Laccuna. "It is most fortunate that we found you here, we have been searching for you for many days now."

"Why?" asked Alistair quietly.

The Laccuna looked suddenly shocked,

"Why?! You do not know?"

"Obviously we do not know, otherwise we wouldn't be asking you. Now I'm not going to ask you a third time, why have you been looking for us?"

"You, you are wanted on the Mainlands for crimes against Thea, the Order has been searching for everywhere for you. I, I apologise for delivering such news but it is common knowledge even in the Castlands and we thought you of *all* people would know."

"We've been a bit busy," snapped Sophie bitterly.

Charity had known it was only a matter of time before the Order tried to get to her. Alistair had warned her as much, and he had been right. Hatred suddenly rose up inside her, a hatred so intense she thought it would burst from her if she opened her mouth.

"How do you know this?" asked Alistair, speaking quite calmly.

"We came across Scouts near the Aguish border. They interrogated us, kept asking if we were hiding you…and we told them no."

"Thank you," said Charity gratefully. "I really appreciate that –"

"We weren't doing you a favour, Mainlander," spat another of the Laccuna. "We had no *idea* where you were!"

He looked disgustedly at Charity, his wild, dirty-blonde hair sticking out like a lion's mane around his grizzled face.

"Why have you sought us out then?" asked Alistair. "Not to chastise us, I assume."

He eyed the lion-like Laccuna who cracked his knuckles in response as the first Laccuna shook his head apologetically.

"No, no, no, sorry, it's just…well, we were told that you would be here," he said, glaring at his bad-tempered companion. "Darion asked us to scout near the Koben until we found you and brought you to him."

"We go nowhere without information," said Alistair dangerously, his hand inadvertently moving along the great cane. "Who is this Darion?"

"He is the leader of a nearby settlement of Laccuna. He's the wisest man in all of the Castlands and he wants to *help* you."

"Help us?" asked Sophie. "Why would a Laccuna want to help us?"

"We do not know the details, only that he asked us to bring you to him. *Please* – we only want to fulfil his requests." begged the first Laccuna looking kindly at all three of them.

Charity saw the concern he displayed and recognised that his words sounded genuine but the other Laccuna looked less impressed, shaking their heads disapprovingly and baring their teeth as their companion continued to prostrate himself in front of Alistair.

"I have been away from my family for so long, I just want this mission to be over. Just come with us, please, I promise you'll come to no harm. I swear it!"

He was almost begging Alistair, who looked down with a look of mingled pity and revulsion at the Laccuna.

The lion-haired Laccuna finally stepped forwards angrily and shoved the speaker out of the way. He spoke not with desperation but utter disgust.

"You're a disgrace, Solkiov, begging these Mainland rats! Have some respect for your brothers and sisters!" He shot the Laccuna named Solkiov another look of revulsion and rounded on Alistair, Sophie and Charity. "Look! If you refuse to come quietly and come in *right now* then we will have to bring you in by force. We don't have time to barter with scum!"

Alistair considered the Laccuna for a while. Charity saw his fingers twitch towards his cane and she wondered when he would spring into action once more but then, to her immense surprise, he released his cane, letting it fall back into its back holster.

"Very well," he said quietly, "Lead us to Darion."

"A wise choice," said the angry Laccuna, looking triumphantly at his brothers. He indicated that they should follow him and turned, shoving the first Laccuna out of the way as he lead them away from the River Koben and towards the rocky hills and peaks of the inner Castlands.

Charity knew that Alistair could have easily bested all of the Laccuna in front of them, so why hadn't he done so? Did he think it was a trap or was there some merit in meeting this Darion? In any case, they were too close to the Laccuna to chat about it so Charity swallowed her questions and followed the group across the dusty land in silence, still staring at her burly protector.

The group were led down a dusty path some three or four miles from where they had made camp the night before. On the way, they passed several other Laccuna, but to Charity's confusion these Laccuna looked nothing like the five that had accosted them near the river. Instead they looked like what Charity would've described as 'perfectly ordinary'. They wore normal clothes, very similar to those seen in any mainland city and lacked sharp teeth or any wild features at all. They were all walking in the same direction and some even smiled and waved as Charity and the others passed them by. She also spotted several large wooden carts on the road drawn by huge Shire horses that clopped past them noisily, apparently en route to the same destination as them.

The closer they got to the settlement the more numerous the Laccuna became, and very soon they were surrounded by at least fifty of them, all bustling and jostling along the rocky path beside them. They had just rounded a small hill when one of the young Laccuna, a small boy, began pointing excitedly into the distance: "It's there, it's there!"

Charity looked to where the boy was pointing and was about to ask Sophie if she could see anything when it came into view, hiding just behind a large hill. It was a large stone embattlement with a set of double doors set into it. The walls were made of rough grey stone and were peppered with turrets and portcullis.

"Have you heard of this place?" she whispered quietly to Alistair.

"No. I had no idea such a large settlement existed anywhere in the Castlands." answered Alistair, his eyes darting around with great interest.

When they finally reached the doors, one of the Laccuna bounded forwards and hammered on it with one hand, a slot opened up and two eyes peered out at them. The slot snapped shut again and the sound of tinkling keys issued from behind the mighty doors, which swung open seconds later. Charity entered the settlement and stared around in surprise. This was not what she had been imagining. There were huts and houses built from sturdy oak and mahogany, all sorts of shops and stalls were also present, just like in a normal town. Most surprising of all were the Laccuna themselves. They weren't scrabbling or fighting with one another, but were going about their lives, some shopping, others talking, some even carrying children around, all shapes, sizes, creeds and ethnicities in the one place, working and living in apparent harmony.

Charity leant over and whispered quietly to Sophie, "I don't understand, what's going on? I thought the Laccuna were, you know, savages!"

Sophie looked at her perplexed. "I know, so did I. Well you grow up with stories of them killing and eating Mainlanders… I never imagined any Laccuna settlement would be like *this*!"

The group leading them had brought them to a small wooden house that looked no different from the many others in the settlement. They pointed inside and only one of them went in ahead, knocking the door as he opened it.

"Darion, we found them," Charity heard him state happily.

"Ah excellent. Thank you my good man," an imperious voice answered from inside the house. "Could you please leave us whilst I discuss some delicate matters with them?"

"Course Darion, we'll be outside if you need us."

He left the hut, bowing his head gratefully. Charity, Sophie and Alistair were lead into the house as the door was shut tightly behind them. Looking around, Charity could see nothing in this room that warranted such reverence from the Laccuna. It had a roaring fire, two bookshelves, a table and chairs and several candles burning about the room. All in all it seemed like a perfectly ordinary Thean house.

"Friends." said a figure standing beside a large squashy armchair near the fire, he turned to face them, thrusting out his arms warmly as he welcomed them into his home.

"You are Darion?" asked Alistair,

"I, am friends, I am. And you must be Alistair Garron," he said, sizing up Alistair with a quick once over. "I had to bargain quite a bit to get them to bring you to me in one piece you know? There is a great deal of Laccuna blood on your hands, isn't there?"

"I…I…what?!" stammered Alistair.

"Ah now, fear not Mr. Garron, I have not searched this long and hard just to bring you here and accuse you! I am well aware that your intentions have always been most pure. Some of our less cultured brothers and sisters can get a bit, ahem, *carried away*, can't they? I daresay they left you with no choice."

"*Carried away?* That's a very charitable way of putting it. The Laccuna have never shown anyone the slightest sign of civility or kindness. Tell me, why do the people of this settlement refute everything I have learnt of them?" asked Alistair suspiciously.

"Oh don't worry, don't worry, I shall explain that in good time, my friend, but first…" Darion turned to face Charity and Sophie now and in the light from the fire she could see that he was actually quite a small, crooked man. He had a balding head, thick sideburns and a black goatee. His fat little belly protruded from a little woollen shawl he was wearing and a necklace of what looked like opals sat around his neck shining in the light of the roaring fire beside him.

"You must be Sophie Pierce," he stated pleasantly.

"Yes, yes, that's right," piped Sophie nervously.

"Hmmm, now what have I heard about you? Ah yes, some *very* interesting things, my dear, a quite gifted Igniculi, is that right?"

"Oh, um I guess," said Sophie going very red.

"Now, now, it is not the time for modesty, Miss Pierce, not whilst the Order chases us at every turn. We must embrace our gifts!"

Sophie nodded in an unsure way and Darion turned his attention to Charity, "And…speaking of gifts…*this* must be…Miss Walters, Charity Walters."

Charity nodded silently, she had no idea what Darion wanted and waited for him to continue but he seemed to be waiting for her to respond.

"Um yes, I'm Charity," she said finally after an awkwardly long silence in which Darion continued to stare at her appraisingly.

"Ah, WONDERFUL!" boomed Darion, so loudly that the fire flickered in the grate. "You have quite a growing reputation in the Castlands, don't you know?"

"Um no, I didn't."

"Why of *course* you do, Miss Walters, of course, a Regalis at your age…" he continued to eye her with an odd mix of interest and surprise. "But alas, your reputation reaches far beyond our borders, doesn't it?"

"I don't really –" began Charity, but Darion cut in.

"However, that particular reputation isn't what one would call welcome, now is it?"

Charity finally understood what Darion was hinting at.

"We didn't do any of those things! The Order is telling –"

"TELLING LIES!" bellowed Darion quite happily, finishing her statement for her and nodding ruefully. "I know! I know, my dear…I know only too well what the Order is capable of and I also happen to know the real reason why you are *here*."

"How do *you* know they're lying?" asked Sophie suddenly.

"Because, Miss Pierce that is their duty – they are there to enforce 'order', to make sure everyone is kept in line. Those lovely Journals you have strapped to yourselves," he flashed a look at Sophie's jacket, where Charity knew she kept her tiny Journal hidden, "they keep you nicely in tune with what's good and just, do they not?"

Suddenly Darion's mood seemed to sour slightly. His jovial manner faded and he glared into the fire for a short moment before continuing.

"You have no doubt been wondering how such a prosperous settlement could remain intact in a wasteland such as this."

They did not respond and so after considering their blank faces he continued.

"Believe it or not, Laccuna are not savages by nature alone. We are in fact outcasts, outcasts from the Mainland all because we didn't pass a fancy little test at birth."

He laughed bitterly to himself and then continued, "Most Laccuna die when they are abandoned, did you know that? Hundreds of children sent out into the wilderness to perish because of a rule enforced by *your* Order. We are the ones that have to patrol the borders and take in the little ones, find them homes, find them families, if it wasn't for *savages* like us, how many would die then?"

"But Laccuna who don't graft have been seen as not worthy!" said Sophie passionately.

"Not worthy?!" laughed Darion, in what Charity thought was a startling impersonation of Cassius' high cold cackle. "What is *worthy* Miss Pierce? Have you ever met a Laccuna and seen for yourself if they are indeed worthy?"

"We've meet them before, and they threatened to cut out our eyes!" said Charity hotly.

"Ah I see, bitter were they? Angry? *Savage?*" Darion whispered vindictively. "Throw any Thean into a sewer and sooner or later he'll learn to enjoy the taste of rat!"

"I don't understand," said Charity confused.

"If you are surrounded by savagery and live in a wasteland then you will grow to suit those conditions, Miss Walters. You'll learn to fight for your food, learn to pick off strangers and mistrust others. The settlement you see here is unlike any other in all of the Castlands and it is the result of years of intense planning and hard work. We managed to get enough materials and like-minded Laccuna to build our village and keep us in relatively comfort, and just like that," he clicked his fingers violently, "The people are…as you Mainlanders might put it, *civilised*."

"I –" began Charity, but Darion interrupted. He looked greatly agitated.

"It is simple, girl. Laccuna are only savage because *you* Mainlanders have forced them to be!"

"You expect to pin the blame for thousands of years of mistreatment on us three?" asked Alistair.

"No, I do not," Darion said, his demeanour softening slightly. "I know it is not *your* fault…and I am not here to lay the charges of the Ivory Order at your door."

"Yes, that would be unwise." said Alistair dangerously,

"Considering the Ivory Order seem determined to *kill* me." said Charity hotly.

"Either that or make everyone think we're criminals!" added Sophie angrily.

"Yes, the campaign to tarnish your good names has been most effective, I daresay many believe you lot to be just as dangerous as us Laccuna." said Darion distractedly. He gave a hollow laugh that was almost a sigh before looking up to find all three of them glaring at him, he composed himself quickly and changed the subject.

"Tell me, have you come across the man named Cassius yet?" he asked wearily, his eyes drawn to the fire once more. He turned to poke the embers with a long metal rod beside his chair.

Charity opened her mouth in disbelief, whilst Sophie gave a little squeak and almost tripped over herself as she made to meaningfully grab Charity's arm. Darion smiled ruefully to himself, "I will take that as a yes."

So Charity told Darion about how Cassius had been tracking them, how he apparently possessed Regalis skills and was now working with the Ivory Order. Darion showed no sign of surprise or shock during her tale but listened intently and then stared into the fire once more before speaking again.

"I am aware of much of what you have said. Cassius is, rather unfortunately, well known to Laccuna."

"How? How do *you* know about him?" asked Charity.

"Because he is one of us…he is a Laccuna!" said Darion simply, a steely look in his exhausted eyes.

"WHAT?" gasped Charity. "He doesn't have Journal?"

She was gobsmacked by the revelation that someone so powerful lacked the most basic thing Theans held so dear.

"Hey! That would explain why he hates Mainlanders so much!" she exclaimed excitedly and Darion nodded in a matter-of-fact-kind of way.

"He was an exceptional case," said Darion, darkly. "One that only comes around every couple of years and not a welcome one. Once he was made known to us, I sent out some of my Laccuna to find out as much about this strange young man as they could. What they found did *not* dissuade me from worry. The story we managed to cobble together is that some years ago Cassius lived on the Mainland. In fact like most Laccuna, it was where he was born, but unlike other Laccuna he was not immediately cast out at birth. Cassius' father seems to have attempted to graft his son with a Journal numerous times. This is unfortunately all too common, as parents refuse to face up the realities of the system in place on the Mainland. Quite understandable really.

"Anyway, no matter how many times he tried, his Father failed to graft the boy with a Journal and was forced to accept the fact that he was a reject, an outcast – in short, his son was a Laccuna. The next step would usually be to abandon the child immediately, cut off all ties and move on with your life, less you tar the family name with such a *travesty.*"

Darion looked disgustedly out of the window as he recounted Cassius' tale, and privately Charity shared his revulsion. She had always found this particular practice sickening.

"For some reason – and we do not know why – his Father refused to send his son into the Castlands. He disobeyed thousands of years of order and routine and kept the infant hidden from all. We have to try our hand at some guesswork here, but we believe that he kept Cassius a secret for seven whole years until finally something made him change his mind. Cassius was brought to the Castlands and left there, alone."

"How do you know he was left there by his Father?" asked Sophie, looking upset.

"Because, thirteen years ago Laccuna found a seven-year-old boy wandering around this very area. Of course our settlement didn't exist back them. The boy was crying for his Father and had no idea where he was or how he had got there. The Laccuna brought him to the nearest settlement for adoption. I only wish my settlement had existed back then, for unfortunately for Cassius, the closest settlement just happened to be one of the more violent in the Castlands.

"This posed a very real problem, however, as things can be a great deal more primal in other areas of the Castlands and children who have grown up accustomed to the mannerisms and etiquette of the Mainland, well they don't quite fit in with the Laccuna. Young Cassius had already become used to being treated like a normal Thean child in a civilised society. All that changed the second he arrived with the other Laccuna. The other children instantly tormented him for his differences. He was beaten and bullied, spat on and reviled... it must've been hell for the boy. I understand most of the elders of the settlement believed he would not last very long, as they had failed to find any Laccuna family that would take in such a fragile boy. Then one day, seemingly out of the blue, something rather unexpected occurred. Cassius started defending himself. Reports suggest that he managed to fight off three attackers, much larger than himself, with nothing but the branch of an Atra tree.

"My scouts spoke to many Laccuna who had watched the boy grow, who told us how he used to practice with the same stick of Atra. He spent hours honing his skills, growing faster and stronger with each day. The years rolled by and soon he was no longer bullied by his peers. Far from it: now he was feared. After nine years he had grown up a stronger man for his trials. He had survived the abuse and learnt to fight back, he was a gifted warrior and although our reports show some inconsistencies, one thing was unanimous from the Laccuna that knew him: no-one dared challenge Cassius anymore.

"This would be disconcerting enough if it wasn't for the other disturbing titbit we discovered. You see by the time he had reached the year of sixteen, Cassius had completely detached himself from the all society. He was completely alone you see; no one wanted to be near him, no one wanted to be seen with him. By now, though, I'm quite sure that even if he was offered help or shelter that he'd have rejected it. I mean, you can almost understand how the boy felt: he was trapped, you see, with no place to call his home, rejected by the Mainland and rejected by the Castlands that had found him. It appears that when he was not tormenting anyone foolish enough to stand in his way, he spent most of his time plotting a horrible revenge on his father, the man who had betrayed him so cruelly and left him to this terrible fate."

The group sat in stunned silence. Alistair and Sophie looked too shocked to speak but Charity was not even thinking about Cassius, a sudden realisation had been building slowly inside her the longer she listened to Darion's tale and now, finally she understood.

"Did he ever find his Father again?" asked Sophie tentatively,

"Yes indeed he did, however dear Cassius was left most disappointed with their reunion." said Darion a savage smile spreading across his face as he spoke.

What? Why?" asked Sophie but it was not Darion who answered, it was Charity.

"He was already dead."

Everyone in the tiny hut stopped and stared at her, dumbfounded.

"How in Thea did you know that?" demanded Darion, looking awestruck.

"I saw him, I…I…met him." said Charity slowly, she finally understood all the things she had seen in her dreams, suddenly it all made sense.

Sophie exploded with questions, "You did?! But how? When? Where?"

"I told you about it, when we first met!" answered Charity,

"No you didn't, I'd have remembered something like *that*."

"I *did*, look it was when I first came to Thea, I was in a small hut, it was just outside Lower Forfal I think. Anyway, there was a man in the hut but he had been stabbed, or at least his Journal had been. He was bleeding all over the place but he wouldn't let me help him, he kept calling me a reader, he was the first person to tell me I was a Regalis." Charity explained, speaking very fast.

"Oh yeah," said Sophie slowly, "you did tell me that."

"Woah woah *woah*, pause your pages for a second girl, how did he know you were a Regalis? And what do you mean by 'when you first *came* to Thea' ?" demanded Darion, waggling an accusing finger at Charity as though it were a sword.

Charity gave a great sigh.

"Well it's kind of complicated, see it all really began back in England, before I even knew what a Journal was. See I'm not really from Thea." She began hesitantly, Sophie flashed her a warning look but Charity ignored her, this was not the time for caution she thought defiantly, it was a time for the truth.

So Charity recounted the story of how she had been in the library at St. August's, how she had come to Thea and how the old man had died as he tried to explain to her what she really was. She talked about the letter she'd found in his Journal, the one that had begged him to bring her to Thea.

"But I never found out how he got me to Thea in the first place, I don't know what he did, I mean if I knew, maybe *I* could do it and find a way back." said Charity exasperatedly.

They all looked at Darion for he was the only one not to have heard Charity's tale, she wondered if he would believe her like Alistair had done or laugh in her face like Sophie. As it turns out he did neither, instead he stood up, walked over to Charity and gently grasped her around her shoulders. In a flash Alistair was on his feet, his cane at the ready but Darion simply peered deep into Charity's dark brown eyes as if trying to decipher something hidden inside them.

"It is said that she had eyes like yours." He whispered hoarsely.

"What?" gasped Charity, unsure what he meant.

"Thea, she possessed the eyes of a reader, she was after all the *first* reader, the *first* Regalis."

Charity did not know what to say to this but Darion appeared to not require a response. He relinquished his grip on her shoulders and turned towards the fire once more.

"When the darkest night falls a little book shall show us the way." he spoke the words like one would a great poem, proudly and with purpose.

"Alistair told me that, he called me Little Book." said Charity quietly, who still did not quite know what this meant she had to do.

"And so he should, there has always been a belief that in Thea's most dire time of need, a reader of unparalleled skill would appear as if from nowhere and bring us back into the light. It appears that from lands beyond our own a Little Book has made its way to us and just in the nick of time too."

"But wait, I don't know if I *am* that person. I mean how do you and Alistair know that this statement is about me?!" asked Charity, voicing something that had been of concern to her ever since Alistair had first called her this.

"We don't *know*," said Alistair quietly, "We *believe*. The letter, whomever sent it knew of your importance and they were prepared to see someone die in order to bring you to Thea."

"But the old man didn't die because I came to Thea, I didn't kill him!" said Charity hotly, she suddenly felt as though she were being accused.

"In a strange sort of way, he did die because you came Charity. Or to put it more accurately he died to *bring* you to Thea." Darion said ruefully to the fire.

"He *died* to bring me here?"

Now it was Darion's turn to sigh, he looked mournfully from the fire to Alistair's side where his brown Journal was clasped to his hip.

"The bond between a Journal and its owner's soul is something more powerful than any Igniculus spell, it is stronger than the most all-consuming love and more potent than the deadliest potion. The only thing that can break the hold a Journal has over a soul is death, and even then it is not always broken as a Journal can hold the memories of its owner for centuries after their passing. To willingly give up the link between man and Journal, to purposefully and intentionally sever the bond is something that no Mainlander would ever contemplate doing. However if one is demented or determined enough then it is possible, an act of desecration of one's own Journal does happen every now and again. It is said that when this harrowing event takes place and if the desecrator wishes they can open up a link, a door to worlds beyond our imagination, to lands and places no Thean has ever travelled. The only problem is that those that claim to have seen such wonders do not live to tell others about it.

"Are you saying he destroyed his own Journal just to bring me here?" asked Charity, feeling slightly sick all of a sudden.

"It appears so. The evidence we have is that Cassius' Father, one Vincent Dunluce took his own life not long before Cassius tracked him down. Everyone had just assumed he had learned of his son's intentions, knew he would soon face him and instead took matters into his own hands."

"Why would he do that for *me* though?" asked Charity, shaking slightly.

"I would imagine it had something to do with that letter, making amends for unleashing his son upon the world, for creating a monster. Thea knows who wrote that letter but it appears they knew just what pages to poke when they wrote to him."

"But why *me*?" asked Charity desperately, "I didn't ask for anyone to kill themselves for me, I didn't want anyone to bring me here in the first place!"

"It is not about what you want, it is about what you have." said Darion, he spoke quite calmly, despite Charity growing redder and redder by the second.

"I don't HAVE anything!" shouted Charity, the words had spilled from her mouth before she could stop herself and she knew at once that she had made a mistake. Darion's eyes widened and his nostrils flared angrily as he turned to face her once again.

"Excuse me?" he said breathlessly, "Did I hear you correctly? You don't have anything. Charity Walters what you *have* is the greatest gift ever bestowed on any Thean since the fallen Goddess herself. You can read *any* Journal, all of Thea's thoughts and feelings are but an open book to you and you have to do is open it."

"I didn't mean - " she started but this time Sophie cut across her,

"And you've got *us*! Don't forget that, you may not have asked to come here but someone obviously knew that something was going to happen and they knew that *you* were the only person who could help."

"I don't...I didn't mean...sorry." mumbled Charity, she didn't quite understand how they could have so much faith on her but she swallowed her objections, if only to continue their conversations about Cassius and his Father.

"So we have established that Charity was brought here by Vincent Dunluce, but hold on there's one thing I still do not understand, Charity, how did you *know* that this man Vincent was Cassius Father? I didn't mention his name earlier."

"Ah…well…I just kind of guessed." said Charity quickly.

"You guessed?" asked Darion looking disbelieving.

"Yeah, just put it all together, the letter, the Journal, all of it just made sense." She said, trying to sound casual but feeling her face begin to burn as she spoke.

"I see." said Darion who did not sound at all convinced.

Charity could not tell them how she had worked it out, telling them she could read was one thing and she couldn't help but feel a swelling of pride at their continued proclamations that she was destined to save all of Thea, that she was 'the Little Book that would light the way'. But how would it be if they knew the truth? That she'd not worked out that Vincent was Cassius Father but that she'd been told by Cassius himself when she had *been* him. Those strange dreams that she'd had, what if they had not been dreams after all? What if she had somehow crept inside Cassius mind and saw everything he had seen, felt everything he had felt and committed every act he had committed. Most concerning of all was the thought that if this was all true and Charity was indeed delving inside the mind of Cassius then what was to stop him doing it to her?"

She shook herself from her thoughts, Alistair had stood up and was talking purposefully with Darion who had seated himself in his chair by the fire.

"Darion, Cassius may be working with the Order but I believe *he* wants to find the Fateweaver and use it for himself." said Alistair very seriously.

"Yes, that is what we feel is the most likely reason for his sudden truce with the Order," said Darion casually. "They have *always* sought out the feather, no matter what the cost."

"Um, Darion," said Charity, in a worried voice. "Cassius might know where it might be, he heard me tell Alistair and Sophie what Calville wrote about it."

"Hold on a moment," said Darion, suddenly awestruck. "You *know* where the feather is?"

"No," sighed Charity sadly. "Well, I mean I..." She faltered, unsure whether to tell Darion about the Journal and her mission from the Order. She looked at Alistair, who nodded approvingly at her.

"Tell him. He needs to know." Said Alistair reassuringly, and so she told Darion about Calville's Journal and how she had been piecing it together on her journey along with Alistair and Sophie.

"Ah, well now that makes things a lot clearer," said Darion, after Charity had finished. "The Order obviously believe *he* is the true Regalis. He fits the mould perfectly. One can see why they believe *he* would inevitably lead them to the feather." He was rubbing his goatee excitedly as he theorised out loud, and spotting Charity added quickly, "Of course I – I mean no offence to you, my dear but you can see why he seems the logical choice, can't you?"

"I fail to see the logic," said Alistair. "The Order's actions do not make sense. They have seen her make progress where Cassius has faltered, so why haven't they attempted to reach Charity and get her back on their side? It is clear, to me, that if anyone is the true Regalis, it can *only* be her!"

"Hmmm," pondered Darion. "The Order does not usually make mistakes when it comes to Regalis... but perhaps they are placing too much store by Cassius' other abilities. His skills as a warrior are something the Order would prize very highly indeed."

"Charity can fight. She's managed to escape from him twice now!" said Sophie, looking proudly at Charity.

"Guys, I...I'm really grateful for the compliments but it doesn't matter," said Charity hotly. "Cassius knows just as much as we do now. He could be finding the Fateweaver as we speak. We have to hurry. We've got to work out where it could be!"

"As for the feather, the plume, the Fateweaver, it will be hidden where true power resides," repeated Darion slowly, Charity having told him exactly what Calville had written four or five times already during her recount of her journey.

"We've been over it a hundred times already," said Charity disheartened. "True power, what is true power?" But Darion did not answer her immediately. He was smiling at her, his eyes sparkling mischievously as he grinned from ear to ear.

"What? What is it? Do you know what it means?!"

"Think about it, girl, what is the most powerful thing on Thea? What controls everything, rules everything, makes people do good things?"

"I don't…"

"C'mon, girl, what controls the people, keeps everyone in line with what is pure and right?"

"Um…"

"THINK GIRL!"

"Journals," said Charity, softly.

"Precisely. And who controls the Journals, who hands them out, who keeps them in circulation, who decrees the laws that our Journals abide by?"

"The Order!"

"Precisely, and the Order gets Journals from…"

Charity looked at him blankly, her spirit dropping, she had no idea where Journals came from.

"The Ordium Tree!" shouted Sophie excitedly. "The Fateweaver is in the Ordium Tree!"

"AH-HA!" yelled Darion, pointing a long fingernail at Sophie.

Charity looked between Sophie and Darion's elated faces. She had heard of the Ordium Tree before, but where? Where had she heard it? She had just opened her mouth to ask Sophie when it came to her – Clergyman Perch had told her about it. He had explained to her that proper Journals could only be made from Ordium, a material that could *only* be found at the Ordium Tree.

"That would seem the most likely hiding place," said Darion happily. "It's quite brilliant really, the one place the Order would never look, right under their noses."

"Under their noses?" asked Charity. "Where *is* the Ordium Tree then?"

"You don't know?" asked Darion, his face falling as he stared at Charity. "Well Miss Walters, I'm sorry to be the one to have to tell you this but the Ordium Tree is in the one place you are least likely to get a welcome reception. The Ordium Tree can *only* be found in the headquarters of the Ivory Order itself…the Order Chapter in Galcia."

Charity stared disbelievingly at Darion. She felt like the heavy weight inside her had suddenly doubled in size and was now threatening to drag her under the earth and suffocate her.

26 – CHARITY'S PLAN

Charity and the others had talked long into the early hours of the morning, before Darion finally announced that they should get some rest. Darion had been kind enough to vacate his quarters for Charity and Sophie, whilst Alistair, who had insisted upon being nearby, was permitted to sleep in front of the dwindling fire, a decision he seemed most content with. For Charity, the prospect of a comfortable night's sleep in a real bed seemed too good to be true, and unfortunately for her she turned out to be right. She had expected to fall straight to sleep the moment her head hit the downy pillow but it was not to be; her head was far too jam packed with information to shut down so easily.

She tossed and turned for what seemed like hours and when she eventually did drift off, she was plagued with a stream of unpleasant dreams and disturbing nightmares. The most memorable of which had starred a grotesque giant tree, the tree was plastered in a withered, rotting bark all except for a gaping hole cut right into the centre of its trunk so that Charity could see straight through it.

She had found herself being chased down a seemingly never ending corridor by the tree, its huge branches flailing wildly, threatening to tear her in half. She remembered how she had tried to run but the tree had been far too fast, it's roots slithered and slimed over the ground as it gradually got closer and closer to her. She had kept hurtling down the corridor, her breath catching in her throat as she ran as fast as her legs would carry her and then a rogue root sprung up in front of her as if from nowhere. She tried to move out of the way but it was far too late and she went tumbling over it and onto the ground, scrambling backwards as the terrible tree advanced towards her. The gaping hole that had split the tree seemed to crack and widen further the close the tree got towards and then without warning a dreadful sound filled her ears. It was a howling, wailing screech and as Charity desperately covered her ears the screaming tree reached its branches high into the air and brought them slamming down towards her, she readied herself for the crash, shutting her eyes fast but it didn't come and when she opened them she was lying in her bed, Sophie snoring loudly in the bed across from her.

Despite this disturbing night's sleep, Charity was still grateful that, when morning came, she didn't have to pack up a campsite and start walking. So it was with a fairly cheerful disposition that she made her way downstairs and sat in the squashy armchair in front of the roaring fire, upon which Darion had begun cooking them breakfast.

Sophie appeared in the kitchen not long after, tousle-haired and yawning widely as she pulled up a spindly wooden chair and sat down.

"Morning!" said Charity brightly, who thought it best to keep spirits up within the group.

"Yeah, morning." She replied sleepily, and then seemingly realising something she glanced bleary-eyed around the room. "Where's Alistair?"

"Don't know."

"He is out," said Darion loudly from beside the fire. He cracked an egg onto a metal plate that was held in place over the roaring flames. The other eggs were sizzling softly and Charity's stomach lurched hungrily and their wonderful aroma filled the tiny room.

"Out? Out where?" asked Sophie.

"He is retrieving something for me."

"What?" asked Charity, curious.

Darion did not answer, but held a finger to his nose and waggled it to and fro.

Moments later, Charity and Sophie had been seated around the small kitchen table tucking into some of the eggs and a large portion of slightly tough bread Darion had pulled from a cupboard. Both girls ate gratefully, as it had been sometime since they had sampled anything close to a home cooked meal. Meanwhile, Darion sat opposite them, a large steaming mug between his hands, watching them carefully.

"Whassat?" said Charity thickly, through a mouthful of eggs.

"Hmm?" said Darion distractedly, and Charity nodded her head at Darion's drink. "Oooo, this is Vather's Vapour. It's an old Laccuna recipe, keeps you warm. Try some, oh but be careful mind, it's not for the faint hearted."

Darion offered the mug to Charity, who peered inside. A dark black liquid stared back at her, she watched curiously as it oozed and belched inside its container, almost as if it were trying to escape. She sniffed the drink with interest and despite its suspicious appearance, Vather's Vapour smelled absolutely wonderful.

"Woah! It smell's like mulled wine and roasted acorns!" she said happily.

"I beg your pardon?!" said Darion who looked as though he hadn't understood a single word of Charity's description.

"Oh, never mind." Charity sighed to herself, "I just mean it just smells great. Doesn't look too appetising though."

"Yes, well…what is it you Mainlanders say, 'you shouldn't judge a book by it's cover'. "

Charity handed back the Vather's Vapour to Darion who drank deeply from the mug, set it down and stared very seriously at Charity.

"You seem impressively unperturbed by our conversation last night."

"Hmm, ye, am fin," said Charity through a further helping of bread and eggs.

"Then I fear you have not understood the severity of the situation, Miss Walters. The Ivory Order Chapter in Galcia is one of the most heavily guarded locations in all of Thea and with you being pursued like you are, well quite honestly, there is *no* chance you being able to get inside the Chapter long enough to find the Fateweaver."

Charity swallowed a particularly large mouthful of food and set her knife and fork down hard. "I *know* that. I assumed that we'd not be allowed to just waltz into the Chapter whenever we liked. I have a plan."

This was perfectly true, she *had* been thinking through a particular idea that had taken hold of her in between bouts of sleep last night. It was certainly not a perfect plan but she thought it had potential and the many hours of interrupted rest she'd had last night had ensured that she had been able to perfect it in preparation for today.

"You do?" said Darion sounding surprised. "Well I myself have been pondering this very problem too. Do continue."

"Ok, *I* think that we should round up as many Laccuna as we can. They'd have to be ones who want to fight back, want to show the Order just what they're made of. We should get those Laccuna together and just swarm the Order Chapter. They'd never expect such an attack, not from Laccuna. When I was in Forfal, Laccuna attacked the Order Chapter there and you should've seen the mayhem it caused. So whilst they're causing a distraction, Sophie, Alistair and I can make our way inside the Chapter and find the Ordium Tree. Then once we get to it, we'll get the Fateweaver and I can put things right again before I go home."

"That is an *interesting* plan, Miss Walters, but I'm afraid it is riddled with holes!" said Darion flatly.

Charity felt her heart sink.

"I understand the theory. I have no doubt whatsoever that I could rally my brothers to mount an orchestrated attack on the Order; their hatred is not exactly a closely-guarded secret and I am sure they would relish such an opportunity. *However* we have no way of getting inside the *city* undetected, never mind the Order!"

"What about the train? That's how we got in," suggested Sophie helpfully.

Darion laughed a wheezy laugh.

"My dear! You expect the Order not to notice a hundred or so Laccuna packed into those train compartments? Not to mention the reality that Laccuna do not carry Odes, so there would be no way we could ever afford to ride it even if we wanted to."

"Well," said Charity slowly, thinking out loud, "There is one way you could ride the train. The storage carriages, they carry stock in and out of Galcia. If we could get inside those carriages then we could ride the train the whole way there and no one would be any the wiser."

"Impossible!" said Darion dismissively. "The Order would notice that many Laccuna sneaking in."

"Not if you did it a couple at a time." She countered excitedly, "Yeah, we just keep sending groups in and they can flow in with everyone else. I've been on the train, and it's so busy no one's going to notice a couple more groups of people wandering about."

Darion was staring at both Charity, his steaming mug still clasped tightly in his hands and a curious expression on his face. Charity thought he looked like he was rehearsing the plan in his head, going over potential problems and pitfalls. They waited several long minutes, no one at the table speaking when finally Darion finally seemed ready to voice his opinion once more.

"It is still an unsubtle plan…however with some variations, it does seem plausible," said Darion scratching his beard thoughtfully. "But *if* we arrive, how would we reach the Order without being noticed? Over a hundred Laccuna marching towards the Chapter, people will panic."

"We use the side streets!" said Sophie excitedly. "There are lots of little passageways and side streets in Galcia. We could split everyone up and then converge at the Order Chapter."

Darion was starting to look more and more convinced and Charity could see a sudden glint of excitement in his eyes now. "Well, yes, I concede that could work, it's incredibly risky mind. But, wait!" Darion seemed to have spotted yet another hole in their plan. "Suppose we get to the Order, what then? Laccuna are no match for Ivory Knights. We've haven't got anywhere near the right equipment, and besides, they would need someone to lead them, someone to command them, tell them where to attack and how to properly defend themselves against the Order troops."

"Don't you have like a general or a leader of some sort?" asked Sophie.

"Of course not. The Laccuna despise any form of organisation, it reminds them of the conformity and rules of the Mainland. Don't let our tiny success here fool you, most Laccuna would rather be found dead than take an order!"

"Couldn't you lead them in battle then?" asked Sophie. "They seem to think you're great, the Laccuna that brought us here called you 'the wisest in all the Castlands' or something like that."

Darion chuckled to himself and smiled kindly at Sophie, "Oh my no! I'd be quite useless, I'm more accustomed to bartering and organising, not commanding or training."

"And you're quite sure they would *need* someone to lead them in battle?" asked Charity.

"I am sure of it. It would be sending them to their deaths to let them go charging in like that without a seasoned warrior at the helm. Without a leader at this very key juncture, I'm afraid your plan is quite useless."

"I will do it." A voice from the doorway spoke and Charity looked over to see Alistair, his cloak blowing in the wind from outside and his cane clasped in his hands.

"You, you will?" stammered Darion.

Alistair nodded but Darion did seem convinced, he stood up and strode to Alistair.

"You have made your feelings on Laccuna very clear Mr Garron. Are you telling me that you would put your honour on the line and lead these Laccuna into battle?"

"I am."

"You would do everything in your power to keep them from harm?"

"I would,"

"And you would swear to lay down your life if necessary for such a cause?"

"Yes, if it means helping Charity and Sophie, then I will do anything."

"Alistair, NO! I didn't mean *you* to - "started Charity, suddenly terrified but Alistair ignored her, speaking to Darion who looked much happier.

"Your men, they can fight?"

"Well yes, some can. They lack a certain discipline but with training I feel most could –"

"Very well," interrupted Alistair. "I will go round up those most eager and begin training at once."

"How long do we have?" asked Sophie.

"I would say about fourteen days. That should be enough time for me to find as many willing men as I can and for Alistair to organise them sufficiently."

"That's two weeks!?" said Charity desperately. "Cassius could solve the riddle at any moment, I mean he's working for the Order and everything! He'll definitely be able to get to the Ordium Tree, and if he can do that, it's all over. We have to act *now!*"

"No," said Alistair flatly. "If we act rashly without planning then we may as well hand you over to the Order right now. We must prepare properly and hope that Cassius fails to find the feather. He is out of our reach, there is nothing we can do right now but do this *right*."

"I…" began Charity, but she fell silent as Sophie nudged her, shaking her head seriously. She watched Alistair and Darion leave, mutinous and convinced she was right but unable to think of a proper argument to convince the others.

She could still hear Darion and Alistair outside the house. They were both chatting animatedly to one another about battle tactics and the potential amount of recruits they could acquire. She looked at Sophie, who was staring out the door, apparently deep in thought. Charity rounded on her furiously.

"Why didn't you let me try and convince them? It could be important!" she snapped.

"It *is* important, Charity. It's the most important thing we've ever done and that's why Alistair is right! If we rush into it, we've not got a hope."

"But Cassius could work it out, at any time, maybe he already has, maybe he's found the tree and he's just trying to find out how to get his hands on it. Can't you see how dangerous, just 'hoping' he won't get it, is for all us?!"

"And if he does get it, we're all done for, I understand that Charity. I think we all do. But if we go barging in with no support and no plan then we're as good as giving him the feather!" retorted Sophie heatedly, her voice rising in agitation.

"What are you talking about? How would us going to stop him *give* him the feather?!"

"Charity, don't you get it? Journals are made from Ordium, the same Ordium that comes from that tree. I'd bet anything that Calville knew that. That's why he left his Journal, so only a Regalis could decipher his clues and work out where the Fateweaver was hidden. It's the only explanation."

"But that makes it worse!" exploded Charity. "If you're right then Cassius is even more likely to find it - he's a Regalis too remember!" She couldn't see how everyone else was being so calm about this, when their very world could be torn apart any moment now.

"NO, CHARITY! Not necessarily. Cassius may be a Regalis but *so...are...you.*" she said in a determined whisper. "That means there are only two people on Thea who'll be able to get that feather from the tree, I'm sure of it."

"But –" stammered Charity, flushing red with frustration.

"IF HE *CAN* find it," yelled Sophie, "then us travelling across Thea and banging down the door of the Order isn't going to stop him. He'll have it whenever he wants it."

"Exactly! So how can you suggest staying here?"

"Charity, Cassius was right, this whole thing, this race for the Fateweaver is much bigger than you. It's much bigger than any of us. If Cassius is meant to find that feather, if he's meant to get it from the Ordium Tree then it's as good as his. He's already there, we're not."

"So…wait…you're saying that when Cassius tries, he'll get the Fateweaver for himself, no matter what?"

"No, not exactly, if he's he's *meant* to get the Fateweaver then I bet it'll be as easy for him as it is to read a Journal. He'll get it on the first try."

"But then we - "

"Charity! Do you think he and the Order are just sitting around doing nothing right now? Of course not, they're probably already trying to procure the feather. Don't you see that all we can do is *hope* he isn't meant to find it, *hope* that he isn't as skilled a Regalis as you and plan a way in for you to reach the tree?"

Charity closed her mouth, repressing the urge to argue further as a sudden wave of understanding washed over her.

"I think…I think I get it," said Charity quietly. She finally understood what Sophie was trying desperately to explain to her. It didn't matter what she did. If it was Cassius who was meant to find the Fateweaver, then it would reach him and there was nothing they could do about it. It was better to hope for the best and plan properly, as Alistair and Sophie had both said, and that way at least she could try finding the feather herself. Charity suddenly felt very foolish for her outburst. She looked at Sophie and for the first time she felt as though she could recognise Sophie as the eldest of the two of them.

"I'm sorry. I just kept worrying about Cas –"

"It is fine," said Sophie in a deep voice that was brilliantly reminiscent of Alistair's booming delivery. She grinned at Charity, who reluctantly grinned back.

"You're quite sure the Ordium Tree is in the Order Chapter?" asked Charity, changing the subject slightly.

"Yeah of course. It was in all the record books I used to write, it's always been there. That's why the Order's Headquarters for all of Thea are *there*, it's the most sacred site for such a place."

"And do you know where it is within the Chapter?" asked Charity hopefully. Instantly, however, she knew from the look on Sophie's face that she did not.

"No, sorry, I just know that it was there *before* the Chapter was built. They built the Chapter around it, you see."

"Right, hmmm, that doesn't really help us," said Charity. "Suppose we might at least go and watch Alistair prepare. We'll need to know exactly what's going on too." Both she and Sophie got up and left the tiny wooden hut, where they were immediately enveloped by bright, warming sunshine.

....

Euphestus cut a dark figure as he swept down the winding staircase, his white cloak billowing out behind him. He moved swiftly and silently. Night had fallen and he wanted no one else to know of his discovery, nobody but the boy. Euphestus came to an abrupt stop at the bottom of a winding staircase. He was standing in front of a pristine white door that was illuminated by the light from a collection of nearby candles. Pushing the door open, he found what he had been seeking. The youth was already here, sitting beside *it*, waiting for him.

"Good, you are here," said Euphestus, sounding relieved.

"Of course. You called? I was in the middle of searching a house."

"That can wait," snapped Euphestus impatiently. "I have solved it. I have found the final resting place of the Fateweaver!"

The youth's eyes flashed dangerously. "Where?" he asked breathlessly.

The hooded man simply turned his head to the magnificent white tree rooted behind the youth. Cassius gasped in disbelief as he turned to face it, his trembling hands outstretched. He moved forward and touched the ivory coloured bark, caressing its surface with surprising tenderness.

"Of course," he breathed slowly. "How do we get it? Do we tear it out?"

"Tear it out! Are you mad, boy?! *That* tree is the most powerful thing we have at our disposal. It keeps all those wretched people out there in line, it keeps The Ivory Order in power."

"Hmm," sniffed Cassius. He didn't really seem to be listening as he circled the great trunk, stroking it's bark with an almost tender touch.

"You…can you feel something?" asked Euphestus, suddenly alert with tension.

"No…nothing," Cassius replied, but Euphestus could detect a trace of hesitation in his wavering voice.

"You're quite sure?" he asked, as Cassius continued to inspect the great tree.

"I… am."

"Cassius, my boy, I want you to see if you can extract the Fateweaver. Take your time, use your Regalis skills – I am sure that they will be the key to finding it. I will be checking on you within the hour, in the meantime if you have need of me, send Anders. I do not want you to leave this room."

A blonde haired guard with a thin moustache had appeared at the hooded man's side. "Your Eminence?" he said, respectfully.

"Ah, Anders, please keep a close eye on our guest. See he gets anything he needs and if there are any problems…" he leant in whispering something inaudible to Anders, who nodded.

After one last hopeful look at Cassius, the hooded man swept from the room, closing the white door behind him. Cassius looked from the beautiful tree to the Ivory Guard now stationed in front of the only exit, and his lips curled into a twisted smile.

....

For the next two weeks Alistair and Darion continued to rush about the Laccuna settlement, busily trying to prepare for the invasion of the Mainland. They spent their time recruiting new volunteers, making armour and weapons from anything they could find that wasn't nailed down, and drilling the assembled Laccuna in the various tactics and plans they would be using in their attack on the Order Chapter. Charity had thought her plan was one that could work, it was certainly the only plan they had, but seeing so many people working so incredibly hard towards making it a reality made her nervous. What if it didn't work? Then all this hard work will have been for nothing and it'll have been *her* fault for suggesting such an idea. The Laccuna did not seem worried about the plan, on the contrary they had been only too eager to help in any way could. After speaking with many of them Charity was not surprised at their eagerness to be involved in an assault on the Mainland, although these Laccuna seemed much more friendly than the ones she'd met previously even they could not hide their hatred for those that had cast out them and their kin. Journals were a symbol for their woes, a stark reminder of their rejection from 'normal' society and they were not shy about expressing how they felt about them.

Regardless of their motive, their passion and work-ethic was incredible and the whole settlement seemed to feed off of this relentless drive for revenge. No more was this more obvious than just before the sun set each night when Alistair would gather all of his would-be soldiers together for combat practice.

The first session had begun with Alistair beating down two newly recruited Laccuna who upon realised he had maimed their friend many years earlier, had come at him with rusty knives. Alistair had deflected their attacks with an almost bored expression, unarmed them with a well timed jab from his cane and then set about pummelling each until they had begged for mercy. Alistair had straightened up, looking suddenly terrifying, his travelling cloak flailing behind him and his fists stained with the men's blood.

"Do you know why you have been stuck out here all of your lives?" he bellowed to the Laccuna assembled around him.

"It is not because of the Mainlanders, or Journals or even the Ivory Order. That is why you *came* to be here not why are you *still* here."

There was a rumble of muttering from the Laccuna, Charity who was standing in the shadow of a large hut, saw mingled looks of outrage and confusion.

"A thousand years. It has been over a thousand years since Laccuna even came close to taking back a square of the land they once called home. Why is this? Can someone please tell me *why* you are still stuck out here?" Alistair glared around at them, as if daring one of them to speak up, no one moved and no one spoke.

"I will tell you then since you all seem to have lost your tongue." Boomed Alistair and he dug his cane into the ground and strode along the Laccuna staring into each pair of eyes as he went. "You lack discipline, you lack organisation, you lack courage but most of all you lack the will to act. All Laccuna do or ever have done is *react*. They react to a feeling of injustice by killing a Mainlander, they react to death by brawling amongst themselves and they react to centuries of exile by simply lying down and licking their wounds."

"Look Garron!" one of the Laccuna fired up, he looks as though he was about to explode but Alistair stepped in front of him, glowering down at the Laccuna who quailed slightly under Alistair's furious stare."

"No." he said quietly, "You *look*. The Laccuna need someone to stop them reacting, they need someone who knows how to act. Someone who can teach you discipline, give you courage, make you work together, well now you have someone."

The Laccuna did not look particularly convinced thought Charity but Alistair was already taking off his cloak and rolling up his sleeves.

"We start now, the Ivory Order have some of the finest warriors on Thea but luckily for you, I can provide you with ample opportunities to get used to fighting *the* finest." Alistair, grinned, looking as excited as a child on Christmas morning, "All of you, try together or one at a time but all I ask is that you try. Now let's go."

It took only a couple of seconds before the first Laccune dove at him, his fists flailing like a Catherine wheel, Alistair caught him by the neck and slammed him into the ground as two more Laccuna came hurtling towards him. The fight lasted no more than ten minutes but in the end Alistair stood triumphantly in front of his troops, his face dripping with a combination of sweat and blood, most of which did not belong to him. He looked around at the Laccuna and beamed at them like they were his own children.

"That was *very* promising. I do believe we may actually stand a chance after all. Now, go and grab your blades," he yanked his cane out of the ground and dusted it off carefully, "This time, we do it for real."

During each subsequent session Alistair would guide the assembled Laccuna in all manner of important battle techniques, such as how to properly defend against an opponent, how to quickly unarm someone, the weak points of Order armour and of course how to fight with a sword, the weapon that all of the Laccuna had been issued with when they joined the group. Charity had thought that Alistair might want to teach them how to use a cane, however he had explained to them on their third session that the Order would most likely be using swords and that since most of the Laccuna wielded knives the progression was not too difficult to achieve in the short time they had available.

Whatever job Charity had been given by either Alistair or Darion, she would always find a way to get herself to somewhere with a good view of the courtyard in time for sunset. For some reason Charity had found herself becoming more and more engrossed in these training sessions, listening intently to the advice Alistair would bellow at his initiates and nodding along to each lesson as though she'd always known each but forgotten them a long time ago.

"NO! Shoulders apart and relaxed. BETTER!"

"Act do not react. You must be the one to dictate the battle, not your foe."

"Use your surroundings to your advantage, move and always keep you blade primed and ready."

"Remember – always anticipate an attack. Your opponent is *always* the most gifted warrior you have ever faced. If you expect the best you will be ready when the day comes, when you must face it."

Charity had found an old stick after watching him show the Laccuna the correct way to hold a sword, "Do not hold it like that son! It is not a knife for cutting you meals, it is an extension of your arm, your means for attack and defence, the only thing that stands between you living and dying."

She copied Alistair's grip and followed his stance from her spot just out of sight of the troops. From that day on she would use the little stick to learn along with the Laccuna, mimicking Alistair as he strode amongst them. Alistair was right, she had thought, her sword even if it was wooden did feel like it was part of her arm. The way she moved it, jabbing slicing and pretending to parry invisible blows felt strangely familiar to her. She practised in every spare moment that she had available during the day and even at night when she was in the privacy of her room, she would leap from the bed to the stool, then nimbly tumble to the floor and back up to her feet, her stick still held in battle position, imagining herself facing off against a horde of terrifying Ivory Knights.

Of course she could only learn so much from watching, so occasionally she snuck down to the yard to practise her own abilities by pretending to 'play' with some of the nicer soldiers in their off time. They placated and condescended to her, barely trying to combat her, until after eight days she had gotten skilled enough to disarm one of them with a well-timed flick of her stick. From that moment on, they took her slightly more seriously. Some still allowed her to spar with them, however, most were far too busy following Alistair's many commands to give her any time.

By the eleventh night Charity had started to sneak in behind the Laccuna and join in with their drills. She thought Alistair had caught her eyes a couple of times but he did not say anything, probably, Charity reasoned, because he was too busy organising the rest of the troop to bother. As the fourteen days rolled by, Charity had managed to improve her own swordplay quite considerably, to the point where she felt that she could even hold her own against one of the better Laccuna soldiers. Of course, she knew that a real sword was nothing like her wooden one, but it had felt so natural that she was *sure* that in a pinch she could at least defend herself if she needed to.

On the fifteenth evening, as the red moon had just slipped into the starry night sky, Charity left Darion's for a walk only to find Alistair siting quite alone on a small bench near the heart of the settlement. She approached him warily, unsure whether he wanted to be left alone or not.

"Alistair?" she said softly.

"Charity," he answered without turning around.

"D'you mind if I sit with you?" she asked tentatively. "I can go if you want to be left alone."

"No of course not. Please, sit," he said politely, budging up and leaving a small portion of bench for her to use. She sat down, looking up at the stars above her.

"Are we ready?" she asked without looking at him.

"As we will ever be."

"Do you – I mean, are you – are you scared?" she asked, stealing a glance at him.

"I am."

"Really?! I would've thought you never get scared," she said shocked.

"Fear is the most crucial tool we have at our disposal Charity."

"What? Why?"

"Fear let's us know we are still alive. It keeps us fighting until our last breath and drives us harder than any rousing speech or passionate love. It is important to face your fears but it is more important to respect them."

"I get it, doesn't stop me being scared though."

"Embrace it Charity. Do you think The Order are scared, do you think they respect the Laccuna? Of course not, and that is why this plan of yours may just work, they will never respect the Laccuna to believe them capable of such a feat."

"What does Darion think of the plan? He's always so busy I never get the chance to ask him."

This was very true. Charity had been trying to grab an audience with Darion for the past four days but every time they were alone and Charity had begun to start a discussion on the impending attack, he would jump up claiming he had forgotten something and rush off hurriedly.

"He feels that the plan is flawed, not fatally, but flawed nonetheless. Portions of the plan are based on conjecture and guesswork but the basic idea is simple enough that it *could* work."

"Well if my idea is so *bad* why doesn't he come up with one on his own?" she asked hotly.

"Because your idea is the only one there is." Answered Alistair calmly, "You were quite right when you stated that the only way in would be on the Imputtian Line. Darion does express the concern, however, that if we were to get to the Chapter you would not be able to find the Ordium Tree – *however –*" he raised his voice slightly, interrupting Charity who had opened her mouth to retort, "I have told Darion that both Sophie I will be there to assist you in any way we can. We all believe in you."

"Oh, well thanks," said Charity sheepishly.

"No thanks is necessary, Little Book. If what we have discovered about the Fateweaver is true than it truly is our only chance before Thea faces its darkest days."

"Do you think The Order has worked out the clue yet? Do you think they know where it is?"

"I do. The Order has some of the finest minds in all of Thea. I believe they will be attempting to find the Fateweaver as we speak and that is why, now that we have enough men, and a plan, it is imperative that we act!"

Charity sat in silence for a long time letting Alistair's words tumble about in her head.

"We leave at dawn," he said quietly. "Go get some rest. You will need it – that is something I *am* sure of."

....

The inhabitants of Upper Forfal could scarcely recall when the town had been so quiet, the Order had driven all commerce away from the once bustling high street and everyone else had quickly learnt to avoid it altogether in favour of the alleyways. As the sun set an unusual sight came into view for the few bold enough to peep out from behind their curtains at the almost deserted cobbles below. A hooded figure, dressed all in white was striding down the street, past the boarded up shop fronts and heading straight for the Ivory Order Chapter.

The Cardinal pushed past the wrought iron gates and moved purposefully towards the main Chapter building, several Order knights bent the knee respectfully as he passed, he nodded silently, this was not the time for pleasantries. He moved inside and made for the third floor where he knew that Perch would be waiting for him as he had instructed. Minutes later he quietly pushed open the door of his private quarters to find Nathaniel Perch sitting beside a large oak book shelf and perusing a copy of 'Offenhert's Ointments for All Occasions Volume Two.' The Cardinal smiled to himself, removing his hood, unclasping his black Journal and placing it on a small table beside the door. He coughed loudly as Perch, who had been so engrossed in his book that he hadn't noticed his arrival jumped as a foot in the air and turned to face the Cardinal, suddenly terrified.

"Your Eminence, f-f-f-forgive me, I had did not hear you enter." He stammered,

The Cardinal did not reply, instead he continued to eye the book still clutched tightly in Perch's right hand.

Perch dropped the book as though it had burned him and hastily made about placing it back on the shelf.

"My most humble *humblest* apologies Your Eminence, I was merely curious. I…I have been waiting ever since your Dove arrived last night."

"You grew bored of waiting," said The Cardinal, his booming voice cracking with amusement as he continued to smile at Perch, "You feel you would have been best suited elsewhere whilst I travelled to speak with you?"

Perch looked suddenly scandalised, "Your Eminence, no, of course not! I would not dare to question your command, I only meant that I was waiting and happened to spot something of interest. I felt that in the circumstances it might have helped with…" but Perch tailed off as the Cardinal strode towards him and pulled 'Offenhert's Ointments for All Occasions Volume Two' from the shelf, looking at it with great interest.

"Yes, I had quite forgotten I owned this volume." He said casually, inspecting the books cover and flicking through its pages, "You thought you would find something for that?" Perch finished, glancing down at Perch's left hand that was covered in thick white bandages that clashed with his glistening robes, he grinned slyly at the shame and revulsion on Perch's reddening face.

"Come come now, that wouldn't do. You did wrong Perch, you committed sins against the Order, you know the punishment for a clergyman just as well as you know there is no cure for it."

Perch instinctively made to grasp his bandaged his hand but the Cardinal shot out his own, grasping Perch by the arm and forcing his bandaged hand up towards his face. Perch howled in pain but the Cardinal ignored him, slowly he peeled back the bandages, unravelling them with such anticipation it were as though he was opening a birthday present. Gradually, as the bandages unravelled and fell to the floor revealing what was left of Perch's hand.

He had sustained many bruises and cuts across the palm and the finger nails seemed to have become clogged with so much grime and dirt that it looked like they were about to fall off at any minute. All of this would have been more than manageable but it was the fingers that the Cardinal was interested in.

"They took the ring finger. Tell me, did they give you a choice?" he asked coldly,

"N-n-no" whimpered Perch, who refused to look up at his maimed hand, instead staring determinedly at the floor.

"Good."

He smiled at Perch's hand and then with one last vindictive look at the snivelling clergyman he released his wrist and strode away from him. Perch, clasped the hand to his chest, shaking like he had been submerged in ice water.

"You know why I have asked to speak with you?" asked Perch.

"Yes, I believe so, Your Eminence."

"Well…" said Euphestus impatiently, "Tell me what you know."

"Ah, ok, well, we brought her in some time ago. It wasn't easy mind, I don't know why but she trusts the girl."

"She is a simple fool." Snapped the Cardinal, inspecting his long white beard in a mirror, "But she is a fool with information. So, out with it, tell me what she has told you."

"I hadn't planned on torturing her, Gisele is, I mean to say she *was* a good friend at one time. She spoke out against our arrest warrant, she besmirched the good name of the Ivory Order so we tried to bring her to the dungeons."

"Tried?"

"Um, well yes, we tried. It was not quite that simple, I don't know if you know Gisele but she's quite the woman. She's a fairly difficult woman to bring anywhere against her will."

"You obviously succeeded though."

"Yes, yes we did, we had to bring two units of Knights out but we got her to the dungeons."

"Perch, I have travelled all the way from Imputtia and I do not have time for a long drawn out explanation. Now tell me what the woman knows or I will lose what little patience I have left."

Perch jumped as though he had received an electric shock.

"Of course, Your Eminence. She told us, after many hours of torture that she had found the girl down at Lower Forfal, down by the little islands that lead out past the harbour. She had come stumbling from a dilapidated old hut and collapsed in front of her. She brought her to the Chapter, she told us that Charity had asked her lots of questions, that she was from Imputtia and wanted to find her way home. She mentioned that the girl seemed to remember very little about Thea, Journals or the Castlands, we suspect that she may have been suffering from amnesia."

"I see, this is indeed valuable information Perch. You have done well. But I think it best if I speak with her, I'm sure given the right *encouragement* I can find out if Charity has been in contact with her, we know that she had few allies on the Mainland, there can only be a few places for her to hide now."

Perch seemed to swell with a renewed confidence, he smiled the first time since the Cardinal had entered the hut and the Cardinal reluctantly returned his smile. Just then there was a knock at the door and Perch ran to open it. A young boy, no older than fifteen was standing in the doorway, his clothes were unmistakably that of one of the Helpers.

"Please, Your Eminence, this came for you, from the Knight patrol, they said it were urgent."

Perch carried the folded note to the Cardinal, looking at the letter as though it might explode in his uninjured hand.

The Cardinal took it wordlessly from him, unfurled it and read silently the words:

'Gisele Corrab has escaped the Chapter. Sweeping the city. Armed escorts are en route to your location.'

He crumpled the note up and dropped it to the floor, he was too furious to speak. This was *his* fault it must be, Perch had failed the Order yet again.

"Your Eminence," said Perch in a quivering voice, "Is everything all right?"

"The knife on the shelf." The Cardinal spoke to the boy in the doorway, "Bring it here and then close the door tightly behind you when you leave."

The boy obeyed, carrying a long silver dagger with an engraved copper handle to the Cardinal who took it from him wordlessly and ushered him from the room.

"Your hand Perch." Commanded Perch who had suddenly turned the colour of his robes.

"But...but...Your Eminence, I...I...I..."

"Perhaps this time the lesson will sink in."

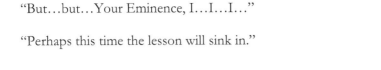

They rose early the next morning. The red moon had just edged beyond the horizon to the west and the sun was peeking out from the east. Charity had butterflies in her stomach and merely poked at the food Darion placed in front her at the dining table.

"Eat girl, you'll be glad of it!" he said coaxingly but Charity couldn't. She felt sick with nerves. It was all very well talking about her plan but now that it was upon her, she felt as though she would give absolutely anything for some more time. Darion stood over her until she reluctantly swallowed some of the dried fruits and beans but before she could finish her meal, Alistair banged into the house.

"Time," he said sternly to the room at large.

Charity hurried to her room, intent on packing the last of her things. She made sure to pack Calville's Journal at the very bottom of her backpack which she had decided to also bring. She knew she had no use for the Journal anymore but simply having it on her person made her feel slightly safer. It had been her one source of guidance on her journey across Thea and to give it up so easily seemed somehow disrespectful. Alistair led them outside and Charity gasped in amazement at the sight that greeted her. About a hundred men stood in neatly assembled rows, kitted out in the oddest collection of make-shift armour she had ever seen. Some had helmets made of wooden panels and nailed on pieces of metal, whilst others had full suits bolted untidily together. The troops were standing to attention as Alistair and Darion walked in front of them and stood observing the miscellaneous collection of Laccuna that was *their* army.

"Men," Alistair said loudly and to Charity's continued astonishment, the Laccuna straightened up obediently. "We stand on the brink of something you have yearned to be a part of for many years. This is a chance, *your* chance, to get revenge on the Theans responsible for your life-long segregation from the Mainland, the Ivory Order.

"Now you all agreed to take on the Order for their crimes against all Laccuna. Many of you asked my motives, why I would side with Laccuna and why the Order suddenly need taken out for good. I promised to tell you the truth but only on the day of our departure, well today is that day so listen up. The item known as the Fateweaver, the feather capable of changing life on Thea as we know it is in fact, quite real – we are sure of it. Furthermore, it is perilously close to falling into the hands of the Order and the one you know as Cassius." Charity saw how some of the soldiers murmured to one another, their looks of shock and fear shared throughout the troop. "If they succeed, if he succeeds on getting his hands on it, then who knows what horrors he could unleash upon all of Thea, Mainlanders and Laccuna alike.

Our plan is simple, we must reach the Chapter and stop Cassius from retrieving the Feather at all costs. We only have one shot at this. We head to the border. You know your groupings by now I assume?" The men nodded. "Stay with your groups until you hear otherwise. I will be leading from the front and Darion will take up the back. Now when we get to Galcia, make sure you follow your routes through the city. Too many people swarming out at once and we'll lose our only tactical advantage. When we reach the Chapter, I will give the signal and then we attack. It is imperative that we get this girl," he pointed over their shoulders to Charity who was standing on the steps of the house, "into the heart of the Chapter before it is too late."

The Laccuna had all turned to stare at her now. She blushed scarlet and smiled nervously; however most of them simply gawked.

"You never told us about her when you recruited us. What's so important 'bout *this* girl?" asked one of the men.

Darion spoke quickly. "This girl is the only one who can stop Cassius, she is the only one who can retrieve the Fateweaver from where it has been hidden."

There was a hushed silence as the Laccuna continued to stare, more interestedly now, at Charity.

"What about the Knights? How many of them will there be? You said you'd know by now." Called another Laccuna, looking concerned.

"We believe the Order Chapter is usually protected by a small battalion of Knights, perhaps seventy or eighty, they don't truly believe anyone would be foolhardy enough to attack the Chapter right in the Order's back garden." He gave a rye smile and continued, "We should have superior numbers, not to mention our sources have informed us that a great deal of the Order's troops have been pushed out to look for Charity. There will never be a better time to strike."

The men roared with renewed approval at these words.

"Are you ready men?" bellowed Alistair,

"YES, SIR!" boomed the Laccuna.

"THEN LET'S GO!"

And with that they tore out of the settlement, still in their neat rows, their weapons and armour clanking noisily as they ran. Charity and Sophie ran after them but Darion grabbed her as she made to pass him by.

"Wait, you'll follow on with me. Come, let's make sure we have everything. Don't worry, when they reach the border they won't enter the station until they know you've arrived."

It took them less than a day to reach the northern border of the Castlands. They managed to make such good time thanks to the Laccuna's superb knowledge of the areas they were traversing; more than once they lead her down intricate passageways, the army slotting into single file, and came out the other side of previously impassable mountains or chasms. Soon though, Charity could spot a familiar sheet of white far off in the distance, and she knew that they were close to the Imputtian Line station and closer to her goal. Her heart had begun to thump horribly in her chest and she tried in vain to think about something else.

At the entrance to the station Charity saw that the Laccuna had all donned travelling cloaks so as to conceal their bulky armour and protective clothing. The effect was not perfect as many of the cloaks were as mismatched and as dishevelled as their gear but in the hubbub of the crowds they would probably be less conspicuous. Groups of about ten or so were stood around the station entrance sporadically chatting to one another and the only man who stood alone was Alistair, his familiar travelling hat pulled low over his face. He was leaning in the half shadow of the large sign that read: 'Imputtian Line Station'.

When Charity moved towards him, he handed her a large black cloth. "Put this on, it'll make you a tad less noticeable."

"What, what is it?" asked Charity, holding the black fabric away from her face with disgust.

"It's a shawl. Put it around your hair, don't want you standing out too much. Sophie help her with it."

"Sure, ok," said Sophie, who looked just as nervous as Charity but seemed to find the task a welcome distraction. When the shawl was delicately tied about her hair, only her white fringe and ponytail were visible. Alistair bent low and whispered to only her and Sophie. "The line should be returning very soon, and when it does, we will go to the first goods carriage. The other groups will follow in intervals."

"Right, got it," said Charity nodding and feeling that she might vomit if she opened her mouth too much.

Sure enough there was a sudden bustling as people began streaming down the huge flight of stairs into the station, as the great white Imputtian train pulled in below. Charity looked at Alistair who nodded resolutely and, her legs now mostly jelly, she moved down the stairs and into the station.

Charity skulked through the bustling crowds, Alistair in front of her and Sophie right behind her as she drew alongside the glistening train which was now belching steam at the front of the myriad different carriages.

"The first one, that grey one, there," said Alistair in a hurried whisper, and he moved forwards towards the carriage. Then with a sideways glance about the station he slide the door open a crack and slipped through and beckoned them both inside. Once they were safely inside he gave another suspicious glance around at the station and withdrew his head into the carriage, shutting the door with a click behind him and immersing them in complete darkness.

"Ah, I can't see a thing!" said Charity.

"We will have to remain like this. We could not afford to bring candles as there is no room for –"

Sophie clicked suddenly and they were bathed in a reassuring pool of light as she held aloft a small flame on the end of her thumb. Charity could see that even in the dim light, she looked positively delighted with herself.

"You've been practising," said Charity, smiling, her nerves momentarily forgotten.

"Yup," grinned Sophie.

For ten agonising minutes they waited in the dim light of Sophie's spark, now and then they would hear muffled shouts from outside and Charity would freeze, petrified that they had been found. The carriage they were travelling in was to be used by just one other Laccuna group but the noise from outside was muffled by the heavy carriage walls so there was no way of knowing who was on the other side or when they would arrive. After about fifteen minutes the carriage door was suddenly dragged open and the light from the station poured inside, temporarily blinding them. Charity had stumbled to her feet, her heart banging rapidly against her chest and dread flooding her brain. Alistair had his cane at the ready and Sophie had her fingers in the familiar Igniculus stance as they prepared to face those at the door. However as the their eyes grew accustomed to the light outside it was not an Ivory Knight that came into focus but several of the Laccuna.

The Laccuna clambered inside and nodding at Charity, Sophie and Alistair as they passed, they positioned themselves near the other door, none of them seemed able to speak to each other. It was either that thought Charity, or they felt as she nervous and sick as she did. Charity stared around the carriage as Sophie walked around it, her spark held aloft, and she was surprised to see that most of the stock that was being transported to Galcia, was piled up near the back of this carriage. She had expected to be crammed tightly in with little room to move but thankfully they had ample, she could even stretch out her legs, if she wanted to. Not long after the first group, a second Laccuna group joined their party, stating that the others were full up, by now however the carriage had begun to shake and vibrate unpleasantly; there was a loud sound of metal crunching over metal and she could feel the carriage lurch forwards as, finally, the line began to move.

This was it. The wheels had been set in motion and there was to be no turning back now, she thought, as she gripped Calville's Journal very tightly in both hands.

27 – FATEWEAVER

Charity knew that as soon as the train got moving they would have no interruptions. Alistair had told them that the goods carriages weren't connected to the glistening passenger ones and as such, didn't get checked until the end of the journey, by which time they hoped to be long gone. They spent their time in silence; neither the Laccuna nor Charity's group had anything to say to one another and Charity spent most of the journey either pacing the carriage or sitting down, deep in thought, dreading what awaited her when the train finally came to a stop. She had felt nerves before but these were different, this was more than idle fretting: she was afraid. Charity was terrified that any one of her friends could get hurt, never mind what might happen to *her,* however this was not the main concern taking up her thoughts as the train trundled relentlessly onwards. The thing she was most afraid of was something that she had struggled to admit even to herself, something that she daren't even think about: what if when she reached the Ordium Tree, nothing happened? No magical feather appeared, as her imagination had told her it would, what if she just stood there stupidly, waiting for something that would never arrive? What if all the sacrifices that had been made and any lives that could still be lost for *her* sake, were to be in vain? All of sudden, an intense wave of panic washed over her. Even though her face remained impassive, she was suddenly drowning under the surface, she wanted desperately to voice these concerns to the carriage at large, to scream it to all the Laccuna and make the whole group turn around and go back to the Castlands, but she knew that this was impossible.

After a short time, during which Charity had continued to desperately rack her brains for some way of getting out of the impending mission, the train began to shudder ominously from side to side. The entire contents of the carriage, them included, were thrown about as the train gave an almighty screech and began to slow. Charity recognised the sound of the great brakes being slammed on, and knew they were closing in on Galcia. In a matter of seconds, or so it seemed to her, Alistair was sliding open the carriage door and pushing her out into the masses of people spilling out from the carriages. Charity made sure Sophie was behind her and made her way for the stairs, passing two burly Knights as she went. One of the Knights glanced at her and for a fraction of a second Charity thought she saw something that looked like recognition in his face but his eyes moved over her, onto the rest of the crowd, and she and Sophie moved on up the ivory split staircase, her heart pounding so hard she thought it might jump out of her throat.

Charity stepped from the staircase and out into the glass-domed city of Galcia. She was surprised to see that none of the shops or stalls were open, in fact even the streets before them were all completely empty. Only the passengers of the Imputtian Line could be seen but even they hurried off into houses and down alleyways, away from where the station led into the city. Soon they was joined by Alistair and Darion, who were then followed by several groups of Laccuna. Once more, no words were shared and after a brief glance at each other, the groups broke apart again, spreading out amongst the city's many darkened side streets and passages. Alistair led her and Sophie down a similar street and Sophie dropped her voice to a low whisper as they walked.

"Where is everyone? Is it too early or something?"

"No," said Alistair, his voice also low. "Darion informed me that Order have been performing searches on random citizens, stopping them in the street and questioning them about your whereabouts. Most people just want to get to their homes and lock the door at the moment."

"But won't that mean we stand out more?" asked Sophie.

"It will, but hopefully they will not be checking the side streets. Also it means that they should not be expecting such a *personal* visit from us, not in their own city."

Charity did not speak, ask questions or even respond as Alistair smiled at her reassuringly. People were being harassed, questioned and driven to their homes because of *her*. Most of them had probably never even heard of her and yet it was her fault their lives had worsened. She felt an incredibly wave of guilt shudder through her and in that moment she resolved that no matter what, she would end this once and for all, she would make sure that no more innocent Theans would be mistreated because for her.

"Shhh," whispered Alistair, looking alert. He was peering around a tight corner as two Ivory Knights approached their street, chatting to one another.

"They reckon the Cardinal has left Galcia," said one.

"What, now? Nah, bound to be nonsense, Galcia's the safest place in Thea," said the other.

"Maybe he's in hiding somewhere less obvious than the main headquarters of the Order!"

"Well what would *he* have to hide from? He's got hundreds of Knights at his disposal, day and night here!"

"I dunno. The girl, maybe he's hiding from her, or Garron. Thea knows what *he's* capable of?"

"Phhf, loada rubbish. The Cardinal knows what he's doing, he's probably setting a plan in motion to make sure those scum are caught!"

Alistair had silently reached for his cane, and as the men rounded the corner to face them, he pounced. Charity saw their looks of surprise for a fraction of a second as Alistair brought his great cane swinging down towards them, and seconds later both Knights crashed wordlessly to the ground.

"Here, take this," he said, removing two swords from the Knight's colossal belts and handed one each to Charity and Sophie.

"What! I can't use this!" said Sophie exasperatedly, holding the Ivory sword away from her with both hands, as if it were a deadly python that might rear back and bite her.

"Just take it, you might need it!" commanded Alistair impatiently.

Sophie had opened her mouth to argue but the look he flashed her with made her drop her protests at once. Charity meanwhile was holding the sword carefully in her right hand, a familiar feeling coursing through her, a feeling she had felt back at Darion's settlement: something about this felt right. Alistair detached two small clasps from the Knight's belts and affixed them to Charity and Sophie's sides. Charity rotated her hips to get a better look at it. It was a small black square a bit like a man's wallet, she thought. The holster seemed to attract the swords as when Charity, under Alistair's instruction, pressed the blade against the black metal, it snapped to her side and remained there quite independently. The little holster also allowed Charity to move just as freely as she would have done without a massive sword attached to her side, and it seemed to shift the sword as she walked, keeping it out of reach of her arms and legs.

"What is this?" asked Charity, "Is it like the Journal clasps?"

"It is a similar design, I believe the sword squares came first and the idea was developed into being used for Journals." Said Alistair distractedly checking all around them for more Ivory soliders.

They pressed on through the streets but saw no more Ivory Order members. Occasionally they would bump into one of the Laccuna groups who had gotten lost in the labyrinthine maze that was Galcia's side streets, but Alistair merely redirected them and they continued along their own path. Before long, the great white palace that towered over Galcia came into closer and closer view. Charity saw, as they drew nearer, that the other Laccuna were waiting for them at a little bridge that connected the rest of the city to the majestic palace. On the other side of the bridge was a great iron door. Charity's heart leapt as she realised that the door was in fact, completely deserted. However, despite their apparent clear path into the Order Chapter, the Laccuna were far from pleased; on the contrary, every face Charity looked at showed a feeling of intense apprehension. Alistair led Sophie and Charity to the front of the crowd, nodding curtly to Darion as they passed.

Alistair stepped in front of the troop, leaving Charity and Sophie at the side. He said nothing but raised one massive hand into the air and brought it swishing down, removing his travelling cloak in a swift flurry of movement. Charity heard herself gasp in surprise as Alistair revealed what lay beneath his cloak. He was wearing a shining suit of armour, but his was nothing like the tattered armour the Laccuna wore. This set of armour was the same glistening white as the Order Knights wore; in fact, she realised as she stared at it, it was *exactly* the same as the Order Knights'. It dawned on her that this must be *his* armour from his short stint in the Ivory Order. Alistair removed his hat and tossed it on top of his cloak, and the Laccuna started imitating him now, removing their own cloaks, revealing their dishevelled armour and unsheathing their swords.

Everything seemed to have gone precisely to plan so far. Charity was amazed that not one of their party had been accosted by Order officials on the journey, and yet she could no nothing to quell the feeling of tension that was coursing through her body. She looked at Sophie who looked just as terrified as she felt. Giving her hand a resolute squeeze, Charity smiled at her despite her nerves. She knew it was almost time. Alistair had turned to face the Chapter across the narrow bridge now, and the Laccuna turned with him, facing the door with determined faces and brandishing their weapons with renewed vigour. The sight of a shimmering Alistair, resplendent in his armour seemed to have given them fresh hope.

Just then, the great double doors swung of the Chapter swung forwards and a sickening sight met their eyes: a cavalcade of white knights all brandishing glistening blades spilled out onto the great bridge, blocking their path. Charity saw too many too count, though Alistair and Darion had said there would be less than a hundred Knights in the city. Charity frantically tried to count the Knights as they continued to pour out of the Chapter and onto the bridge, each clad in the same untarnished attire as Alistair. Charity couldn't keep track of the number of knights, but she was sure of one thing – the Laccuna were heavily outnumbered. She glanced quickly at their own hastily assembled army. Some of the men were flinching tetchily, perhaps their minds daring their legs to run. Their faces were worried but unwavering and Charity saw that they *all* stayed standing on the bridge, poised for battle. Alistair turned to look at Charity and Sophie, she tried to read his face, had he known about the change in numbers? But he was, as usual, quite unreadable, and he bent low to them, not looking at them but keeping his blue eyes fixed on the white wave of Knights in their way.

"Stay close to me. I will get you into the Chapter and then you must go alone. I will be needed out here. Don't stop, don't look back, just go! Do you understand?"

Charity nodded silently.

"Answer me – I…I want to hear you say it," he said, and despite the situation erupting around them, Charity couldn't help notice the melancholy in his voice.

"Yes…" she croaked back.

"Thank you…" he said smiling at her. Then he turned to the Laccuna and bellowed in a voice so mighty that it seemed to fill the entire dome that enshrined Galcia: "LACCUNA CHAAARRGE!"

As if a starter bell had rung, the two forces hurtled forwards, the Laccuna screaming with fury and fervour, the Knights rushing forwards to meet them with cries of 'For the Order!' and 'For Galcia!'. The first blades collided with an almighty *CRASH!* and with that the battle had commenced. Charity wordlessly grabbed Sophie by the hand and, ducking, pulled her through the tangled bodies and swinging swords, all the while glancing around at the battle around them.

She looked over and just caught a glimpse of Alistair, who was roaring loudly as he swung his cane forwards into an oncoming Knight. His stick struck the metallic armour and it split into several pieces, and the man flew back, throwing off several other Knights who all fell to the ground in a heap. Charity did not look back to see how the rest of the Laccuna fared, she only saw the door ahead of her. Alistair, meanwhile, had forged onwards, grunting and slicing through the knights on the bridge as if they were made of grass. He crashed into two smaller knights as they tried to flank him, and as they split apart noisily Charity had to jump back in order to avoid being knocked off the bridge. Out of nowhere, a huge blade came hurtling towards Sophie, who screamed in terror and jumped out of the way just time. Charity ran at the wielder of the sword, a burly Knight who had spotted them worming their way through the ruckus. She slid under the Knight's opened legs and cracked him hard on the back of the knee with the hilt of her sword. The man howled in pain as his knee collapsed under the strain, he teetered for a moment and then, *WHAM!* he flew off the edge of the bridge, as a nearby Laccuna smashed into him with incredible force. Sophie shouted something to Charity, but she couldn't hear her over the yells and crashes of metal around them. Sophie helped her to her feet and pointed towards the Chapter door, now only a fifty feet from them.

They reached the door as the last of the Knights seemed to emerge from the doorway. Alistair swung his cane forwards in a great sideways arc and three more Knights crumpled to the ground. Out of breath, but smiling, he turned to look at them, just as a massive fist came hurtling out from behind the door and caught him on the side of the head. He crashed into the ground dazed but conscious, as a mountain of a man stepped out from great hall ahead. He was at least Alistair's height, perhaps larger and had a great dirty black beard that took up most of his face. Charity saw as he stomped towards them that he carried no weapons, instead seeming to prefer his massive boulder-like fists. The stranger bellowed with mirth as Alistair righted himself, shaking his head dazedly.

"A Garron is it? Well let's see you fight like a true Thean!" he coaxed Alistair, who was still getting to his feet shakily. "C'mon, drop that walking stick o' yours, son!"

Alistair stretched himself up to his full height, wordlessly threw his cane aside and stepped forward, his fists raised.

"Alistair...you don't have to..." began Charity.

He flashed a meaningful look at her. "No time, GO!" he shouted and as the great Knight turned to look at them scuttling into the Chapter, Alistair cracked a powerful fist across his face. Charity heard the crack behind her as his fist collided with the man's jaw but to her astonishment, his booming laugh was still echoing in the doorway as she and Sophie pelted forwards.

Charity tore up the first staircase they came across. She had absolutely no idea where she was going but she yearned to escape the noise of the battle outside. Together they tore through the house, looking for some sign of where the Ordium Tree could be housed, checking up and down staircases, inside ornately decorated rooms and down long, deserted corridors. All the inhabitants of the Chapter had apparently made their way outside to the bridge, as the Chapter seemed completely empty; indeed the only noises that could be heard were those from the raging battle just outside. Despite herself Charity listened for a sound, some hint or clue as to how it was progressing, but the screams and sounds of metal clashing horribly with flesh were disturbingly ambiguous.

"I have no idea where the tree is!" Charity said to Sophie desperately, after finding themselves at the bottom of a staircase they had climbed twice before. "Do you have *any* idea?"

"No! I kinda thought you'd just, get an idea when we got here, like a feeling, you know?"

"Well if I am, it's not a very strong feeling." Charity had started to wonder if she should go back outside and help, as they weren't making much headway here, but then again what use could they be even if they did go back? Sophie could barely hold the sword Alistair had given her and although she might be able to disarm one solitary Laccuna swordsman, she was certainly no match for an entire army.

"Well come on, let's try up here…again," said Sophie resolutely and Charity followed. There seemed to be no alternative.

Charity and Sophie climbed yet another winding staircase and ran down a long corridor that seemed somehow familiar – was this another dead end? This corridor was lined with small circular windows and all along the walls were pictures of old men in white uniforms with the Order's now familiar, symbol of an open Journal and a red moon emblazoned on them.

Then Charity heard it. Someone was ascending the stairs behind them, she could hear the floorboards creak wearily under their weight as they climbed. She looked at Sophie, who was frantically staring up and down the corridor. Charity spied a door near to them and bolted through it, keen to avoid any unwanted attention. She burst into the room, slamming the door open but to her horror they made it only one step inside the room before running headlong into someone dressed head to toe in Ivory armour. Charity fell to the floor and stared up at the huge Ivory Knight, who looked around, affronted at the interruption. He eyed them both with surprise and then slowly realisation dawned on his exposed face.

"My, my, my, if it isn't the one who we've been looking for all this time," he said in a gruff voice, his face split in an unpleasant smile.

Charity made for her sword but the Knight grabbed her arm with a gloved hand, he snatched her sword from it's square and tossed it aside, then turning back to her he thrust her hand back at her and she fell to the floor at his feet.

Sophie had started to back out of the room just as a second Knight appeared behind the first, blocking her exit. He grabbed her roughly by the hair and trailed her towards Charity. Sophie screamed in pain as he threw her to the carpeted floor.

"That's the other one *too!*" said the second Knight excitedly.

"Imagine just bumping into these two!" said the first. "How much do you reckon we'll get when we bring this little lady to the Cardinal?"

"Ohhh," said the second, rubbing his unshaven chin thoughtfully, "more than a thousand Odes each, I reckon."

"Enough to retire that's for sure!" laughed the first, thumping the other guard happily on the arm but not taking his eyes from Charity, who still lay prostrate at his feet.

"Do we need both of 'em?" asked the second Knight, now pointing his blade at Sophie, who was raised her hands in surrender.

"No, that's *right*, his eminence just wants the white haired one." He tugged at Charity's black headscarf which slipped off her head revealing the rest of her glistening white hair. "Charity Walters I believe." He spoke her name in a high, song-song voice. "Right bunch of trouble you've caused. Bet you don't know how many shifts we've had to take just to look for *you!*"

He kicked her hard in the stomach. Charity grimaced in pain but held her tongue. She would not scream. She would not give this man the pleasure.

"If it were up to me, I'd kill ya both, here and now," the first Knight said vindictively, waving his great blade about. "But since his Eminence only wants *you*. I reckon we'll just have to enjoy killing the small one twice as much for the both of ya."

His face cracked into another wicked smile and the second knight laughed stupidly, still jabbing the knife threateningly at Sophie who squealed and squeaked in terror with every thrust.

"This one's more fun anyways, Gregory," he said, kicking her hard on the back. She rolled over, clutching her sides and howling in pain.

Charity felt a rage unlike anything she had ever felt. She felt so angry that she thought her fury would come spurting out of her like a volcano. She could feel herself getting angrier and angrier with every whimper Sophie uttered, feel the rage building up inside her, and when just when she felt her rage could not build up any more, a bang like a firework echoed about the tiny room. The second knight yelled in pain and surprise as he flew through the air, hitting the nearby wall with a tremendous crash. He had just begun scrambling to his feet when his whole body was suddenly enveloped in bright orange flames. The first Knight looked on terrified, he gazed in horror from his burning companion to the two girls. He only had time to utter one word before something bounded forward from out of nowhere and pinned him to the ground.

"Sparks."

Charity thought for a moment she had gone mad. A fiery red wolf that seemed to bristle and burn with the same orange fire that had affected his friend had leapt straight at the Knight, engulfing him in similar flames and then disappeared into the air in a puff of smoke. At first, Charity thought Sophie had performed some amazing feat of Igniculus magic, but she was still rolling around the floor in pain and had only now looked up to see what was happening.

Before long the two knights were burnt black, their limbs twisted in apparent agony as stream of acrid smoke drifted from their corpses and all around the tiny room. Suddenly a voice spoke from the doorway.

"It is very impolite to treat ladies like that."

Slowly Charity could just make out a figure stepping towards them through the smoke.

"Ladies, I believe you are in need of some assistance."

It took Charity a couple of seconds to realise who had emerged from the haze of acrid air but as it slowly disappeared she recognised who it was and what must have happened. Ruven of the Igniculus Temple was standing serenely before them, his black cloak swirling around him, his beard and shoulder length black hair unaffected by the sudden change of temperature in the tiny room.

"Ruven? What are you doing here?" asked Charity, helping Sophie gingerly to her feet.

"Doing my duty as a citizen of Thea. I was contacted by Silvus some time ago and he informed me of your *situation*. The Order is clearly out of control and we must act if we are to remain untainted by their actions. The Igniculus are behind *you*, Charity! You can be sure of that."

"Thank you, Ruven. That means so much!" She was still shaking slightly as she reattached her blade to the sword square.

Ruven waved a hand airily and stepped forwards to take Sophie by the arm, and together they walked her out of the room and back into the corridor.

"How did you know we'd be here?" asked Charity.

"Darion sent me a dove some time ago, we go a long way back you know. When I saw the battle begin I knew it was time to act. I moved quickly to find you amongst the fighting but you had already gone."

"Did you see Alistair? Is he ok?" she asked quickly.

"I didn't. I only saw death and destruction. The only thing I am sure of is that the battle was still on-going when I entered the Chapter in search of you. But why are you *here* in the first place?" he asked, eyeing her with surprise.

"We found out where Charles Calville hid the Fateweaver," she said in rush.

Charity had no idea whether Ruven was trustworthy or if she should be telling *anyone* what she had discovered, but his sudden rescue coupled with the impossibility of their situation made her more desperate than ever for any form of help.

Instantly Ruven's manner changed. He became incredibly serious, his wide smile slipping off his face as he fixed them with a look of utter disbelief.

"You found Calville's Journal? His missing pages?" he asked, seizing Charity roughly by the hand, Sophie still hanging limply from her shoulder.

"Yes, look." Charity pulled out the Journal to show him, and he touched the golden writing tenderly with a long finger, staring longingly at the heavy book.

"I don't believe it. Thea be praised…tell me, is what Silvus said true? Was Alistair accurate?"

"I dunno, what did he tell you?"

"He left word with Silvus, he claimed that *you* were the Regalis the Order were searching for…" he let the statement hang in the air, his face seized with anticipation.

"Well I am!" said Charity assuredly. "Or at least I was. They changed their mind after they sent me out, they sent a man called Cassius after me, but we managed to find the last pages, we know where the Fateweaver is hidden."

"Astonishing, simply astonishing."

"Yeah, well Calville left a clue we *know* the Fateweaver is here, we know it's in the Ordium Tree…but, but we don't know where in the chapter it's kept," she said desperately.

"But my dear girl, I know where it is." Said Ruven who looked on the verge of blissful tears, "Come, come follow me."

"You do!?" shouted Charity. "Oh Ruven thank you so much!"

"We have no time for thanks, dear girl. Come let us make haste, I'll hold your friend up, c'mon!"

They travelled downwards, back the way they had come, descending three more staircases until the light from the windows had been replaced with lit lamps all along the halls and corridors. Down, lower and lower they ventured, deep into the bowels of the Chapter and what must be a mile underground, Ruven holding up Sophie on his own now and Charity following along in their wake. Eventually after they had walked entire length of the palace they came to a dead end. An ancient looking stone wall met Charity's eyes, it would've been quite indistinguishable from a cliff face where it not for the pure white door placed right in its centre.

"This is it," said Ruven in a voice of hushed reverie. "The Ordium tree is housed at the very bottom of the Chapter. The roots reach deep under the ground after all, so it needs to be close to Thean soil. After you, my dear. I will support Miss Pierce through." Ruven kindly held the door open for Charity. She walked over the threshold into a dazzlingly white room, the light temporarily blinding her as she stumbled forwards groping for something to guide her as she walked. As her eyes adjusted to this new light, she could just make out the blurry form of a colossal tree, as white as the floor, walls and ceiling that surrounded it. She took a step towards the tree and before she knew what was happening, something had slammed into her with such force that she had been lifted into the air and across the room. Charity crashed onto the tiled floor and felt several of the fingers of her left hand snap loudly as she planted them to break her fall. She screamed in agony, clutching her broken hand tenderly with the other. Looking up, she saw Sophie and Ruven standing at the doorway just as a huge blast struck the ceiling above them, and a ton of white marble, stone and dust descended upon them. Charity screamed once more, still clutching her broken fingers, as her best friend and rescuer were plunged out of sight by the falling masonry. She got to her feet with difficulty as a cold laugh started up from the clouds of dust billowing beside the ruins of the doorway.

She knew he was there before he revealed himself, some part of her had always known he would be here waiting for here. Cassius moved from beyond the dust and debris, his face as gaunt as ever and Charity saw that he now bore a large scar just below his ear, a lasting effect from his battle with the Sloaks. He approached her without a word, his sword already drawn. Charity's eyes flashed around the room searching for a way out, but she saw nothing but a crumpled figure on the floor in the corner and the pile of rubble where the door had been.

"I have been thinking things over and I must admit that I am surprised, Charity, that it has come to this," he said, his face unreadable. "To think a talentless little *wench* would have been able to stumble her way to the most secretive part of the Ivory Order is quite unbelievable, wouldn't you say?"

Charity pulled herself to her feet. To her surprise Cassius did not try to stop her, but stood quite still, watching her. She straightened up facing him, fear and fury fighting it out inside her.

"You have not answered my question, Charity," he said in a saccharine voice that was almost as disturbing as his normal tone. "Would you not say that all this," he gestured at the walls around him, to the Ordium Tree, to Charity, "is quite unbelievable?"

"Yes, yes I would!" she said ferociously. "It's *more* than unbelievable, it's incredible, it's amazing, it shows me that people will *never* stop surprising you and that we can do more than you could ever do! And that's why even if you do kill me, someone else will rise up and stop the Order. We'll keep coming, Cassius, we'll keep coming until we're all dead!!"

She was bellowing the words at Cassius, screaming at him without meaning to. He had stopped walking towards her now and stood stock-still waiting for her to finish, a curious expression on his pale face.

"Ah I see, you still believe I work *for* the Order. I understand now," he said with the air of one remembering he had forgotten something important. "Now it all makes sense. My dear Charity, do you think that if I had the Fateweaver, I would so readily hand it over to the fools that seem to control this worthless world? No…I…why *I* could make this world great, I could make this world into a place unlike any other, I could make it…flawless."

"Flawless?"

"Oh my yes, just imagine it, a world without conflict, a world without division. No more Mainlanders and Laccuna, with the feather, I could unite them both in death. Death shows no favourites you see, death has no *rules* or *regulations,* death is above all, fair."

"You're mad." Muttered Charity, horrified.

"No Charity, I am not mad, I am the only one on this Goddess forsaken rock that isn't. I shall give you an example, a tree in your forest begins to rot, it's poisoned, it's sick beyond repair, it's unworthy to stand with the others. If you leave it be then the entire forest will die, what do you do?"

"You chop down the tree."

"WRONG!" shrieked Cassius, his voice echoing off the tiles and around the chamber, "One tree in your forest is tainted, you cannot be sure what others have the disease you need to start over, the answer is simple and yet few see it as clear as I do. You see Thea is my forest Charity."

"You don't mean…" began Charity, her mouth falling open.

"And *every* forest needs a fire." Whispered Cassius, looking more unhinged than she had ever seen him before.

"Yes, when I find the famous feather, I believe I'll start with my dear brethren before moving onto the Mainlanders. Who knows, I may let those friends of yours watch."

"You're wrong!" Charity shouted, "The Fateweaver isn't meant to be used!"

"What on Thea are talking about, girl? Of course it is!"

"No!" Charity said angrily, her face flushed.

Cassius was mad, she'd known that long ago, but his terrible plans had shown a side to the Fateweaver she'd rarely thought about. The terrible potential of the feather had finally been revealed to her, and with that Charity realised something. She understood now, she finally understood why Charles Calville had gone to all this trouble to hide the Fateweaver after he had searched so long for it. He didn't want to hand it to a worthy successor, he wanted to get rid of it so no one would ever find it again.

"Calville knew the feather's power was too great, that's why he hid it. He meant that no one should use the Fateweaver ever again!"

"A weak man with a weaker conviction," spat Cassius. "I am worthy to wield such a power because I am the last true Regalis!"

"Is that why your Father abandoned you?" bellowed Charity. Immediately Cassius face darkened considerably, the very air around him seemed to crackle with fierce electricity as he glared at Charity with his piercing black eyes.

She had no idea what had made her say it but something inside had urged her to do so.

"What…did…you…say?" Cassius whispered so quietly she could barely hear him.

"Your father. Did you know I met him before he died, before he killed himself, Cassius?" Charity kept her voice light and conversational as if they were merely talking about their prospective holidays. "Do you know *why* he did it, Cassius? I'll tell you, shall I?"

"Shut your filthy mouth!" he snapped ferociously.

"He killed himself to summon me to Thea! All because he knew that the only way he could make amends for having such a failure of a son, was to bring *me* to the attention of all of Thea."

Charity stared into Cassius' cold, black eyes, willing herself to sound composed, confident. "He was ashamed of you, Cassius!" she whispered softly.

"LIES!" snapped Cassius, but Charity could see his muscles tensing as he strained to keep himself stationary, his dark eyes locked upon her own brown ones. She tried not to blink, to meet them dead on, to prove she was unafraid. Silence filled the glistening room. Cassius had yielded for a full minute, as still as a statue and bristling with barely suppressed anger and then, as if an imaginary starting pistol had been fired, he suddenly burst forwards and charged at her.

Charity saw his feet moving, saw his arms raise the great glistening sword and swing it down towards her, and with a massive effort she managed to pull the sword from her side and hold it aloft with both hands, blocking the blow. The vibrations rocked her back and she stumbled onto one knee. Cassius, who clearly hadn't been expecting such a move, fell back also, his face apoplectic with shock and rage. Charity held the sword in front of her with a shaking hand, just as she had watched Alistair do so many times.

"It's not lies I'm afraid…it's all true…would you like to know what his last words were, Cassius?"

"I said, SHUT UP!" and he attacked once more. But Charity was ready this time. She sprang back to where the great Ordium Tree was positioned, its roots were spread out all over the tiled floor. Some had even penetrated its surface creeping underground, and she had to watch where she moved so as not to stumble over them. Charity watched Cassius' movements carefully. She had watched Alistair enough over the past few days to mimic some of his movements on the battlefield and although she had practised using nothing but a stick, the heavy blade seemed somehow just as light in this moment. Cassius sliced and jabbed at her, angrily lashing through the air but to her immense surprise she managed to block every blow. She seemed to be able to predict just where he was going to strike.

Cassius fell back, his face was incandescent with rage. "You have been practising," he wheezed through gritted teeth. "But still, you will not best the greatest swordsman in all of Thea!"

Again he flowed forwards, spinning and jabbing his great blade. Charity dodged the first two blows with her blade, blocked the third but was caught on the arm with a glancing edge as he brought it down for a fourth. She felt the searing pain and saw the red blood stain the perfectly white floor beneath her. Cassius could sense her weakness. He barged forwards and leapt into the air. Charity raised the blade again to block the blow but this time, his momentum was too powerful, and as his blade clashed noisily with her own she felt her sword shatter into a thousand tiny pieces. Cassius righted himself and spying her solitary Ivory handle still clutched in her hand, his face broke into a triumphant smile.

"At last…once I have killed you I can finally take my place as the one true

Regalis on Thea."

"You'll never get the Fateweaver! If you haven't got it by now you don't stand a chance, don't you see you're not *meant* to have it!"

Cassius laughed mirthlessly, his eyes still fixed upon Charity. "Oh it may take time, girl, I don't doubt *that* but with you out of the picture, that is precisely what I will have. Yes…soon the Fateweaver will be mine to wield…very soon indeed."

Cassius looked almost giddy with joy, his thin face curled in an unpleasant grin.

She tore her eyes from Cassius' triumphant face. The Journal had spilled from her bag as she fell and was glistening on the floor beside her. It had served her so faithfully but she had failed it, she knew that now. Charity grimaced as she pulled herself to her feet once more, one more time just to face him, her arms and legs bruised and beaten, her face dripping with sweat. She was completely unarmed but she had survived, she had survived up until the very end. She took several long drawn out breaths. She understood what had to be done now, something inside her head told her it was the right thing to do and so she obeyed it, without question. Throwing the broken hilt to the floor, Charity ran, ran as hard as her legs would allow her, ran straight at him as he readied himself, still grinning maniacally.

Thoughts wove their way into her head as she hurtled towards him. Alistair bravely wielding his cane against the army of White Knights, Sophie who had been through everything with her, and lastly of home, her home with her mother and father. She knew how she would get there at last. Sprinting forwards, her head bent down, she tore towards Cassius. But he was ready. With an almost lazy flick of the leg he kicked her into the air. She flew upwards, suspended ridiculously for a second or two, before Cassius slammed a fist into her side and she crashed through the air, colliding with something rock hard.

She looked up, dazed. Straight above her head were hundreds of white pages, or were they leaves? She couldn't quite tell from where she lay. As her vision became clearer, Charity realised that she was slumped at the base of the Ordium Tree and that the leaves, instead of being made of foliage, seemed to sprout leaves of paper, each one filled with words and intricately written passages. Looking forwards she could see Cassius stalking towards her. She attempted to move but her legs were badly sprained and she could barely lift herself off her back. This was it, she thought to herself, she had given it her all but in the end it was for nothing. She placed both hands at her sides and felt two of the large, white roots of the Ordium Tree underneath. She gave one last mighty effort and attempted to lift herself upright but the pain in her legs and from her broken fingers coursed through her like lightning. She fell back to the ground grimacing in anguish; Cassius was mere feet from her now, his face triumphant and his blade drawn.

Then, all of a sudden, something extraordinary happened. Charity felt a small tingling sensation, a vibration emanating from the tips of her fingers right through her hands. Looking down she saw that it was not her hands that were shaking, but the roots of the Ordium Tree that were vibrating softly under her touch. First the roots and then the trunk behind her back followed suit, and very soon the entire tree was shaking and vibrating like a pneumatic drill was penetrating its surface. Charity looked up at the leaves, which were rustling noisily, and the branches shook and swung as if they were about to fall off. Cassius had stopped walking now and was staring at the tree in bewilderment.

"What did you do?! Stop it! STOP IT!" he screamed at her, his gaunt face full of fear.

All of a sudden the tree stopped its shaking and fell still once more. Charity looked up, confused, sure she had done something wrong, and then she saw it, a glint of gold, a flash of colour sparkled in the depths of the colourless tree. Something small and delicate floated down towards her. It fell like a leaf on a windless day, slowly drifting down in a lazy motion and landing right on Charity's lap. She stared down in utter disbelief, and as she reached out a hand and touched it, a wonderful tingling sensation spread through her entire body.

The Fateweaver, the most powerful artefact in Thean history lay, quite innocently, upon her St. August's school skirt. She picked it up very slowly and examined it as if she had all the time in the world.

The Fateweaver was about the length of her hand. It was small and golden in colour with three coloured blotches set through each side: one, white, one red, and one blue. Its ends were curled and longer than any other feather she had ever seen and the golden fibres of feather seemed to curl up at the bottom, meeting at a perfectly sharp point.

A tap of metal on stone brought her back to her senses, and she tore her eyes from the feather's captivating presence and looked up. She was surprised to see that she was not alone; the feather had demanded her attention so fervently that she'd completely forgotten about her imminent peril. Cassius was still present but this was a different man than the one that had stood there moments before. He looked shell-shocked, frozen in place like an absurd wax figure. His voice seemed to have faltered and his blade hung limply at his side.

With a trembling hand she held it aloft in the bright light of the room and as she moved it, she saw that it left behind a golden residue in the air around her. She gripped it tightly between her finger and thumb.

"Please…" he begged, his eyes suddenly filled with a fear more resolute than she had ever seen, his face as gaunt and lined as his father's had been.

Charity gritted her teeth. She knew what she had to do, had known ever since she saw the first glint of gold sparkle within the Ordium Tree. She rolled up her left sleeve and laid her arm flat on her legs, then scribbled a command on her outstretched arm. She felt a sudden stab of unimaginable pain, her arm burning so much that she dropped the little feather to the floor. Cassius was shrieking out in pain as he was lifted off the ground, as if suspended by invisible strings. His screams filled the empty room, bouncing off the walls and making the very tiles shake and rattle. Charity tried to tear her eyes from his face, but she could not. She saw a sudden burst of light issue forth from with his chest, followed by a second and third shaft, and soon Cassius was bellowing in agony as the light enveloped him. The light was too bright, it was blinding her, and as Charity closed her eyes she heard a colossal bang reverberate in the chamber. She heard Cassius howl in agony and then just as quickly as they had started, the screams stopped and the light extinguished itself. Charity heard a heavy clatter and when she opened her eyes once more she saw nothing but an empty room and one lonely sword.

28 – THE LEGEND OF LITTLE BOOK

Charity pulled herself to her feet with exceeding difficulty. Her legs were in tremendous pain but she managed to right herself and make her way over to the blocked doorway, the feather now safely concealed in the pocket of her skirt. She listened hard. She could hear voices issuing from beyond the rubble.

"She's in here. Quickly we have to hurry, *he's* in there with her."

"C'mon, move!"

"Ow, outta the way."

"Ready, one, two three, GO!"

A colossal bang shook the whole room and Charity took several steps backwards as some of the rubble crumbled away, revealing part of the now very battered door.

"One more should do it. Ready men? Three, two, one!"

With another huge bang, the stones blocking the doorway were smashed into smithereens and a group of people stormed noisily into the white chamber. Charity couldn't see anyone due to the huge cloud of dust descending upon her but before it could clear two figures bounded forwards and pulled her into a bone-crushing hug. She recognised them both immediately. Alistair and Sophie hugged her tightly and Charity hugged them back with all the force she could muster. When they released her Alistair grabbed her and looked deep into her eyes.

"Where is he? Did he escape? What happened?"

Charity told them about how she had managed to stop Cassius and how the Ordium Tree had dropped the Fateweaver right into her lap. The assembled crowd gasped in unison as she pulled it out of her pocket as and waved it about. The gold residue gave off a particularly mystical effect, she thought to herself. Some of the men she now noticed were Laccuna. Darion and Ruven were there and she also spotted, with a shock of recognition, Thomas the young Igniculus boy who they had met in Silvus' Supplies.

"Oh Thea, it *is* real?" said Sophie, shaking her head in disbelief.

"What did you write on your arm Charity? Where did you send him?" asked Darion looking awestruck.

"I wrote: *'Cassius was cast from Thea'*. I didn't know if it would work or not, it was the only thing I could think to write," she said honestly.

Alistair looked around the room and smiled kindly at her. "I would say that you did brilliantly…Little Book."

"To Little Book!" one of the Laccuna shouted proudly.

"TO LITTLE BOOK!" the rest of the group chorused, Sophie and Alistair included, as Charity beamed around at all of them. The party made their way out of the room, passed what looked like a large stone battering ram and back up the many staircases to the bridge outside the Order Chapter. On the way Charity quizzed Alistair, Sophie, Ruven and Darion about what had happened whilst she had been with Cassius.

"It was utter carnage, and many good men were lost," said Darion sadly. "Alistair was exceptional though, he must've taken out about fifty Knights by himself before that big one got to him."

"I saw him, just before we entered the Chapter. What happened?" asked Sophie excitedly.

"He was a brutal opponent but nothing I couldn't handle," said Alistair with a wry smile.

"Boxed his ears in, didn't he?" said Darion, "Never seen anything quite like it!" he added proudly, slapping Alistair on the back.

"Down in the chamber, when the ceiling fell, it missed us by inches," said Ruven. "I tried all my Igniculus conjuring to break through but it was no use, so Sophie and I left and we managed to help finish off the last of the Knights."

"They weren't expecting a hundred fiery eagles to rain down upon them!" said Alistair, laughing now.

"Yeah and that was just Sophie!" said Ruven. The group laughed as Sophie looked proud but extremely embarrassed.

"She was quite something, I'll say!" said Darion. "Well, after that, most of 'em ran off. Only a couple stayed and well, let's just say Laccuna aren't famed for leaving survivors..." he finished darkly.

"What will happen to the Order now?" asked Charity.

"Well it seems the rest of the Chapters don't know too much about this. We'll have to keep a close eye on the place. Ruven has said he'll take over the Order duties for Imputtia in the meantime, give out the Journals, make sure the citizens of Galcia get back to normality, you know?"

"It would be an honour," said Ruven dramatically, bowing with a swish of his black cloak.

"We're going to tell people though, first thing to do is get the word out about the Order. Make no mistake girl, you've changed things, forever." said one of the Laccuna.

"But what about you, what are *you* going to do, girl?" asked Darion. "That feather you've got is one powerful little trinket. You could do all sorts of good for this place."

"No," Charity said flatly and they all stopped walking to stare at her, surprise and shock on every face. "I'm going to use this feather for two things. One will be to get home and the other will be to make sure no one ever finds it again. I'm going to destroy it."

"WHAT?!" asked Sophie incredulously. "Destroy it, but why?!"

"This thing isn't meant for anyone to use. Think about it, the power to do anything you want, it's too much, no, if this exists people are just going to come after it and if it ever fell into the wrong hands then it would be *my* fault. It has to go…forever this time."

"Men, Ruven, Darion, could we have a moment with Charity?" said Alistair suddenly. "She has something to do and I feel it would be best if we did it alone."

The rest of the group trooped off, still uttering their congratulations, leaving Charity, Sophie and Alistair alone on the bridge under the starry night sky.

Alistair had made sure they were indeed quite alone before he spoke. Sophie meanwhile looked like she had just come to a sudden, unpleasant realisation.

"I agree with you, Charity." said Alistair very seriously.

"You do?"

"Yes, no one is safe if that feather can be used by Thean hands. Our only choice is to destroy it."

"Ok then I'll do it," she said resolutely. "You're sure it'll just disappear if I write on my arm like before?"

"I believe so. That was quite ingenious using your own flesh as paper."

"Yeah, it just came to me."

"Very well," said Alistair heavily. "If you are ready, Charity, then I think now would be the best time."

"Now...?" she spluttered.

"Yes. This is not over. The Order *will* return, and they will not wait long before they send larger numbers to find you, to find this." He indicated the tiny feather. "We *must* make sure that the feather is destroyed whilst we have the opportunity."

"I know..."

"Then you know what you must do," Alistair finished solemnly, as he placed a mighty hand on her shoulder.

"WAIT! Does that mean you're...leaving?" said Sophie suddenly.

Charity froze, staring at Sophie.

"I always just thought that even if we did manage to succeed that you'd…I dunno…change your mind, maybe decide you wanted to stay."

"Sophie, I would, I mean, I want to, I really do!"

"Then just stay!" stammered Sophie, but Charity ignored her, ploughing on.

"Sophie, I can't believe I've been so lucky to have friends like you and Alistair but…" she looked into Sophie's emerald green eyes and as the impending reality of what she was about to do came crashing down upon her, she struggled desperately to fight back tears, "I have a family back home. They'll be looking for me. I must've been gone months – they'll think I'm dead!"

"I know, but it's just…oh, Charity."

Sophie flung herself forwards and onto Charity's shoulder. She began to weep silently on her shoulders, shuddering as she poured her feelings out onto Charity's shirt. Charity returned her hug but kept her eyes locked on Alistair, his dependable, unshakeable manner stopped her from breaking down and she wished she could have borrowed some of his strength at this moment.

After some time Sophie managed to calm herself enough to release Charity, sniffing loudly and wiping her eyes with her sleeve. She looked very seriously at Charity.

"I'll never forget you," she said, her lip quivering again.

"Me neither." Charity pulled her school tie from her bag and handed it to her. "Something to remember me by, when I'm gone." Sophie accepted the stained tie like it was a glistening crown, taking it with trembling hands and grasping it tightly to her chest.

"Thank you, Charity," she managed to utter, in a constricted whisper.

Charity then turned to Alistair, who was standing very still. He gazed down at her, his great head bowed sadly. Then meeting her gaze, he thrust his hand forwards in a handshake gesture.

"It has been an honour, Charity Walters" he said stiffly, but she brushed his hand out of the way and hugged him as tightly as she could.

"You're my best friends, you know that?" she said, her head buried in his rough woollen cloak.

"I do," he said very quietly.

"Me too," Sophie echoed.

Charity released Alistair and took two steps back onto the bridge. She looked at her two best friends for what she knew would be the last time. Taking the Fateweaver in her hand, she outstretched her left arm once more.

"Please do me one last thing for me?" she asked in a trembling voice.

"Anything," replied Alistair.

"Close your eyes, I…I don't want you to see me go."

Charity saw their eyelids close, Sophie's tears streaming down her thin face now. Alistair placed a shaking hand on her shoulder and pulled her close.

"Goodbye," Charity said, tears burning her own eyes now.

"Goodbye…Little Book," said Alistair.

Charity scribbled onto her arm with the Fateweaver, **'Charity Walters went back from where she came and the Fateweaver was turned to dust.'**

All of a sudden everything went black. Galcia had disappeared in a rush of sound and colour, her two friends had gone and been replaced with nothing but blinding, scalding light. Charity tried to open her eyes but found she couldn't. She could feel hands brushing her face, feel the winds blowing around her but still she could not see where she was. She could feel herself falling, further and further, and although she continued to strain her eyes against the blinding light she could see nothing. Finally, after a long time she felt herself drop onto something soft and squishy. She managed with a great effort to force open her eyelids. They creaked open slowly and Charity stared at her surroundings. She could see once more.

She blinked. She was still in her St. August's uniform but the multi-coloured plume had disappeared from her hand now. Shafts of moonlight were shining in through the open window and as she got up from where she lay to get a better look around her, a dozen or so heavy books fell off her. Her fingers on one hand were swollen and bruised and her back ached dully in about a dozen places. Charity straightened up and stared out of the window at the starry sky. A single ivory coloured moon lit up the night sky and illuminated an opulent building of red brick that took up most of the horizon. The building was surrounded by rich forest greenery and just beyond the clumps of trees and bushes an old iron sign swayed peacefully in the night air. Charity could just make out the words 'St. August's School for Young Ladies'.

It came upon her so quickly she barely had time to steady herself as she felt her legs buckle. Her head was swimming. The library seemed to turn upside down in an instant and then everything went black.

The End

ABOUT THE AUTHOR

Stuart Montgomery was born in Larne, Northern Ireland on 9th October 1987. He graduated from Stranmillis University College in 2010 with Bachelors of Education and has been teaching in primary schools across the country ever since.

He is also partial to cats and fudge.

Printed in Great Britain
by Amazon